Heart's Blood

Juliet
Marillier

TOR

First published 2009 by Pan Macmillan Australia Ltd

First published in Great Britain in 2009 by Tor
an imprint of Pan Macmillan Ltd
Pan Macmillan, 20 New Wharf Road, London N1 9RR
Basingstoke and Oxford
Associated companies throughout the world
www.panmacmillan.com

ISBN 978-0-230-01791-7 (HB)

Calligraphy by Gaye Godfrey-Nicholls of Inklings Calligraphy Studio

1 3 5 7 9 8 6 4 2

A CIP catalogue record for this book is available
from the British Library.

Printed and bound in Great Britain by
CPI Mackays, Chatham ME5 8TD

Visit **www.panmacmillan.com** to read more about all our books
and to buy them. You will also find features, author interviews and
news of any author events, and you can sign up for e-newsletters
so that you're always first to hear about our new releases.

To Saskia and Irie
with love

acknowledgements

Gaye Godfrey-Nicholls of Inklings Calligraphy Studio provided expert guidance on all aspects of scribing. John Aris helped me with the Latin invocation. The members of my writers' group assisted me through this book's bumpy road to completion, sharing practical advice, moral support and strong coffee. My multi-skilled family helped with everything from brainstorming to proofreading. My editors, Anne Sowards at Penguin, Julie Crisp at Tor UK, and Mary Verney at Pan Macmillan Australia, worked cooperatively to produce a single editorial report, making my life much easier. My agent, Russell Galen, continued to provide excellent support. A big thank you to all.

chapter one

t a place where two tracks met, the carter brought his horse to a sudden halt.

'This is where you get down,' he said.

Dusk was falling, and mist was closing in over a landscape curiously devoid of features. Apart from low clumps of grass, all I could see nearby was an ancient marker stone whose inscription was obscured by a coat of creeping mosses. Every part of me ached with weariness. 'This is not even a settlement!' I protested. 'It's – it's nowhere!'

'This is as far west as your money takes you,' the man said flatly. 'Wasn't that the agreement? It's late. I won't linger in these parts after nightfall.'

I sat frozen. He couldn't really be going to leave me in this godforsaken spot, could he?

'You could come on with me.' The man's tone had changed. 'I've got a roof, supper, a comfortable bed. For a pretty little thing like you, there's other ways of paying.' He set a heavy hand on my shoulder, making me shrink away, my heart hammering. I scrambled down from the cart and seized my bag and writing box from the back before the fellow could drive off and leave me with nothing.

'Sure you won't change your mind?' he asked, eyeing me up and down as if I were a prime cut of beef.

'Quite sure,' I said shakily, shocked that I had been too full of my woes to notice that look in his eye earlier, when there were other passengers on the cart. 'What is this place? Is there a settlement close by?'

'If you can call it that.' He jerked his head in the general direction of the marker. 'Don't know if you'll find shelter. They've a habit of huddling behind locked doors at night around here, and with good reason. I'm not talking about troops of armed Normans on the road, you understand, but . . . something else. You'd far better come home with me. I'd look after you.'

I slung my bundle over my shoulder. On the tip of my tongue was the retort he deserved: *I'm not so desperate*, but I was not quite brave enough to say it. Besides, with only four coppers left and the very real possibility that pursuit was close behind me, I might soon be reduced to accepting offers of this kind or starving.

I stooped to examine the weathered stone, keeping a wary eye on the carter. He wouldn't attack me, would he? Out here, I would scream unheard. The stone's inscription read *Whistling Tor*. An odd name. As I traced the moss-crusted letters, the man drove away without another word. The drum of hoof beats and the creak of wheels diminished to nothing. I took a deep breath and ordered myself to be strong. If there was a sign, there must be a settlement and shelter.

I headed off along the misty track to Whistling Tor. I had hoped to reach the settlement quite quickly, but the path went on and on, and after a while it began to climb. As I made my way up, I could see through the mist that I was walking into ever denser woodland, the dark trunks of oak and beech looming here and there above a smothering blanket of bushes and briars. My shawl kept catching on things. I wrenched it away with my free hand, the other holding tight to my writing box. I stumbled. There were odd stones on the path, pale, sharp-edged things that seemed set down deliberately to trip the unwary traveller.

The last light was fading. Here under the trees, the shadows and the mist combined to make the only safe speed a cautious creep. If only I were not so tired. I'd been up at first light after an uncomfortable night spent in the rough shelter of a dry-stone wall. I'd walked all morning. At the time, the carter had seemed a godsend.

Footsteps behind me. What now? Hide in the cover of the trees until the person had passed? No. I had made a promise to myself when I fled Market Cross, and I must keep it. *I will be brave.* I halted and turned.

A tall man emerged from the mist, shoulders square, walking steadily. I had just time to take in his impressive garb – a cloak dyed brilliant crimson, a chain around his neck that appeared to be of real gold – when a second man came up behind him. Relief washed through me. This one, shorter and slighter than the other, was clad in the brown habit and sandals of a monastic brother. They halted four paces away from me, looking mildly surprised. The deepening dusk and the rising mist rendered both their faces ghostly pale, and the monk was so thin his features seemed almost skeletal, but his smile was warm.

'Well, well,' he observed. 'The mist has conjured a lovely lady from an ancient tale, my friend. We must be on our best manners or she'll set a nasty spell on us, I fear.'

The red-cloaked man made an elegant bow. 'My friend has a penchant for weak jests,' he said. He did not smile – his face was a sombre one, thin-lipped, sunken-eyed – but his manner was courteous. 'We see few travellers on this path. Are you headed for the settlement?'

'Whistling Tor? Yes. I was hoping to find shelter for the night.'

They exchanged a glance.

'Easy to lose yourself when the mist comes down,' the monk said. 'The settlement's on our way, more or less. If you permit, we'll walk with you and make sure you get there safely.'

'Thank you. My name is Caitrin, daughter of Berach.'

'Rioghan,' said the tall man in the crimson cloak. 'My companion is Eichri. Let me carry that box for you.'

'No!' Nobody was getting his hands on my writing materials. 'No, thank you,' I added, realising how sharp I had sounded. 'I can manage.'

We walked on. 'Do you live somewhere locally?' I asked the two men.

'Close at hand,' Rioghan said. 'But not in the settlement. When you get there, ask for Tomas. He's the innkeeper.'

I nodded, wondering if four coppers would be enough to buy me a bed for the night. I waited for them to ask me why a young woman was out wandering alone so late in the day, but neither of them said a thing more, though each glanced at me from time to time as we walked on. I sensed my arrival was a curiosity to them, something that went beyond the obvious puzzle of my appearance. When I'd fled from Market Cross I'd looked like what I was, the daughter of a skilled craftsman, a girl of good family, neat and respectable. Now I was exhausted and dishevelled, my clothing creased and muddy. My boots had not handled the long walk well. The manner of my departure had left me ill equipped for travel. Of my small store of coins, all but those four coppers had been spent on getting me to this point. A new idea came to me.

'Brother Eichri?'

'Yes, Caitrin, daughter of Berach?'

'I imagine you are attached to a monastery or similar, somewhere near here. Is there also a Christian place of scholarship and retreat for women?'

The monk smiled. He had teeth like miniature tombstones; they made his features look even more gaunt. 'Not within several days' ride, Caitrin. You seek to enter a life of prayer?'

I blushed. 'I would hardly be qualified for that. What faith I once had, I have no longer. I thought it possible such a place might offer refuge . . . Never mind.' It had been a mistake to ask such a question. The less people knew about my woeful position the better. I'd been stupid to give these two my real name, friendly as they were.

'Are you in need of funds, Caitrin?' Rioghan's question was blunt.

'No.' The carter had made me wary. Rioghan's good manners did not necessarily mean he was trustworthy. 'I'm a craftswoman,' I added. 'I earn my own living.'

'Ah.' That was all he said, and it pleased me. No intrusive questions; no laughter at the idea that a woman could survive on her own without resorting to selling her body. For the first time in many days I felt almost at ease.

We walked on in silence. I could not help staring at Rioghan's crimson cloak. The fabric was silky and sumptuous, most likely a cloth imported from a far land at fabulous cost. But the garment was sadly worn, almost to holes here and there. Did Rioghan have nobody to do his mending? A person who wore such an extravagant item, not to speak of the gold around his neck, must surely have servants at his beck and call.

He saw me looking. 'A badge of authority,' he said, and there was a note of terrible sadness in his tone. 'I was once a king's chief councillor.'

It was hard to find the right response without asking awkward questions. Why once and not now? Rioghan did not look terribly old, only sad and unwell, his pallid complexion adding to that impression. Connacht was ruled by kings of the Uí Conchubhair; Ruaridh had been high king for many years. There would be chieftains ruling each region in these parts. As I had travelled westwards I had seen palisades of sharpened sticks encircling villages. I had seen folk digging trenches and raising defensive mounds around the mud and wattle strongholds of local leaders. If ever a king needed his chief councillor it was now, with the Norman invaders eyeing this last untouched part of the land. Had Rioghan fallen out of favour with his leader? Been supplanted by an abler man?

'I'm sorry if I was staring,' I said as we took a branch of the track that headed downhill. Below us, looming shapes in the mist suggested we were at last close to the settlement of Whistling Tor. 'That is such a fine red. I was just wondering what the dye-stuff was.'

'Ah,' said Rioghan. 'You're a weaver? A spinner?'

'Neither. But I'm interested in colours. Is that the village?'

The two of them halted on either side of me and I paused, looking ahead. A formidable barrier surrounded the modest settlement, a conglomeration of sharp-pointed stakes, iron bars, splintery old gates and other lethal bits and pieces. The mist shifted around it, revealing here a broken plough, there a great jagged stone that must have taken the efforts of eight or ten men to haul into place. As a fortification against the Normans the barrier probably wouldn't last long, but it made a powerful

5

deterrent to travellers. The place was set about with flaming torches on tall poles.

'It seems the folk of Whistling Tor don't like visitors,' I said flatly. 'Since I'm with you, I suppose it will be all right.' Within that wall I could see men moving about, but the mist made details obscure. I headed on down the hill towards the barrier, my two companions behind me.

I was about twelve paces from the wall when something hurtled over it towards me. I ducked, shielding my head. A sizeable stone hit the ground not far away, followed by several smaller ones. Someone shouted from within the barrier, 'Not a step further! Spawn of the devil, away with you!'

Blessed Brighid, what was this? Trembling, I peered out between my sheltering hands. Four or five men stood on the other side of the fortification, their faces uniformly ash white, their weapons at the ready: a pitchfork, a scythe, an iron bar, a club with spikes. 'Away with you, scum!' yelled one, and another added, 'Go back where you belong, into the pit of hell!'

Had the mist transformed me into a monster? *Run, Caitrin, run!* No; I must be brave. I cleared my throat. 'I'm just a . . .' I faltered. *A wandering scribe* might be the truth, but nobody was going to believe it. 'A traveller. On my way to visit kinsfolk. My name is Caitrin, daughter of Berach.' Curses, I'd done it again, used my real name. *Pull yourself together, Caitrin.* 'I need shelter for the night. I mean no harm here.' I glanced over my shoulder, wondering why Rioghan and Brother Eichri had not spoken up on my behalf, but nobody was there. While the inhabitants of Whistling Tor village were hurling stones and insults, my two companions had made a silent departure.

All alone. No one to turn to but myself. That was nothing new; I had been all alone at Market Cross, in a house full of folk. Should I run? Where? *Speak up, Caitrin.* This couldn't be what it seemed, surely. It was some kind of mistake, that was all. 'It's the truth!' I added. 'Please let me in.' I remembered something. 'Might I speak to Tomas?'

The men of the settlement stood close together, eyeing me. They looked both combative and terrified. This didn't make sense. What did they think I was, a one-woman raiding party? I shivered, hugging my shawl around me, as they held a muttered consultation.

'Where did you say you were headed?' The man with the club asked the question without quite looking me in the eye.

'I didn't,' I said. 'But my mother's kin live in these parts.' That was not quite a lie: my mother's family had indeed lived in the far west of Connacht, but there were none of them left now, at least none I knew of.

'Fetch Tomas,' someone said. A lull, then; no more missiles thrown, but plenty of talk in low, agitated voices on that side of the barrier, while on this side I stood waiting as the last light faded. I wondered how much longer my legs would hold me up.

'What are you?' A new voice. Another man had joined the first group, an older man with a more capable manner. 'Ordinary folk don't come to Whistling Tor. Especially not after dark.'

'Are you Tomas?' I asked. 'My name is Caitrin. I've been on the road all day. I just need somewhere to sleep. I can pay.'

'If you mean no harm, prove it,' someone called out.

'How?' I wondered if I would be subjected to a search or other indignities when I got through the defensive barrier. Well-born young women did not usually travel alone. It would be plain to everyone that I was in some kind of trouble. After today it was all too easy to believe men would interpret that as an invitation.

'Say a Christian prayer.' That was the man with the club, his voice still thick with unease.

I stared at him. Whatever these villagers were afraid of, it seemed it was not the Normans, for the most part a Christian people. 'God in heaven,' I said, 'guide and support me on my journey and bring me safely to shelter. Blessed Saint Patrick shield me. Mother Mary intercede for me. Amen.'

There was a pause, then the man with the club lowered his weapon, and the older one said, 'Let her through, boys. Duald, make sure the barrier's properly sealed afterwards. You can't be too careful in this mist. Go on, let her in.'

'If you're sure, Tomas.'

Various bars and logs and pieces of metal were moved apart, and I was admitted to the safe ground within. 'This way,' Tomas said as I murmured thanks.

7

He walked by my side through the village. The houses were bristling with protective measures, the kind used by superstitious folk: triangles of iron nails, bowls of white stones set under steps, other charms to ward off evil. Doors and shutters were tightly closed. Many were barred with iron. What with the shifting light from the torches and the gathering mist, there was a nightmarish quality about the place. In the centre of the settlement stood a bigger building, solidly built of mud and wattle and roofed with rain-darkened thatch.

'Whistling Tor Inn,' my companion said. 'I'm the innkeeper; my name's Tomas. We can give you a bed for the night.'

Tears pricked my eyes. I'd been beginning to think I had strayed into a different world, one where everything was awry. 'Thank you,' I said.

The inn was locked up. A wary-looking woman opened the door at Tomas's call, and I was ushered into a kitchen where a warm fire burned on the hearth. Once we were in, the woman set a heavy bar across the front door.

'My wife, Orna,' Tomas said. 'Here.' He was pouring me a cup of ale. 'Orna, is that soup still warm? This lass looks as if she could do with a meal.'

My heart sank. I made myself speak up. 'I have only four coppers. I don't suppose that's enough to pay for soup as well as a bed. I can manage without food. I just need to get warm.'

The two of them turned searching looks on me. I could see questions coming, questions I wouldn't want to answer.

'That's all right, lass,' Orna said, shifting a pot onto the fire. 'Where are you headed? We don't get many visitors here.'

'I'm . . .' I hesitated, caught without a satisfactory answer. I could hardly tell them the truth: that I had left home with no plan other than to set as much distance between myself and Cillian as I could. But I did not feel comfortable lying. 'I have kin in these parts,' I said. 'A little further on.'

'You'll likely not get another ride for a long while,' said the innkeeper.

'Is Whistling Tor so far off the main roads?' I asked.

'Not so far that a carter couldn't bring a person down here quickly enough,' said Orna, stirring the pot. A savoury smell arose, making my mouth water. 'But they won't do it. Folk skirt around us. Nobody comes here. This place is under a curse.'

'A curse?' This grew stranger and stranger.

'That's right,' said Tomas. 'Step outside that barrier at night and you put yourself in deadly danger from what's up the hill there. Even by day, folk don't pass the way you came if they can avoid it.'

'The name is unusual. Whistling Tor. The hill you mention is the tor, I suppose. But why whistling?'

Tomas poured ale for himself and his wife and settled on a bench. 'I suppose it once was a bare hill, the kind you'd call a tor, but that would have been a long time ago. The forest has grown up all over it, and it's full of presences. Things that lead you out of your way, then swallow you up and spit out the pieces.'

'What do you mean?' I asked, not sure I wanted to know the answer.

'Manifestations,' said Tomas weightily. 'They're everywhere; there's no getting rid of them. They were called forth long ago; nigh on a hundred years they've plagued this place.'

'Nobody can say exactly what they are,' put in Orna. 'All we know is, the hill's swarming with them. All kinds, from little tiny ones that whisper in your ear to great slavering monsters of things. Here, get this into you.' She put a steaming bowl of soup in front of me, with a wedge of coarse bread beside it. Monsters or no monsters, I set to with enthusiasm as my hostess went on. 'Whistling Tor, that's fair enough. The wind does make an eerie sound in the trees on the hill. But Whispering Tor would be closer to the mark. Go too far up there and you'll start to hear their little voices, and what they tell you won't be pleasant.'

It was hard to know what question to ask. 'How did they get there, these . . . presences?'

'They were called forth in the time of my great-grandmother, and they've been here ever since, them and the curse that came with them. It's hung over us like a shadow for close on four generations.'

'So the barrier around this settlement, and the guards, are not to protect you against Norman attacks?'

'Folk say those poxy iron-shirts won't come so far west.' Tomas took a mouthful of his ale, watching me as I ate. 'Myself, I'm not so sure. I've heard that some of the chieftains are calling their men to arms, and one or two have brought in fighters from the isles, big brutes of *gallóglaigh* with heavy axes. If the Normans come to Whistling Tor, we're done for. There's nobody to protect *us*; no leader, no fighters, no funds to pay for help.'

'What about the high king? And don't you have a chieftain of your own? Can't he protect you?'

'Huh!' There was profound scorn in Tomas's voice. 'Ruaridh Uí Conchubhair isn't interested in the likes of us. As for a chieftain, the one we've got makes a mockery of the title. He's worse than useless. Stays holed up in his big fortress, on top of the Tor there,' he waved in the general direction of the woodland path I had taken to reach the settlement, 'surrounded by his malevolent creatures. Sends his man down for supplies, pays a few measly coppers now and then to get a bit of work done, but take action? Make an effort to defend his people? Not likely. Takes his tributes in good grain and livestock, gives back nothing at all. Hasn't set foot beyond the hill since I can remember, and that's a good while.'

'That man's warped and twisted like thread gone awry on the loom,' put in Orna. 'The curse got *him* with a vengeance. But maybe we shouldn't be speaking of this. I wouldn't want to give you nightmares.'

I refrained from telling them that my own story provided more than enough material for night after night of bad dreams. Their fanciful tales were a welcome diversion from the problems that would face me tomorrow. For, after all, I could pay for only one night in the safety of this inn. 'I did meet two men on my way here,' I said. 'One was a monk. They guided me down to the settlement, but they left rather quickly when your friends out there started throwing stones.'

The effect of this was startling. Both Tomas and Orna formed the sign to ward off evil, each looking at the other. 'A monk, was it?' Tomas sounded disturbed. 'Thin sort of fellow, big teeth?'

'That's right. His name was Brother Eichri. He seemed friendly. They both did.'

'Anluan's cronies, the two of them,' said Tomas. 'If that's what Duald and the others spotted, it's no wonder they were throwing things.'

'Anluan?' The conversation was proving hard work.

'Our chieftain. So-called chieftain. I can't think of one good thing to say about the man, crooked, miserable parasite that he is.'

'More soup?' At Orna's question her husband fell silent, but the anger in his words vibrated through the warm air of the kitchen.

'If you came here through the woods,' he said after a little, 'it's just as well you didn't meet the dog.'

'I don't mind dogs,' I offered cautiously.

There was a meaningful pause. 'This is not so much a dog as a . . . *Dog*,' said Orna.

'A really big one?'

'Big. You could say that. The creature can take a fully grown ram in a single bite. In the morning, all that's left is a few wisps of wool.'

Now they really were trying to scare me. If every hapless traveller who wandered into the settlement was regaled with such stories, it was little wonder the place had so few visitors.

'There's a bed made up in the back room,' Orna said, seeing that I had finished my supper. 'It's nothing fancy, but you'll be warm.'

'Thank you,' I said, feeling very awkward. I was new to being utterly without resources; new to having no shelter beyond dawn tomorrow. New to being all alone. 'I appreciate your kindness.'

'Fallen on hard times, have you?' asked Tomas.

Maybe he meant well. After the carter, I was not prepared to put it to the test. 'A temporary setback,' I said, hearing how unconvincing it sounded. 'I would like to sleep now. I need to be able to lock the door. Especially with those things about, the ones you mentioned.' I did not for a moment believe in tiny beings that whispered in one's ear, or in monstrous dogs. But I had learned about the human monster, and I needed a bolted door before I could sleep.

'It's the cold, creeping ones that are the worst,' said Orna. 'They sing to you, lull you with their voices, and the next thing you find yourself wandering on a little path to nowhere. My own uncle fell prey to them. You can't arm yourself against them. If they want you, they get you.'

I began to wonder if this whole episode was a crazy dream brought about by exhaustion and sorrow. 'If Whistling Tor is so beset by these creatures,' I asked, 'it seems strange to me that the village still exists. That's if I understood you right, that these . . . manifestations . . . have been plaguing the region for almost four generations. I'd have thought people would have packed up and left long ago.'

'Leave Whistling Tor?' The innkeeper's tone was full of amazement. It was plain that he had never considered such a prospect and found the idea unimaginable. 'We couldn't do that. Whistling Tor's our place. It's our home.'

'The sleeping quarters are through this way,' Orna said briskly, as if that topic was too painful to dwell on. 'Brace the bar across the door and don't open up until daylight.'

I did not dream of creeping presences and dogs that devoured sheep whole, but of Market Cross and of Ita. My kinswoman sought to rule me even in my sleep, her tongue a whip scourging me for my imperfections. *You're nothing*, her dream voice reminded me. *You're nobody. Your father shouldn't have filled your head with wild ideas and impossible aspirations. Women don't earn a living at men's crafts. Berach should have had you learn a housewife's skills, not train you into a little copy of himself, just as if you were a boy. Be glad you have responsible kinsfolk to take care of you, Caitrin. It's not as if you've demonstrated an ability to look after yourself since your father died. Be grateful Cillian is prepared to give you his name . . .*

In the dream, I had no voice. I could not scream a protest, I could not say that the idea of marrying Cillian filled my heart with terror. I could not tell her that turning my back on my beloved craft meant betraying my father. But then, in the long, waking nightmare that had unfolded after Father's death, I had not once spoken out. My voice had been muted by grief and by a numb refusal to accept that all I held dear had been suddenly snatched from me. Even now, I did not quite believe that in a single season the bright promise of my life had turned to ashes.

Now Ita and I were in a tiny cell with iron bolts on the door. It was bitterly cold; I was clad only in a shift of scratchy homespun. Ita was shaving my head with a big knife. *You've run out of choices, Caitrin, you disobedient girl. You must go into the priory. You'll have plenty of time there to consider the result of your folly.* A nun's grey habit was laid out across the pallet. *On second thoughts,* Ita's dream voice said, *we'll do it this way.* The floor of the cell opened under my feet. I fell, half-naked as I was, and a forest of bony hands stretched out to rake my flesh with long nails as I passed. A howling filled the air, a wretched, despairing noise. Slavering mouths surrounded me, sinking their pointed teeth deep into my arms, my legs, the tender parts of my body, until I felt the flow of hot blood all over me. *You're nothing! Nothing!* A derisive, shrieking laugh. Down I fell, down, down, knowing that when I landed I would break in pieces . . . *Sleep,* whispered someone. *Long sleep* . . .

I woke, heart hammering, skin damp with the sweat of terror. Where was I? It was pitch-dark and I was trembling with cold. An icy draft swept into the cell-like chamber where I lay. A cell . . . the priory, oh God, it hadn't been a dream, it was true . . . No, I was in the inn at Whistling Tor, and I had kicked my blankets onto the floor while I slept. My bundle and writing box were beside me, the proof that at last I had taken control of my life and fled Market Cross. Tears filled my eyes as I reached for the blankets. It was all right. I was safe. The nightmare was over.

It had been worse than usual, perhaps thanks to Tomas and Orna's tales, and I had no wish to lie down and close my eyes again. Besides, it was too cold to sleep. A clammy chill was seeping right into my bones. I huddled into the blankets and applied my mind to the dire situation I had brought on myself. I had no resources beyond my craft and my common sense, and even that had deserted me lately. I must think of tomorrow. How to get a ride when folk seldom visited Whistling Tor. How to pay for it with no funds. And the big one, the one that kept my belly churning with fear and my head racing to find solutions: how to stay one step ahead of pursuit.

My head began to turn in circles. My father lying pale and still on the workroom floor. Ita's voice, always her voice, issuing decrees, giving orders, making things happen, too soon, much too soon, while shock and sorrow rendered me incapable of standing up for myself. And as soon as my sister was gone, the blows. Ita was a master of slaps and pinches. And Cillian . . . Cillian had marked me. The bruises on my skin – blue, black, yellow, an angry patchwork – would fade. There were other hurts, deeper ones, that would be harder to lose. *You did it, Caitrin,* I reminded myself. *You got up and walked out.*

Dawn came at last, but I did not unbar my door until I heard folk moving about outside. While I discounted the horror tales of suppertime, my dream made me reluctant to venture out until the local people deemed it safe to go abroad. Just as I was removing the iron bar, Tomas came to knock on the door.

'There's a fire on,' the innkeeper said. 'Come through when you're ready. I've got a bit of breakfast for you.'

'I can't pay any more.'

'No extra charge, lass. You need something in your stomach.'

I could have wept. It seemed so long since I had been amongst kind people. Soon after, I was sitting at a table by the window of the inn, looking out as I worked my way through a platter of coarse bread and sausage.

The mist was clearing. I could see the houses of the settlement, and behind them a stretch of the makeshift fortification. Beyond that, the ground rose towards a wooded hill. At the very top, sections of a high stone wall could be glimpsed above the canopy of oaks and elms. Towers loomed. The place looked big, grand. Without a doubt, this was the fortress Tomas had mentioned, the one that housed the crooked, inept chieftain of Whistling Tor. Stone: that was unusual. The Normans built in stone. Our own chieftains constructed their fortresses of mud and wattle. This place was substantial. Situated as it was, strategically high above the surrounding terrain, it would make an excellent base for a regional commander, and I wondered if the Norman leaders knew about it. For such a prize they might well venture into the west.

The slopes below the wall were thick with vegetation. Birds were flying in and out. The tale of dangerous creatures in the woods had painted the ancient fort as grim and forbidding in my mind, but the green growth softened it. All the same, it looked set apart, lonely somehow; even without last night's tales, I thought I would have sensed a sadness about the place.

Outside the window Tomas, an apron around his waist, was speaking to a man I had not seen last night, a large, square-jawed individual with knives at his belt and a heavy axe slung on his back. He had on a worn but well-cared-for leather breastplate over practical garments of wool; it was the garb of a warrior. His hair was more grey than fair, and hung to his shoulders in thick twisted locks. As he and Tomas entered a dispute of some kind, Orna came out carrying a bundle, which she more or less dropped at the stranger's feet. She did not look at him or speak a word, just scurried back inside. The men's conversation reached me through the open window.

'What about someone to help with the livestock, at least?' the visitor asked. 'That boy you sent me didn't even last two days.'

'They're afraid, Magnus. You can't expect folk to stay in that household of freaks, not to speak of what's in the woods on every side. And it's not as if your master pays them a fortune for their labours.'

'You know quite well that the most a lad or lass should expect for that kind of work is a bed and two square meals a day, with perhaps a little something to take home on feast days. We need help. It's perfectly safe. Anluan's folk don't attack their own.'

'I can't help you,' Tomas said flatly. 'You might tell Lord Anluan that ordinary people are sick and tired of being harassed by those creatures in his woods, and they're still wearier of his failure to do anything about that or about any of the misfortunes that have beset the region since his sorry ancestor unleashed hell in Whistling Tor.'

'Come on, Tomas. You know how things stand. Ask around the neighbourhood for me, will you? I can't manage without a lad to give me a hand, and we could do with a girl to help around the house as well. And there's another thing. Anluan needs someone for a special job, over the summer. Someone who can read Latin and write. Write properly, I mean. *Fast and accurate*, that's what he said.'

My heart began to race.

Tomas snorted in disbelief. 'Wouldn't you need a cleric for

that?' he asked. 'You won't get any of *them* near Whistling Tor, the way things stand. You're wasting your time. All right, I'll ask. But you know what the answer will be.'

As I gathered my belongings, the visitor hefted the bundle onto his shoulder and headed off in the general direction of the fortified barrier. By the time Tomas came back in with a load of firewood, Magnus had disappeared from view.

'That man who was outside,' I said. 'Magnus, was it? Did he say they needed a scribe up at the fortress?' I prayed that this was the gift it appeared to be: a remarkable opportunity of both hiding place and paid work.

'He did say that.' Tomas set down the wood and regarded me, hands on hips. 'Someone who can read Latin. Why he asked me, I can't imagine. It's hard enough to find him a simple cowherd, let alone a scholar. Sounds like it's a big job, whatever it is; could take the whole summer. I'll tell you the truth, Caitrin. There's not a soul in the region would agree to spend a season in that place, not for all the silver in Connacht. Not that it matters, since none of us can read anyway, Latin, Irish or anything else.'

'Who is Magnus, exactly? A servant? He works for the chieftain, Anluan, is that his name?'

'Steward, I suppose you could call Magnus. Been there since Irial's time. Hired as a fighter; stayed on when Irial died. Magnus is a foreigner, one of the *gallóglaigh*. Doesn't do much fighting now. More of a farmer and jack of all trades. I can't imagine why he stays.'

'So there are ordinary folk living on the hill, not just these . . . presences?' I'd have to run to catch up with Magnus before he disappeared up the path into the woods.

Tomas's gaze sharpened. 'Magnus is the most ordinary it gets up there,' he said.

'I must go after him,' I said. 'I can do the job. I can read and write. I'm a trained scribe, and I need work. Will the barrier still be open?'

'You can read?' Tomas's incredulity was not so surprising; people tended to respond like this when they heard about my skills. 'A young woman like you? That's the strangest thing I ever heard.'

'What you told me last night was a lot stranger,' I said. 'Tomas, I have to run or I won't catch up with him.'

'Whoa, whoa, now wait a bit.' Tomas looked genuinely alarmed. 'That story you heard last night might have been hard to swallow, but it was simple truth. You'd only need to spend a few days here to discover that for yourself. I'll accept that maybe you're a scholar – why would you lie about such a thing? – but as I said to Magnus, no scribe in his right mind would touch this job. I didn't take you for a fool, lass.'

'I have to tell you something,' I said, deciding to risk part of the truth. 'I'm being followed and I don't want to be found. I didn't do anything wrong, but there's someone after me and I need to get away. And I do need paid work, quite badly. Will you ask the men to let me through the barrier, please?'

He didn't like it, and nor did the men who were on duty by the fence this morning, a different group from last night. But the barrier was still open. They were just beginning to replace the iron bars when I got there.

'You'd be safe enough with us in the village,' Tomas protested. 'I told you, nobody comes here.'

I pictured Cillian and his friends, big, strong individuals with limited imagination. Cillian would come after me, I knew it in my bones. If only out of pride, he would come. 'I'll take my chances with the fortress,' I said, not letting myself think too hard. 'But thank you. You've been kind.'

'Good luck to you then,' Tomas said. 'Stay on the path. Head straight uphill. My advice is, put your fingers in your ears and run. If you catch up with Magnus you might have a chance of reaching the top in one piece.' He sounded doubtful.

As I walked away I heard a man offer a wager: ten coppers that I wouldn't make it to the fortress. Nobody seemed inclined to take him on.

There was no sign of Magnus. I headed up the pathway under the trees. The mist had cleared. The sun was out, but the air was chill. I passed the point where I and my two companions had taken the downward branch last night and went on up. My legs began to ache, for the path was steep as it wound around the hill.

The way narrowed. Other paths went off to left and to right.

At the side of one I saw a pile of white stones. Next to another the foliage of a strap-leafed plant was knotted together, as if in some secret sign. I did not take either of those ways, but held to what I thought was the main track, though there was a similarity about them that seemed designed to confuse. Peering uphill between the trees, I tried to convince myself I could glimpse the fortress wall. It could not be much further.

Something brushed against my right cheek. I slapped at it, not keen to reach my destination covered in insect bites. Another, on the left side; I swatted, hurting myself, but caught nothing. A moment later there was a hissing in my ear and I started in fright, whirling around. There was nothing there, only the stillness of the woodland, such a profound hush that not even birds raised their voices. Whatever that had been, it was more than a troublesome midge. The sound came again, a wordless whisper. The hairs on the back of my neck prickled in unease. I picked up my pace, striding forward. Whatever it was stayed with me, a rustling, a shivering, the sensation of something cold and fluid clinging around my shoulders. 'You're imagining things,' I muttered to myself.

And then there was no mistaking it, for there were words, soft against my ear, intimate, wheedling: *This way . . . Take this little twisty path . . .*

Nothing to be seen, only the voice. Something compelled me to look to the right, where a smaller path soft with ferns made a tempting way into a deeper part of the woods. On either side the trunks of beeches glowed green with moss under the filtered sunlight. Shuddering, I turned away, heading in the opposite direction.

No, this way! It came in a different voice, lower, more hushed, a gentle, persuasive tone. *Over here . . . Follow me . . .*

This way, thisss way . . . Now it was a chorus, a clamour all around me; the forest was full of voices.

'Stop it!' I cried, feeling both alarmed and a little foolish. 'Leave me alone!'

Something tugged at my right arm, almost dislodging my writing box. Bony fingers dug into my flesh, putting me sharply in mind of last night's hideous dream. I wrenched myself free.

Something clutched my left arm, then put its hand on my waist, fingers creeping. I ran, my bag bouncing on my back, my feet slipping on a carpet of forest litter, my skin crawling with disgust. I skidded through puddles and blundered against rocks, I whipped past briars and bruised myself on branches. My head had room for nothing but the need for flight. My body seemed full of my pounding heart.

I came up hard against the trunk of a birch and stood there, my chest heaving. The voices had fallen silent. On every side was a dense blanket of bushes, ferns and creepers, and the trees like a waiting army. The path was nowhere to be seen.

It should be a simple choice, even so. Go steadily downhill and reach the village, where a humble admission that I had made an error would gain me admittance. Or keep on uphill and try to reach the fortress. I looked around me again. Curiously, there no longer seemed to be an obvious up or down about the hillside. Each time I blinked or turned my head, objects seemed to shift. A gap between the trees disappeared as quickly as it had come into view. A rocky outcrop by which I could fix a path turned before my eyes into an impenetrable mass of thornbushes. I might walk and walk in this place and never reach any destination at all.

You didn't listen, whispered a little voice. *You didn't take heed. You do not belong here.*

'Lost, are you?'

I started violently, whirling around at the rough, booming voice. Between two massive oaks stood an extraordinary man. I hardly had time to take in his squat build, his ruddy cheeks like ripe apples and his mossy, green-grey beard. I glanced only briefly at his odd garb: a rough tunic and breeches of skins, a garland of leaves and twigs on his wild thatch of hair, festoons of greenery wreathed around his neck. As he took a step towards me, I saw what was coming up behind him. If the man was unusual, the dog was monstrous. The moment I set eyes on it I believed the whole story, rams, wisps of wool and all. It was a powerfully built animal of brindled hue, short-haired, its muzzle of the shape that men favour in a fighting dog, with the kind of jaws that grip fast and cannot be prised apart against the creature's will. Its ears were small, its eyes mean, its posture one of imminent attack. It was four times as big as any dog I'd ever clapped eyes on.

'He won't bite,' the man said, offhand. 'Which way are you headed?'

I swallowed. It was not much of a choice: put my fate into the hands of this pair, or stay here and let the eldritch voices lead me on a long walk to nowhere. 'I'm trying to get up to the fortress,' I said, struggling to keep my voice steady. If the dog knew I was afraid, it would be more likely to attack.

'You're far off the path. Here.' The strange man extended a knobbly hand, grasped mine and helped me over a fallen tree trunk. 'It's not a long walk if you know how to do it. Track's neglected. Folk don't come this way. Follow me.'

I walked behind him, and the dog walked behind me, growling deep in its throat. Without quite looking, I knew its little eyes were fixed intently on me.

'Hush, Fianchu!' the man commanded, and the growling died down, but it was still there, a subterranean threat. 'He's not good with strangers,' my companion said. 'If you're a kindly soul, he'll warm to you in time. Talk to him, why don't you?' He paused, and I halted, not prepared to turn around in case the hound launched its considerable bulk straight at me. 'Go on, try it,' the man added, not unkindly.

Under the circumstances I could hardly refuse. 'Fianchu, is that his name?' I asked.

'He's Fianchu, and I'm Olcan.'

'My name is Caitrin,' I said. 'I've come to see your chieftain about a scribing job.' I turned very slowly towards the dog. It was two strides away and had gone into a sitting posture. 'Nice dog, Fianchu,' I muttered insincerely.

'That's it.' There was a smile in Olcan's voice. 'Keep it up, see, he likes it.'

Fianchu's stumpy tail was beating a little rhythm against the forest floor. His mouth was stretched in a grin, revealing a set of efficient-looking teeth. Encouraged, I continued. 'Such a good boy, sitting so politely. Good Fianchu.' I reached out cautiously.

'Careful!' said Olcan. 'He has been known to snap.'

Hoping very much that I was not about to lose a hand, I held my fingers where Fianchu could smell them. I watched him without looking him directly in the eye. 'Good boy. Nice gentle boy.'

The hound sniffed at my hand, then put out his massive tongue to lick it.

'Looks like he's taken to you,' said Olcan, grinning widely. Fianchu had gone down into a lying position, his massive head right beside my foot. I scratched him behind one ear and he drooled.

'To tell the truth,' my companion went on, 'I wasn't sure if he'd make friends or take a bite out of you. Looks as if you've got the touch.'

'Good,' I said a little shakily. 'Do you live at the fortress, Olcan? Do you work for the chieftain?'

Olcan gave me a complicated look. 'I'm no man's servant,' he said. 'But I'm one of Anluan's folk.'

Soon we were back on the path, which wound steeply upwards through small groves of elder and willow. Whistling Tor was far bigger than it looked from down in the settlement. At last, above us between the trees loomed the massive bulk of the fortress wall.

'Gate's around that way a bit,' Olcan said, halting. 'Don't go back downhill.'

'Thank you,' I said. 'I'm most grateful. Where exactly –'

But before I could ask for further directions, he turned on his heel and strode back down the hill, Fianchu padding silently after him. I was on my own again.

chapter two

skirted the wall, telling myself to breathe slowly. Those voices, those creeping hands . . . I had been too quick to dismiss Tomas and Orna's stories as fantasy. And afterwards, I'd been so alarmed by the appearance of Fianchu that I hadn't even thought to ask Olcan what the mysterious presences were. I understood, now, why people never came up here. If Olcan hadn't appeared at the right moment to rescue me, I'd probably have become so hopelessly lost I'd never have emerged from the woods again. I just hoped I would get the scribing job so I didn't have to walk back down the hill today.

I paused to tidy my hair and straighten my clothing. I practised what I would say to Lord Anluan or to whomever I met when I finally reached the front door. *My name is Caitrin, daughter of Berach. My father trained me as a scribe. He was famous throughout our area for his fine calligraphy and undertook commissions for all the local chieftains. I can read and write both Latin and Irish, and I'm prepared to stay here all summer. I am certain I can do the job.* Perhaps not that last bit – it implied a confidence I did not feel. Ita had told me often enough that women could never ply such crafts as penmanship as well as men could, and that I was deluding myself if I imagined I was any different. I knew she was expressing society's view when she said that. Any commissions I had fulfilled had always been presented to customers as my father's work. It had irked Father that such subterfuge was necessary if we wanted fair payment. Folk believed, generally, that all I did was mix inks, prepare quills and keep the workroom tidy.

Lord Anluan would likely be no different from others we had worked for. He might well find it hard to believe that anyone other than a monk could read and write, for secular scribes such as my father were a rare breed. As for convincing this chieftain to employ a young woman for such work, that might not be so hard, I thought, in the light of the difficulty Magnus seemed to be having in finding helpers who would stay.

Further around the wall there was an arched opening with the remnant of iron fastenings to either side. If there had been a gate to block this entry, it had long since crumbled away to nothing. The fortress would once have provided an impregnable refuge, a safe retreat for the inhabitants of local farms and settlements in time of war. The stone blocks that formed it were massive. I could not for the life of me imagine how they had been moved into place.

Everything was damp. The stones were covered with creeping mosses; small ferns had colonised every chink and crevice, and long-thorned briars clustered thickly around the base of the wall, a forbidding outer barrier. I looked up at the towers and was seized by dizziness. Fine day or not, their tips were lost in a misty shroud.

Narrow slit windows pierced these towers, designed for the shooting of arrows in defence. There were some larger openings lower down, and from the gateway where I stood I glimpsed someone moving about inside, perhaps a woman. *Magnus is the most ordinary it gets up there*, Tomas had said.

I advanced cautiously through the gap. The space enclosed by the wall was immense, far bigger than it had seemed from outside, and there were buildings of various kinds set up against the bastion, here on one level, there on two, with external steps of stone. In one place these went up to a high walkway, a place where fighting men might be stationed in time of siege. Not that such a presence could be effective now, when anyone could wander in without a by-your-leave. The high, round towers were situated at the corners of the wall and had their own entries.

I would have expected a chieftain's stronghold to have a courtyard inside, a place where warriors on horseback and oxen drawing carts could be accommodated, and where all the bustle and activity of a noble household could unfold. There was nothing like that here. Instead, the whole place was grown over with trees of various kinds – I saw a plum, a hazel, a weeping willow – and under them were bushes and grasses alive with insects and birds. I advanced along a flagstone path, my skirt brushing the thick foliage of bordering plants, and saw that beneath this lush, undisciplined growth there were traces of old gardens, lavender and rosemary bushes, stakes for beans now leaning on drunken angles, patches where straw had been laid to shelter vegetables of some kind. On a weedy pond, two ducks swam in desultory circles.

The main door might have been anywhere. All was swathed in creepers and mosses, and every time I glanced across at the biggest of the buildings, the one I thought most likely to be the entry point, it seemed to be in a slightly different place. *Use your common sense,* I ordered myself grimly as I noted the position of the sun relative to the towers I had just passed. Towers and walls didn't move. This place might be odd, but nowhere was as odd as that. I passed a hawthorn bush over which a lonely shirt had been laid to dry. The garment was sodden from last night's rain. I still couldn't see the front door.

A scarecrow stood amidst the ill-tended plants near the path, a crow perched on each shoulder. It was an odd thing in a voluminous black cloak and a silk-lined cap. I went closer and the sun broke through the mist above me, striking a glint from a decoration that circled the neck of the effigy. Saints preserve us, if those were real jewels the manikin was wearing a king's ransom.

The scarecrow raised a long-fingered hand to cover its mouth politely, then gave a cough. I felt the blood drain from my face. I stepped back, and whatever it was stepped forward out of the garden, flinging its cloak around itself in an imperious gesture. The crows flew up in fright. I stood rooted to the spot, unable to speak. The thing fixed its dark, assessing eyes on me and smiled without showing its teeth. There was a greenish pallor about its skin, as if it had been left out too long in the rain.

'Excuse me,' I babbled stupidly, 'I didn't mean to disturb you. I'm looking for the chieftain, Lord Anluan. Or Magnus.'

The being lifted its hand, pointing towards a wall that seemed to enclose another garden. Through an archway mantled by a white-flowered creeper wafted a scent of familiar herbs: basil, thyme and wormwood. The inner wall was covered in honeysuckle.

'In there? Thank you.' I scuttled away, eyes averted. *You need this job, Caitrin. You need this hiding place. You vowed you would be brave.*

The walled garden was almost as unkempt and overgrown as the area outside, but I could see it had once been lovely. A birch tree stood in the centre, and around it were the remnants of a circular path lined with stones, and beds of medicinal herbs hedged with bay. The bay was running riot and the herbs were sorely in need of a trimming, but it was clear that this little garden had been more recently tended than the wilderness beyond its walls. An ancient stone birdbath held its share of avian visitors; someone had cleaned and replenished it not long ago. A wooden bench stood under the tree, and on it lay an open book, face down. I froze. But there was nobody in sight; it seemed the reader had tired of study and left this sanctuary.

I put my bundle and writing box on the bench and walked slowly around the path, liking the methodical way the garden had been laid out. Its untidiness did not trouble me; it was only in the practice of my craft that my mind required complete order. This haven had been planted by a skilled herbalist. There was everything here for a wide range of uses, both culinary and medicinal. Belladonna for fever, sorrel for the liver. Figwort, meadowsweet, heart-of-the-earth. And over there . . .

Heart's blood. In an unobtrusive corner, half hidden beneath the spreading silvery-grey leaves of a gigantic comfrey plant, grew a clump of this rarest of herbs. I'd never seen the real thing before, but I knew it from an illustrated treatise on inks and dyes.

I moved closer, crouching down to examine the leaves – they grew in characteristic groups of five, with neat serrations along each delicate edge – and the stem with its unusual mottled pattern. No buds yet; this rarity bloomed only in autumn, and then briefly. It was the flowers that made it a herb beyond price, for their crushed petals, when mixed in specific proportions with vinegar and oak ash, produced an ink of rich hue, a splendid deep purple favoured by kings and princes for their most regal decrees and beloved of bishops for the illustrated capitals in missals and breviaries. The capacity to produce a supply of heart's blood ink could make a man's fortune. I brushed my fingers gently against the foliage.

'Don't touch that!' roared a deep voice from behind me. I leaped to my feet, my heart thudding in fright.

A man stood on the pathway not three arms' lengths from me, glaring. He had come from nowhere, and he looked not only angry, but somehow . . . *wrong*.

'I wasn't – I was just –' Suddenly I was back in Market Cross, with Cillian's cruel hands gripping my shoulders as he shook me, and Cillian's abusive words ringing in my ears. 'I – I –' *Pull yourself together, Caitrin. Say something.* I stood frozen, my stomach tying itself in knots.

The stranger stood over me, fist clenched in fury, eyes glowering. 'What are you doing here? This place is forbidden!'

I struggled to find the words I had prepared. 'I'm a . . . I've come to . . .' *Get a grip on yourself, Caitrin. You are not going back to that dark place.* 'I'm a . . . a . . .' I forced the memory down, making myself look up at the man. His appearance was unsettling, for although his features were above the commonplace in beauty, they were at the same time somehow skewed, as if the two sides of his face were not a perfect match for each other. I noted the red hair, as ill tended and overgrown as his garden, and the fair complexion, flushed by anger. His eyes were of an intense dark blue and as inimical as his voice.

'You're a what?' he snarled. 'A thief? Why else would you be here? Nobody comes here!'

'I wasn't trying to steal the heart's blood plant,' I managed. 'I'm here about the work. The position. Reading. Scribing. Latin.' I faltered to a halt, backing away. I could feel his rage quivering in the air of the peaceful garden.

He stood there a moment, staring at me as if I were the oddity and everything else here completely normal. Then he lurched towards me, one arm outstretched as if to seize hold of me. The cold fear washed through me again. 'It doesn't matter,' I squeaked. 'I must have made a mistake . . .'

I backed further, then fled for the archway. Curse it! Curse this place, and curse Ita and her son, and most of all, a pox on me for daring to hope that I might have found sanctuary and for being wrong. And now I had to go all the way through that wretched forest again.

'Wait.' The man's tone had changed. 'You can read Latin?'

I halted with my back to him, my stomach churning. I couldn't seem to catch my breath. My lips refused to form the simple word, *yes*, but I managed a nod.

'Magnus!' the man roared behind me, making my heart jolt with fright. I drew a shaky breath and turned to see him heading off towards a door at the other end of the garden, an entry direct into the most substantial of the buildings backing onto the fortress wall. Despite his height and strong build, the man's gait was markedly uneven, and the odd slope of his shoulders was quite pronounced. *Warped and twisted like thread gone awry on the loom.* If that had been Anluan, neither of us had made a good first impression.

As I'd been told to wait, I waited, but not inside the forbidden area. I collected my belongings and went to stand just beyond the archway, one eye out for any further oddities. That was where Magnus found me a little later. He had shed his weaponry but still made a formidable figure with his twists of hair, his broad shoulders and well-muscled arms. One of the *gallóglaigh*, Tomas had called him. They were mercenary warriors, islanders descended from Norsemen and Dalriadans. I wondered how this one had ended up at Whistling Tor.

'A scribe,' the big man said flatly, fixing shrewd grey eyes on my face, which no doubt was unusually pale. 'How did you know about the work we needed done?'

'I'm sorry if I've upset anyone,' I said. 'My name is Caitrin, daughter of Berach. I stayed last night at the village inn. I couldn't help overhearing your conversation with Tomas.'

His gaze had sharpened as I spoke. 'I'm told you were

attempting to steal a precious plant from our garden,' he said. 'That's not the act of someone who's seeking employment.'

'I told that man I wasn't stealing! If you're talking about heart's blood, the time to steal it would be autumn, when it's flowering. The value's all in the blooms. For the ink, you know.'

There was a moment's silence, then Magnus's strong features creased into a smile. He looked like a man who didn't smile much. 'All right, maybe you are a scribe,' he said. 'That doesn't explain how you got here.'

'I walked. I did lose my way, but a man helped me. A man with a dog. Olcan and Fianchu.'

Magnus's eyes widened.

'As you see, I got here safely,' I added.

'Mm. No fear of dogs, then. Well, I've been ordered to take you indoors, and I imagine he'll want a sample of your writing. This way.'

'I'm not sure I want to stay. That was him in the garden, wasn't it? Lord Anluan? He scared me. He was so angry.'

'You look cold,' Magnus said. 'My name's Magnus. I do everything here, more or less. Steward, guard, farmer, cook, cleaner . . . You may as well come in and have something to drink, since you've got this far. Don't let Anluan upset you. He's not used to folk, that's all. We're a bit out of practice.'

I drew a deep, unsteady breath. His manner was reassuring: blunt but kind. He seemed the sort of man who would be truthful. 'All right,' I said. 'If you're sure it's safe. There are some very odd-looking folk here. Not that looks should matter, but . . .'

'I'll take that for you,' said Magnus, pointing to my bag. I passed it to him and we headed along the path. 'If you're planning on staying to do the job, you'll need to learn not to let appearances upset you,' my companion added. 'We're all oddities here.'

'The folk in the settlement said you were the most ordinary person on the hill.'

Magnus gave a short, mirthless laugh. 'Ordinary, what's that?' he said grimly. 'As it is, you may not be here long enough to meet us all. Once you see the job he wants doing, you'll very likely change your mind. Anyway, you may not be up to the standard he requires.'

'I was trained by the best.'

'Then you've nothing to worry about, have you?' Now he sounded amused. 'There's one thing you need to remember.'

'Oh?' I fully expected the kind of instructions people got in dark tales; Whistling Tor seemed just the place for them. *Don't touch the little key third from the right. Don't go into the chamber at the top of the tower.* 'What is that?'

'Stay out of Irial's garden,' Magnus said. 'Nobody goes in without Anluan's invitation. You broke that rule. You upset him. He's had enough people take one look at him and run off in disgust, without you adding yourself to the number.'

'I wasn't disgusted, just scared. He came out of nowhere and he shouted at me. I'd already seen Olcan and the dog, and a scarecrow that walked around and showed me the way. And there were voices. And hands. They were all around me in the forest, trying to entice me off the path.'

'If you're so easily frightened,' Magnus observed, 'you won't last here more than a day or two. Might be kinder to leave without getting his hopes up too much. I don't want you to get started on the work, then bolt because you can't cope. I'm surprised you plucked up the courage to come at all.'

'I can cope,' I said, stung by the criticism. 'I didn't know I was trespassing. I walked up intending to find you and ask you about the job. The folk in the village had plenty to say about this place, but I dismissed most of it as wild exaggeration. After Fianchu, and those voices, I realise I may have been wrong.'

'Ah. No doubt Tomas regaled you with stories about Anluan's disfigurement and his general ineptitude as a leader?'

'More or less.' I was ashamed now. My parents had taught me not to judge on appearances. 'They implied his – condition – was part of a family curse.'

'Make your own judgements, that's always been my philosophy.' Magnus's mouth was set in a tight line now. 'Maybe that's why I'm still here and nobody else is.'

When I had looked at Anluan's curiously unbalanced features, had my own face shown a revulsion that was all too familiar to him? What must he have thought of me? 'I heard that the scribing work will take the whole summer,' I said. 'I know you experience some difficulty in getting people to stay here. I am available to work right through until autumn if that's what is required. Provided you can assure me that I will be safe here, I won't bolt. I'll stay until the task is completed.'

'Mm-hm.' Magnus ushered me up some steps and into what was evidently the living area. I followed him along a dark hallway and then through a series of chambers of austere appearance. There were no rushes on the floor and the rooms were almost bare of furniture. The stone walls had a damp look about them. I spotted a tall bronze mirror propped in a corner, its surface partly covered by a cloth. Images moved in it, things that most certainly did not exist in this near-empty chamber. I hesitated, my gaze drawn towards it, my flesh crawling with unease. 'We'll go to the kitchen,' Magnus said. 'You'll be wanting to get warm.'

The kitchen was down another hallway and through a heavy oak door. A meagre fire struggled on the hearth. On a well-scrubbed table lay the bundle of supplies Magnus had carried up from the village, its contents as yet unpacked. My companion hung a kettle from an iron support over the hearth and added wood to the fire. I watched him, my head full of awkward questions.

Magnus rummaged on a shelf, produced a little box and spooned something from it into an earthenware cup. As he worked I looked about me, noticing that this chamber, too, had its mirror, a three-sided, polished piece of some dark metal I could not identify. It seemed an ordinary one, the reflection showing a section of wall and roof, but the light was odd, as if the image within the metal showed the room at a different time of day or in a different season. It was hard not to stare at it.

'This is a restorative mix,' Magnus said, stirring. 'Should put a bit of heart back into you. You look as if you need it.' When the kettle was steaming, he filled the cup and put it on the table beside me. 'It's safe to drink,' he added. 'By the way, you might want to avoid looking in the mirrors for a while. They can be confusing. You'll get used to them in time. If you stay, that is.'

'I see.' It was troubling how strongly the polished surface drew the eye, as if it might have enticing secrets to yield. I changed the subject. 'Are you the one who tends the herb garden, Magnus?' I asked. 'Irial's garden, is that what it's called? I noticed it's quite well kept compared with . . .' My voice trailed away as I realised the implied insult in my words.

'That garden's his domain,' Magnus said. 'But I do everything else.' He glanced around the kitchen, plainly seeing it through my eyes. It was clean but remarkably bare, the shelves near empty, the cooking pans, platters and cups lined up neatly. My sister's kitchen, at home in Market Cross, had been a place of warmth and light, savoury smells and bustling activity. That was before Father died; before Maraid abandoned me to Ita and Cillian. Going into that kitchen had felt like being hugged against a mother's heart. This chamber was cold, despite the fire. There was no heart here.

'I meant no criticism,' I said awkwardly.

'Not your fault, is it? At least, now you're here, I can take looking for a scribe off my list of duties. That's if he'll have you. I'd best go and speak to him.'

I sat alone before the fire while he went off to find his master. I tried the herbal draught, which was bitter but not unpleasing. I imagined Maraid here, setting a jug of wildflowers on a shelf, hanging a bright weaving on a bare wall, singing as she chopped onions and leeks for a pie. But then Maraid would never be in my current situation. She was far too practical. All she had done was fall in love with a travelling musician and end up poor. *She's her mother all over again*, I could hear Ita saying. *A slut born and bred, can't help herself. And you'll be the same, mark my words. Your kind of looks attract the wrong sort of man, the sort with only one thing on his mind.*

I was about halfway through the drink when my gaze crossed the mirror once again and I saw reflected in it the form of a woman standing very still in the doorway behind me. Somehow she had got there without a sound. I jumped up, spilling the contents of my cup. 'I'm sorry,' I said, looking around for something to clean up with. 'You startled me.' When she did not reply, I added, 'My name is Caitrin, daughter of Berach. I'm here about the scribing job.'

She stood watching in silence as I found a cloth and wiped the tabletop. Under her scrutiny I straightened, turning to face her. This was no serving woman. Her manner was regal and her clothing, though plain to the point of severity, was expertly cut

31

and fashioned of finest wool. The gown was dove grey, the over-dress a slightly darker shade; her hair was concealed by a light veil. Under its neat folds her expression was coolly judgemental. Anluan's wife? She was quite young, perhaps not much older than me. How old was the chieftain? Between the unkempt hair, the scowl and the oddity of his features, all I could say was that he was probably no more than thirty.

The woman clasped her hands together, gazing at me with lus-trous grey eyes. Her features were neat and small. She held herself very straight. Anluan's sister, perhaps? Could she be Magnus's daughter?

'I'm just waiting for Magnus to come back,' I said, forcing a smile. 'He said I could sit here.'

The woman did not smile. 'I'm sorry,' she said crisply. 'We won't be needing you.'

After a moment's stunned silence, I protested. 'Magnus implied that I could have the job if I was able to do it. I should at least be given a trial –'

She took a step back, as if to allow me to pass her on my way out. 'We won't be needing you. It was a mistake.'

I stared at her. The promise of work, of funds, of safety from Cillian, the hope of a refuge for a whole summer, all dashed because of a mistake? 'But Magnus came down to the settlement asking for someone who could read and write Latin,' I said, feeling my face flush. 'I can do that. I should be given a chance to prove myself, my lady.' I considered telling her the truth and casting myself on her mercy. Somehow I didn't think that would get me very far. 'Even if there has been a mistake, I'm certain I can make myself useful here.' After all, Magnus had said they needed a boy for the farm and a woman for the house. If I could be safe, I'd be prepared to scrub floors all summer, even with this chilly woman giving the orders. 'Please, my lady,' I said. Her intense, wide-eyed scrutiny unnerved me. 'At least let me speak to Magnus again.'

'There is no need to speak to anyone else,' she said. After a moment she added, 'You are disappointed. Understand that it is best that you do not stay.'

Tears stung my eyes. I was reaching for my belongings when Magnus strode in the back door and set a quill, an ink pot and a scrap of parchment on the table. 'Write something,' he ordered. 'Straight away, he said, to prove you can work quickly as well as accurately. If it's good enough, he'll consider giving you a few days' trial.'

I glanced over at the woman. Her lips were pressed tightly together; a little line had appeared between her brows. 'I was told I wasn't required,' I said quietly.

'It's all right, Muirne,' said Magnus. 'Anluan wants to see her work.'

I drew a shaky breath. 'You said *if it's good enough*. Good enough for what?' I asked, putting my writing box on the table and undoing the clasps. 'Unless I know what this task is, how can I judge what sample to provide? Latin or Irish? What hand? What size?' I got out a medium goose quill and a pot of the black ink I had mixed myself. 'If it's all right with you, I'll use my own things.'

Magnus waited, arms folded, as I produced Father's special knife and refined the quill.

'What does he want me to write?' I asked, glancing up at him.

'He didn't say. Just show what you can do.'

'But how can I –'

'Best get on with it or I'll have to tell him you were slow.'

'Slow-witted, you mean, or slow at my craft? I am neither. But this is like sewing a coat for a man you've never seen, when you don't know whether it's for going fishing or parading around court to impress people.' The task was not made any easier by the silent watcher in the doorway.

'Do you want the position or don't you?' Magnus asked flatly.

I could not tell them how desperately I did want it, ill-tempered chieftain, disapproving noblewoman, animated scarecrow and all. Anluan had scared me, true; but nothing could be as terrifying as what I had left behind me. A sample: what would he expect? Should I provide an apt Latin quotation? Draft a letter? In the end, the quill moved almost despite me, and what I wrote was this: *I can read and write fluently in Latin and Irish. I'm sorry if I upset you. I would like to help you, if you will allow that. Caitrin.*

My script was plain and neat; I had the knack of keeping it straight even when there was no time to score guidelines. At the top of my sample I added the name *Anluan*, and decorated the capital with a little garland of honeysuckle around which a few bees hovered. The *C* for *Caitrin* I made into a slender hound sleeping in a curled position, tail tucked over its legs. I dusted on some fine sand from the bag I kept with my supplies, and the piece was more or less ready.

'Was that quick enough?' I asked as I passed the parchment up to Magnus, surprising an unguarded smile on his lips. 'Hold it flat, it won't be completely dry yet. If he's so particular, I imagine smeared ink will rule me straight out of contention.'

He bore my handiwork away and I waited again, uncomfortable under the eyes of the woman in the doorway. I couldn't think of anything appropriate to say, so I remained silent and, for a while, so did she. Then she advanced into the kitchen, moved some cups around on a shelf and said, with her back to me, 'You won't stay. Nobody stays. You will end up disappointing him.' Her tone was odd, constrained. Magnus had said something along the same lines: that it would be better to leave now than to get Anluan's hopes up only to desert him later. I didn't want to make an enemy of Muirne or Magnus. If I got the job, we'd be living in the same household all summer.

'If he wants me, I will stay,' I said, but as the time drew out I wondered whether it might be better if Anluan sent back a message that I wasn't up to the job. Magnus would probably escort me down the hill if I asked him to. Tomas had said the village would shelter me. How likely was it, really, that Cillian would come so far west in his efforts to track me down?

I tried to weigh up Whistling Tor with all its peculiarities, including the curse Tomas and Orna had mentioned, and the situation I had run from. People in Market Cross had believed it fortunate Ita and Cillian were there to tend to me in the helpless fog of grief that had followed my father's death. Ita liked to make sure folk understood. Someone had come to the house asking for me; perhaps several people. I'd not been myself at the time, and I couldn't remember clearly. I did recall Ita's voice, sharp and confident. *You can't see her. She can't see anyone. You know how highly strung Caitrin always was. Losing her father has turned her wits. She's in no fit state to make her own decisions, nor is she likely to be for some time to come. I will nurse her and provide for her, of course; my son and I will be staying in this house to ensure Caitrin is properly looked after. And I'll set my mark to any legal papers on her behalf. Poor Caitrin! She was such an accomplished girl.* If people couldn't see me, they couldn't see the bruises. If people couldn't hear me, it didn't matter if I spoke sense or nonsense. Anyway, I wouldn't have had the courage to speak up. Because the worst thing wasn't Cillian's fists or Ita's cruel tongue. It was me. It was the way the two of them turned me into a helpless child, full of self-loathing and timidity. It would be a mistake to think I'd be safe in the village with Tomas and Orna. Cillian would pursue me. Ita was determined that he and I would marry. *It's best for you, Caitrin,* she'd said, and I'd been too sad, too confused to ask for a proper explanation. It couldn't be about worldly goods. Father had left Maraid and me almost nothing.

'A scribe,' said Muirne, turning to fix her large eyes on my face. 'How did you learn to be a scribe?'

'My father taught me.' I had no intention of confiding in her; not before I found out if I was staying or going. 'He was a master craftsman, much in demand around the region of Market Cross.'

'There are many papers. It's dusty. Dirty. Hard work. Not a lady's work.'

My smile was probably more of a grimace. 'In this particular field, I am a very hard worker. I hope I will get the opportunity to prove it to you.'

Her neat brows lifted, and a little smile curved her lips. A moment later, she was gone as silently as she had arrived.

'Come with me. I'll show you where you can put your things.' Magnus spoke from the other doorway.

I jumped to my feet. 'Does that mean I've got the job?'

'A trial period. I'm to show you what needs to be done – you may change your mind once you see it – and you can work on it for a few days. He'll assess your progress and decide if you're up to completing the work by the end of summer. There's a chamber on the upper floor where you can sleep.'

I hurried after him, questions tumbling over one another in my mind. 'What exactly is it I'll be working on?' I asked.

'Records. Family history. They've all been scholars after their own fashion, from Anluan's great-grandfather down to him. He's got all manner of documents in there, some of them not in the best condition. Needs sorting out, putting straight. It's a mess, I warn you. Enough to dishearten the most orderly of scribes, in my opinion. But what do I know of such matters?'

As he talked, the steward led me along a hallway and up a precipitous flight of heavily worn steps to an upper floor, where several chambers opened off a long gallery. Large spiders tenanted each corner and crevice of the stonework. Leaves had blown in through the openings where the gallery overlooked the garden, to gather in damp piles against the walls. There was a forlorn smell, the scent of decay.

'Here,' said Magnus, ushering me through a doorway.

The chamber was bare, cold and unwelcoming, just like the downstairs rooms I had seen. It was furnished with a narrow shelf bed and an old storage chest. I did not think anyone had slept here for a very long time. 'I'll bring you up some blankets,' my companion said. 'It gets cold here at nights. There's a pump outside the kitchen door; we use that for washing. And you'll need a candle.'

'Has this door a bolt?'

'This may not be your run-of-the-mill household,' Magnus said, 'but you'll be quite safe here. Anluan looks after his own.'

On this particular point it was necessary to hold my ground. 'Anluan can hardly be expected to patrol up and down this gallery all night making sure nobody disturbs us,' I said.

'No,' Magnus agreed. 'Rioghan does that.'

'Rioghan!' I was surprised to hear a name I recognised. 'I met him yesterday. At least, I think it must be the same man. A sad-looking person with a red cloak. I didn't realise he lived here at the fortress.'

'He's one of those who live in the house,' Magnus said. 'I'll introduce you to all of them at supper, when we generally gather. More live out in the woods, but you won't see them so much.'

'Did you really mean that, about Rioghan walking up and down the gallery at night? I'm not sure I'd be very happy about that, even if it did make things safer.'

'Rioghan doesn't sleep. He keeps watch. He may not be on the gallery – he prefers the garden – but he'll be alert to anything unusual. As I said, it's safe on Whistling Tor provided you belong.'

36

'I don't belong, not yet.'

'If Anluan wants you here, you belong, Caitrin.'

'I still want a bolt for my door.'

'I'll put it on my list of things to do.'

'Today, please, Magnus. I understand you are very busy, but this is a . . . a requirement for me. Something I can't do without. Perhaps I can return the favour in some way.' As soon as this was out I remembered the carter's words: *There's other ways of paying.* 'For instance, I could chop vegetables or sweep floors,' I added.

'I'll bear it in mind. Well, make yourself at home. There's a privy out beyond the kitchen. When you're ready, come down and I'll show you the library. You'll be wanting to make a start.'

Some time later, clad in the spare gown I had brought – a practical dark green – and with my hair brushed and replaited, I stood with Magnus on the threshold of the library and found myself lost for words.

I had always valued order. The skilled exercise of calligraphy depends in large measure on neatness, accuracy, uniformity. In our workroom at Market Cross, the tools had been meticulously maintained and the materials stored with careful attention to safety and efficiency. It had been a haven of discipline and control.

Anluan's library was the most chaotic place I'd ever had the ill luck to stumble into. It was a sizeable chamber. Several big tables would have made useful work surfaces had they not been heaped high with documents, scrolls and loose leaves of parchment. This fragile material was strewn about apparently at random. Around the walls stood sundry chests and smaller tables, their tops as heavily laden as those of their larger counterparts. I suspected every receptacle would reveal, on opening, a welter of entangled materials.

I walked in, not saying a word. There were glazed windows all along the western side of the chamber. In the afternoons the light would be excellent for writing.

'The things you'll need are in that oak chest,' said Magnus, pointing to the far end of the chamber. 'Pens, powders for ink and so on. He said even if you've brought your own, they'll run out quickly. There's a good stock of parchment, enough for the job, he thinks. If you need more of anything we can get it, but to be honest I'd rather not have the trouble.'

I eyed the disorder around me, trying hard to view it not as an obstacle but as a challenge. 'What exactly is it I'm supposed to do here? Is Lord Anluan going to explain it to me himself?' A family of scholars, Magnus had said. I thought of the very detailed instructions Father and I had received for our commissions, the minute attention some of our customers had paid to the niceties of execution. 'Where is the material I have to transcribe?'

And when Magnus just looked at me, then cast his gaze around to take in the entire chamber, long scrolls, thick bound books, tiny fragments, loose bundles of parchment sheets, I felt hysterical laughter welling up in my throat.

'*All* of this?' I choked. 'In a single summer? What does this man think I am, a miracle worker?'

Magnus lifted a scrap of vellum by a corner and blew on it, setting dust motes dancing in the light from the window. 'Trained by the best, didn't you say?'

'I was. But this . . . this is crazy. How do I know where to start?'

'You don't have to write everything down. It's only the Latin parts he wants, seeing as he was never taught that tongue. It's Nechtan's records, the oldest ones. There's some in Irish, and he's read those, but he thinks some of the Latin documents are his great-grandfather's as well. He needs you to find those and put them into Irish so he can read them for himself. They're mixed up with all sorts of other things.' Magnus glanced at a row of small bound books that had been set by themselves on a shelf, and his expression softened a trace. 'Pictures, recipes for cures and so on. Notes, thoughts. Each of the chieftains of Whistling Tor made his own records. But the library's never been organised. The oldest pieces are crumbling away. If it was me doing the job – not that I'm a reading man, myself – I'd see some merit in making a list of what's here as you go through it, so you'll know where to find things later. Makes sense, doesn't it?'

'Perfect sense, Magnus. Thank you for the suggestion.' I took one of the little bound books from the shelf and opened it flat on a table, revealing a charming illustration of some kind of medicinal herb. Beside it, in spidery writing, were instructions for preparing a tincture suitable for the treatment of warts and carbuncles. 'I wish someone had done that before now. Made a list, I mean. You said Lord Anluan and his family were scholars.'

Perhaps I had sounded too critical. 'He did make a start himself.' Magnus's tone was forbidding. 'Or tried to.'

'Tried to.' If what Tomas and Orna had told me was true, this chieftain must have a lot of time on his hands. They'd implied that he did not perform any of the duties a local leader might be expected to undertake, such as riding forth to make sure his folk were well, checking on his fields and settlements, establishing defences against possible attack. 'This is a big task, Magnus. It looks as if I'll have to sort out the entire contents of the library before I start on the translation. Is there anyone here who could help me?'

'Shall I go and tell him you can't do the job?'

'No!' I found that I was clutching the plant book to my chest, and set it down. 'No, please don't. I will do my best.'

Magnus's gaze was assessing. 'Is it the law you're running from, with your need for a locked door and your wish to take on a job nobody else would want?'

He was too perceptive by half. 'If you don't ask awkward questions, I won't,' I said.

'Fair enough.'

'But I must ask just one. Why doesn't Lord Anluan come and talk to me about this himself?'

'Anluan doesn't see folk from outside.'

This flat statement sounded remarkably final. How could I do a good job without talking to the man who wanted it done? No awkward questions. That meant I could take this line of conversation no further.

Magnus had moved over to the window and was staring out. The library overlooked the herb garden in which I had encountered the reclusive chieftain of Whistling Tor earlier. From here I could not see the clump of heart's blood, only the profusion of honeysuckle and the riotous growth of more common herbs.

'You shouldn't judge him,' the steward said quietly. 'He's got his reasons. You're our first visitor in a long time, and the first ever to come without some coercion. And you're a woman. It was a shock.'

'To me, too,' I said, deciding not to point out that if one advertised for a scribe, one should not be surprised to see one turn up on the doorstep, so to speak. I was learning that the rules of this household bore little resemblance to those of the outside world. I moved to a small table by the window, which stood out for being the one tidy place in the chamber. The oak surface had been wiped clean, and on it stood a jar fashioned of an unusual green stone with a swirling pattern, containing several inexpertly trimmed quills and a knife. Perhaps Muirne was responsible for this little island of order. Beside the jar lay two sheets of good parchment, covered in writing. I picked one up. 'Whose hand is this?' I asked.

'Anluan's,' said Magnus. 'Nobody else here can write.'

One look told me why Anluan had done no more than make a start on the daunting task. True, he could write, and if I really put my mind to it I could read what he had written. It was the worst hand I'd seen in my life, so undisciplined that the letters seemed to be trying to crawl right off the page.

'Don't look like that,' Magnus said. 'You're a scribe, and he's a fellow who's lost the use of his right hand.' There was no judgement in his voice, only sorrow.

'I'm sorry . . .' My voice faded as I began to read.

Autumn begins to bite hard. I am in the final stages of preparation. With each new dawn, my mind and body are more fiercely driven by this. Knowledge beyond the earthly; a discovery to surpass any made hitherto by mortal man in this world. What if it is true? What if I can open this portal into the unknown? Where might I journey? What wondrous events might I witness? And when I return, how will I be changed?

I have despatched Aislinn to gather wolfbane.

'I'll leave you to it then. I've got things to do.'

I glanced up, one finger keeping my place on the page as I nodded to Magnus. He said something about supper, but his words faded into nothing as I was captured by the narrative before me.

40

Another day. Another step. As the time for the experiment draws closer, my helpers desert me, too blind to share my vision to the end, too feeble to bear the weight of my aspirations. They have allowed the superstitious tales of the local populace to influence them. My steward left me this morning. I can no longer serve you, those were his weakling words. No matter. I need no lackeys. I will do this alone, and when it is done I will have a parade of followers, a retinue of attendants, an army worthy of a king. They will be mine to lead, and those who doubted me, those who had not the stomach to stay the course, will choke on their cowardice. I will open this portal, and I will walk

I had reached the end of the second page. A dark and fascinating tale; I wanted more. But there was no more, not here at any rate. It couldn't be Anluan's account of his own experience, surely. He had not seemed at all the kind of man who would write thus, in an archaic and grandiose way, nor could I in my wildest imagination think of him commanding an army of any kind. This must be a partial transcription of some older document. To discover the rest of the story, I would have to hunt down Anluan's source.

In the window embrasure beside the table where the chieftain had been working stood a little old chest. It was marginally less dust-coated than the others and seemed the obvious place to start looking. I reached out to see if it would open, then withdrew my hand. The box had a powerful aura, enticing and repellent at the same time. It made my skin prickle with unease and my heart race with anticipation.

The voice of reason told me there was no need to open it right now. There were small mountains of other documents to sort, not to speak of sweeping the floor, wiping away the dust that coated every surface, airing the room, establishing a storage system so I would know where to find things. I cleared a space on one of the bigger tables by the crude method of pushing everything else out of the way and got out the folding wax tablet I kept for making notes. It had seen good use over the years. I had learned my letters on it, my small hand wielding the stylus at first awkwardly, later with more control, as I formed the foundations of my craft. The tablet was shaped like a book, with a hinged wooden cover. A leather strap held it closed when not in use, and the stylus had its own pocket. The wax surfaces, protected thus, had remained clean and serviceable. I would use this to keep daily records of my work and to note down which documents were located where. Parchment and vellum were too costly to be squandered on such ephemeral writings. I opened the tablet, glanced around the library and sighed. I could feel that box calling to me. *Read*, it whispered. *Read and weep.*

I wouldn't be able to set my mind to any other work until I dealt with this. I moved to the window and opened the box. No demons sprang forth. Inside, an assortment of items was neatly stowed. For the most part the contents were leaves of parchment, rolled in bundles and tied with disintegrating cords. Herbs had been sprinkled between the bundles long ago. These had dwindled to dust, but a faint sweet scent lingered on the pages, which were starting to crumble away at the edges. I reached for a bundle, then froze, gripped by a sense that someone was watching me. My skin prickling, I straightened and looked about me. The door to the garden stood ajar, but if someone had been there, he had vanished between one breath and the next. A faint scent of herbs lingered, sage and rosemary. I glanced out the window, but could see nobody. *Get a grip on yourself, Caitrin. This place is odd enough without adding your own imaginings.* I bent again to my task, lifting out each bundle of documents in turn and setting them side by side on the table. At the very bottom of the box was something wrapped in black cloth. I hesitated, then picked this up and placed it before me, unfolding its shroud with hands that were not entirely steady.

Perhaps I should have known it would be a mirror. This one was of obsidian, and something about it made me uneasy. The enigmatic black surface showed little reflection. I had read of such a mirror somewhere, I was certain. A dark mirror, used for divination. The artefact was in a silver frame crawling with eldritch creatures, each no bigger than a joint of my little finger, their eyes set with miniature stones of red or green. I blinked and stared anew. Hadn't that gnome-like homunculus been at the bottom of the mirror last time I looked? And what about that being that was part sprite, part lizard? It had been curled up on itself and now it was looking right at me . . .

I shook my head to clear it of such fancies. I would begin to sort these loose sheets, starting with the ones in the worst state of repair. If Anluan had any sense, that would be where he had begun his own somewhat limited attempt to do the job, so I would perhaps find the next part of that intriguing narrative somewhere amongst these deteriorating pages. So he'd lost the use of his right hand. I pondered this, wondering whether, if I tried using my left, my writing would be even more wayward than his. I had heard that a person could learn to use the other hand just as well, given time. Perhaps Anluan had not had time. Or perhaps he had lacked the will. He'd given up trying to talk to me quickly enough.

All of the documents from the little chest seemed to be in the same writing, a bold, regular hand. The style of script was antique and the penmanship was that of a scholar. The pages were so brittle there seemed a danger they would fall apart before I could get the job done, and the ink had faded badly. Little life remained in these records.

I skimmed the pages. One or two were in Latin, but most were in Irish and dealt with nothing more nefarious than an account of the daily life of house and farm:

> *. . . a good crop of new lambs, most of the ewes have dropped a pair, some three . . . weather mild, fewer losses than last year . . .*
>
> *. . . dispute with Father Aidan, who considers my area of study perilous. Nothing new in that.*
>
> *Fergus got an excellent price for our calves at this year's market.*
>
> *I have a son. They tell me he is healthy, though he appears red-faced and small. I am surprised, not at his fighting spirit, but that my wife has at last proven herself useful at something.*

That jolted me. I had been beginning to warm to the writer, an ordinary man making a record of losses and gains on his farm – sheep, cattle, where had they been kept? – and debating issues with the local priest. But after that callous remark, I found I could not like him at all. *My area of study.* Likely the writer was one of the unusually scholarly chieftains of Whistling Tor.

> *He is to be named Conan, for my father.*

43

I began on the second bundle of papers. For these the scribe had used Latin and a different style of script to go with it, a rounded half-uncial rather than the common hand of his Irish writings. Or perhaps this was a different writer. The pages seemed of similar age, the ink equally faded.

Autumn of the thirteenth year of the tenure of Glassan son of Eochaid as high king. We approach the time known as Ruis, in Christian nomenclature All Hallows. A time of transition, when we step into the dark. A time when end is beginning and beginning end.

Not only was this Latin, but the style of expression was more formal. I smoothed the page out carefully. The parchment had been scraped back and reused at least once, perhaps several times; it seemed there had not always been a ready supply of materials at Whistling Tor. I tried to guess the document's age. Glassan son of Eochaid. A hundred years, give or take a little? Hadn't Tomas or Orna said something about a hundred years of ill luck? I couldn't find the writer's name anywhere on the pages, but perhaps if I read on, it would be there.

The dark mirror flickered. I turned to look over my shoulder, half expecting to see Muirne there with her neat clothing and dis-approving expression. But there was nobody; I was alone in the library. I turned back and my gaze caught a touch of red, not in the mirror but out in the garden. Had it been Anluan whose pres-ence I had sensed before, standing in the doorway watching me without a word? He was seated on the bench now. He had his left elbow on his knee, his right arm across his lap, his shoulders hunched, his head bowed. White face, red hair: snow and fire, like something from an old tale. The book I had noticed earlier was on the bench beside him, its covers shut. Around Anluan's feet and in the birdbath, small visitors to the garden hopped and splashed and made the most of a day that was becoming fair and sunny. He did not seem to notice them. As for me, I found it dif-ficult to take my eyes from him. There was an odd beauty in his isolation and his sadness, like that of a forlorn prince ensorcelled by a wicked enchantress, or a traveller lost forever in a world far from home.

I must stop being so fanciful. Less than a day here, and already I was inventing wild stories about the folk of the house. This was no enchanted prince, just an ill-tempered chieftain with no manners. If he'd been spying on me, that was his prerogative as my employer, I supposed; after all, I was on trial. I turned my attention back to the documents. The words on the page swirled and moved, and I rubbed my eyes, annoyed at my lack of concentration.

I have applied myself assiduously to the great work of preparation. I keep the door locked. That does not stop the ignorant from seeking my attention with intrusive knocking. The child was sick – some minor malady, a cough, a slight fever. It was inappropriate to call me; trivial domestic matters are for others to deal with. It is for precisely this reason that our principal place of experimentation is situated beneath the floor level of the house, guarded by bolts and key, and by charms and wards to keep out marauders of a less earthly kind. The minds of ordinary folk cannot comprehend the nature of our work . . .

Something moved on the surface of the obsidian mirror. I glanced quickly, started with shock, stared deep, the hair standing up on my neck. Surely not . . . but there it was. Within the dark stone was the image of a man standing in an underground chamber, a long, shadowy place lined with shelves on which stood crucibles, flasks, jars of powders and mixtures, books . . . so many books in one place, their covers stained and worn as if from long and frequent handling. Anluan . . . No, this man was much older. In the uneven light from candles set around the chamber, his features became those of a carven saint: the eyes deep and penetrating; the mouth thin-lipped, disciplined; the bones of cheeks and jaw jutting beneath the pale skin. With long-fingered, dexterous hands he sorted implements on the bench before him, knives with odd-shaped blades, pincers, screws, other things whose uses I could only guess at. *This one.* He selected a gleaming instrument like a miniature scythe. *I'll get my answer from the old hag with this one.*

A chill ran through me. I shut my eyes, opened them again in disbelief, my gaze moving between the lines of black script and the gleaming surface of the dark mirror. What was this? I could see the work chamber of the document as if I were standing right there opposite the writer. I could see his long, ascetic face as he pondered the dilemma facing him. And I knew his thoughts; knew them and felt the edge of a terrible darkness touching my mind. How could this be? I was here, in the library by full daylight, and yet I was in that underground place, my hands feeling the touch of cold metal as the man took up his blade; my mind knowing his evil purpose. The mirror . . . the mirror held the memory of time past, and as my eyes fell on it once more I felt the man's presence as if he and I were one. Now there was no looking away.

The old woman lies on the table, grimly silent. He'd been confident of achieving success before Aislinn got back with the herbs, but the crone is holding out beyond all expectations. She knows, of course. Of all the local women who dabble in a little white magic, this one has the reputation as the most experienced, the one who will understand without a doubt exactly what is meant in the grimoire by *potent powders of summoning*. But this wrinkled ancient with her parchment skin and her crooked fingers isn't giving the secret up easily. Perhaps she is so old she no longer fears death; she may be using what arts she has to dull the pain. She's already endured techniques that would make grown men soil themselves.

He's conducted such interrogations before, though not often. They follow a logical sequence. If a person holds out to the point where one risks losing him without a result, it becomes more effective to transfer one's attention to someone else, someone with whom one's subject has a bond – the husband or wife, a child, an aged parent. There is a weak chink of that kind in the strongest armour. But this old woman has no family. She's lived by herself in the woods for years.

He sighs. His hands are filthy. It will take vigorous scrubbing to get the blood out from under the nails. The crone's breathing is a squeaking rustle, another irritant. He doesn't look at her; such disorder offends his eye. And now Aislinn is coming back, he can hear her at the door.

'Are you done, my lord?' the girl asks politely, coming in and locking the door after her. She is thorough as always; he has trained her well.

'I haven't got a thing.' There's no need to pretend with Aislinn. She knows everything about him, to the extent that a simple village girl can understand a mind like his, a mind that soars above those of ordinary folk like a great eagle above the creeping, crawling creatures of the earth. His thoughts reach for the high, the impossible, the stuff of dreams and visions. 'I don't want to kill the witch before she's given me the answer – I can't understand why she would hold it back, she's near death anyway, why take such valuable information to the grave?'

'I have something that may help,' Aislinn offers unexpectedly, her tone sweet. 'I went back to her cottage after I gathered the herbs I needed. And I found this.' She holds up a bundle, and the woman strapped onto the table lets out a hissing sound, her reddened eyes rolling towards what the girl is carrying.

'Ah!' His breath comes out in a rush of triumph. He takes the little dog from Aislinn and carries it over to the tabletop, close to the woman, so she can see. A warmth floods through his body, the anticipation of success. 'Aislinn, you may go out if you wish.'

'I'll stay and watch, Lord Nechtan.'

The creature in his hands is quite small. It is not yet frightened – it has recognised its mistress and is straining to get close enough to lick her face. 'I think we may be ready to talk,' says the chieftain of Whistling Tor. And when the woman replies only with a moan of horror, he gets out his thin-bladed knife, weighing it casually in his free hand. 'I'm an artist at this. Watch me and learn.'

When it is over, he disposes of the debris while Aislinn cleans. The crone was all too ready to gasp out the names of the ingredients once he began to work on her creature. Aislinn has written them down in her little book, precise by measure, each in its turn. There was just time to get the last. Now he and the girl are the only living beings in the subterranean chamber, save things that scuttle and crawl in the corners and rustle in the walls. Not many of those: Aislinn keeps it spotless.

He watches her now as she scrubs the table. What a difference a year or two can make. Aislinn was a child when she first came to his notice; he did not expect a serving girl to show such intense interest in the maps and charts spread out in the chamber whose floor she was sweeping. He did not expect the orphaned daughter of humble villagers to be such a quick learner, thirsty to master reading, writing and numbers, then move into more esoteric branches of study. His protégé has been clever, eager to please and a great deal more patient than he is, which makes her an invaluable assistant. Time has passed, and Aislinn is no longer a child. Her hair is a fall of liquid gold; her pert buttocks move to and fro as she swings the brush. He's suddenly hard for her, desire thrumming in his blood. No doubt she would be as quick to learn the arts of the bedchamber as she's been with sorcery, and what pleasure he would take in the teaching.

But no. He cannot allow himself this; there are priorities. He must obey to the letter the information he got from Saint Criodan's: the vital knowledge that was so astonishingly expensive to acquire. *Let me show you the woeful state of our roof, Lord Nechtan; it will be quite costly to repair.* Who would have believed Brother Gearalt would hold out for such a generous donation to the monastic funds before opening the doors to that secret collection within the foundation's library? Oh, a dark collection it was, full of intriguing surprises. The good brother didn't let him take the book away. He was given only long enough to find and read the one form of words. It was enough. He knew what he wanted.

'How quickly can you make up the mixture?' he asks Aislinn.

'It might take a number of days, Lord Nechtan.' The girl pushes her hair back from her brow. He imagines the pale strands drifting across his bare body; he thinks of her under him, yielding. 'Goldenwood has to be gathered in a particular way. And some of the ingredients need grinding thrice over.' After a moment she adds, 'I can stay on and work late. I can sleep in the corner there.'

There's a pallet each of them has used from time to time when an experiment needs watching; they take turns to rest. Now that she's older, that no longer seems wise. But time is of the essence, for All Hallows is drawing close. The pieces must be ready to slot in place by then or there will be a whole year more of waiting. Another whole year of Maenach stealing his cattle as if he has every right to do so. Another whole year of being ostracised because nobody understands the significance of his work. A year of slights and offences, injustices and dismissals. It is unthinkable. 'So close,' he muses. 'Less than a turning of the moon and then, such power . . . Power such as none of them can possibly dream of, Aislinn, the capacity to dominate not only wretched Maenach and the rest of my neighbouring chieftains, but the whole district, the whole of Connacht, the whole of Erin if I want it. Against my army, none will stand. It will be a force worthy of a great hero of mythology, such as Cu Chulainn himself. I can hardly believe it is within my grasp . . . We must not waste a moment. This must be precise in every detail.'

They go back to work. Aislinn mixes powders, grinds dried berries, measures liquids with meticulous attention. He pores over his notes, though he has long since committed the charm to memory. He knows it deep in the bone, a potent, living thing. It is his future. It is his raising up and the doom of his enemies. It is, purely and simply, power.

The light in the underground chamber dimmed. The image wavered and faded, and with a shudder I came back to myself. Here in the library the sun was streaming in the window to set a brightness on the parchment before me. It was glinting off the surface of the obsidian mirror, on whose border the little creatures were now huddled or curled into postures of sorrow or fear, heads under wings, hands over eyes, arms around one another, as if what had been revealed were too piteous to behold.

Oh God, oh God . . . Tears spilled from my eyes. Foul thoughts and obscene images crowded my head. I felt filthy, soiled, wretched. Bile rose in my throat, bitter and urgent. *Out! Out of this cursed place!* I blundered across the chamber, bruising my hip on the sharp corner of a table, and stumbled out into the garden, where I sank to my knees and retched out the contents of my stomach under a lavender bush. My gut heaved and heaved again. Between the spasms I fought for breath.

A hand on my shoulder. I started violently, Nechtan looming in my mind, and the hand was withdrawn.

'What is it? You are ill.' A man's voice. I had forgotten Anluan, in the garden. 'I'll call for Magnus,' I heard him say.

'No!' Through the paroxysms of my gut and the dark visions in my head, I had enough awareness to know I did not want the all-too-busy steward called away from whatever he was doing to tend to me. 'I'm sorry. I know I shouldn't be in your garden. I'll be all right in a moment –' As if to make me a liar, a new fit of choking and retching gripped me. My nose and eyes streamed.

Anluan crouched down beside me and, rather awkwardly, held out a handkerchief. 'Muirne!' he called.

I looked up, mopping my face ineffectually, and saw that she was standing beyond the bench in the shadow of the birch tree. I had not seen her when I looked out before.

'Fetch water,' Anluan said. It was an order, and Muirne obeyed in silence, going out through the archway.

In time the spasms died down. I wiped my nose and eyes anew and rose shakily to my feet. Anluan got up too. He did not try to touch me again.

'I'm sorry,' I managed. 'I'll go now. I know you don't like people to be in this garden . . .' I glanced over my shoulder towards the library door. There was no way in the world I was going back in with that thing lying uncovered on the table. I took a step or two along the path, thinking I would make my escape into the main part of the grounds where I could recover in private. Everything swirled and went hazy around me. 'I need to sit down,' I said.

'Sit on the bench, here.' Then, after another awkward silence, 'I do not know how to help you. Have you eaten something that disagrees with you?'

I looked at him properly then. It seemed quite the wrong question. 'The mirror,' I said, shaking my head in a vain hope that the images might flee. 'That mirror in the little chest, with the documents you were working on . . . How could you do that to me? How could you leave it there, knowing what power it had? It pulled me in; it made me feel . . .' That had been the worst part of it, the sensation that I actually *was* that evil man and was thinking those thoughts and doing those things myself, because I wanted to. Here in the garden birds were singing, plants were growing, the sun was shining. But a shadow had touched an inward part of me, and I did not think it would be easily banished. 'It made me feel dirty,' I said in a whisper.

'What mirror?' asked Anluan. When I only gaped at him, he added, 'This house is full of such artefacts. Magnus was supposed to warn you not to look in them.' He had seated himself on the other end of the bench, as far from me as he could manage, and was not meeting my eye but glaring across the garden at nothing in particular. There was neither sympathy nor apology in his expression. 'You've been hired to read the documents,' he said, 'not to meddle with what doesn't concern you.'

His anger tied a new knot in my stomach. *Be brave, Caitrin. Stand up for yourself.* 'The mirror was stored with the documents,' I said shakily. 'I wasn't meddling, simply being thorough. How could I possibly be prepared for what happened?'

He did not respond. I worked on my breathing, wondering how long it would take Muirne to bring the water. Then Anluan said coolly, 'I need a scribe with fortitude. Perhaps you are not suited to Whistling Tor.'

A little flicker of anger awoke in me. 'I have plenty of fortitude for reading, writing and translation, my lord. Magnus did warn me about the mirrors. But . . . perhaps he didn't know about this one. It was . . .' I shuddered and put my hands over my face, but the sickening images still paraded before my eyes. 'It showed me what was in the documents as if I were really there. It put someone else's thoughts into my mind, as if he and I were the same . . . Lord Anluan, I'm not prepared to go back into the library while that mirror is there on the table. It would be unreasonable to expect that. What I saw was . . . disgusting. It was evil.'

After a silence, the chieftain of Whistling Tor said, 'What are you telling me? That despite your claims of expertise, you do not wish to do this work after all? Hah!' It was a derisive bark, bitter and painful. 'This is no surprise. You're running away as everyone else has done. Nobody stays here.'

'Magnus stays,' I pointed out. Talking to Anluan was a little like reasoning with an angry child. 'And I'm not running away. I didn't say I was leaving.'

'If you will not enter the library, you cannot complete the task.' A silence. He glanced towards the archway, shifting restlessly on

51

the bench. 'I need the work done. There is nobody else to do it. Tell me what you saw in this mirror. What can be so horrifying that it turns a capable scribe – if that is indeed what you are – into a quivering, vomiting wretch?'

I swallowed the retort that sprang to my lips. 'I've no wish to think about it, let alone talk about it. My lord,' I added belatedly, not wishing to provoke his anger further. 'Could you arrange for the mirror to be removed before I continue with the work?'

'Ah. So you will go back into my library?'

An image of the future came to my mind. Say no, and I'd be on the road again with no money, no friends and pursuit getting closer every day. I would indeed be running away, for as long as it took Cillian to find me and drag me back to Market Cross. 'I might consider it, under the right conditions,' I said.

'Tell me what you saw in this mirror,' Anluan said, and fixed his unusual blue eyes on me with some intensity. I returned his gaze, thinking that if there were not that lopsided quality to his face, he would be quite a fine-looking man, his features strong, his skin of the very fair kind that flushes easily. His mouth was well shaped, though more given to solemnity than smiles. But all was awry, as if frost had blighted him on one side only, leaving a creature who was two in one, strong and weak, sun and shadow. I was staring. Remembering what Magnus had said, I turned my eyes away.

'Did you really not know it was in the chest?' I asked him. 'Magnus told me the transcription on the little table was yours. The documents you were working on were in that same box.'

'Would you accuse me of lying?' His tone was wintry. 'Answer my question. What did the mirror show you?'

I forced myself to tell the tale of blood, death and vaunting ambition. Anluan listened in silence to my halting account, and when I was finished he said calmly, 'You must continue the work. I will put this mirror away before tomorrow.'

'Thank you,' I said, but I needed more than that. 'What can you tell me about Nechtan? Magnus explained that his documents are the ones you want me to look at. It will be easier to pick them out if I know a little of his history. Magnus told me you are the only person here who can read, my lord. Otherwise I wouldn't trouble you with my questions.'

'Nechtan was my great-grandfather. The oldest writings are his. You will find a few by my grandfather, Conan, and then there are my father's notebooks.'

'What was your father's name, my lord?'

'Irial.' His tone shut off further questions. 'I will deal with the mirror now. You should take time to compose yourself. Start the work afresh tomorrow, and heed Magnus's warnings in future. Stick to the job you've been hired to do, and don't interfere with what doesn't concern you. You can't expect to understand everything here at Whistling Tor, and there's no need for you to do so. It's a place unlike other places. Or so I'm told. I need you to stay. I need the work done.'

He rose and limped into the library, leaving me alone in the walled garden. Irial's garden, Magnus had called it. *My father's notebooks*. It seemed likely Irial had written those meticulous botanical notes I'd looked at earlier, and executed the tiny, exquisite drawings that accompanied them. I glanced at the little book Anluan had left on the seat, wondering if he had been reading his father's work. It was bound in fine calf leather, tooled with a pattern of leaves, but when I lifted the cover to peep inside, the writing I saw crawling across the creamy parchment was not the spidery script of the gardener's notebooks, but Anluan's irregular, laboured hand. Someone gave a little cough. I shut the book hastily, not wanting to be caught prying. Muirne was standing about four paces from me, a cup in her hand. She had a disturbing ability to move about with scarcely a sound.

'Thank you,' I said, getting up to take the water from her. Her fingers were cold. 'I'm much better now.'

'You saw something that scared you.' It was a statement, not a question. 'A mirror?' When I nodded, she said, 'There are many stories here. Many memories. This is not an easy place.'

'I'm beginning to realise that,' I said, glad that she was taking the time to speak to me, even if her manner was a little odd. 'I suppose I'd better go; I know this is Lord Anluan's private garden. Will someone call me when it's suppertime?' I took a sip, then set the cup down on the bench.

'I suppose someone will,' Muirne said.

'Thank you.' Should I add *my lady*? I had no idea where she belonged in this unusual household, only that if I did not make an effort with her, the summer was going to seem very long. I had thought she might be Anluan's wife, but he had treated her like a servant. I smiled at her, then walked out under the archway with my mind full of unanswered questions.

chapter three

I couldn't pluck up the courage to explore, even though Anluan had given me the rest of the day off. I retreated to my unwelcoming bedchamber and sat on the pallet, thinking. Even with the mirror gone, I could hardly bear the idea of stepping back over the library threshold. The job would surely involve delving deeper into Nechtan's extremely unpleasant life. The little chest might well contain the next part of his journal, in which the experiment he was working up to might be explained in full, repellent detail.

The thought disgusted me. And it fascinated me. To my horror, I realised I wanted to read on. Did Nechtan and his assistant open whatever portal it was and bring forth a fearsome army? Was that even possible? If I used the mirror again, would it open the same window into that man's dark thoughts? What might I see there?

I shuddered, remembering. Sickening as the scene in the vision had been, equally appalling was the fact that Nechtan had evidently taught his assistant not just the skills of sorcery but also his own warped moral codes. She was the one who had fetched the little dog; that had been her idea. She had chosen to stay in the chamber and watch as Nechtan demonstrated his expertise in torture. In the mirror vision, she had been a presence in the shadows, a figure leaning over to scrub the table, a fall of golden hair. I had never quite seen her face. But her voice had revealed her approval, her admiration, her slavish willingness to help. If Nechtan was the one who had made her that way, Anluan's great-grandfather had truly been an evil man.

As it began to grow dark, I ventured out to fetch water from the pump, carried it up to my chamber in a bucket and washed my face and hands. I combed and plaited my hair, pinning the braids up on top. With no fresh gown to change into – the one I'd worn for travel needed sponging and airing – the best I could do was give the green one a brushing down. If I stayed here, I was going to need additional clothing to see me through the summer. I had a nightrobe and a change of smallclothes. Apart from those, my pack had held only an embroidered kerchief that had belonged to my mother and the doll Maraid had sewn for me after Mother died. Róise was only a handspan tall. Her features were worked in fine thread and she had dark silky hair, the same colour as mine. Her nut-brown skirt was made from one of my mother's, her cream linen tunic from one of my father's shirts. A favourite blue ribbon of Maraid's formed her sash. I could not look at Róise without thinking of my family. The doll made me sad and happy both at once. In the dark time I had clutched her to my breast all night long. I had soaked her embroidered face with wretched, helpless tears.

I set Róise on the pillow. She looked somewhat out of place in this bare, dim chamber. I must ask Magnus for a lamp, or at least a candle; those steps would be treacherous at night. As for the question of clothing, the first spell of wet weather would see me in difficulty. I had not anticipated spending so long in a place where there would be no opportunity to sew or to borrow suitable garments. It was further evidence of how poorly I had planned my flight from Market Cross. Perhaps the practical Magnus would have an answer. He'd probably tell me to ask Muirne. A chieftain's wife – if that was what she was – generally did distribute her own old clothing to the poor and deserving, but even on the unlikely chance that Muirne would put me in that category, there was no way her garments could be made to fit me. She was of slight build, while I had a smaller version of my sister's figure, my bosom and hips generous, my waist narrow. Ita had once remarked that it was a whore's body.

Suitably tidied, I made my way to the kitchen where the table had been cleared of cooking paraphernalia and was set with seven bowls, seven spoons and seven goblets. Magnus was stirring a pot on the fire.

'Can I do anything to help?' I asked.

Before he could answer, a familiar figure in a red cloak and gold chain made a regal entrance into the chamber.

'Rioghan!' I exclaimed, finding myself well pleased to see a familiar face, even one fairly new to me.

'Welcome to Whistling Tor, Caitrin,' Rioghan said, and swept into his well-practised bow. 'What a delight. We see few visitors here, and even fewer comely women.'

I felt myself blush scarlet.

'You're embarrassing the girl, Rioghan,' said Magnus, setting his pot on the table. 'She's not one of your flirtatious court ladies.'

'I was merely speaking the truth,' Rioghan said. 'Please be seated, Caitrin. There is a woeful lack of ceremony to our repasts here. Our welcome is nonetheless genuine.'

'Thank you,' I said, and sat. The king's councillor took the place opposite me.

The forest man, Olcan, came in next, with Fianchu in close attendance. The enormous hound went straight for a corner by the hearth, where a meaty bone lay beside a pile of old sacks. Fianchu settled on the sacks and began a purposeful crunching.

'Ah, Caitrin,' said the forest man. 'So you found the house. Staying?'

'For a trial period. I've been given some work to do in the library.'

'Good,' observed Olcan, seating himself beside me. 'Hope you stay awhile. Fianchu likes you. Don't you, boy?'

Intent on his bone, Fianchu made no response.

'That smells good, Magnus,' I said.

'The meal will be humble, alas,' said Rioghan in melancholy

tones. 'Times have changed at Whistling Tor. This was once a fine household, Caitrin. Supper was consumed in the great hall. Ale flowed copiously. The floors were thick with sweet-smelling rushes. Bards entertained the crowd with harp and pipe. After the meal there was dancing.' He sighed.

Magnus had begun to ladle out the contents of the pot, serving each of us in turn. It seemed odd to me that we were starting without Lord Anluan or Muirne, for both of whom, by my count, places had been set. But it was not for me, the newest arrival, to say anything about it. When I heard footsteps in the hallway I thought they had arrived, but it was Brother Eichri who entered, looking even thinner and paler than before. There was a transparency about his skin that enabled me to see clearly the bones beneath. His high frontal tonsure rendered his head skull-like. Yesterday he had worn a cape over his habit. Now, with that garment gone, I noticed that in place of a monk's cross he was wearing a peculiar necklace. There were odd little objects hanging from it, things I was not sure I wanted to identify. They reminded me of the unpleasant scene in the obsidian mirror.

Brighid save us, the man was gaunt. His bones seemed to jangle as he settled himself on my other side. 'Caitrin, daughter of Berach,' he said with a toothsome smile. 'What a pleasure. Villagers scare you off, did they?'

'No, they let me in,' I said, realising that I had in fact shown some courage over the last day or so. 'I stayed down there overnight and came up this morning.'

'She's working here,' Magnus said. 'Scribing for Anluan. Trial period. Remember your manners, you two.'

'I'm happy to see you again, Brother Eichri,' I said. The presence of a holy man in this place of shadows and whispers was reassuring.

Across the table, Rioghan's dark brows shot up to supercilious heights. 'Brother?' he echoed. 'He's long since relinquished any claim to such a title. Eichri might more accurately be dubbed sinner, evil-doer, transgressor, apostate, criminal –' He halted, perhaps seeing my expression.

'I thought the two of you were friends,' I said, shocked by his outburst.

'They are,' said Magnus, setting a platter of bread on the table. 'They go on like this all the time. Don't let it bother you.' He sat down beside Rioghan. 'I heard you had a little problem with a mirror.'

'I did.' The memory made me shudder. 'What it showed me was so horrible I'm afraid I bolted out into the herb garden and was violently sick. Fortunately, Lord Anluan was there and I was able to explain what had happened. He said he'd put away the mirror before I have to start the work again.'

I became aware that all eyes were on me with varying degrees of amazement in them.

'Have I said something wrong?' I asked.

'Only surprising,' said Magnus. 'Go on, eat, it's getting cold.'

I eyed the others. Magnus had dipped his spoon in his bowl, about to start. Olcan was helping himself to bread. Eichri and Rioghan were glaring at each other across the table.

'Do Lord Anluan and Lady Muirne eat separately?' I asked.

Eichri surprised me by giving a snort of laughter.

Magnus said, 'They'd usually sup here with us. It's a small household and we don't stand on ceremony. But Anluan's uncomfortable with folk from outside. He may not make an appearance tonight.'

'He will,' Rioghan said instantly. 'I wager a gold piece to whatever you can offer, Brother.'

'He won't,' Eichri retorted. 'I stake the finger bone of a virgin martyr, Councillor.'

'A what?' I spluttered.

'Oh, he'll have one,' Rioghan said. 'He's got all sorts.'

And when I took another look, I saw that the items suspended on the cord around the monk's neck included an assortment of dainty bones. Maybe they were human and maybe they weren't. It was one of many questions I knew I would not ask.

'By the way,' Magnus said, dipping a chunk of bread in his bowl, 'Muirne's not the lady of the house, though she may act as if she is.' This was directed to me.

He offered no further explanation, and it seemed inappropriate to ask for one. Perhaps Muirne was a kinswoman of limited means, the kind who often finds shelter in the household of a nobleman. That would go a certain way towards explaining her manner.

A slight stirring of the air; I glanced up to see the familiar grey-clad figure in the doorway, her large eyes on me. It felt curiously as if I had summoned her with my thoughts. She advanced into the chamber, going to the shelves and picking up a tray.

'He's not joining us then?' asked Magnus.

'He'll eat in his chamber tonight.' She brought her tray over to the table. 'He's weary. Out of sorts.' In a sequence of movements so neat and effortless that I could see they were part of an oft-repeated routine, she took up Anluan's bowl and held it while Magnus filled it. She added spoon and knife to the tray. Magnus cut a wedge of bread; Muirne placed it neatly beside the bowl. Once or twice she glanced my way, and I could see in her expression that I was the reason for Lord Anluan's absence. Muirne took her tray to the bench, picked up a jug, filled his lordship's cup.

'Pay up, Councillor,' Eichri said, rubbing his bony hands together in glee. 'Let's see the colour of your gold.'

Rioghan sighed, reached deep within the folds of the crimson cloak, and sent a shining coin spinning across the table into the skinny fingers. 'It's the same hue it was yesterday,' he said in resigned tones. '*Brother.*'

'I hope Lord Anluan will be feeling better soon,' I made myself say as Muirne headed for the door, intent on her mission. She left the chamber without a word. Perhaps she had not heard me.

'Ale, anyone?' asked Magnus, getting up to fetch the jug. He glanced at me. 'Don't mind Muirne,' he said. 'We're none of us accustomed to visitors. She worries about Anluan, doesn't like to see him upset. She's a good-hearted little soul.'

I was hungry; not surprising after what had occurred earlier in the day. Magnus and Olcan ate steadily, in the manner of people who have done a full day's physical labour, but Rioghan and Eichri only picked at the small servings they'd been given. I expected Muirne to return and eat with us, since she had taken no provisions for herself, but the meal progressed and she did not come.

'You're a fine cook, Magnus,' I said. The supper was somewhere between a soup and a stew, heavy on vegetables and light on meat, but seasoned with an interesting blend of herbs. 'This is a delicious meal.'

'Enjoy it while you've got it,' he said. 'Fresh provisions today. Now it's steadily downhill until next time I pay a call on Tomas.'

'But you must grow a lot of things up here,' I ventured, thinking of the farming activities I had read about earlier.

'I do what I can. Olcan helps me.' Magnus dipped his bread into his bowl. 'We've got chickens, a couple of cows, some other stock, and the vegetables, of course. Still, we can't work magic. You a cook?'

'Not much of one. My sister used to do all that.'

'Your sister, eh?' Rioghan leaned back in his chair, examining me. 'Is she made in the same mould as you, all curves and curls?'

I could not summon the light response required. Instead, Ita spoke in my head, her voice a derisory whisper: *See the way men look at you? You're made to be a whore, Caitrin. Be thankful Cillian wants to wed you. Without him you'd be headed down a path to ruin.*

'You're upsetting the young lady, Councillor.' Eichri's cavernous voice was stern.

'Maraid does look quite like me, only bigger,' I said. I must find a new line of discussion. 'How long have you lived at Whistling Tor, Brother Eichri?'

They laughed, the monk, the councillor, Olcan and Magnus all together.

'Seems like forever,' Rioghan said in dour tones. 'We're sick to death of the fellow.'

'Too long,' Eichri said. 'Yet, it seems, not long enough.'

There was nothing I could say to that, since I had no idea what he meant, only that it sounded very sad. 'I – Magnus, you said something before that suggested . . . I don't want to pry, but aren't there any other folk living here, apart from yourselves, I mean? It's such a big house. How can you manage without grooms, farmhands, people to wash clothing, scrub floors, tend to stock?'

Magnus broke a piece of bread between his big capable hands. 'It's just us,' he said, glancing around the table. 'Us and the ones out in the forest.'

'That makes you a delightful surprise, Caitrin,' Rioghan put in. 'Our dusty old web has caught a splendid butterfly.'

'As to how we manage, a man does what he has to,' Magnus said. 'We work hard.'

I drew a deep breath. 'Magnus,' I ventured, 'you mentioned *the ones out in the forest.* Who are they?' Feeling the pressure of four men's eyes on me, I added, 'It's just that when I was first coming up the hill, when Olcan and Fianchu found me, I'd been hearing strange voices, voices that made me lose my way. And I'm sure I felt . . . hands. Down in the village, people were talking about a curse, about fearsome beings on the hill. If I'm to stay here, I would be happier it I knew exactly what these things are.' Or maybe not, I thought as soon as I had spoken. If the vision in Nechtan's obsidian mirror was any indication of what I could expect at Whistling Tor, perhaps blissful ignorance was preferable.

The four men looked at one another. Each of them seemed to be waiting for someone else to answer.

'In that mirror earlier,' I said, trying not to see it again, 'a man called Nechtan, Anluan's ancestor, was talking about an . . . army. He was preparing an experiment, and hoping the result would make him powerful. That could have been about a hundred years ago, by my calculations. The folk in the village said the whole place had been under a curse for a hundred years. I thought . . . well, I suppose it is none of my business, but I do have to read the family documents, so . . . does the curse date from Nechtan's time? Is it something to do with those whispering voices and creeping hands? These others you mention, the ones who live out there?' I could not believe I was asking such questions. The old Caitrin, the confident, serene one, would not have hesitated; she would have sought out whatever information she needed to do a good job. I lifted my chin. I could be that woman again if I tried.

Olcan had his elbow on the table, his mossy head resting on one hand. 'Big story, Caitrin,' he said. 'All you need to know is, the Tor's old. It's older than the memory of any ordinary man, older than the most ancient story that was ever told around the fire at suppertime. A hundred years is just an eye-blink to this place. There's a lot of memory in these walls; there's a lot of power in these stones. Yes, there are one or two folk living out in the woods who are not quite your usual man-at-arms or kitchen maid. Some of them you'll see, some you'll hear, some may pass you by without being noticed at all. You shouldn't be afraid.'

'Folk,' I managed. There were goose bumps all over my body. 'What sort of . . . folk?'

'All sorts, Caitrin,' said Magnus calmly. 'Nothing to worry about. You're on the Tor as Anluan's invited guest. While you're here, Anluan keeps you safe. Nobody and nothing can touch you.'

It was not a restful night. The bedding I had been given failed to keep out the chill, and when I did manage to drift off into sleep, Nechtan tangled with Cillian in my dreams, jolting me awake with my heart pounding and my body drenched in nervous sweat. When I could bear it no longer I got up, slid back the newly installed bolt on my door, and went out to the gallery that edged the upstairs rooms. I stood with my bare feet in the litter of leaves and twigs and gazed out over the gentle chaos of the garden, the trees and bushes illuminated by the cloud-veiled moon to shades of uncertain blue and grey. By the pond, a figure in a red cloak paced to and fro, to and fro. It was true, then: there was an all-night sentry on duty. I watched him awhile, and at one point he looked up and raised a pale hand in greeting. The cold forced me back to bed, where I tossed and turned until morning.

As soon as it was light I made my way down to the kitchen, where Magnus already had the fire burning and water heating.

'We don't gather for breakfast,' the steward said. 'If you want water to wash, you'll have to wait. I can't spare the time to pump it.'

'I'll do it myself,' I said, hoping this did not break any rules.

He spared me a glance. It was not unfriendly. 'Good for you. The pump's out the back door in the yard. Take that bucket there, it's lighter to carry than the other. I'll be leaving a pot of porridge beside the fire. Help yourself when you're ready. Don't know how early you plan to start work.'

'Early,' I said. 'There's a lot of it.'

I made the mistake of rolling up my sleeves before I left the kitchen, and was instantly aware of the big man's stare. I turned away, but not before he had seen the bruises on my arms.

'Who did that?' asked Magnus, an edge in his voice that would have made a grown man tremble. 'Who set those marks on you, Caitrin?'

'It doesn't matter,' I muttered, hauling my sleeves back down. I headed for the door out to the yard, but he was there before me, his solid form blocking the doorway.

'Yes, it does. We knew you were running away. Stands to reason, doesn't it? Why else would anyone want to stay up here all summer, except to escape from something? Rioghan told me you were all over bruises.'

'Rioghan?' How could he know about the marks Cillian had left on me, the ones that showed on my arms, the many, many more that were concealed under my gown?

'Last night, in the garden,' Magnus said, and I remembered that I had been standing on the open gallery in my night attire while the councillor patrolled the garden below. Rioghan might have seen a good expanse of arm, shoulder, upper chest. 'Who hurt you?'

'It makes no difference who,' I said. 'The bruises will fade. They'll be gone soon.'

'Of course it makes a difference. Someone beat you, not once but over and over; that's blindingly obvious.'

'It's not important,' I murmured. 'Really.'

Magnus put his big hands on my shoulders. Despite the gentleness of his touch I could not help flinching. He spoke quietly, leaving his hands where they were. 'It's important to us, Caitrin. Maybe you've had nobody to stand up for you; maybe you've been all on your own. But you're at Whistling Tor now. You're one of Anluan's folk. If a man thought to set a violent hand to you now, he'd soon find you're not on your own any more.'

My eyes were suddenly brimming with tears. I could not find any words. As he released his hold and stepped back, I simply nodded, picked up my bucket again, and went out.

By the time I had performed my ablutions and returned to the kitchen, Magnus was gone. I ate my porridge, then headed for the library.

On the threshold I hesitated, glancing over at the table where I had been working before. The pages of Nechtan's account were still spread out there. At one end of the work space lay a considerable pile of other loose leaves, and the stone jar had been placed on top of these so draughts could not scatter them. There was no sign of the mirror.

I took a deep breath and went in. The chest in which I'd found Nechtan's writings was on the floor, its lid closed. In the centre of the table was a scrap of parchment on which a couple of lines were written in an unmistakable hand.

Mirror in chest. All papers here.

I was filled with gratitude by this terse note, though I would have been happier if he had taken the mirror right out of the library. I knew its capacity to entice, even from within a box. Never mind that. I'd made a plan for the day's work and I would get on with it. Sort through the papers from the chest this morning, reading anything in Latin. Start on cleaning the library this afternoon.

As the morning passed, I realised there was an aspect of this kind of scholarship that I had not anticipated: boredom. The tale of Nechtan's cruelty had been unpleasant but dramatic. It would have captured my attention even without its attendant vision. What I had before me today was entirely mundane and prosaic. A particularly hard winter, with stock losses. A good harvest of pears. An uneventful ride to visit a chieftain named Farannán. Unspecified trouble brewing in the southeast. Nothing about Nechtan's family, the wife he had dismissed so cruelly, the new son. No reference to the experiment or to his quest for power. Who would have thought that the enigmatic, ruthless figure of the vision could be so . . . ordinary?

I was falling asleep as I read. I glanced out the window, wondering if Anluan was in the garden again, but there was no sign of him. A light rain had begun to fall; the greyish-green fronds of chamomile and wormwood bowed down under its gentle persistence. I turned my gaze back to the page, where Nechtan set out a dispute over access to a particular grazing area. My eyelids drooped.

I woke with a crick in my neck and an uncomfortable awareness that I had been sleeping with my head pillowed on my arms for quite some time – the light in the library had changed, and my body was aching with cramps. Sitting up, I realised I was no longer alone. Anluan was standing in the doorway to the garden, watching me. Under the scrutiny of those piercing blue eyes, I wilted. This was not a good start.

'You sleep soundly,' he observed.

'I'm sorry. I was awake most of the night. It was cold. And . . .' No, I would not tell him about the flight from Market Cross and the exhaustion that was more than physical. I would not speak of the nightmares. 'Thank you for putting it away, Lord Anluan,' I added. 'The mirror, I mean.'

'Mm.' He still had his eyes fixed on me. Their look had become wary, puzzled, as if he was trying to work out exactly what sort of creature I was. 'Not Lord, just Anluan. We don't use titles in this household. You'd best get on with your work.'

'Yes, I . . . May I ask you a question, Lord . . . I mean, Anluan?' Did this chieftain really mean me to call him by his given name?

'A question. What question?' His tone was less than encouraging.

'I was told – the others told me, over supper last night – of certain . . . presences, in the woods. I was warned of the same thing down in the settlement, and I thought the folk there were exaggerating, the way people do sometimes, to tell a more entertaining story. But it seems it's true.'

Anluan regarded me, and all I could read on his uneven features was a profound desire to be somewhere else. After a long pause he said, 'You like to talk.'

'I don't know what you mean,' I said, taken aback.

'You find it easy to talk.'

'Not always.' Cillian used to wait until Ita went out somewhere. He would only hit me in private. I was accustomed to being so frightened that I couldn't move, let alone speak. I had despised myself for staying mute and frozen as he hurt me, but the little voice inside me, the one screaming *No!*, had been drowned out by the terrified hammering of my heart. After I told Ita the first time and she wouldn't believe me, after I learned she was blind to the bruises, I never tried to tell again. 'But . . . it would be useful if you could answer some questions for me, since you are the only person here who can read and write. If I'm to make sense of these records . . .' My voice trailed off; his expression was becoming more distant with every word I spoke.

'The task is simple enough,' Anluan said, not moving from his stance by the door. 'Sort, read, translate. Your job is unrelated to these tales and rumours. What is your question?'

'It is . . . I . . . you say, *tales and rumours*.' Tension coiled in my stomach, a familiar sensation. 'Is it not true, what the others said about the strange beings in the forest?'

The crooked mouth went into a tight line. I had angered him. I felt myself shrink down, although he had not moved. 'What does that matter?' Anluan snapped. 'Can you do this work on your own or can't you?'

I made myself breathe. *It's not Cillian. Be calm. Speak up.* 'I – I –' My voice was a feeble squeak. I cleared my throat and tried again. 'I can do it on my own, yes, though possibly not by the end of summer. If you could help – if . . .' I clutched my hands together; he would think me a halfwit if this was the best I could do. 'It would help if I knew which was Nechtan's script,' I managed. 'I noticed he used two different hands, one for Irish and one for Latin, or so it seemed.'

Anluan wrapped his good left arm over his weak right one, under the cloak he seemed to wear even indoors. 'The documents from the chest, those I placed on the table for you, are all Nechtan's,' he said, his tone marginally quieter. 'Yes, he used two styles. Conan had an Irish hand similar to his father's, but you'll find his script less even. Irial's writing was informal and much finer. He preferred a narrow quill.' Then, with a cursory nod, the chieftain of Whistling Tor was back out the door into the garden, leaving me to my labours.

Weighing up the odd conversation, I considered it a small victory that he had given me a useful answer to my second question. Nechtan, Conan, Irial. There were three records to be found here, four distinct hands, and only one set of documents to be translated. I could speed up the job considerably by sorting all the loose leaves first, storing them in an orderly fashion and making a catalogue as I went. Not so hard.

I set to work once more, leafing through the records and trying by guesswork to put them in chronological order. It was only when I heard Fianchu barking somewhere outside that I realised I had been staring at the same sheet for some time, while my mind wandered over Whistling Tor and its extremely odd chieftain, a man who was not only one of the rudest I'd ever met, but who seemed incapable of carrying on a normal conversation. What ailed him? The crooked face, the damaged arm and leg would stop him from conducting such physical activities as were expected of a man in his position: hunting, riding, fighting. Did he also have some impairment of the mind that skewed his perceptions and made him susceptible to sudden bursts of ill temper? I recalled a young man known as Smiling Seamus, back at Market Cross. The tale went that the midwife had dropped Seamus on his head soon after birth; whatever the cause, he had grown up different from other folk, slow to learn, almost like a child, but amiable in temperament. Anluan was the opposite of amiable. And he was a scholar. On the other hand, some of his utterances were almost like a child's, oddly direct, as if he saw the world through simpler eyes than most. There was certainly something strange about him, something not quite right.

I made myself get up, stretch and walk around the library. I needed to tackle this a different way or I'd make no progress at all. Gritting my teeth, I swept the contents of one of the bigger tables into a pile at one corner. Then I began working my way through them, picking up each little book or scroll or parchment sheet, wiping off the dust with a fold of my skirt, reading a few lines, then setting the piece in the appropriate group. The work table soon held three piles of material – Nechtan's, mostly loose leaves of deteriorating parchment, spotted brown with age and, where folded, falling into pieces; his son Conan's, a far smaller heap; and a group of documents whose writers I could not identify. Many of these were in Latin; I glimpsed the words *diabolus* and *mysteria* and shivered. Somewhere in here there might be a key to Nechtan's unusual activities, the ones of which the local priest had so disapproved. Somewhere he might have written more about the experiment, the army he intended to summon or conjure, the immense power he would then be able to wield against his fellow chieftains. And somewhere there might be a link with the family curse and these mysterious beings that Anluan didn't want to talk about. That was foolish of him, really. Here I was with his family records, after all. If there were dark secrets in the history of Whistling Tor, wasn't this library the likeliest place to discover them?

I did not make a pile for Irial. The notebooks of Anluan's father were already collected on their own shelf in a corner of the library. When I opened the covers of one or two, I saw that the lover of plants and their lore had written the year and season on the front page of each. Irial's books were not dusty. Someone had wiped the leather covers clean and set the volumes vertically, with stones at either end to hold them in place. Above the neatly organised books, a bunch of dried flowers and foliage in a jar and an unlit lamp shared their own shelf, and on the flagstoned floor in front there was a woven mat, its colours darkened with age and wear to a uniform purple-grey. The area was almost like a shrine.

Irial's books were works of art. His botanical drawings were finely detailed and drawn with both accuracy and charm. He'd used a crow quill sharpened to a point. It was quite plain the artist had loved what he did, unusual as such a pastime might be for someone in his position. It made me wonder what sort of leader Anluan's father had been. Perhaps he, too, had failed to carry out the duties the folk of Whistling Tor expected of their regional chieftain. Tomas and Orna had been blunt about Anluan's inadequacy in that regard. Perhaps his father had spent hours in the garden and in the library, pursuing what had obviously been an activity he enjoyed with a passion, and had neglected his district and his folk. Perhaps he had never taught Anluan how to be a chieftain.

Something caught my eye, and I turned the little book in my hands sideways. Irial had written his botanical notes in Irish, which made sense – this language would render his work accessible to a wider readership. But in the margin, in a script so small and fine that at first glance it seemed decoration, not writing, was an annotation in Latin. *The most potent remedy known to man cannot bring her back. This is the hundred and twentieth day of tears.*

A chill went down my spine. What was this? Another secret, something so private the writer had chosen to set it down in this odd, almost cryptic fashion? Whose loss had Irial mourned for so long?

I moved the notebooks over to the work table, where the light was better. At around midday, Magnus brought me food and drink on a tray, which made me feel guilty for causing him more work. I went out to the privy and returned immediately to the library. There were many, many margin notes, scattered apparently at random through the botanical notebooks, all of them Latin and written in that minute script that tested the most acute of eyes.

It is the forty-seventh day of tears. To see her face in his wounds me.

I long for an ending. Sweet whispers. I must not heed them. The five hundred and third day of tears. Holy Mother, how long had the man gone on grieving?

The notes did not follow the same chronological sequence as the little books. I imagined Irial going back to his old records day by day in the time of his sorrow, setting each observation on a page chosen at random. The last entry I could find was five hundred and three. I searched for the first, and eventually found this: *The fifteenth day. My heart weeps blood. Why? Why did I leave them?*

And then this: *She is gone. Emer is gone.* Beside it, in a different ink, a scrawled number two. On the day he lost her, perhaps he had been incapable of writing.

I returned to my chamber when I judged it to be almost time for supper. Now both my gowns were the worse for wear, the brown still stained from my journey, the green dusty after my long day's work. I brushed down the skirt as well as I could, and washed my face and hands. It must still have been evident that I had been brought to tears by Irial's notes, for the moment I appeared in the kitchen Magnus set down his ladle, ushered me to a chair and set a brimful cup of ale in front of me.

'What's wrong?' His broad features wore a frown of genuine concern. When I did not answer immediately, he added, 'Come on, get it off your chest.' His manner was kindness itself.

'I'll be fine. I read something that made me sad. Something that reminded me of home.' I knew about loss. I knew about the numb sorrow that went on and on. 'Magnus, what can you tell me about Anluan's father?'

'Irial?' He turned back towards the fire to stir his pot, but not before I had seen the change on his strong features. Here was another with an abiding sadness. 'What do you want to know?'

I realised, to my surprise, that in Magnus's company I felt safe. On the other hand, anything I told Magnus, Anluan would know before morning. I did not want to share today's reading matter with the lord of Whistling Tor. 'Was his wife called Emer?'

'She was. Who told you that? Not him, surely. He never talks about her and seldom about his father.'

'I saw a reference to her in the documents. When did she die, Magnus? How old was Anluan?'

'This job of yours, it's going to open up old wounds.'

'I suppose it will, and Anluan has already told me I must read and write and not think about what I'm doing, more or less. But I don't see how I can transcribe family history if I don't know how it all fits together.'

'I did warn him the process might be painful,' Magnus said. 'The lad was seven when his mother passed away; nine when his father followed her. Irial did his best for as long as he could. After that, all the boy had was me. Irial hired me as a fighting man, not to bring up his son.'

I was silenced. Nine, and both parents dead – it didn't bear thinking of. At least Maraid and I had had our father until we were young women, though the loss of him had been no less crushing for that.

'Irial was a good man,' Magnus said. 'A fine friend, a loving father. Whatever it is you've found, you'd best not speak of it to Anluan. He's already –'

Sounds in the hallway indicated the arrival of the rest of the household, and our conversation came to an abrupt end. Fianchu erupted into the room, bounded over to me and licked my face, almost sending me sprawling, then went to his usual spot by the fire. Olcan, Eichri and Rioghan came in after the hound, greeted us and took their places. We waited briefly, but Anluan did not make an appearance. Magnus began to cut up a leek and cheese pie to accompany the soup, and there was Muirne in the door-way. She was in the same grey gown and overdress, or perhaps another, identical in colour and cut, for it was immaculately clean and appeared newly pressed. Her snowy veil looked freshly laundered. Her gaze passed over us, revealing nothing.

'He's not supping with us tonight?' Magnus queried.

'He's tired. His leg aches.' I watched as she performed the same routine as last night's, holding the tray as Magnus served Anluan's meal, filling the cup, checking that everything was placed precisely so. She left without another word.

My four companions made good company. Magnus kept me well supplied with food and ale. Olcan regaled me with Fianchu's exploits for the day. Eichri and Rioghan exchanged barbs across the table and moved their food around on their platters, but I did not see either eat a bite. As the meal drew to a close, I plucked up the courage to ask Magnus a new question.

'I came here with only a small bag, as you probably saw. I'll need at least one more change of clothing to get through the summer, and I have no funds to buy cloth, even supposing they have some down in the settlement. Would there be any old things here? Something I could alter, perhaps, just to get by?'

'I don't know.' Magnus sounded doubtful. 'We wear everything until it's falling apart, then we use it as cleaning cloths and suchlike. You can sew?'

'My sewing is certainly better than my cooking. Do you think Muirne might be able to find something for me?'

'You could ask,' Magnus said. 'She'll know where such things are, if we have any.'

'I don't think she approves of my being here,' I said, hoping this did not sound discourteous. 'It might be a little awkward.'

There was a little pause, then Magnus said, 'She's devoted to Anluan, Caitrin. She looks after him, tends to him, keeps him company even when all he's fit for is staring at his boots. He can be as miserable as a wet winter day. It takes an unusual person to tolerate such a man. Anything that upsets him, she'll disapprove of. Don't take it personally.'

'She surely won't object to finding you a gown or two,' said Rioghan. 'There must be old things stored away. If anyone knows where, it will be Muirne. She knows every corner of Whistling Tor.'

Lying awake in bed some time later, I thought of sad Irial and his lost Emer, and that little boy left an orphan at nine years old. Before he could properly read and write. Before he had the least idea of how to be a chieftain. Most of what Anluan had learned he must have taught himself, unless Magnus had found him a tutor.

If he had, the fellow hadn't stayed long enough to teach his charge Latin.

I wondered in what corner of the fortress Anluan and Muirne had their private apartments and how they had spent their evening. I thought of the beings out in the woods, the ones nobody seemed prepared to talk about. I considered Nechtan's experiment. What exactly was this army he had tried to bring forth? With my mind full of puzzles, I fell asleep to the melancholy call of an owl, somewhere out on the wooded hill.

chapter four

I spent a number of days struggling to impose order in the library. I set a restriction on myself: read only enough of each document to determine where it fitted into the records, then put it aside for later. It was all too easy to become engrossed and lose track of time. The mirror stayed in its box, out of sight, while I dusted and sorted and made notes. The moment I stepped over the threshold each morning I could feel its presence.

By suppertime each day I was filthy and exhausted. I sat quietly as the men talked. I noticed there was no longer any mention of the curse, the family history, or the mysterious presences out in the woods. Magnus made sure I ate properly. Olcan brought me gifts – a curiously patterned stone, a handful of freshly picked berries. The interchanges between Rioghan and Eichri remained combative in tone, but it was becoming plain to me that the councillor and the priest were old and devoted friends. To me, they showed unfailing warmth and courtesy. As for Fianchu, he had accepted my presence as a member of the household. When I appeared, he would rise from his corner to greet me, then turn his attention back to his bone.

Each evening, Muirne fetched Anluan's supper and took it away. His quarters were in the south tower; I had seen a lamp burning there late at night. I wondered if he planned to shun the supper table all summer, until the intrusive stranger had departed. I was somewhat uncomfortable to be the cause of such disruption to the household routine. On the other hand, I was beginning to feel at home here, odd though the place was. At long last there were moments during the day when I forgot Cillian; times during the night when I woke, not to the sweating terror of the familiar nightmare, but to an astonished calm – the realisation that I had escaped, that I was no longer in the dark place, that perhaps, finally, I was safe.

From time to time, as I sat in the library working, I had a sense of being watched. At first when this happened I would glance up quickly, sure that the silent Muirne must be in the doorway with her big eyes fixed on me, or that the mercurial chieftain of Whistling Tor had come to check if I had fallen asleep on the job again. But I never saw anyone, and after a little I became almost used to that uncanny sensation that I was not alone. Uncanny: if this place was anything, it was that. The scarecrow was often in the courtyard somewhere, birds perched on its hat and shoulders. It generally favoured me with a little bow when I walked by, and I responded with a nervous smile or greeting. When I plucked up the courage to ask Olcan what this being was, exactly, the forest man replied, 'Something old and harmless. A bit like me, really.'

My clothing grew dirtier by the day, until I could bear it no longer. I arose very early, planning to find Muirne before I began work. Magnus was already off on his round of chores. I ate my porridge seated alone at the kitchen table, trying not to look into the triangular mirror, which this morning seemed to reflect the chamber at dusk, everything shadowed in purple, grey, deep blue. Whoever had fashioned these artefacts must have possessed exceptional skills. I wondered if it was possible for an ordinary man to teach himself such arcane craft, or whether the knowledge must somehow be bought. Perhaps they were Nechtan's own creations.

When I turned to go, Muirne was in the doorway watching me, as if she had known I wanted her.

'Good morning, Muirne,' I said, making myself smile as I rose. 'I have a request. I'm wondering if there might be some spare old clothing in the house, something I could alter to fit myself – a gown or two, perhaps a shift. I didn't expect to be staying in one place all summer and I haven't brought much with me.'

She eyed me up and down, and for a moment her eyes were Ita's, assessing my body as unacceptable, the sort of form that was designed to draw attention for all the wrong reasons.

'I realise your old things wouldn't fit me. But I thought maybe . . .'

'Of course, Caitrin. Come with me.' She turned and was off at a brisk walk, leaving me to scurry along in her wake. I followed her through one deserted chamber after another. Like the hill itself, this house was far bigger than it seemed from the outside. There were so many twists and turns that I completely lost my bearings. Eventually Muirne led me through a massive arched doorway and into a chamber of grand proportions, where natural light spilled down through jagged holes in the roof to pool on the flagstones. Rain had come in through the openings and the place smelled of mould. There was an eerie stillness here; the soft sound of my footsteps seemed an intrusion.

'This way,' Muirne said, and headed directly across the chamber towards another door at the far end. I stepped after her somewhat awkwardly. The floor held various piles of debris: half-burned lengths of wood; rolls of ancient, stained fabric; broken glass. And along the sides of the hall stood . . . mirrors. Many, many mirrors, some covered with cloths, some in full view. They were of varied sizes and shapes, the biggest taller than a tall man, the smallest the size of a lady's hand. Their gleaming surfaces called to me; I felt the pull of them.

'Muirne . . .?' I whispered, frozen where I stood.

'What?' When I did not reply, she halted and turned. 'Come. It's this way.'

'The mirrors,' I managed. 'I don't want to . . .'

Muirne's neat brows went up; her lambent eyes were incredulous. 'The mirrors can't harm you,' she said. 'Just don't look in them.'

I swallowed hard and moved on, trying not to glance to either side. But the mirrors made it difficult. From either side of me came their voices, *Look here! Look here!*, and try as I might, I could not ignore their pleas. With my skin crawling and my heart beating like a drum, I glanced to the right and into the surface of a tall, thin artefact in a dark metal frame. A figure stared back out at me: myself, yet not myself, for though she wore my clothing and bore the shape of my features and my body, she was white-haired and old, her skin wrinkled with time, her mouth not full-lipped and red like mine but seamed and tired, the flesh of her face fallen onto the bones, so I could see death's touch on her. She smiled at me, revealing shrunken gums in which a few blackened teeth still maintained precarious hold.

My heart knocking, I walked on. Here to the left, a round mirror, artfully made, on a curious three-legged stand with little iron feet. The surface highly polished metal, perhaps bronze; in it, smoke and fire, and from it a roaring, crackling sound, as if I were looking, not into a reflection, but through a window to a scene of terror and destruction. And amid the flames a woman's voice crying out: *Help! Help me!* The words turned into a hideous, wrenching scream, and I knew the fire had taken her. I ran after Muirne, glimpsing here a clutching hand, there a pair of anguished eyes, there a scene of snow falling over pines, there a maelstrom of twisting, tangling monsters.

At the far door I stopped to recover myself, leaning on the frame, eyes clenched shut, chest heaving. I told myself I would not be sick again, not indoors, and not in Muirne's company. I fought to get my breathing under control.

'I'm sorry,' Muirne said, fishing a handkerchief from her pouch and putting it in my hand. 'I did not realise you were so disturbed.' She waited patiently while I mopped my eyes, blew my nose and tried to compose myself. 'Would you prefer to leave the clothing until later?'

'No,' I gulped, opening my eyes and squaring my shoulders. 'Let's go on. Muirne, is that the great hall? Was there a fire at some stage?'

'Yes.' She offered no more.

We went on through a maze of passageways, then up a long spiral of narrow stone steps. Without ever going outside, we had reached one of the towers. The treads were as worn in the middle as the ones leading to my bedchamber. There were landings, some with rooms opening from them, but Muirne did not pause long enough for me to get more than a quick glimpse in. I had thought perhaps this was the north tower, but where I caught a view from a window I saw no trace of the sea, only dark forest untouched by the light of the rising sun. Another showed mist hanging low over bare fields, which was entirely wrong for any side of the fortress, as far as I knew. The higher we climbed, the harder the claws of unease gripped my stomach.

We reached the topmost landing. There was a low door leading from it.

'It's in here,' said Muirne.

The little chamber held two storage chests and a colony of spiders, but nothing else save a steep stairway in one corner leading to a trapdoor up above. It was open; I glimpsed pale sky.

'You wish to climb up?' Muirne asked. 'There is a wide view from the top: the hill, the settlement, the region all around.'

No! shrieked a little voice inside me. After the mirrors, I simply wanted to get my clothing and go. But Muirne was making an unusual effort to be friendly. I should do the same. 'All right,' I said. 'Provided it's safe. You go first.'

I was somewhat relieved, on emerging at the top of the tower, to find that it was securely edged by a waist-high stone wall. I had wondered if the view would be as odd and changeable as the vistas from those windows, but I looked out over the hillside and, turning, saw slow smoke rising from the morning fires of the settlement at its foot, and sheep grazing on level ground to the north of the wooded rise. In the distance was a blue-grey smudge that must be the sea. It was not so very far off. To the northeast, along the coast, I could see another settlement with a defensive palisade around it. 'What is that place, my lady?' I asked.

'It lies beyond the borders of Anluan's territory.' Unspoken but plain in her tone was, *Therefore it does not matter.*

I looked closer to home. The garden still slept. Down below the towers the sun had not reached the wilderness of bush and briar, the dark pond and the shadowy edges of the woodland. I caught a glimpse of Olcan striding out through a little archway in the fortress wall with a scythe over his shoulder. Fianchu bounded ahead.

'Where is the farm?' I asked. 'Magnus spoke of cows and other stock.'

'Down below the wall.' She was thrifty with words.

I tried to engage her in conversation. The summer would be much easier if we were on good terms. 'I've been surprised that they can keep all this going when there's so little contact from the outside.'

Her features tightened. She had perhaps taken this as a criticism of her beloved Anluan. 'That need not concern you,' she said. After a moment she seemed to relent. Putting a hand on my elbow, she steered me to a vantage point from which I could glimpse a cleared area in the woodland, beyond the opening Olcan had used. 'If you find cows and the men who tend them interesting,' Muirne said, 'you can walk to the farm that way. It isn't far.'

'Through the forest?' I queried. 'But what about these presences everyone mentions, the ones that the villagers think so dangerous? I know they're real; I heard them myself, coming up the hill. I felt their touch.'

'The path to the farm is a safe walk; just remember to take the left fork where it branches. But these villagers are correct. There are many perils in these woods. To tell you the truth, Caitrin, I am surprised you have stayed here so long.'

She was still holding my elbow, and it made me uncomfortable. 'Long?' I echoed. 'I've only been here a few days.'

'For Whistling Tor, that is long.' She released my elbow, but as I made to turn, her hand fastened on my shoulder. I gave an involuntary yelp, part pain, part fright; it was exactly the spot Cillian had most favoured for gripping while he shook me. I was seized by a sudden mad conviction that she was about to push me over the parapet wall.

'Oh, did I hurt you?' Muirne's grip slackened. 'Or did you think you might fall? It's a long way down, isn't it? Best step back from the edge.'

I turned and breathed again. What had got into me? She'd think I was a bundle of nerves. 'Could we go down and look at the clothing now?'

'Of course, Caitrin.'

The two chests in the tower room were full of women's garments: gowns, tunics, shoes, head-cloths, under-shifts. Muirne crouched to lift out one item after another and spread them on the floor around her. Her expression was bland, her hands careful.

I knelt to examine these unexpected riches, my attention drawn by a bundle in the hue of wood violets. Unrolled, it proved to be a gown of soft wool that looked as if it might fit me quite well. There was a long over-tunic in a lighter shade that seemed to belong with it. I knew the outfit would look well with my rosy colouring and dark hair. Somewhere in the back of my mind, I heard Ita saying: *It's a pity you take after your mother. That mouth, that complexion, that figure, they're sure to get you into trouble.* With a sigh, I set the garments down.

'These things are lovely,' I said. 'But they seem too fine for me to use.' Some of these items were very old; here and there the cloth had worn perilously thin. Like the documents in the library, these garments had not much life left in them.

'This would be suitable.' Muirne held up a severe gown of dull dark grey, the kind of thing a housekeeper might wear.

'It certainly wouldn't show the dirt,' I observed. 'But even the most creative seamstress could not make that fit me.' I could see at a glance that the garment had been made for someone tall and slender. 'I wonder if I might salvage some of these other things. They are going to rags, but there are enough good pieces to make up into a useful gown or two. Someone would have to lend me a needle and thread.'

Muirne made no response.

I tried again. 'Do I need to ask Lord Anluan's permission before I take anything?'

'No,' she said, sounding suddenly frosty. 'My permission is adequate.'

'Of course – I'm sorry – forgive me, my lady. I'm a newcomer to the house and I don't quite understand how things are done here.'

'Take what you need; nobody wants these old things,' Muirne said abruptly.

'Th-thank you,' I stammered.

'There's no need to thank me,' she said, getting up and moving to the door. 'You know I don't like your being here. I made that clear the day you arrived. I suppose we must make the best of things.'

I stared at her. The sudden hostility had come from nowhere, and I wondered for a moment if I had misheard. 'I don't know why you would disapprove,' I said carefully. 'Anluan has a job to be done, and I'm qualified to do it. I mean no harm to anyone. He wants me here.'

'He should not have employed you,' Muirne said. 'Your presence wearies and disturbs him. This work on the documents is a misguided venture. He made an error of judgement.'

It seemed important to speak out on this particular point, even if she snapped my head off. 'Muirne,' I said carefully, rising to my feet so I could look her in the eye, 'I realise there are still aspects of the household and the Tor that I don't fully understand. But one thing is plain to me. Anluan is a grown man. It's appropriate for a man to make his own decisions. He's entitled to hire a scribe to translate his documents if he wants to. He's the chieftain of Whistling Tor, not a helpless child.'

Something flickered in her lovely eyes. 'How can you understand?' she said. 'This place is not like the outside world, Caitrin. If you have any wisdom at all, remember that some secrets are best not revealed. Some tales are best left untold. Now I must go; I am required elsewhere. You can find your own way back.' Before I could say another word, she went out the door.

Rather than obey my instincts and bolt downstairs, I decided to wait until I could be sure she was gone. Her cryptic warnings had unnerved me; I needed time. Plainly she had convinced herself that my presence in the household was bad for Anluan. He did often seem weary and despondent, that was true. And he never seemed to do very much. Most days he spent time in Irial's garden, where I could see him from the library window. Sometimes he would write in his little book, but more often he simply sat on the bench, staring into space. Tomas and Orna had implied he left the Tor only rarely, if ever. Such isolation must be bad for him. No wonder his manner was so odd. I vowed to myself that I would stay, dire warnings or not. Perhaps by the end of summer I could both finish the job and make friends with Muirne. She was the only female in the household. It must get lonely. Perhaps she had simply forgotten how to talk to another woman.

Now that she was not watching me, I took time to examine the garments more carefully. Not only could they help clothe me for the summer, but they might also provide insights into the history of Whistling Tor. The library held the ink and parchment records set down by men. But that was only half the story. Women talked to their daughters and granddaughters, weaving memories. If no living women remained, one might still learn something from what they had left behind: a garden planted in a certain pattern, a precious possession set away with careful hands, a gravestone for a beloved pet. And clothing. I did not know who had owned these gowns, these delicate undergarments, but perhaps they had something to tell me.

It seemed to me that this apparel had clothed three different women. The newest garments included the violet gown I so liked and a russet one of the same size and style. There was a head-cloth that matched the violet, embroidered with jewel-bright flowers. This woman had loved colour.

The oldest gowns were tattered and decaying. Their fabric was dark and plain, but had once been of good quality – this had helped preserve them, I thought. The woman who had worn these had been tall and thin, someone with neither the time nor the inclination for frivolity. There was a third set of clothing, in better condition than the dark things but older than the colourful ones. These garments had been made for a small, slight person. I mused on what I knew of the family at Whistling Tor. Perhaps this tower room contained items from the wives of the three chieftains who had preceded Anluan. Nechtan the sorcerer – his was the tall, serious wife. The son, Conan, whose birth had been acknowledged in Nechtan's records – his wife had been the little woman. And the bright things, those I had planned to take away and wear, had belonged to Irial's beloved Emer: Anluan's mother.

The door creaked, then slammed shut, startling me. I had felt no draught. My heart began to race. I got up and strode over to pull on the handle. It refused to budge.

'Muirne, are you still out there?' I called.

No response. She'd probably gone so far down the stairway that she couldn't hear me. 'Muirne! I can't open the door!'

Silence. She was gone; I felt it. I mustn't panic. The door could not have locked itself. It must simply be wedged by the force of the draught that had blown it shut. I tried again, hauling with all my strength, but the thing wouldn't move an inch. Perhaps the wood was warped by damp – this did seem a curious place to store clothing, with that trapdoor to the elements. The trapdoor! Thank heaven for that. I could climb up to the roof, then shout until I attracted someone's attention. Embarrassing as that would be, it would be better than waiting until Muirne realised I had not returned from our exploration – that might take all day.

I climbed the steps, one hand on the stone wall for balance, and set my other hand to the square of wood, which Muirne had pulled across the opening when we came down. There was no bolt or catch to hold it in place, but try as I might I could not move it. I needed a stick or other implement to help me; my efforts with the door had taken all the strength out of my arms and my back was aching. I looked around for an old poker or length of firewood, anything useful, but there was nothing in the little chamber but the two chests and clothing spread out everywhere. And a mirror. Why hadn't I noticed that before? It hung on the wall by the steps, tiny, oddly shaped, in a frame of weathered wood. The surface glinted dimly in the light from the narrow window. Whatever I did, I must not look in it.

Breathe slowly, Caitrin. I took stock of the situation. Eventually someone would notice I was gone. Eventually someone would ask Muirne if she had seen me. I just had to wait. This calm advice did nothing to cool my flushed cheeks or slow my racing heart. Something was wrong here. Someone meant me harm. I recalled a tale of an unwanted wife who had been walled up in just such a tower room to starve to death while her husband enjoyed himself with a younger and more fecund bride. Nothing I could do. Nothing. No way to help myself. I knew this feeling well; it had shadowed every moment in Market Cross, once Ita and Cillian came. *You are powerless. Useless. Hopeless. You are nobody.*

I descended the steps and went over to the window. 'I'm not at Market Cross,' I muttered. 'I'm here. I can be brave. I can.' The window looked down onto a section of roof; nobody was going to see me from below. I tried the door again. Had Muirne used a key to let us in? It wasn't possible, surely, that she had done this on purpose.

There seemed no option but to wait the time out. I folded the violet gown and the russet, placing them on a spread-out shawl. I added some shifts and smallclothes, then tied up the bundle. I packed the other garments neatly away into the chests. Magnus and Olcan were probably both out on the farm, with my activities the last thing on their minds. Anluan had not troubled himself to attend supper even once since my arrival; how likely was it that he would check whether I was at work today? As for Eichri and Rioghan, I had no idea how or where they spent their days. Rioghan probably caught up on sleep; those nights spent pacing the garden must take their toll. I kept my eyes off the mirror.

Time passed in an endless slow sequence of little sounds, creaks in the walls, rustling in the corners as of small furtive creatures about their business. We had not brought a candle or lamp with us and the chamber was dim. The patch of light from outside shifted slowly across the floor. In my mind, Muirne was speaking to Anluan. *Your little scribe's gone already*, she was saying. *She couldn't bring herself to stay. Packed up her bags and was off down the hill at first light.* I saw Anluan looking at the welter of documents in his neglected library.

A pox on this accursed place! Even when I was sitting all alone, something played havoc with my thoughts. I kept seeing the visions from those mirrors in the great hall: myself as a wizened crone, the same age as the poor soul Nechtan had tortured to death; a woman trapped in a terrible fire, screaming for help that did not come. Worst of all, I could hear a voice from the mirror on the wall, the one I was trying so hard not to look at. It did not speak aloud, but secretly in my mind. Its tone was a woman's, sharp and practical. *Use me, Caitrin. You got yourself into this silly predicament. Use me and escape. Stay there staring at the floor and you may stay there forever.*

'I'm not looking in any mirrors,' I said aloud. No doubt the thing was bursting with visions of murder and mayhem.

Just turn your head, Caitrin.

I forced myself not to do so, but I must have moved a little. Something caught the light from the window, something shiny hanging from a nail in the wall just above the mirror. A key.

There, said the mirror voice. *Off you go now, and tell no tales or they might come back to haunt you.*

I snatched the key without looking at the mirror's surface. My hands were shaking as I inserted it in the lock. The door opened smoothly. 'Thank you,' I muttered, grabbing the bundle and going out. The landing was empty. I locked the door behind me and slipped the key in the pouch at my belt.

I was not setting foot in the great hall again, ever. Instead of retracing my steps along the route Muirne had used, I looked for a door at the foot of the tower and found one, unbolted. Why hadn't she chosen this far simpler way? I ran through the grounds – the scarecrow lifted a hand in greeting and I nodded as I passed – and back in the front entry. Once inside the house I discovered that even this shorter path had its difficulties. Doors seemed to be in unexpected places, steps led up where before they had gone down, windows let light onto formerly dark landings. It was like the day I had first come up the hill, when my surroundings had seemed to change at random. By the time I reached the library, through a process of trial and error, it was at least midmorning.

I halted on the threshold. Anluan was seated at one of the larger tables, writing in his little book. He had not seen me. His left hand curled around the quill, holding it in a death grip; there must be pain in his fingers and all along the forearm. I studied the angle of the page, the slant of the pen, and wondered how hard it might be to correct the bad habit of many years. He had forgotten to conceal his right hand; he was using it to keep the page steady as he wrote. Though the fingers lay unmoving, they did not look in any way deformed. There was a certain grace in the curve of the hand. There was beauty in the very concentration on his face, an intensity of purpose that made him look different; younger. *There is another man here*, I thought. *One whom folk seldom see.*

I must have moved or made some small sound, for he looked up and spotted me before I could retreat. With a practised gesture he whipped a fold of his cloak over the limp right hand, then closed the book. 'You're late,' he said.

'I'm sorry. Muirne took me to look at some old clothing. Then the door shut of itself. It took me a while to get it open again.'

He said nothing, simply regarded me gravely.

'May I ask you a question?' Such opportunities were rare indeed, so I might as well seize this one.

'You have too many questions.'

This felt much like reaching out my fingers to Fianchu, not knowing if he would make friends or bite. I pressed on. 'I walked through the great hall just now. I saw some things in the mirrors, I couldn't avoid them. And there was a mirror in the tower room. It – it seemed to speak to me; it told me how to open the door. Did Nechtan make those mirrors? How could he learn to do such things?'

Anluan's sigh was eloquent. *I am weary of this. Why don't you do your job and keep quiet?*

'Did he have a hereditary gift of some kind, or did he study the art of . . .' I found I could not quite say what I had intended.

'Go on,' Anluan said. 'You think my great-grandfather was a sorcerer? A necromancer? Hereditary gift, you say. Perhaps you see evidence of the same dark talents in me. No doubt those folk down the hill have a theory as to what secret practices may have warped me in both body and mind.'

I stared at him aghast. His brows were knitted in a ferocious scowl, his eyes were blazing, his tone was full of bitterness. So quick to anger. So quick to assume the worst. 'The villagers had plenty to say, yes,' I told him. 'But I prefer to make up my own mind. And I haven't been at Whistling Tor long enough to do that yet.'

His sapphire gaze remained on me as the silence drew out. Finally he said, 'Magnus told me you were ill treated, before you came here. Beaten. Who would do that?'

This was a blow in itself. 'It's in the past,' I muttered. 'I don't want to talk about it.'

'Ah,' said Anluan. 'So you may ask questions but I may not?'

'Didn't you say my work amounted to *sort, read, translate*?' I snapped. There was no need for him to ask about my situation, absolutely none. 'All you need to know about me is that I have good eyes and a steady hand.'

'It doesn't matter what I said. You ask about sorcery. You suggest a hereditary talent. You leap to conclusions, just as the

86

superstitious folk of the village do, and assume I possess the same interests and qualities as my great-grandfather.' Anluan was on his feet now, his jaw tight, his left hand bunched into a fist. I felt Cillian's grip on my shoulders and took an involuntary step backwards. 'You are as quick to judge as other folk. They make their assessment in a moment and it stands for a lifetime.'

'You've done the same,' I said. 'You seem to have reached all kinds of conclusions about me and what I'm thinking. But you know nothing about me.'

'Then tell me,' said Anluan.

A trap: I had walked straight into it. I moved to the window and looked out. It had begun to rain; the drips trickled down the glazed surface like slow tears. After a little I said, 'I'm a scribe. I'm eighteen years old. There's nothing else to tell.' My voice was less even than I would have wished.

'I was wrong about you,' Anluan said quietly. 'Sometimes you find talking the hardest thing in the world.'

I went to the table where I had been working the day before, opened my writing box, took out my father's knife and began preparing a quill. The familiar tools of my trade brought back a sudden sharp memory of home, Father and I seated side by side, intent on our work, and, in some other part of the house, Maraid busy with broom or duster, or chopping vegetables for the evening meal she would insist all of us attended together, no matter how pressing the need to complete a commission. *Suppertime is family time*, my sister would say. *Nothing's more important than that.*

Anluan was scrutinising me; he had not missed the change in my mood. 'What?' he demanded.

'It's nothing.' I willed my memories into a locked corner of my mind. 'I'd best get on with my work.'

'You answered a question for me, so I will answer yours,' Anluan said gravely. 'Did Nechtan study the dark arts? I believe so. I reveal no secrets when I tell you this; I anticipate that when you read his Latin notes you will discover references to it. Has the family an inherited talent in sorcery? I hope not. I have never put it to the test and I don't intend to. If your imagination has painted you a picture of hidden torture chambers in this house, you should disregard it.'

'Imagination? I didn't invent that scene of torture, I saw it in one of your mirrors. Haven't you ever used them yourself, my – Anluan?'

A shudder went through him. 'I have not, and I will not. As that man's kin, I would never take such a risk.'

'I see.' This was dark indeed. He feared that if he used Nechtan's artefacts, he might become his great-grandfather all over again. 'Have you thought of destroying the mirrors? I saw something very unsettling in the great hall. I cannot imagine why anyone would keep such malign objects.'

'I said I'd answer one question, not a dozen.' He'd put his shutters up already; the interchange was over. 'Return to your work. I will not trouble you further.'

At the precise moment he spoke, there was Muirne at the garden door, waiting for him. I could not see a drop of rain on her clothing, yet beyond the window the foliage was dripping. As Anluan reached the doorway she slipped her hand through his arm, and they went out together, he bending his head as she said something, perhaps: *You're tired. She's upset you.* A moment later they were gone.

For the rest of the day I allowed myself to read. There was a sequence of records written in Irish by Anluan's grandfather, Conan, that had caught my interest earlier, and they soon had me deeply absorbed. Conan's style was less fluent than his father's, and his writing less regular; he had perhaps been more man of action than scholar. His account was compelling:

Still they dog me and will not be ruled. A battle with the folk of Silver-lake ten days since. At first the host followed, obeying my commands. But at the point of closest encounter my control over them faltered. The spell of mastery was broken and they rampaged wildly, heedless of whom they attacked. They hacked and stabbed at the enemy, my own personal guards and each other without discrimination. There was no choice but to flee the field. By the time I drew the host back within the boundaries of the hill I had lost every one of my guards, and the villages on either side of the road had been laid waste. Folk cursed me as they died. Tonight I will study the grimoires again. I fear there is no way to rein these creatures in. If my wretched father,

God rot his stinking bones, could not harness them, why would I do any better?

These creatures. Was he referring to the army with which Nechtan had hoped to dominate his enemies? *The host.* It sounded wayward, destructive, terrifying. *There is no way to rein these creatures in.*

I glanced out the window, then back at the parchment before me. The forest was close; it encircled the fortress of Whistling Tor. Nobody could go up or down the hill without passing under those trees. Could some kind of ravening horde really be still living in the woods out there, something capable of inflicting death and destruction more or less at random? Perhaps Conan had been a drunkard or a madman, given to wild imaginings. I rather hoped so.

I recalled that Nechtan had referred to a book hidden away in the monastery's secret collection, containing a particular form of words he needed for his experiment. A book of magic: a grimoire. If spells really existed for calling forth eldritch forces such as those Conan referred to, then one had to suppose there were also counter spells, charms for banishing them. Maybe there was a Latin grimoire here in the library somewhere; could that be what Anluan was hoping I would find? It seemed unlikely. If the family had possessed a book with such a charm in it, surely as soon as Nechtan discovered that he could not control the army he had conjured, he would have sent it straight back where it came from.

The documents chronicled Conan's continuing struggle with what he had been bequeathed.

Many days of rain. They say the river will flood soon. A losing battle to persuade the villagers up onto the hill where they will be safe. I sent Enda down again, since he at least can make the trip without an unwelcome retinue. The people barred their doors against him. There will be drownings.

An unwelcome retinue – the host again? Surely they hadn't followed Conan wherever he went? Reading further, I found references to a great flood, and also to Conan's wife:

Three children of the settlement were swept away in the rising waters. Líoch wept and upbraided me for not doing more. I bade her be glad our son is here in the fortress and safe, and not to chide me for the burden my wretched father laid on all of us. What does she expect: that I should loose the host to wreak havoc where it will, as he did? I asked these folk to come to my house; I bade them come, and they would not. If their children drown, be it on their own heads.

The books reveal no answers. If my father ever had what I need, he hid it from me. Such an act does not surprise me. The man was riddled with hatred.

News from the southeast: a new incursion. I do not know how I can bring myself to lead the host out again. But they are all I have. Irial is young yet. What if I am slain?

Night after night a whispering in my ear. It tempts me to despair; it holds out the reward of oblivion. I will not heed it. My son needs his father. Yes, even such a father as I. For me there is no hope. But I can hope for him.

There was so much sadness in these records. The more I read, the more I thought of the current chieftain, a man whose moods seemed to span a narrow range – at one end, sorrow, at the other, fury. Yet his father had been the peaceable, orderly maker of those botanical notes, creator of the lovely garden in which I had seen Anluan sitting as if enchanted into a forlorn shadow of a man. *I wish I could teach you to smile,* I thought. *But I fear it might be impossible.*

I worked until it was too dark to read. I would not have a lamp in the library; it was much too dangerous with the documents there. As I left, I slipped one of Irial's notebooks into my pouch. I would read it later, in my chamber, by candlelight.

I was last to supper, and tonight of all nights Anluan had decided to make an appearance. He sat at the head of the table, Muirne at the foot, though she was seldom in her chair – it became clear that in her presence nobody else would serve his lordship. She ladled his food, filled and refilled his cup, cut his bread and sliced his meat. I watched with some fascination, wondering how long it would be before he lost his temper and told her to stop fussing. In fact, she might have been invisible for all the attention he paid her. Had the memory of our trip to the tower not been so fresh, I could almost have felt sorry for her. The chieftain of Whistling Tor had not changed for supper. His red hair was unkempt, his chin rough with stubble, and he wore the same clothing he had had on in the library earlier. His shirt had a fraying cuff and needed laundering. Muirne's outfit was spotless, as always.

'How's the work progressing, Caitrin?' Magnus asked with a smile. 'You look a little tired.'

'I'm perfectly well,' I replied, before Anluan could seize the opportunity to suggest I was not up to the task. Honesty compelled me to add, 'I had a little problem this morning; one of the doors stuck, and it meant I started work late.'

Muirne spoke up, surprising me. 'I heard about that, Caitrin. I'm sorry I left you there on your own – if I'd realised . . .'

'It's all right,' I said. Of course she hadn't shut me in. It was this place, with its secrets and oddities. It was enough to make the sanest person think mad thoughts. 'I managed to open the door eventually; I found a key.'

Anluan's attention was on me instantly. 'A key? I thought you said the door stuck. Where was this?'

Think fast, Caitrin. To tell the whole truth would cast Muirne in a bad light before the man she adored; at the very least, she would appear inconsiderate. 'In the north tower,' I said. 'I forgot where Muirne had put the key when she left, and I'm afraid I panicked.' A look of astonishment passed briefly over Muirne's usually impassive features. 'It was nothing really,' I went on. 'After that I spent the day reading, but tomorrow I must do some more cleaning. Dusting the shelves wasn't enough; they need a good scrub.'

'Don't wear yourself out,' Magnus said, scrutinising my face. 'Olcan or I could maybe help with that part of things. Pity we can't get serving folk to stay up here any more. You shouldn't be troubling yourself with mopping and dusting.' He glanced at Anluan, but the chieftain was studying his platter and did not appear to have heard.

'I couldn't ask you to help, Magnus,' I told him. 'You've got more to do than anyone. I'm not averse to physical work; I'm a craftswoman, not a pampered young lady. But it is unfortunate people won't come here to work. I could get the scribing job done much more quickly with an assistant, someone who could read a little.' Since Anluan was not cutting me off as he often seemed wont to do, I asked a question that had been on my mind earlier, as I realised how slow the job was going to be on my own. 'Have we reached the end of my trial period yet? I will be happier once I know my services will be retained for the summer.' I addressed this to a point halfway between Magnus and Anluan.

'It scarcely matters,' Anluan said, lifting his head to look at me. 'There's a familiar pattern here at Whistling Tor; it never changes. You have lasted a little longer than some of us expected, but you won't stay. We're all trapped in a net of consequences, condemned to paths outside our control. It's the way of things.'

'Are you saying that we can't escape our lot, whatever it is? Do you really believe that?' Not so long ago I might have agreed with him. But I had escaped the trap that was closing around me in Market Cross. If one could summon the will, it could be done.

'I cannot speak for you,' Anluan said. He had given up all pretence of eating; his knife and spoon lay on the table. 'It is true for all of us sitting here tonight, and for all who live on Whistling Tor.'

I remembered something. 'Including the village, if what Tomas and his wife told me is true,' I said. 'The way they spoke about Whistling Tor, it seemed they both love and hate the place. They were shocked when I asked them why they didn't pack up and go somewhere else.'

'It's all they know,' said Magnus. 'The demon at home, the familiar one, is always preferable to the one out in the unknown world.'

'That's what I thought once,' I said, a shiver running through me. 'Now, I'm not so sure.'

Anluan's gaze was fixed on me; I could feel it even when my head was turned away. 'You say you'll stay,' he said. 'You won't. It runs against the grain of things.'

This remark was greeted with silence. Why did none of them contradict him? Patterns could be broken; paths could be changed.

All it took was courage. I had to stand up to him. I could not accept this. 'Rioghan,' I said, 'I wish to make a wager. If I lose, I will repay you at the end of summer. Will you lend me a silver piece?'

The king's councillor smiled. 'Of course, lovely lady.' A shining coin flew across the table to me and I caught it, weighing it on my palm. 'Your wager is not with me, I presume?'

'It's with your chieftain here. He says I won't stay. I wager I will stay until the scribing job is done. His lordship can put up whatever stake he pleases.'

There was a delicate silence. I hardly cared whether I had offended Anluan. It was time someone challenged him.

'I have nothing to offer,' he said flatly.

'Want to borrow –' began Eichri, but I cut him off.

'I'm not in the least interested in acquiring any finger bones or other items of that sort,' I said. 'I'd settle for an apple from the garden; they should be ripening up by the time the job is done. Or perhaps Anluan could write something for me.'

Silence again; this time it felt as if all of them were holding their breath. Anluan's face darkened. His lips tightened. His left hand, resting on the tabletop, became a fist.

'You mock me?' he asked, and in an instant my sudden surge of bravery was over. In his tone were all the times Cillian had hurt me, and the times Ita had hurled insults at me. I became the girl who had once crouched in a corner of her bedchamber weeping, unable to move. I had a good answer for him, but it refused to come out.

'Explain yourself!' demanded Anluan.

Trembling, craven, despising myself, I got to my feet and made for the door, a mumbled apology on my lips.

'Stop!' It was a command, and I obeyed. I was right by his chair. I kept my gaze on the stone floor. I counted the beats of my heart. 'If you run from a simple question, why should anyone believe you will not run from Whistling Tor at the first difficulty?' Anluan's tone was like a flail.

'I didn't run,' I whispered, finding a last shred of courage hidden deep. 'You know that. The day I looked in Nechtan's mirror, you were there.'

Another silence, this time of a different quality. Magnus cleared his throat. I stood where I was, ready for another blast of angry words.

'If you require me to wager, my stake is heart's blood,' Anluan said, his voice quieter. 'Last out the summer and you'll be here to see it bloom. You'll be here to pluck the flowers and make ink. When the work is finished you can take it home with you.'

Olcan whistled. 'That's some wager,' he said.

My head was reeling. If I could work out how to make even one good pot of ink, I would not have to worry about money for years to come. Anluan must have no idea of how valuable the stuff was. 'I can't accept that,' I said shakily. 'It would be worth a fabulous amount. It wouldn't be right for me to take it.'

'It is what I offer,' said Anluan. 'The argument about value is irrelevant. You won't stay.'

'All right, I accept,' I retorted. 'I will prove you wrong.'

He shrugged. It was an awkward gesture, emphasising the uneven set of his shoulders.

'Heart's blood ink, eh?' Eichri chuckled. 'Fine colour; comes up beautifully on vellum. You know how to make the stuff, Caitrin?'

'I'll know by the time the flowers are out,' I said. 'With a whole library full of documents, there must be instructions somewhere.'

That night I had the bad dream again, the one in which Ita threw me down a well of tormenting demons. I woke drenched in sweat and shivering at the same time. Beyond my bedchamber door the moon shone down into the garden. Knowing I would not sleep again, I took off my clammy nightrobe, put on a shift and wrapped my shawl around me. I went out to stand on the gallery overlooking the courtyard, wondering how long it would be before I could hear an angry voice without turning from courageous, resourceful woman to powerless, hopeless child. Perhaps brave Caitrin was only a fantasy. Perhaps the cringing, whimpering girl who had failed to stand up to her abusers was the real me. If so, my parents must be looking down on me in shame.

In the courtyard Rioghan was pacing, the red of his cloak muted under the moon. In the stillness I heard snatches of his speech. 'Go in from the west instead, splitting the force into three parties . . . No, devise a decoy, take the enemy by surprise with a flanking action, then strike with catapults . . . He would still have fallen. My lord would still have fallen . . .' He walked further down the garden and his voice was lost for a little. Then he turned on his heel, restless as a caged animal, and paced back. 'We should have checked the signs . . . Why did I tell him it would work?'

My own troubles paled by comparison with such distress. It seemed he was revisiting, over and over, the circumstances of some terrible error of judgement that haunted him. Perhaps every single night was spent in this painful search for answers. I wondered if going down to talk to him would be any help at all. It would be a distraction, at least. I was about to do so when I had the sensation that someone was watching me. I glanced about, hugging the shawl around me more closely, aware that under it I was scantily clad. There was nobody on the gallery; nobody on the steps. While moonlight bathed the garden in an eerie glow, under the trees it was shadow dark. I imagined folk standing there, clad all in black; I could almost see them. *Don't be foolish, Caitrin.* The rampaging host of Conan's records would hardly be up here, inside the courtyard walls. Maybe there were creatures of some kind out in the forest beyond the fortress, but they couldn't be the ones he had spoken of. It had been years and years ago – Anluan's father had been a child. Besides, a host of hacking, stabbing warriors could hardly be living just out there without my having seen or heard something of it.

One thing I knew with certainty: I was not the only sad and troubled soul in this place. Perhaps I would never quite be free from the shadows of my own past, but that didn't mean I must stand by in the face of other folk's misery. I found my cloak and went down to talk to Rioghan. He was still muttering to himself.

'If I had put archers on the northern hill . . . Or perhaps taken action far earlier, set a permanent guard at the bridge, that might have delayed the onslaught . . . He would still have fallen . . .'

I was standing right beside him and he had not noticed me. His fists were clenched, his eyes full of shadows.

'Rioghan,' I said quietly.

He started. He had been far away.

'Caitrin! You're up late.'

'I can't sleep.'

'A familiar state for me, alas, but not so for a young thing like yourself. You have bad dreams?'

'Sometimes. Troubles and terrors grow stronger in the dark, when I'm alone. Then, when I sleep, the bad things from the past come flooding in. But it's worse for you. It seems you have that even when you're awake.'

'It is true, Caitrin. I cannot be bitter. This is my lot. My own action, or failure to act, earned it for me.' Rioghan settled himself on a bench that was damp with dew and motioned for me to sit beside him. I did so, feeling the chill as it seeped through cloak, shawl and shift to sink into my bones.

'Whatever you did, or think you did,' I said, 'it's in the past now. We all make mistakes. Sometimes we can compensate for them later. Or we can come to terms with our errors and move on.'

Rioghan gave a great sigh, spreading his pale hands in a gesture of helplessness. 'My deed cannot be made good,' he said flatly. 'My lord is gone. He is dead, long dead, and the sward green over his dear bones. I held him in my arms as his lifeblood ebbed away; I wear this cloak in token of that. I cannot bring him back. I cannot expiate my sin, yet I am compelled to try. My mind will not let me rest. There must be something I could have done, some way I could have acted, something I could have changed to snatch victory from bitter defeat. I was his most trusted adviser. How could I have got it so wrong?'

'What happened? Who was your lord?'

'Ah, Caitrin. A precious jewel, a man who blazed like a bright star in the firmament. His name was Breacán, and he was king of northern Connacht. Long ago, you understand. Long, long ago. This region was Breacán's home territory. The kingship was his by force of arms, but he was a good man. He ruled with justice and compassion. Many was the encounter I planned for him, the strategy I devised for him, and all executed with the brilliant flair and perfect judgement that were part of his very being. As a team we were unbeatable. Until that day.'

'He fell in battle?' I knew little of the history of this region. I could not work out how many years had passed since the events

96

he referred to. Rioghan's age was hard to guess; it could have been anything from five-and-thirty to perhaps fifty. The curious pallor of his skin and the sorrowful lines of his expression gave him something of Anluan's look. Perhaps the entire household was bonded by sorrow.

'Let me show you.' Rioghan squatted down and, by moonlight, proceeded to lay out a miniature battlefield with sticks, stones and little mounds of earth. Despite the lateness of the hour and the fact that I was cold and damp, I soon became fascinated. I watched Breacán's forces advance down a broad valley, advance intelligence having told them their enemy would be encamped near the far end and ill prepared for their arrival. I saw, at the same time, how the enemy had secret lookouts high on the flanking hills and a message system involving the flashing of silver discs in the sunlight, something Breacán's men did not detect until they were trapped between two parties of assailants, summoned by this method from hideouts at either end of the valley.

'It was a rout, Caitrin,' Rioghan said. 'And I was the one who led them into it. Mine was the counsel that told my lord, *This is safe; we have the numbers*. When others advised casting an augury to determine the wisdom of the advance, or recommended desisting from the manoeuvre until we had obtained clearer information from certain captives, I insisted we continue. I was so sure my plan was right. I was duped. A man I had trusted had lied to me. That, I did not learn until my lord had been cut down before my eyes, and his loyal men, men who had been my friends, lay slain by his side. The enemy spared this wretched councillor. They wanted one left to tell the sad tale. I laid my lord over his saddle and conveyed him home. I was alive where so many better men had perished through my ineptitude. I wished with every breath that I, too, had been slain on that field of bloody sacrifice. But it was not yet my time.'

'It's a sad story,' I said. 'But you were not the only one responsible. If someone gave you false information, the blame was partly his. And folk didn't have to listen to you; they didn't have to do what you said if they disagreed with you. Everyone has responsibility for his own actions.' I saw myself crouched helpless and silent under Cillian's blows. 'But sometimes we can lose ourselves.

Out of fear or sadness or guilt, we become less than we should be. It can be hard to find the courage to move on.'

'There now,' Rioghan said, rising to his feet and reaching out a hand to help me up. 'I should not have troubled you with this, Caitrin. My sorry tale has made you sad. Or is it your own woes that weigh you down? You are safe here. Anluan looks after all of us.'

'Your story made me think, that was all. Uncomfortable thoughts. I've wanted so much to be brave, and I can't always manage it.'

'Dear lady,' Rioghan murmured. 'Nobody at Whistling Tor means you any harm, you must believe that. Your presence is like a sweet fresh breeze blowing through this weary old place.'

This made me smile. 'Rioghan?'

'Yes, Caitrin?'

'You have a new lord now. Breacán is gone. I know Anluan isn't a king or a warrior. Perhaps he has some disadvantages. Some flaws. But he is worthy of your loyalty.'

'He has it,' Rioghan said. 'Don't doubt that.'

As I went back to my chamber, I realised this was true. Anluan's tight circle of retainers had all chosen to share their damaged lord's lonely existence on the hill. Magnus had been a warrior. He could have left when Irial died. Instead, he had stayed to help his friend's son grow to be a man. At some stage, perhaps loyalty had become love. Whatever it was, it had endured some sorry times. I recalled the lines I had read in Irial's notebook after supper, by lantern light.

One touch, that is all I ask. One touch; one embrace. Reach out to me, beloved. Where are you? The ninety-first day.

Day two hundred and sixty. Winter. In the garden the birch twigs glitter with frost. My heart will see no spring.

I had not been long at work the next morning when Anluan came into the library, moving to stand by the window and gaze out into the garden. 'Magnus said I must apologise,' he said abruptly.

I was too surprised to respond.

'He says I misjudged you. If I did, I am sorry.' His tone was all sharp edges.

I drew a deep breath. 'You were so angry,' I said. 'It frightened me, and when I'm frightened I find it hard to speak properly. I didn't mean any insult to you last night when I spoke of writing.' I chose my words carefully. 'I'm a scribe. I've worked very hard to learn my craft over the years. I consider a page of script one of the finest things a person could wager. And I would never mock a man for the fact that his writing was a little irregular. Besides, that could be remedied.'

'Huh!' Anluan turned on his heel and stalked away across the library. 'You think a bunch of old rags can be made into a silken robe? A worm-eaten apple into a glossy, perfect fruit? Impossible. Why do you imagine I've employed you?'

I took a deep breath and then another. 'As an apology, that was somewhat lacking,' I said, forcing myself to challenge him. 'I doubt Magnus would be very impressed by it. If you don't like the way you write, learn to do it better. I could teach you. It would require concentration, calm, and regular practice. I suppose you might find that difficult, but once you mastered the technique, I believe it would come quite naturally.'

A lengthy silence; he was standing by the far wall, half in shadow, and I could not read his expression. No doubt an explosion of some kind was imminent. My body was tight as a bowstring, waiting for it.

'Again you judge me,' he said quietly.

'Not so harshly as you judge yourself. With . . .' I had ventured into far deeper waters than I'd intended. At this point, going on might be safer than going back. 'With courage and hope, we can conquer our fears and do what we once believed impossible. I know that's true.'

'Courage. Hope.' His voice was shaking, and not entirely from anger. 'Easy for you to say such words, with your background of family, of comfort, of warmth and rightness. You understand nothing.'

This was too much. 'That's not fair!' I lashed out, springing to my feet. 'You can't know how much I've longed for those things, family and . . . and safety and . . . If I still had that, why in God's name would I be here?' I turned my back on him, wrapping my arms around myself and wishing I could unsay the words. I willed him to go away.

After some time, he said, 'So you stay in my house, not out of a desire to help, but because what lies behind you is worse than the chaos you find here.'

'I didn't come here just for payment or a place to stay. I love my craft more than anything in the world; it's all I have left. I do want to help you. I wrote that in the sample piece and I was telling the truth.'

He said nothing, and when I risked a glance, he was simply standing there, watching me. It seemed to me that a wrong word would set him in flight.

'If you had time, I could teach you to write more evenly, and in a way that would not hurt your hand and arm. You could practise a little each day.' And when he did not respond, I added, 'If you worked with me in the library, I would be able to ask your advice on the documents. It would help me very much if you were here to answer a question or two.'

'I think not.' Anluan moved to the doorway. 'I do not believe I could be of much assistance to you. I'm easily tired. I cannot . . .' A thought half spoken there, but his glance downwards completed it for me. The lame right leg, the useless right hand would make many of the simplest tasks difficult or impossible: lifting a pile of books, for instance. And he did get tired. I had seen that for myself. Perhaps he had some malady that went beyond the physical limitations. It was not something I could ask about.

'As for my script,' he added, 'I fear no tutor could mend that.'

Such was the look on his face, yearning and desolate, that I swallowed the denial that came to my lips. He was not speaking of learning to write, but of something far bigger. Whoever took Anluan on as a student must first teach him hope.

'Well,' I said to his departing back, 'you could let me try.'

Magnus and I became friends. Aware of the heavy load he carried, I made a habit of rising early so I could help him in the kitchen before starting work in the library. He would not let me prepare the porridge or mix up the mash for the chickens, but mending was a different matter; it was one of his most detested duties. Gradually I worked my way through a pile of neglected garments. The alteration of clothing for my own use I had done as quickly as I could after the disturbing visit to the north tower. With the russet and the violet along with my own two gowns, I was well supplied for rest of the summer, even when the weather made getting things dry a challenge. Once or twice I had helped Magnus launder garments – mine, his and Anluan's – and hang them over the bushes in the courtyard. I wondered when and where Muirne attended to her washing. She had a series of identical grey outfits, and I had never seen them other than perfectly clean and neatly pressed. Had we not been on Whistling Tor, I would have assumed she had the exclusive services of an expert laundress.

I saw little of her, or of Anluan. Sometimes they would be in Irial's garden, sitting under the tree, he writing in his little book, she hovering close by. Often I would see a lamp glowing in Anluan's quarters, late at night when the household was abed. But apart from Magnus's warm kitchen, the house felt empty, echoing, forlorn. When we gathered for supper, without our chieftain or his constant shadow, the talk was of the day's work: vegetables to be planted, stock to be tended to, a bridge to be mended. And in my case, the documents. There were always the documents.

I continued to sleep poorly, the old nightmares haunting me. I would wake with a start, my heart hammering, sure I had glimpsed a dark figure in the doorway. I would hear creaking footsteps on the gallery outside my chamber, or the soft swishing of a garment. Sometimes there was a stirring in the air, a presence I could sense close by, but I never saw anyone, save for Rioghan with his steady pacing in the courtyard below. Well, I had been warned Whistling Tor was a strange place. I should probably count myself lucky that this was the worst I had encountered.

I was attending to the cuffs of a shirt one morning when Magnus said, 'It's time I went back down the hill for supplies. Maybe tomorrow. Anything you need?'

'Linen thread, if you can get it. That's all. I don't need any writing materials.' The translation of Nechtan's Latin notes was progressing slowly, thanks to my tendency to get lost in one tale or another while reading.

'You could come with me if you want.' This was offered with some diffidence.

I looked up, but he was stirring the porridge on the fire, his back to me.

'I don't think Anluan would approve,' I said. 'He expects me to work every day, I'm sure.'

'That's as may be,' Magnus said, turning to put the pot on the table. Steam arose from the contents, along with a wholesome smell. 'It wouldn't hurt to remind him that you're your own woman. At least, that's my opinion. He still doesn't believe you'll keep your word about staying here. If you come down to the settlement with me, pass the time of day with the folk there, and then come back of your own free will, it might show him that you've the fortitude for the job even when the opportunity to escape is offered to you on a platter. And another thing. It would be good for the locals to see with their own eyes that a young woman can stay up here for a month or so and emerge, not only completely unscathed, but calmer and happier than she was when she headed up the Tor.'

'I've never felt like a prisoner here, Magnus. I know I'm free to go. It happens to suit me to stay, not just because the work needs doing, but . . .' In fact, the likelihood of Cillian finding me at Whistling Tor was now much diminished. My trail must surely have grown cold.

'Free to go. I hope that doesn't mean you'd think of walking down the hill on your own. You're safe up here; Anluan ensures that. But if you wander off into the woods without his knowledge, you could soon find yourself in trouble.' He passed me a bowl of porridge.

'If it really is so dangerous, how do you get to the village and back in one piece?'

Magnus smiled. 'Never had any trouble yet, and I've been doing it since Anluan was knee-high. Must be something about the way I look. And if you're with me, you'll be all right. Think about it. I expect you wouldn't mind a chat with some womenfolk. Muirne's hardly the most sociable of girls.'

'Magnus.'

'Mm?'

'Why won't anyone tell me what they are, these things in the woods? Every time I ask for explanations, I get a vague reply about beings or creatures, and how they're of various kinds, and then someone changes the subject. But in the documents they're described as a fearsome army, a force nobody can control, something that was so powerful and destructive that everyone in the neighbourhood must have known about it.'

He looked at me, grey eyes steady. 'There's two ways you might find out the answer to that, Caitrin. It might be somewhere in those documents you're working on. Or he might decide he's ready to tell you.'

'Oh.' I considered this as he ate his way steadily through his porridge. 'Could you answer a question?'

'Depends what it is.'

'Is Anluan the only person here who knows what they are?'

'No, lass. We all do.'

'So he's ordered you not to talk about it, not to tell me.'

'I need to explain something to you, Caitrin. You might be tempted to think Anluan is somewhat less than a grown man. He hasn't had much to do with the world outside, and it makes him . . . odd, sharp, not quite in tune with folk like yourself, folk from beyond the hill. He's got his reasons, strong ones, for being the way he is. I've tried to help him. I haven't always done a good job of it. He can seem a bit like a child sometimes, quick to anger, all too ready to see a chance remark as a slight. But don't make the mistake of thinking anyone else is in charge here. Anluan's the leader of this household. He makes the rules and the rest of us abide by them.'

After a little I said, 'I see. Very well, I'll come with you tomorrow. Shall I tell him or will you?'

Magnus grinned. 'I will. But I'll wait until suppertime. Now I'd best be gone.' He rose to his feet, and I thought it was perhaps not so surprising that whatever lurked in the woods had left him alone, for even in his old working clothes he was every inch a warrior.

A familiar mist wreathed the trees and clung to the bushes as Magnus and I made our way down to the settlement. It was early; I had been astonished to see Anluan standing in the archway, a sombre, cloaked figure, watching us as we went.

'We'll be back before midday,' Magnus had called, but Anluan had said nothing at all. I imagined he disapproved of my going; he had not come to last night's evening meal, but I knew Magnus had told him the plan.

I walked close to my companion, fearing whispering voices and creeping hands, or worse. After a while Magnus said, 'They don't tend to come out when it's me, as I told you. Scarcely a peep out of them. Besides, you're one of Anluan's folk now; that protects you.'

'That's very . . . inscrutable,' I said, lengthening my stride to keep up.

'I wouldn't be taking you if it wasn't safe.'

The simple logic in this was reassuring. I relaxed somewhat. 'You never married, Magnus?' I asked him.

'Never met the right woman. Not a lot of them to choose from in these parts.' This was spoken with good humour, but it seemed to me a terrible waste. He would have made some woman a fine husband, and not just because he was so handy around the house.

'I'm sorry,' I said, meaning it.

'Not your fault, is it? I made my choice and I'll live with it. He needed me. Still does, I believe.'

'You're all very loyal to him.'

'He's a fine lad. If you stayed long enough, you'd come to know that.'

'Magnus?'

'Mm?'

'Was Anluan born with his disability, the weak arm and leg and the crooked shoulders?'

Magnus walked on as if I had not spoken, and I wondered if this was another of those questions that would never be answered. Then he said, 'He was born as straight as any other child. He fell ill. This was after both Emer and Irial were gone. A palsy. We nearly lost him. Tried to get help, but nobody would come.'

Nobody comes here. I tried to imagine how that would have been: the boy lying between life and death, and only the ill-assorted inhabitants of the fortress to tend to him. 'But surely –' I began, then stopped myself. If I had learned anything by now, it was that this place ran by its own rules, and perhaps always had.

'He's got kin,' Magnus said. 'But things are complicated. Maybe one day he'll trust you enough to tell you. He was very sick. We got him through it. It was a grim time. He regained the power of speech, though that was a slow process. He was left with his weakness. It's a hard thing for a boy of thirteen to come to terms with, that he'll never be an able-bodied man. Still weighs heavily on him, as no doubt you've seen. I did my best.'

'I know, Magnus.' After a moment I asked, 'What kin?'

'At the time of Anluan's illness, Emer's brother was chieftain of Whiteshore, that's our neighbouring territory to the northeast. If you went up the north tower you'd have seen it. The fellow had never approved of Emer's marriage to Irial. He'd cut off all contact between the two territories. We sent a lad from the settlement with a message, when Anluan was hanging between life and death. They wouldn't let him through the gates.' He glanced at me, his strong features set. 'Ask the folk down the hill why these things happen, and they'll tell you Whistling Tor is cursed. It's near enough to the truth. Fear kept folk away then, and it keeps them away now. Emer's brother is gone; his son, Brión, is chieftain of Whiteshore now. A better man than his father, from what I've heard. But that gap's never been bridged. Fear keeps Anluan a prisoner.'

'And you with him,' I said softly.

'Couldn't leave the boy on his own, could I?'

We walked on. I pondered the fear that made the Tor an island cut off from the outside world. It was, no doubt, based on the supposed presence of an eldritch host in these woods, a host that had once been real, unless the written records of both Nechtan and Conan had been the ravings of madmen. And yet here we were, halfway down the hill, with not a single monster to be seen. The forest was peaceful under the morning sun; birds exchanged eloquent calls up in the canopy. Certainly, this was a melancholy place. But there were no –

'Magnus?' My voice had gone small and shaky.

'Mm?'

'There's a man under the trees, over there – in a dark cloak –' Even as I pointed, the figure I had seen became no more than a shadow.

'Just keep your eyes on the path,' Magnus said. 'Nothing to worry about.'

Something rustled, and I whipped around the other way. A woman this time, half glimpsed amid ferns, white face, staring eyes, enveloping hood. Even as I looked, she was gone. A phantasm, perhaps conjured by my fearful imagination out of the glancing of light on stones or the dance of leaves in the wind.

'Take my arm, Caitrin.' Magnus's voice was steady as a rock. 'Look ahead. Remember what I told you. You're one of Anluan's folk now, and you're safe with me.'

And by the time we were twenty paces further down the hill, there was nothing to be seen. I knew better than to ask questions. We covered the rest of the distance to the settlement in silence, and the bristling barricade was opened to let us in.

My arrival in the settlement was greeted with expressions of astonishment. Clearly, nobody had expected that I would survive my trip up the hill in one piece, let alone return apparently none the worse for wear. Tomas, it emerged, had taken the risk of accepting Duald's wager that I would reach the top alive, and now stood to collect his winnings.

'I had my doubts,' he told me as Magnus and I waited outside the inn while folk went off to pack up the supplies we needed. 'I won't deny that. But you seemed so set on getting there, I thought, if anyone can do it, she can.'

'Thank you for your faith in me,' I said. 'Might I go inside and talk to Orna awhile? We're in no rush to get back.' Judging by what I'd seen of Magnus's last visit here, we were likely to be handed our provisions and seen swiftly back out through the barrier. Now that we were here, I found that I did, in fact, want some female conversation, even if it was full of dire warnings about uncanny warriors and giant dogs.

'Why not?' said Tomas, glancing sideways at Magnus. I sensed it was not usual for my companion to be invited in; I had not forgotten how fearful Orna had appeared in his presence last time, as if Magnus had brought the taint of the Tor into the settlement with him.

'Take your time, Caitrin,' Magnus said. 'I'll be out here if you need me.'

Inside the inn, Orna was scrubbing the floor, while a red-haired woman worked energetically with a long-handled brush, cleaning away cobwebs. Both stopped work to stare at me as I came in.

'By all the saints and crawly creatures,' Orna said, sitting back on her heels. 'You're back.'

'I am, and hoping you may have time to sit down and talk awhile. Maybe some ale? Magnus has funds.'

'Of course.' Perhaps aware that I must have an interesting tale to tell, at the very least, Orna got up and fetched the ale jug, introducing her friend, Sionnach, as she set three cups on the freshly scoured table. 'Now tell us,' she said. 'What did you think of Lord Anluan? What's it really like up there?'

It transpired, as I told them what little I believed Anluan would think it reasonable for me to tell, that very few people in the village had ever seen him in the flesh. There were some young folk who had done a day or two of work up on the Tor before they fled in fright, Orna said, and some old folk who recalled seeing Anluan as a child, but Orna, Tomas and Sionnach had never clapped eyes on him, and neither had any of their friends.

'So he never comes down here,' I said. 'Not at all.'

'Not at all. We see Magnus. Sometimes we run into the fellow with the dog, a curse on the two of them. But not *him*. Not the chieftain who's supposed to be leader and protector of us all. A pox on the wretched, twisted freak. But you'll have seen for yourself what he is.' There was a question in Orna's voice; she and Sionnach were both waiting eagerly to hear my tale.

'Anluan's an ordinary man,' I said, realising as I did so that this was an inadequate description. 'He has a slight physical deformity, but it does not make him a monster. He is a little – well, he has a tendency to lose his temper rather easily. But he's no freak. I think he has the makings of a good chieftain, but . . . there are some difficulties. I don't see much of him. I work on my own most of the time.' I felt a sudden sense of disloyalty; it would be wrong to talk too much, to expose more of the wounds that lay on Anluan and his loyal retainers. Somewhere in my mind was the big question, the question of *why*. I did not think it would be answered here, where talk of curses and monsters loomed so large. 'I've been doing some mending for the household up there,' I said brightly. 'I don't suppose you have a supply of linen thread, or some fine needles?'

They were only too happy to oblige. Orna got out her sewing box and Sionnach ran next door to fetch hers. A lively discussion of hemming methods ensued, during which I managed to insert some careful questions about recent visitors to the settlement, and whether anyone might have been asking about a young woman travelling on her own. The reply was not unexpected: that nobody came to Whistling Tor. It must be somewhat of an exaggeration. Certain supplies would have to be brought in, and certain goods must go out, accompanied by people to convey them. But there was no reason for Orna to lie about this. She and Tomas knew I did not want to be found, and as innkeepers they would be more aware than most of any comings and goings in the district. 'Though there have been some rumours,' she added darkly. 'They say the Normans are getting closer. A troop of them was seen riding on Silverlake lands. There's talk they might press on right into this region. Sets a chill in the bones, doesn't it? Who'd stand up for us if they came?'

Probably thanks to my presence, Magnus was eventually invited inside the inn, where he and Tomas, with a couple of other men, sat with us women over ale and oatcakes. I noticed how skilful Magnus was at extracting information without quite asking for it. By the time we got up to leave, he had discovered the name of the Norman lord whose warriors had been seen at Silverlake – Stephen de Courcy – that there had been twelve men in the party, and that Tomas's informant had been a monk from Saint Criodan's, where the Normans had stopped to say prayers and ask for directions. There had been no formal visit to Fergal, chieftain of Silverlake; not yet.

As we were leaving the inn, Orna took my sleeve and held me back while the men went on ahead. 'Are you sure you want to go back up there, Caitrin?' she murmured. 'What about those . . . things?'

I saw the fear in her eyes, and the amazement that I would choose to return to the Tor of my own free will in the face of such abominations. 'I've seen very little,' I told her. 'Perhaps it's not as bad as you think. On the way up I did hear some voices, it's true. And this morning I kept imagining I saw folk in the woods. But I've seen no evidence of a . . . host. Nothing truly fearsome.'

'They're fearsome all right. I'd say ask my grandmother, but she's gone now. They're not just wild tales, those accounts of folk ripped limb from limb and whole villages laid waste. They're all true. Just because you haven't seen it for yourself, that doesn't make it any less real. I don't know how you can be so cool and calm about it.'

I thought of Conan's records, the misguided attempt to use the host in battle, the despair over the future of his people and his family. 'I'm not doubting you, Orna. I've been told that Anluan will keep me safe.'

Orna shook her head, lips tight. 'Anluan, eh? And how will his lordship do that, with his weak arm and his twisted leg? There's only one way a man like that can protect you, Caitrin, and that's by sorcery. Everyone knows what Nechtan was. This is his kin; this is a man not to be trusted. Be careful, that's all I'm saying. If you wanted to stay here with us, we'd fit you in somewhere. You don't have to go back up there.'

'Coming, Caitrin?' Magnus was waiting at the door, sack of supplies over one brawny shoulder.

'I'm coming.' I turned back to Orna. 'Thank you, you've been very kind. I'm sure I'll be all right. I hope this Norman threat comes to nothing. Perhaps I'll see you again next time Magnus comes down.'

'We'd like that.' Her plain features were transformed by a smile. 'Wouldn't we, Sionnach? Not good for you on your own up there, no other women, household full of who knows what. Make sure you do come.'

I felt refreshed by the change of scene, though the news about the Normans was worrying. After an uneventful walk back up the Tor, we came into the courtyard to see Anluan in the archway

109

again, as if he had not moved all morning. He offered no greeting, just nodded when he saw us.

'I need to talk to you,' Magnus told him. 'Got some news.'

They headed off in the direction of the kitchen, and I went to the library, where I spent the afternoon leafing through inconsequential farm records. I could not get Orna's words out of my mind. *There's only one way a man like that can protect you, Caitrin, and that's by sorcery.* I did not want Anluan to be a sorcerer. I wanted him to be a chieftain; I wanted to see him become the person I glimpsed sometimes beneath the forbidding exterior, a man who was sensitive to the moods of others, a man who could make leaps of logic, a man who . . . Well, that was none of my business; I had not been hired to deal with the disorder in this chieftain's spirit, only that in his library. *Wretched, twisted freak.* If he were ever to become what he should be, it would only be by a daunting effort. He would have to battle years of prejudice and misunderstanding. Hardest of all, I thought, would be learning to believe in himself.

'Another dumpling, anyone?' Magnus dipped his ladle into the cook pot. 'I'll be in need of some help as soon as this wet spell's over. Best keep your strength up.' Tonight we were all assembled for supper. The rain had begun in early afternoon and was still falling steadily outside.

'I'll give you a hand if I can,' I said.

Anluan turned his gaze on me. 'You're not being paid to chop wood and herd cows.'

'Thank you for the offer, Caitrin,' Magnus said with a smile. 'Anluan may not be aware that you've been helping out with this and that for some while now. If that's cause for another reprimand, the fault's mine for accepting assistance when it was kindly offered. As for the farm work, Olcan will help me.'

'Your family home has a landholding, Caitrin?' Anluan's question was harmless on the surface, but I knew he had not asked it casually.

'A small one, yes. A house cow, geese and chickens, a plot for vegetables.'

'And your father's name is Berach,' said Muirne.

'Was. My father died last autumn.'

A brief silence. 'You have a sister, I remember that.' Rioghan this time. 'A more generously built version of yourself, I believe you said. Are there brothers as well? I suppose not, or we'd have had them rampaging up here trying to fetch you home.'

This guessing game was like being prodded from every side with sharp bodkins. It was the first time they had asked me outright about my home situation. 'No brothers. Just my sister and me.'

'And where is she, Caitrin?' asked Muirne.

'Married and gone. She wed a travelling musician.' *Married, gone and left me. Left me to Cillian.*

Anluan rose abruptly to his feet; the rest of us, after a startled moment, did the same. 'This is a fine meal, Magnus,' he said, gathering his cloak around him, though the chamber was warm. 'I'm sorry I can't do justice to it. I will retire now. As for Caitrin, she should not be wasting her time with domestic work. She has more important duties.'

I opened my mouth to protest, but Magnus spoke first. 'Noticed how nicely mended your shirts are these days?' he asked quietly. 'That's Caitrin's work.'

Anluan's fair complexion flooded as red as that of a small boy caught peeking curiously at his sisters bathing. Without a word, he turned his back and left the room. True to pattern, Muirne followed.

The rest of us relaxed. Magnus brought out another jar of ale; Olcan shared the remnant of the bread amongst the five of us. Eichri whistled a tune under his breath. It did not sound like a religious melody.

'Your story intrigues me, Caitrin,' Rioghan said. 'You came to Whistling Tor all alone. You have no resources, or you wouldn't have needed to borrow the price of a wager. Your father was a master scribe, you say. We don't doubt that, since he taught you, and we've heard Anluan praise your skills at what, for him, is unusual length.'

If Anluan had spoken thus, it certainly hadn't been in my hearing. Despite the way the conversation had turned so quickly back to the topic I did not want discussed, I felt a glow of pleasure at his recognition. 'Father was very highly regarded,' I said. 'I don't want to talk about him. It's too soon.'

'I know that, Caitrin. There is just one question that is exercising my mind, and it is this: if your father was what you say he was, how is it that his death has left you apparently penniless?'

'Rioghan.' Magnus's tone was deceptively quiet. 'That's enough.'

'Ale, Caitrin?' Olcan refilled my cup. 'How about a tale, a cheerful one for a wet night? Clurichauns, warriors, princesses enchanted into the form of birds, what's your fancy?'

'I understand there are some things you can't talk about,' I said, taking a risk, 'but would you be prepared to tell me about Irial?' I glanced at Magnus, wondering if this might be as distressing for him as talk of Market Cross was for me. 'I've been reading his notebooks,' I went on, 'and I think he must have been a lovely person, gentle and wise and . . . sad. Were the rest of you living here when Irial was chieftain? How did he meet Emer?'

'We were here,' said Eichri quietly. 'Emer's father was Iobhar, chieftain of Whiteshore.'

'Irial must have been on better terms with his neighbours than it seems Nechtan and Conan were.'

'He worked hard at that, Caitrin.' Magnus set down his ale cup. His grey eyes were sombre. As soon as he spoke the other three sat back, as if in recognition that this was his story to tell, not theirs. 'He hired me in an attempt to shore up the defences of his holding, not just the Tor but the surrounding farmland and the settlements that fall within his domain. Nechtan had lost hold. He had relinquished stock and territory along with the trust of his fellow chieftains. Conan was unable to make good his father's losses. When Conan died and the responsibility passed to his son, Irial was determined to set things right, despite the risk. Resources were tight; he could not hire a whole company of *gallóglaigh*, only the one warrior to help him. I had two lads with me at first, but they left; couldn't cope with the oddities of Whistling Tor. In those first years Irial put everything he had into trying to rebuild the alliances that had been broken since Nechtan's time. It was hard. Conan had made some bad errors. People didn't trust Irial; they feared Whistling Tor and its dark tales. I made visits on his behalf, spoke to folk, explained what he was about. Iobhar of Whiteshore was the best of the local chieftains. He was prepared to listen, despite the barriers to trust. We managed a council, just the one, at Whistling Tor, and Emer came with her father.'

'She was a lovely girl,' put in Rioghan with a sigh. 'You remind me of her, Caitrin, especially when you wear that violet gown. Emer's hair was not dark like yours, but flame red. A sweet lady. The moment Irial clapped eyes on her he loved her, and she fell for him just as quickly.'

'Folk were surprised when Iobhar agreed to the match,' said Magnus. 'He knew he wouldn't be seeing much of his daughter once she was wed to a chieftain of Whistling Tor. She did go home a few times in the early years. She took Anluan to visit his grandparents when he was an infant. I escorted them; it was safer for Irial to stay here. Emer liked to see her family, but all the time she'd be counting the days until she got back to Whistling Tor. Irial was fortunate in her. There aren't many women would be prepared to live in such a place, however dearly they loved a man. Emer transformed his life. They had a few good years; they had Anluan. And then she died. We won't speak of that.' Magnus turned away, but not before I saw the tears glinting in his eyes.

'I'm sorry,' I said, getting up to put an arm around his shoulders. 'It wasn't fair of me to ask for the tale. Most people wouldn't have had the courage to stay on. You did the right thing, Magnus.' I glanced at the others. 'Anluan's lucky in you, all of you.'

'There now, Caitrin,' said Olcan, wiping a hand across his rosy cheeks, 'you'll have us all blubbering like babies. Magnus, how about some mulled ale? No more sad tales tonight.'

Magnus said nothing, but he got up and set an iron poker in the coals, then began to assemble an assortment of herbs and spices on the table.

'You've been working hard, Caitrin,' said Eichri, changing the subject. 'How is the stock of materials holding out?'

'Quite well. I will keep careful count of what I use. I know I must make the supply we have last all summer.'

'As to that,' said Eichri, 'more can be procured if you require it. If you want vellum, parchment, inks, tools, speak to me.'

'You'd best watch yourself,' Rioghan said to the monk. 'It ill becomes a man of the cloth to indulge in thievery. You have more than enough black marks to your name already, Brother.'

'Who said anything about stealing, Councillor? I might borrow a little here, a little there; only what can be easily spared. Saint Criodan's will never miss it. All those monks think about is how long it'll be until they can get up and ease their aching backs.'

'Aren't monks supposed to regard the exercise of calligraphy as an act of worship?' I asked, not at all sure how much of this conversation was serious.

'Not being a scribe myself, I couldn't tell you.' Eichri's toothy grin was full of mischief.

I remember something. 'Saint Criodan's. That's the place where Nechtan was shown a secret library. A collection of . . .' No, I did not want to speak of this after all.

'No talk of Nechtan,' said Olcan. 'Magnus, that smells like spring and summer all wrapped up together. How about a song or two while we wait for it to brew? I've always liked that one about the lady and the toad.'

I woke late the next morning somewhat the worse for wear. The rest of the evening had passed in convivial style with the four of us offering Magnus varied advice on the preparation of the mulled ale, then trading songs and stories until the brew was fully consumed.

I made my way, yawning, to the library, but my head felt too fragile for scribing. After last night's revelations, I was drawn to Irial's notebooks. There was a charm about them that was soothing to the heart. If it had not been for the melancholy counterpoint of the Latin margin notes with their tale of loss, the books would have provided the perfect path to peace of mind.

Irial had labelled each drawing with various names including those used by local herbalists, such as fairy's kiss, rat's ears and prince-of-the-hill. Below these he had made observations on the shape, colour and texture of leaf, stalk, flower, seeds, root, and had listed the plant's uses both medicinal and magical. Some could be steeped in water to make healing poultices or restorative teas. Some might be burned on a brazier to restore calm or bring good dreams. I sat at the small table by the window, where the light was best, and read the pages properly this time. Here and there were margin notes in Irish rather than Latin. These did not form a litany of his grief over Emer, but dealt with practical matters. *I have used this to beneficial effect.* And next to another drawing. *Olcan tells me his folk combined this herb with bay to induce a state of trance.* I wondered when I might turn a page and see before me a formula for heart's blood ink.

After some time my head began to throb. Fresh air might help; I would take a walk. I went back through the house to fetch a shawl from my chamber, then headed out into the main part of the grounds. I passed Muirne coming in.

'Muirne, do you know where Anluan is today?'

'He's resting, Caitrin.'

No sign of anyone this morning; even the scarecrow was absent. Perhaps my companions from last night had been felled by the same headache that had interrupted my work.

The sun was out, sending dappled light down through the trees. It had been raining again and the air was fresh. I made my way along one of the overgrown paths, thinking how quiet it was. In fact, it was unnaturally quiet. Where was everyone? Surely Magnus wouldn't let a headache keep him from his daily work. Suddenly I felt ill at ease, my skin prickling, my palms clammy.

A single furtive footfall. My heart lurched. Before I could turn, someone grabbed me from behind.

chapter five

I fought. I had not known I could fight so hard, clawing, biting, kicking like a wild creature in a trap. Cillian, it was Cillian, I knew his voice, the voice of my worst nightmare. 'Get a gag on her!' he ordered someone sharply. I twisted and wrenched one way and another, but there was no escaping the strong arms holding me, the cruel hands biting into me.

I got one scream out before a cloth went over my mouth and was knotted so tight it made my gorge rise. Cillian had four others with him, all familiar to me from Market Cross, big men with knives, clubs and wooden stakes. He held me while one of his cronies bound my hands behind my back and another tied my ankles together. I kept struggling until Cillian hit me over the ear, making my teeth rattle. My body was tight with terror.

'Stop fighting, stupid fool,' Cillian hissed. 'You've led us on enough of a dance.' He slung me bodily over his shoulder, with my head hanging down behind, and strode off towards the gap in the wall. My heart hammering, my flesh clammy with cold sweat, I willed someone to come, anyone. *Help me! I can't go back, I can't, I can't* . . . There was a swaying view of boots tramping and the stones of the pathway. *Please, oh please* . . .

'How dare you! Release her immediately or face the conse-quences!' A commanding roar: Anluan's voice.

Cillian halted. Around him, his men did the same. He turned. Upside down, I saw the chieftain of Whistling Tor standing in the archway of Irial's garden. Anluan's face was ashen pale, his eyes incandescent with rage. Nobody else was in sight; he was con-fronting them alone. A rush of warmth ran through me, and with it a new fear.

'I said, release her!'

Cillian put me down but kept a punishing grip on my arm. My eyes met Anluan's as he limped towards us, head high, gaze fierce, cloak swirling around him.

They laughed, Cillian first, then the others.

'You planning to fight all of us at once, cripple?' My captor's tone was mocking. 'From what I heard down the hill there, you've about as much strength as a wet piece of string. Cursed, they said. Only takes one look at you to see what the curse is, freak. Come on, then, fight me! Let's see what sort of a man you are!' A roar of appreciation from his cronies.

Anluan had halted ten paces from us. Now he took one step forward. His tone was level. 'This is your last warning. Untie Caitrin's bonds and set her free immediately, or pay the price for trespass.'

More sniggering. 'He's got the manner of it, surely,' Cillian drawled, 'but not the manhood to carry it out. You've got the wrong end of the stick, *my lord*. Caitrin here is my close kin. No doubt she's told you some wild story, but the truth is, she had a loss and it sent her right out of her wits. The silly girl ran away. I'm here to take her home where she can be looked after.'

He made to pick me up again and for a moment his attention left Anluan. Mine did not. The chieftain of Whistling Tor advanced no further. Briefly, the blue eyes went distant. He raised his left hand and clicked his fingers.

'Whaa–!' shouted one of the men, and another cursed explo-sively. Olcan had appeared from nowhere and was standing in front of us, a sturdy, short-legged figure. His face was not genial now but wore a fearsome grimace, and in his fist was a big shiny axe. A rope leash was wound around his other hand. The leash

117

was taut – Fianchu was straining towards the intruders, teeth bared, tongue slavering, little eyes full of murderous intent. Cillian turned, taking me with him, and there was a general scramble for weapons until the men's eyes fell on what was behind. A tall horse stood there, a horse all bones beneath a pale translucent skin. Its eyes glowed red. The rider was in the habit and cape of a monk. Within the shadow of the hood his face was skeletal; his eyes glinted with an eldritch light.

'Don't be afraid, Caitrin,' Eichri said, then showed his teeth in a ghostly rictus of a grin. The horse did likewise, uttering a sound that was more rattle than neigh, and reared up. Cillian's party scattered, shouting.

'Release her.' Anluan's voice was quieter now, but it cut through the general mayhem like a knife through butter, and this time Cillian obeyed, gesturing for one of the others to untie the rope around my ankles. The spectral horse was circling, its progress audible as a clatter of bones, and I saw that Eichri was carrying a long, pale sword.

'Oh God, oh God!' someone screamed, as behind the rider a swirling mass flowed out from under the trees around the courtyard, not mist, not smoke, but something full of gaping mouths and clutching hands, something with a hundred shrieking, moaning voices and a hundred creeping, pattering feet. Cillian's men struck out wildly with their weapons, but the blanket of ill-defined forms continued to advance until it was close to swallowing all of us. The uncanny sound reverberated through my head, blotting out reason. With my heart pounding fit to leap out of my chest, I kept my eyes on Anluan's. If he was not afraid, I told myself, then I would not be afraid. I belonged to his household now, and he had told me I would be safe.

A parting shove, and I found myself sprawling on the ground as Cillian and his men fled through the gap in the fortress wall and down the hill, pursued by Eichri at full gallop with the amorphous host following behind. Unleashed, Fianchu pelted off in their wake, baying. Olcan marched at the rear. As Anluan hurried to my side, his limp more pronounced than usual, Magnus appeared from the general direction of the farm, striding towards us.

Anluan had knelt to lift me to a sitting position, his touch gentle.

118

'You're safe, Caitrin,' he murmured. 'The host will not harm you; they obey my commands. There is nothing to fear.'

With his good hand he managed to unfasten the gag while Magnus untied my wrists. Down the hill, a cacophony of shouting, barking and metallic clashing had broken out. The two men helped me to my feet. My breath was coming in gasps; the tears I had held back so that Cillian would not see me defeated were flowing in earnest now.

'Inside,' Magnus said. 'We can rely on the others to see off our unwelcome guests. Did I hear that fellow say he was your kinsman, Caitrin?'

'Not now,' said Anluan. After helping me to my feet he had backed off, as if wary of touching me. 'Take it slowly, Caitrin. You've had a bad shock. Magnus, go on ahead and brew a restorative for Caitrin, will you? We will follow.'

I was crying so hard I couldn't even frame a thankyou. It had been so close. What if Anluan hadn't come out? I might even now be on my way back to Market Cross. How in the name of God had Cillian found me? Had the villagers betrayed me, when only yesterday they had been all sympathy? And how had Cillian managed to get up the hill? Now that it seemed to be over, I had begun to shake. As we headed for the front entry, Anluan moved closer, half lifting his arm as if to put it around my shoulders. I edged away, fighting for self-control, and he did not complete the gesture. 'I never even saw Cillian coming,' I sobbed. 'I was stupid to go out there on my own, stupid!'

'This was no fault of yours,' Anluan said quietly as we went into the house. 'I am sorry I was slow to reach you. I heard you cry out and I ran. But I could not run fast enough.'

'You got there in time, that's all that matters.' I paused to wipe my face on my sleeve. 'Anluan, those beings . . . and Eichri . . . I don't understand any of it.' One thing was glaringly apparent: Eichri was no ordinary monk, nor even an ordinary man. 'How did you do that? That . . . summoning? They were there so quickly. Olcan appeared from nowhere.'

'It is a thing I can do.' He seemed reluctant to say more.

'Was that the . . . the host? Nechtan's host?' I had hardly thought to be afraid of them. Mind and body had been possessed by the old fear, the fear that had driven me from Market Cross to seek safe haven here. That terror still trembled through me: the knowledge that if I were taken back home, I would lose myself forever.

'It is the same force you have seen mentioned in the documents,' Anluan said. 'Nechtan's army, such as it is. Sometimes biddable, sometimes unruly. Stone is no barrier to them. I thought it better that you did not know . . .' As we walked into the kitchen he swayed, and after seating me on a bench he sank down beside me and put his head in his hands.

'Anluan, what's wrong?' His sudden collapse frightened me.

'He'll be better soon,' Magnus said, spooning powders into a jug. 'It's a natural reaction: the exercise of power can be draining.'

'I can answer for myself, Magnus.' Anluan's voice was not much more than a whisper. 'Caitrin, it is past time for an explanation, I know.'

'You're not well,' I said.

'It's nothing. I cannot give you answers to everything, for there are some questions here that have none. Those entities you saw just now – we don't quite know what they are, only that they're wayward and difficult to govern. There is a passage in Conan's records that you may have read, in which my grandfather attempted to ride forth with them to fight a battle.'

'He lost control,' I murmured. 'And they ran riot.'

'There are many such descriptions in the documents. These beings have been on the hill since Nechtan's time. The common belief is that he summoned them by an act of dark magic. They are not monsters, despite the impression they gave just now. That was simply trickery, an illusion that can be used to strike fear into an adversary.' He did not clarify who created this illusion, himself or the host, and I did not ask. Touch too closely on his own astonishing role in this, and the flow of words would likely dry up.

'The host is bound to the chieftain of Whistling Tor, whoever he may be,' Anluan said. 'I can exercise a certain control over their actions. It is done by . . . by thoughts, by concentration . . . Not sorcery; a knack. When I do this, it weakens me. As you see.'

'Don't try to talk,' I murmured. 'There's no need to tell me all this now.'

'I will tell it.' His tone had sharpened. I felt the considerable effort he exerted to make himself sit upright, straight-backed on the bench. 'Caitrin, you have seen that I can command these forces. I can call them to my aid. But this . . . relationship . . . does not end with the occasional deployment of Nechtan's host to rescue a friend in trouble or to keep out unwelcome visitors. You know that in the past the host has run amok and caused unspeakable harm. There is an evil amongst them, something that has the capacity to rule them if allowed to go unchecked. Its exact nature, we have never known – my theory is that Nechtan's original experiment went wrong somehow, and that instead of the mighty and biddable army he desired, he got a force that was more burden than asset. There is a constant need for me to maintain order on the hill. I can never afford to relax my control completely. You have observed, no doubt, that I am often tired. I have been ashamed of this. When I look at myself through your eyes, I see a weak man, a lazy man, one who spends much of his day inactive. There is a reason for it, beyond my physical affliction. Every moment of every day, a part of my mind must be fixed on Nechtan's host. If I ever lost control of them, their minds would be influenced by the evil that dwells somewhere amongst them. They might leave the Tor and run riot in the fields and villages beyond. Should I let that happen, the region would be doomed.'

Throughout Anluan's extraordinary speech, Magnus had calmly mixed his powders, added hot water from the kettle on the fire, poured the result into a pair of cups and set them on the table. Now he was getting out a jug of ale.

I tried not to show how horrified I was. 'Why didn't you tell me this before? And what about Eichri? He was . . . he is . . .'

'He's one of them,' Magnus said. 'Rioghan as well. Those in the house, the inner circle, are different from the rest. They're friends and allies. They were in the forest with the others at first, but over time they attached themselves to the chieftain's household. Their resistance to the evil I spoke of is strong. In will and intent, in loyalty, they are not so different from human retainers. There's no need to be afraid of them.'

'Olcan, too? Muirne?' I had lived among them without realising they were . . . what, exactly? Ghosts? Demons? I thought about Rioghan's unusual pallor, Eichri's gaunt appearance and

Muirne's gift for moving about without a sound, and realised I'd been blind. No wonder the villagers had started throwing stones at me – it was not the young female traveller who had scared them, but her uncanny companions.

'Not Olcan,' Magnus said. 'He's something different. Old as the hill itself. And this was a strange place even before Nechtan did whatever it was he did.'

'It's . . . it's hard to believe,' I said, shivering. I thought of the meals Magnus served, hardly more than a mouthful for Rioghan, Eichri or Muirne, and that never actually eaten. Had that pretence been all for my benefit, to stop me from learning the truth about Anluan's strange household? Or had it been played out nightly for years and years? 'Hard to accept.' I glanced at Anluan. 'I don't know what to say.'

There was a silence as Magnus pushed the cups towards us and fixed Anluan with a particular look. 'Drink it,' he said. 'You too, Caitrin. First the draught, then the ale. You need food as well.'

'Why didn't you tell me earlier?' I asked.

Anluan picked up his cup and drained it, then jerked his head towards the door. To my surprise, Magnus went out and closed the door behind him, leaving the two of us alone at the table.

'If I'd told you, you would have gone away,' Anluan said simply. 'I forbade the others to tell you for the same reason.'

I sat there for a little, saying nothing.

'Finish your drink, Caitrin,' he said. 'And answer me a question. Was that the man who put those bruises on you, before you first came here?'

'Yes. He is a kinsman, that part of what he said is true. But his assurances that he would look after me were lies. They never did that, him and his mother, they only . . .' My tears were closer than I had realised; I floundered to a halt, blinded.

We sat in silence for a little, and I made myself sip the herbal draught. It was strong and tasted of peppermint.

'You have surprised me,' Anluan said quietly. 'I thought you might turn tail and run, the moment we freed you. Of course, with your abusive kinsman heading down the hill, you would not wish to follow. The thought of this Cillian makes your face turn pale, your tears spill, your hands shake.'

I set down the cup and clutched my hands together.

'And yet, when you ask me about the host,' he went on in tones of wonder, 'you are your capable self. How can this fellow and his supporters be more frightening to you than that force you saw manifest from nothing?'

'I knew you would keep me safe,' I said simply.

A tide of red flooded his pale cheeks. He fixed his gaze on the tabletop.

'I know it must seem odd that I am so afraid of him, of Cillian, I mean.' My hands were twisting into the fabric of my skirt. I made myself fold them in my lap and drew a deep, unsteady breath. I had never told anyone this; I had not thought I ever would. 'It's not only him, it's the whole thing. Just thinking about that time, before I came here, turns me into . . . into a different person. A person I hate to be, a person I'm ashamed to be. That other Caitrin is powerless. She's always afraid. She has no words.' The moment I'd heard Cillian's voice, I'd been back there, crouched in a corner, folded up on myself, eyes screwed tight, pressing Róise to my heart, willing the world away. Praying with every fibre of my being to be taken back to the past, before Father died, before *they* came. 'When you and I first met in the garden and you were so angry, for a little I felt like that again. And then today, as soon as I heard Cillian speak, I . . .'

'I hardly know what to say.' Anluan spoke with some awkwardness, as if he thought his words might offend me. 'Your kinsman was right when he called me a cripple. I cannot ride, I cannot run, I cannot lead an army into battle. Not an army made up of earthly warriors of Magnus's kind, anyway. But this force I can command. On Whistling Tor, the host is obedient to my will. While you stay here, I can keep you safe. I hope you will stay, Caitrin, now that you know the truth. We want you here. We need you.'

There was a lump in my throat. 'I did say I'd stay for the summer,' I told him. 'Nothing's happened to change my mind. I'm planning on winning our wager.'

'Wager? Oh, heart's blood ink. Then I must allow you to be in Irial's garden, so you can observe the plant's progress. You spoke of trust. That is my proof of trust. You may wander there freely. I do not think we will disturb each other.'

At that moment the door opened and there was Muirne. She halted abruptly when she saw the two of us sitting side by side at the table, then she moved forward, eyes on Anluan, brow creased in concern.

'You're unwell.' She was by his side, leaning over, assessing him without touching. 'You need rest.' The limpid eyes turned towards me. 'Perhaps it's best that you go, Caitrin.'

I rose to my feet, despite myself. He did look exhausted, his skin a waxy white, his eyes shadowed.

'No,' Anluan said. 'Stay, Caitrin,' and he put out his hand to touch my arm, holding me back. In the moment before he withdrew his fingers, it felt as if he had put his hand around my heart. 'I don't need you at present, Muirne.'

She opened her mouth as if to argue the point, then shut it. 'Very well,' she said, and headed towards the inner doorway.

'Close the door behind you,' said Anluan without looking at her.

From the doorway she gazed back at him, her expression one of sorrowful reproach. It was completely wasted. Anluan's gaze was on me, and I saw in his eyes that whatever it was that had just happened, it had changed things between us forever. Muirne gathered her skirts and left the chamber without a word.

'Maybe she's right,' I said shakily. 'You do look very tired.'

'I'm fine.' His voice was no steadier than mine. 'You'd better drink the rest of that draught. Magnus won't be best pleased to find it only half finished.' As I obeyed, he added, 'You could practise being brave a little at a time.'

'What do you mean?'

'Choose a small fear, show yourself you can face it. Then a bigger one.'

'It's not so easy.' I could not fight Cillian; he was twice my size. I could not fight Ita. I could not fight death.

'No. I don't suppose it is easy. Not for anyone.'

'Will you do it too?' It felt odd to be talking to him thus, as if we were friends; odd but somehow right.

He hesitated. 'I don't know.' A wayward lock of hair had fallen over his brow; he used his good hand to push it back in an impatient gesture. The blue eyes seemed turned inwards, as if he could see a long list of impossible challenges: *Stop covering up your right hand. Learn to control your temper. Go down to the settlement and meet your people. Be a leader.*

'We should eat something,' I said, trying for a lighter tone. 'I don't know about you, but I didn't have any breakfast.' Magnus had left freshly baked bread to cool. I fetched a platter, a jar of honey, a sharp knife. Anluan poured the ale, sat down, looked at me.

'The bread smells good,' I said.

I saw on Anluan's face that he recognised a challenge when one was offered. Narrowing his eyes, he took up the knife in his left hand.

I had not thought how infuriating, how humiliating it must be to attempt such a task when one has little strength in the fingers of one hand. He struggled to hold the loaf steady as he cut. A flush of mortification rose to his cheeks. I had to clutch my hands together on my lap, so badly did I want to reach out and help him. When he was done, he picked up my share on the blade of the knife and passed it to me like a trophy of battle. I accepted it without fuss and busied myself spooning on honey. The kitchen was full of a deep quiet.

I slid the pot of honey across the table to my companion. I took a bite of my bread. 'Thank you,' I said, and smiled.

Anluan dropped his gaze. 'I would fail at the first real challenge, Caitrin. You heard how they ridiculed me out in the courtyard. Without help, I could not have rescued you. What the villagers said about me was accurate. As a man, I am useless.'

'You walked out to face those men on your own, with no weapons. I didn't see the least fear in your eyes.'

'I was not afraid for my own safety. I did fear for you. Caitrin, what the outside world believes of me is true. Without the host, I have no power at all. I am a cripple, a weakling and a freak.' He did not speak in self-pity but as a flat statement of fact.

'You should take your own advice,' I said, struggling to sound calm and practical. 'Practise courage in small steps. You've just achieved one. The next might be to do something about your writing.'

'Oh, no,' said Anluan. 'Your turn next. But not now. Let's enjoy our meal in peace.'

Suddenly I was not quite so hungry. If I could think of a list of challenges for Anluan, I could surely imagine a list for myself: *Make friends with Muirne. Talk about your father. Use the obsidian mirror again.* I looked across the table into Anluan's eyes, and he gazed back. The odd little smile broke forth on his lips, and the blue of his eyes was like the sky on a warm summer's day.

'All right,' I said. 'If you can, I can.'

As we were finishing our belated breakfast there was a scratching on the door that led out to the yard. When Anluan went to open it Fianchu barrelled into the chamber looking mightily pleased with himself. He came straight to me and stood with tongue lolling while I gave him a congratulatory scratch under the chin. On the step stood Olcan with his axe over his shoulder.

'All done,' he said. 'They won't be troubling you again, Caitrin.' Then, seeing my expression, he added, 'Oh, we haven't killed anyone. A bruise here, a scratch there, that's the extent of it. I'm sorry you had a fright.'

'Thank you, Olcan,' said Anluan. 'I must confess to experiencing a strong desire to kill, not so long ago. If that man ever crosses my path again, I may give a different set of orders. Where is Eichri?'

'Settling that uncanny steed of his, I expect. Caitrin, you're still looking peaky. You should go up to your bedchamber and have a good rest.'

'I don't think I could rest.' The prospect of being alone with my thoughts was not at all appealing, but I was in no fit state to work.

'There is something I should show you, Caitrin,' Anluan said, rising to his feet. 'Can you manage a walk?'

I had not expected to find myself heading down the track through the forest again. The knowledge that I was walking in Cillian's footsteps made me cold to the marrow. He and his friends couldn't be far away. If they saw me out in the open, mightn't they make another attempt to grab me, despite what had happened earlier? To speak of this was to admit how little courage I had. It was to seem to doubt Anluan's capacity to protect me.

Hugging my shawl around me, I kept pace with my taller companion. Anluan was attempting to minimise his limp; I could see his effort in every step he took. I tried to concentrate on the warmth of the sun and the beauty of the trees in their raiment of myriad greens. I brought my wayward thoughts under control by considering how to make an ink the precise shade of beech leaves soon after their first unfurling.

'That pathway leads to caves,' said Anluan, pointing along a barely discernible track overgrown with brambles. 'Some extend deep underground. The tale goes that Olcan's kind once dwelt there. If you ask him, he will give you an answer that is neither yes nor no. There are no others like him here now, only those folk you saw before. They will not show themselves to you unless they choose to do so.'

'Or unless you summon them.'

'What happened this morning was unusual. When I saw you captive, it became necessary to call them.' He hesitated. 'Do not imagine that I ever relish the exercise of such power. That I do not fully understand the nature of my control over them must be a peril in itself. Yet I must do it, Caitrin. Every day I impose my will on them, as I told you, so that they will not fall under the influence of the evil amongst them. As chieftain of Whistling Tor, I have no choice.'

We walked on. Above us, sunlight filtered down through the branches of willow and elder; a stream gurgled somewhere nearby. The warbling song of a thrush spilled through the air. 'I don't want to trouble you with too many questions,' I said. 'But there's one that seems important. When you spoke of this before, you implied that you cannot step outside the tight boundary of the fortress and its land or the host will escape your control. When your grandfather tried to lead them into battle the result was catastrophic. You spoke once of being trapped. Is that true? Is that the reason you can't –' I fell silent.

Anluan kept walking. 'The reason I cannot be a leader? The reason I must let my territory and my people fall prey to flood, fire and invaders? Come, we are almost at the foot of the hill: the margin between a safe place and a place of peril. I will show you.'

'But –' I could see the settlement across the open ground ahead, the view framed by a pair of sentinel oaks. Smoke was rising from hearth fires; men stood guard behind the fortifications.

'You believe your Cillian might still be there?' Anluan's voice was calm.

'It's the obvious place to run to. He must have been there this morning. They must have let him in and told him I was up here. Otherwise how could he have known where to find me?' I had halted on the path. My feet were refusing to carry me a step further. 'I'm sorry,' I said as panic rose in me, threatening to blot out reason. My skin was clammy, my throat tight. 'I don't think I can go on. I'm – this is – Anluan, I can't do it.'

'Come, Caitrin. One step at a time, as we agreed.' He reached out his hand. I took it and was drawn on down the path, towards the edge of the woods. If we stood in that gap we would be in full view of anyone who might pass between the forest and the settlement. I clung to his hand, my stomach churning.

'You may be right about your attackers,' Anluan went on. 'Perhaps they went to speak to the innkeeper. Maybe he told them you'd been there and had headed up to the fortress. But it's clear Tomas didn't pass on the warning he's so ready to give to other travellers: that these woods are dangerous; that few who attempt to reach my house alone arrive there unscathed. It seems to me the villagers do not want you hurt any more than I do. As they would see it, they were directing Cillian and his mob straight into the path of the host.' He halted abruptly between the marker oaks. 'I cannot go beyond this point where we stand. Imagine a line encircling the hill at this level. The chieftain of Whistling Tor must not cross that line. Each of my forebears, from Nechtan forward, attempted to do so, and each time the result was disastrous. No wonder our own people revile us. When my father . . . when he . . .' There was a note in his voice that turned my heart cold. His hand had tightened on mine; he was hurting me. 'It can't be done,' he said flatly.

'This is the curse,' I breathed. 'Not being able to leave; being forever tied to these beings. Giving up your whole life to them. That is . . .' I could not find a word for it. Terrible, cruel, tragic: none seemed sufficient.

'Unfortunate?'

'Unfortunate indeed,' I said, 'if there really is no remedy for it.'

'Remedy?' The word burst out of him, scornful, furious. He dropped my hand as if it might burn him. 'What remedy could exist for this?'

I said nothing. I had hoped that after what had just unfolded, he would spare me his sudden bursts of anger. It had been too much to expect.

'Hope is dangerous, Caitrin,' he said after a little, his voice calmer. 'To allow hope into the heart is to open oneself to bitter disappointment.'

That shocked me into a response. 'You don't believe that,' I said. 'You can't.'

'The curse condemns the chieftains of Whistling Tor to lives of sorrow. If there were a way out of this, don't you think my father, or his father, or Nechtan himself would have found it? If we could run this household as other chieftains do theirs, sending emissaries, receiving visitors, employing stewards and factors to help us fulfil our responsibilities, matters might be different. But you've seen how it is. Nobody stays. Since Nechtan's time, fear and loathing have kept them away. I don't need false hope from you, Caitrin, only neat script and accurate translation. You can't understand this. Nobody from outside can.'

He was wrong, of course. I knew exactly how it felt to be hopeless and alone. I knew about sorrow and loss. But Anluan was in no state of mind to hear it, nor was I prepared to lay my heart bare before a man whose mood could turn so abruptly from sun to storm. 'If you think your situation is beyond remedy,' I said quietly, 'why bother with translating the Latin? Why trouble yourself, or me, with reading the documents at all?'

He made no answer, simply stood there gazing towards the settlement as if it were a far-off, unattainable land of legend.

'There might be a description of what Nechtan did,' I went on. 'There could be a key to undoing it. You have your life ahead of you, Anluan. You mustn't spend it as a slave to your ancestor's ill deed.'

'Come,' he said, as if I had not spoken. 'You'll be tired. We should return to the house.'

We walked some way in silence, save for the songs of birds in the trees around us and the soft thud of our footfalls on the forest path. About halfway up the hill I stopped to catch my breath.

'It's so quiet,' I said. 'So peaceful. If I hadn't seen the host with my own eyes, I'd find it hard to believe there was anything living in these woods beyond birds and a squirrel or two.'

'They are here.'

An idea came to me, perhaps a very foolish one. 'Are you able to – to bring them out and talk to them? They came to my rescue. I should thank them.'

Anluan's eyes narrowed. '*Thank* them?' he echoed. 'It would be the first thanks they had ever received, I imagine. Curses and imprecations have been more common over the years. Besides, they acted at my bidding. Without my control the host might just as easily have set upon you.'

Very likely this was correct, but a stubborn part of me refused to accept it. If everyone at Whistling Tor, from its chieftain down, kept acting in accordance with the fears and restrictions built up over a hundred years, then Anluan's gloomy predictions must come true and he would be the very last of his line. He would indeed be trapped, and his household with him. If there was any way to prevent that, we should surely do our best to find it.

'I'd like to try it, if you agree,' I said. 'Can you make them come out again?'

Anluan gave me an odd look, mingling disbelief and admiration. He raised his left hand and clicked his fingers.

They did not flow forth in a mist-like mass this time, but appeared one by one, standing under the trees, as if they had been there all along if only I had known how to see them. When Anluan had brought them rushing to my aid they had screamed, wailed, assaulted the ears. Now they were utterly silent. Not creatures of ancient legend; not devils or demons. All the same, my skin prickled as I looked at them: here a woman carrying an injured child, there an old man with a heavy bag over his shoulder, his back bent, his limbs shaking; under an oak, a younger man whose fingers clutched feverishly onto an amulet strung around his neck. There were warriors and priests here, little girls and old women. The more I gazed at them, turning to look on all sides, the more of them appeared, until the forest was full of them. Ghosts? Spirits?

Eichri and Rioghan could lift cups and platters, open doors, help around the house and farm. I had touched both of them, and Muirne, and found their forms solid, if unusually cold. This host was somewhere between flesh and spirit, I thought. Not spectres, not living human folk, but . . . something in between. Whatever had gone wrong when Nechtan performed his rite of summoning, this sad throng was the result.

My mind showed me Rioghan endlessly pacing the garden as he sought a way to atone for his terrible error. I looked on the forlorn faces, the stricken eyes, the damaged bodies, and a profound unease came over me. I sensed their sorrows, their burdens, their years of waiting for an end that never came. If they were ghosts, or something similar, they were unquiet ones, still on their journey to a place of peace.

The silence was broken by a rustling, a slight, restless movement. The host was waiting. I cleared my throat, not sure if I was afraid or not, only feeling the deep strangeness of it all. I glanced at Anluan. He was watching me intently, just as the others were.

'You're safe with me,' he said, then lifted his voice to address the crowd. 'This is Caitrin, daughter of Berach. She came to Whistling Tor as my scribe. She has something to say to you.'

An ancient man-at-arms put down his club and leaned on it. The woman with the hurt child sank to the ground and settled there, cradling it in her arms. A young warrior with a stain of red all across his shirt leaned against a willow, watching me with restless eyes.

I trusted to instinct and let the words form of themselves. 'You helped me just now when I was in trouble,' I told the assembled host. 'You did a good thing. I suppose each of you has a story, and I think some of them must be sad and terrible. I'm here at Whistling Tor to help Lord Anluan find out about his family's past, and about what has happened here on the hill since . . .' Something stopped me before I spoke Nechtan's name. '. . . since you first came here. I hope that a way can be found to help you. I hope that before the end of summer it will be possible to repay the good deed you did for me today.'

None of them spoke, but there was a universal sigh, soft and sorrowful, and then they dispersed. They did not walk away or

131

wink instantly out of sight, but faded gradually until their forms were no longer discernible against the dark trunks of the trees or the green of the foliage.

'You speak to them of hope?' Anluan sounded both astonished and displeased, and my heart sank.

'There's always hope,' I said. 'There's always a reason for going on.' Once, when she was called to the door, Ita had left a carving knife unguarded on the table. I could have done it. I could have plunged the blade into my chest. My hand had itched to seize the weapon. To end the pain . . . to set myself free . . . But I had not done it. Even in that time of utter darkness, somewhere deep inside me the memory of love and goodness had stayed alive. 'There is hope for everyone.'

'Doesn't the presence of these beings on the hill convince you that for some, life is without hope and the place beyond death still darker?'

'You believe they are spirits of the unquiet dead?'

'Speak to Eichri or Rioghan. They are something of that kind, but their forms are more substantial than one would imagine ghosts or spirits to be. They do not eat; they do not sleep. Yet they can touch; they can laugh; they can plan and debate and trade insults – at least, those who dwell in the house can, and I suppose it is true for the rest as well. They can feel sorrow, guilt, regret. It seems all were once ordinary men or woman who dwelled in these parts.'

'That's . . . astonishing. And sad. A hundred years of waiting in the forest for . . . for what? Is there no way to release them?'

'Come, let's walk back,' Anluan said. 'Don't be so swayed by sympathy that you convince yourself these folk are harmless. They can attack, as you have already seen; they can kill, maim, destroy. Some of them were good people, perhaps, when they were alive in the world. But they are subject to influences more evil than you could imagine. It takes all my strength, all my will, to combat that. The situation is beyond remedy, Caitrin. Even your persistent hope cannot stretch so far.'

After we had climbed in silence for a while, I said, 'Rioghan and Eichri are good people. Funny, kind, clever. I cannot imagine either committing evil acts. And Muirne . . . while she and I are not exactly friends, I've seen how she looks after you, cares for you.'

'They've made a choice to be part of the household, perhaps because of some particular strength of will. Rioghan and Eichri clutch at life with all they have. Muirne has a long history of tending to the chieftains of Whistling Tor; she is a kindly soul, if wary of outsiders. You should not make the error of thinking the rest of them are the same.'

We emerged from the forest just below the fortress wall. Anluan sank down on a stone, suddenly fighting to catch his breath.

'I shouldn't have made you do it again so soon,' I said, crouching beside him. 'Call them forth, I mean. It's too much for you.'

'I hate this,' Anluan muttered. 'This weakness, this . . . Why can't I . . .'

I caught myself about to behave as I had seen Muirne do under similar circumstances, fussing over him, offering support and sympathy. I made myself step back and, instead, settled cross-legged on the ground nearby. I would wait quietly until he was ready to move on. And while I waited, I would think about the words I had just addressed to the host, and whether they had implied a promise I had no capacity to keep.

chapter six

It felt distinctly odd to face the assembled household at the supper table in the knowledge that three of them were, if not exactly dead, most certainly less alive than Anluan, Olcan and I were. All eyes turned on me as I came in, last to arrive after falling asleep in my chamber and barely waking in time to brush my hair and make my way down. Muirne's neat features gave nothing away. Anluan looked exhausted but managed a nod of acknowledgement. Olcan smiled, genial as ever, and Fianchu got up to give me his usual slobbery greeting. The pallid faces of Eichri and Rioghan wore guarded expressions; it was clear they did not know how I would respond to the startling revelations of the day.

'Recovered, Caitrin?' asked Magnus, who was carving a joint of mutton. 'That was quite an experience. I hope you got a rest.'

'I fell asleep. I'm sorry if I'm late.' I took my place beside Eichri without fuss.

'Anluan tells us you gave some kind of undertaking to the host today,' said Rioghan. 'I wish I'd been there to hear it.'

'I didn't promise anything,' I said. 'I'm hardly in a position to do that. But Whistling Tor is such a sad place. I know how it feels

134

to be sad. If I can help anyone here, I believe I should try my best to do so. If we could uncover the whole of Nechtan's story, we might find that matters are not as hopeless as they seem.' I glanced at Anluan. 'It's possible the Latin documents may contain a . . . solution. Something that could end the suffering of those folk out in the forest.' I looked down at my hands, suddenly embarrassed. 'And yours, I suppose. Put that way, it sounds arrogant.'

'You can't imagine you will find a counter spell.' I heard in Muirne's tone how unlikely this was. 'There can be no such spell, Caitrin, or it would have been put to use long ago.'

I felt my cheeks flush with mortification. It was with precisely this in mind that I had made the host my foolish offer of help.

'Arrogant, no,' Magnus said. 'Ambitious, yes. If the rest of you want my opinion, Caitrin's arrival amongst us has marked a big change, and maybe a change we all need. Speaking of which, Caitrin, Anluan has asked if I'll go down to the settlement again in the morning. I'll make sure your unpleasant friends are right out of the district, and at the same time I'll enquire about how they knew where to find you. We don't take kindly to folk who betray friends. But we won't leap to judge, either. I'll talk to Tomas and Orna, find out what's been going on.'

'Thank you, Magnus,' I said. 'It would set my mind at rest if I could be sure Cillian is gone. As for the host and a counter spell, I know it's an unlikely chance. But what we need could be there among the documents. Perhaps it's hidden in some way. Encoded.' I was bursting to ask them what they were, how they felt, where they had come from. Seated at the table by lamplight, with Magnus calmly serving supper as if everything was just as it had been, I found I could not quite get the words out. Instead I asked, 'Do you believe Nechtan used dark magic of some kind when he brought forth the host?'

'It's what folk say.' Eichri shifted in his seat; there was a grating sound, bone on bone. 'But until you find a record spelling out exactly what he did, nobody can be quite sure. Saint Criodan's is full of stories about him, though any monk who had personal dealings with him is long gone, of course. He was generous towards the foundation; he paid for a new building to house the library and scriptorium. Quite the scholar.'

The vision from the obsidian mirror came back to me, complete with every detail, and I set my knife down, finding I was not hungry after all. 'He paid for knowledge,' I said. 'A secret book, kept under lock and key. It contained something he needed, perhaps a spell, though it seems unlikely that a monastic foundation would have grimoires. He didn't bring the book back here, but he got the information he wanted – he must have made a quick copy or memorised it. It would almost certainly be in Latin. Even if that's not amongst the documents, there may at least be a description of the . . . procedure. I don't know quite how to say this, but . . . it seems you were . . . called back, as those others in the woods must have been. What can you remember?'

'We were somewhere else, and then we were here,' Eichri said. 'My earthly life, such as it was, remains vivid in my memory. The moment of my death . . . One does not forget that. But the time between then and my return is blurred. I recall being somewhat taken aback not to find myself sizzling in the flames of hellfire or condemned to some other dire punishment. That still awaits me, perhaps. It is possible Nechtan's ill-executed experiment bought all of us time to make amends. To win ourselves a better conclusion when it is time to go once more.'

'It may never be time to go,' said Rioghan gravely. 'Muirne is right, Caitrin. If Nechtan had possessed a charm of reversal, a form of words to banish the unruly host – I do not use the term *unruly* for myself or Muirne, you understand, but only for my clerical friend here and that rabble out in the woods – he would surely have used it as soon as he realised he hadn't got what he wanted. We've already been on the hill for twice the natural lifespan of a man. We might be here forever, performing a good deed a day and getting no benefit at all from it.'

'So you were in some kind of middle realm, between this one and the next?' I queried. 'A waiting place?'

'Hell's antechamber,' observed Olcan dryly.

'Or heaven's,' I said. 'If it is possible to call folk back, as it seems Nechtan did, then Eichri may be right. Perhaps this second sojourn in the world of the living offers a chance to win a passage, not to perpetual suffering, but to eternal rest.'

'For me there can be no such reprieve,' muttered Rioghan. 'Nor for *him*, I think.' He gazed at Eichri. 'His crime was too obscene for such a second chance to be possible. Besides, in all the years he's been hanging about here, I've never observed the least sign of contrition. There's no hope for you, Brother.'

'Hope of what?' Eichri's lips stretched in a mirthless smile. 'A place in heaven? I never expected that, even when I was a living man, Councillor. At least I had the honesty to acknowledge that I was bad to the core. Hence the surprise when, on falling to the ground with such a pain in my chest that I knew I would never rise again, I did not find myself roasting nicely in the Devil's flames, but . . . well, as I said, we are not sure of that part. Whatever came next, it was evidently not memorable.'

'Interesting idea,' said Magnus. 'For folk who are neither sinful enough to go straight to perdition nor saintly enough to rise to God's right hand, there's a future of utter tedium. A soul might work extremely hard to escape such a fate. Not being a godly man myself, I can't say if it's plausible. What would you have to do, Eichri, to be washed clean of your wrongdoing?'

A rattling shiver passed through the ghostly monk. Then Anluan said, 'I do not know if it is true that a man can be absolved of any sin if he atones for it in some way. What is your opinion, Caitrin? Are you a woman of religious faith?'

'I was once,' I told him. 'When my father died, it was a blow. What unfolded from that day almost destroyed my belief in God. But I believe we all have an inner goodness; a little flame that stays alight through the worst of trials. So perhaps my faith is not altogether gone. As for whether good deeds can cancel out wicked ones, I cannot say.' I thought of Ita's biting tongue and Cillian's cruel hands. I remembered Nechtan's heartless act of torture, which he had believed perfectly justified. 'Perhaps there are some evils that can never be erased,' I said. 'As for religious faith, a lack of it shouldn't stop us from doing good deeds for their own sake.'

Anluan had set down his knife with his meal barely touched. 'If a man takes his own life,' he said, 'that, surely, can never be acquitted. It is the ultimate sin, don't you think? Such a person must go straight to hellfire, that's if one believes in such a phenomenon. Or to oblivion. Or to be born again as the lowliest of creatures, a slug or marsh fly, perhaps.'

The others had gone unnaturally still. They were waiting for my response with a degree of interest that was suddenly intense. I did not like the look on Anluan's face. His mood had changed abruptly. He seemed strung so tight that he would snap if I gave him an answer he did not care for.

'Slugs and marsh flies have their places in the great web of existence,' I said. 'How should I answer, Anluan? As a devout Christian would, or as a person whose faith is, at best, shaky?'

'Answer honestly.'

'Very well.' My supper companions were all staring at me. 'I do not view suicide as wicked, just terribly sad. There is only one death, but it is like a stone cast into a pond – the ripples stretch far. Such an act must leave a burden of sorrow, guilt, shame and confusion on an entire family. A natural death, such as my father suffered, is hard enough to deal with. A decision to end one's life must be still more devastating for those left behind. I cannot imagine the degree of hopelessness someone must feel to contemplate such an act. Even in the darkest time, even when God was utterly silent, I never . . . there was always something in my life, something I can't even define for you, that stopped me from taking that step. The thought of such utter despair chills me. I hope that is honest enough for you.'

'Excuse me.' Anluan was on his feet and out the door almost before I had time to blink. His faithful shadow rose from the table and hastened after him.

Dismay must have been written all over my face. Magnus poured a cup of ale and set it in front of me, while Eichri wrapped his bony fingers around mine.

'I'll have Muirne's supper,' said Olcan. 'Pass it up, Rioghan, will you?'

'If he didn't want an honest answer he shouldn't have asked for one,' I said, furious with myself for upsetting Anluan again, when he had been so open with me earlier.

The silence that followed was like the first ice of the season, brittle and dangerous.

'Anluan won't tell you this,' Rioghan said, 'but Irial died by his own hand. He used poison; we never found out exactly what kind. It must have been easy for him to concoct, since he was so knowledgeable about plants and their uses. Sixteen years ago, that was, and as clear in our minds as the day it happened. He was still alive when we found him out in the garden. It was . . .' He shivered. 'It was bad. I'll never forget his skin, all blue-grey like one huge bruise. His eyes went cloudy. Whatever it was that he took, it affected the lungs. He found it harder and harder to catch his breath. It seemed to me there was something he wanted to tell us, but his voice was gone.'

I could think of nothing to say. I probably should have guessed that this was the explanation for Irial's outliving his beloved Emer by only two years.

'There's more,' said Olcan. 'On a dark day, long ago, I found Conan out in the woods with a very efficient stab wound to the heart and his hunting knife still in his hand. He may not have been the sort of fellow folk warmed to, but at least *he* waited until his son was a man. It's a pattern those of us who are close to Anluan don't much care for.'

Sixteen years. That meant Anluan was only five-and-twenty. 'I'm sorry,' I said. 'This must be distressing for all of you.'

'You're one of us now,' Magnus said quietly. 'It's good that you know. We don't like him upset, that's true. But he did raise it, and he did ask you to be straight with him. That's not a blunder, Caitrin, it's two steps forward. He's trying hard. But you'll have to go carefully. He bears a lot of scars.'

'I suppose Irial simply couldn't go on without Emer. But it seems a terrible thing to do when his son was so young, only a child.' It had troubled me, reading his record of grief, that Irial had barely mentioned his boy. It was another reason not to draw the margin notes to Anluan's attention.

Magnus sighed. 'When she died, Irial's whole world fell apart. He never got over the loss of her. Two years, he held on, but the world grew darker and darker for him. Not that I ever expected he'd act as he did. I thought he had the strength to endure it for Anluan's sake. I'd give a lot to be able to turn time backwards. I'd like to talk to Irial, say all the things I should have found time to say while he was still here.'

'I should go and find Anluan,' I said, getting up. 'I should apologise.'

'I wouldn't.' Magnus's grey eyes were sombre. 'Talk to him tomorrow, by daylight. He's best alone tonight.'

'He's not alone,' I pointed out. 'He's got Muirne.'

Perhaps there was something in my tone that revealed what I really thought about this: that Muirne's presence was likely to make him more, rather than less, despondent. With Irial's story fresh in my mind, and Conan's, Anluan's dark moods had begun to take on a troubling significance. I bitterly regretted upsetting him.

'Don't much care for Muirne, do you?' Olcan asked with a smile.

'She doesn't like my being here,' I said. 'That makes it rather difficult to be friends. I understand a little better now that Anluan has told me more about the host. Muirne is devoted to him, that's obvious. She thinks my presence will exhaust and weaken him, and perhaps there's some truth in that. I suppose she fears that if he gets too tired, he may not be able to keep the host in check.'

'Take my advice,' Magnus said. 'Give Anluan time to think this over. He respects your judgement, Caitrin. But it's new to him, this talking openly about the past. He's never dared hope for a different kind of future.'

'He did hire me.'

'True,' Eichri said, 'though that may have been more act of desperation than act of hope. He thinks the world of you, Caitrin. Don't doubt it, despite the way he snaps. But you're an exotic creature to Anluan, a curiosity from a far-off land. You challenge him in more ways than you could imagine.'

I looked from one member of this inner circle to another. Their love for their chieftain shone in their words and on their faces.

'Very well,' I said. 'I won't trouble him tonight.' No doubt there would be a light burning in Anluan's quarters, visible through the tangle of foliage in the courtyard as usual. I wondered if he wrote in his little book by lamplight or simply stared into the flame. Maybe, like Nechtan, he pursued branches of study that could not be carried out more openly. There were no grimoires in the library. That didn't mean there were none in the house. I had been taking Irial's notebooks to my bedchamber, a different one each evening. Anluan might have a whole private collection in his quarters. Might not such a collection include Nechtan's books of magic?

I excused myself, lit my candle with a taper from the fire and went up to my bedchamber, wishing my mind had not travelled down this last path. Anluan had said he did not use sorcery to command the host, only a knack. I had believed him. But he had made the others conceal the truth from me so that I would stay at Whistling Tor. That was only one step from a lie. Perhaps he had lied about the sorcery. He'd seen how horrified I was by the mirror vision. If he were a practitioner of the same dark arts as Nechtan, he'd hardly be open about it.

My chamber door was ajar. Inside, a child in a white smock was sitting cross-legged on the floor, in the dark, with my little doll Róise on her lap. The girl's hair was white, too, drifting in a pale cloud around her head and shoulders. She was crooning a wordless lullaby. The hairs on my neck rose. A glance around the chamber told me she'd been investigating all my things. Clothing spilled out of the storage chest, my comb lay on the floor and the bedding had been disordered with more violence than such a fragile being seemed capable of. I took two steps into the room. The child raised her head, fixing shadowy eyes on me.

'Hurt,' she whispered. 'Baby's hurt.' Her skinny hand moved tenderly to stroke the silken threads that formed Róise's hair. Even by the fitful light of my candle I could see that the doll was the worse for wear. Some of her hair had been pulled right out and her skirt was in shreds. My stomach tight with unease, I cast my eyes around for knives, bodkins or other dangerous implements. 'Oo-roo, baby, all better soon,' the child sang, rocking the doll in her arms.

A rustling sound behind me in the open doorway. I whirled around.

The young warrior in the bloody shirt stood there, the one from out in the woods. His arms were wrapped across his chest. A febrile trembling coursed through his body. Whatever it was that shook him so, rage, fear, a malady, it possessed him utterly. Brighid save me, what had I begun?

'Tell me the truth.' His voice was dry and scratchy, as if he'd been long out of the habit of using it. He cleared his throat and tried again. 'Can you give us what we need? Or did you speak lies and false hope? We have waited long.'

I almost yelled for Magnus. The young man had a sword and a dagger at his belt. He sounded desperate. He looked poised on the brink of violent action. But I did not call out. I was the one who had set this in motion and I must be brave enough to deal with the consequences.

'I wasn't lying,' I said, doing my best to hold his nervous, darting gaze. 'I'll do my best to help you. Tell me, what is it you need most?'

For a moment his eyes were full of whirling visions, images of pain and struggle.

'Sleep.' He spoke the word on a sigh. 'Rest. That is what we long for. It is what we crave. Tell the lord of Whistling Tor to let us go.'

'He would if he knew how,' I said. 'I'll help him search for a way. But . . . I must be plain with you. I am only a . . . I am not . . . I have no position of authority here at Whistling Tor. I cannot swear to you that there's a remedy to be found. All I can promise is to do my very best for you.'

The young man bowed his head. With a sound like shivering leaves he faded away before my eyes. I turned my attention to the child and to my disturbed chamber. Since I could think of nothing appropriate to say to a small ghost girl – I could hardly tell her she should be tucked up in bed by now – I began methodically to set my belongings to rights. First the blankets; I gathered them and began to fold. A moment later the child had set Róise carefully down and was holding two corners for me, her sorrowful eyes intent on my face. We moved towards each other as in a dance; I gathered the top edges together, the girl took up the lower corners and we repeated our measure. I laid the folded blanket on the foot of the bed and picked up the second.

'Thank you,' I said. 'You're a good helper.'

'Baby's hurt.' Her tone was mournful. She glanced at Róise, who now sat on the floor with her back to the storage chest, her embroidered eyes fixed on us.

'She's only a doll,' I said cautiously. 'I'll mend her. But I'm sad that someone damaged her. My sister made her for me. Róise is my memory of good things.' It was hard to know how much to say. The girl seemed harmless. But she'd been in my chamber and the fact that she was helping me now didn't make up for what she'd done to my belongings. 'Please pick up the comb and put it on that chest.'

She did not put the comb away, but brought it to me, then turned her back in clear expectation that I would tidy her wispy pale hair for her. I set the second blanket down and began a careful combing.

'Where's my mama?' the child asked suddenly.

My heart turned over. 'I don't know, sweetheart.' Her hair was as flyaway as thistledown; the candlelight seemed to shine through it.

There was a long silence as I gently combed, and then she said, 'I want Mama. I want to go home.'

Tears sprang to my eyes. I knelt down and put my arms around her. She was ice-cold, preternaturally cold, and although she had substance, she felt nothing like an ordinary child – she was far less solid in form than Rioghan or Eichri. I suppressed a horrified shudder. There was nothing I could say that would help; no promise I could make that a small child might understand. I could not send her home. She had no home. I could not find her mother. I could not offer her a place to stay, a bed to sleep in. She was a spirit child; she did not belong with me.

'Your hair looks lovely now,' I said. 'My name is Caitrin. What is yours?'

Her voice was like the passing of a breeze in the grass. 'I don't remember.'

Down in the garden, Fianchu exploded into a fanfare of barking, seeing off some night-time creature. In my arms, the child vanished. One moment she was there, the next I was holding nothing at all.

'Caitrin?' Olcan called from outside.

My skin in goose bumps, I went out to the gallery. He and the dog were coming up the steps.

'Thought I might leave Fianchu with you tonight,' Olcan said. 'You'll be nervous after what happened earlier with your unpleasant kinsman and his cronies. You needn't have this fellow in the bedchamber with you, though that'd be his preference without a doubt. You can leave him out here when you bolt your door, and he'll sleep across the threshold.'

'Thank you.' Fianchu's presence would be more than welcome. 'I had visitors just now. From the host. Will Fianchu keep them away as well?'

'You'll be safe, Caitrin. You're Anluan's friend. They won't harm you.'

I considered this as I lay in bed a little later with the door shut and bolted and Fianchu on my side of it, comfortable on one of the two blankets, for I had not had the heart to shut him out. If dogs had been able to smile, he'd have had a big grin on his brutish features. Everyone seemed sure that Anluan could protect me; that his mastery over the host meant the uncanny presences of Whistling Tor would not harm his household or the chieftain himself unless he crossed that invisible line he had shown me. I wondered about that. The young man in the bloody shirt had seemed almost inimical when he accused me of lying. There had been anger in his voice when he bade me tell Anluan to let the host go. Anluan was Nechtan's descendant, and Nechtan was the one who had brought these folk forth and, I assumed, condemned them to their strange existence on the hill. Were we really safe from them? Or might it take only a wrong word or a trivial error of judgement to turn them into the chaotic, destructive horde of Conan's account, a force that destroyed friend and foe alike? When they had confronted Cillian this morning, they had looked ravening, fearsome, malevolent.

My mind went to Anluan. I recalled his courage as he stepped out to face my attackers, all alone. Now he was alone once more, probably in his quarters brooding over his father's sad end. Alone save for Muirne. Solicitous, protective, devoted Muirne. Even if she had been a living woman, as I had believed until this morning, she was wrong for him. 'He needs someone as perfect for him as Emer was for Irial,' I told the enormous hound. 'Someone who will be kind to him, but not too kind. Someone who won't mind living in this strange place. Someone with the patience to help him learn.'

Fianchu made no comment, only lifted his head, sighed, and stretched out luxuriously on the blanket.

'Someone who respects him,' I added. 'Someone who sees him as strong, not weak. Someone who needs him as much as he needs her.'

The dog was asleep. I blew out my candle and pulled the blanket up to my chin. 'And no, I don't mean myself,' I murmured. 'I'm not so foolish as that. Though I'd surely do a better job of it than *she* does.'

Despite Fianchu's protective presence I slept badly. I rose at dawn with the tangled remnants of my nightmares hanging close about me. When I opened my door to let the dog out there was a sudden movement along the gallery, a blur, as if a ghostly presence had kept its own watch outside the door.

Mist shrouded the garden, creeping into every corner. Within the shifting shapes of it I could see them: the wounded, the sorrowful, the furious, the desperate folk of the hill. Their eyes were fixed on me. There were no threats, no entreaties, indeed there was no sound from them at all as they passed, but I heard the unspoken words in my heart: *Find it. Find a way.*

'I will,' I muttered, more to myself than to the host. 'If I can, I will.' But as I threaded my way through the maze of chambers and passages towards the kitchen, I reminded myself, uncomfortably, that I was here at Whistling Tor because I had run away from my own problems. The host had been on the hill for a hundred years. It had blighted the lives of four chieftains, their families and the folk of the region. Anluan had hired me to translate Latin for him, not to achieve what nobody else had been able to do in all that time.

Magnus was in the kitchen making up the fire.

'I'm off down to the settlement soon,' he said. 'You sure you're all right, Caitrin? You're not looking well, even now. It's not every day you discover all of a sudden that you're living alongside – well, I've never been quite sure what to call them. Must have been unsettling, at the least.'

'I slept badly. That's nothing new. Yes, it was a strange day. It wasn't the host that most disturbed me, it was the way Cillian managed to find me, just when I was starting to feel safe. When

145

Tomas and Orna first sheltered me, I told them I was running away and expected to be followed. It's hard to believe they would tell him where I was.' Even in this quiet chamber, with this kindly man as my only company, the words did not come easily. 'It had been quite bad, at home, before I came here,' I made myself say. 'It took me a long time to be brave enough to leave. I was so terrified he'd drag me back, I hardly thought to be afraid of the host.'

The fire was blazing now. Magnus set the kettle on its hook. 'If that fellow's typical of your kinsfolk, you're best off without them, in my opinion,' he said. 'What is he to you, Caitrin? A cousin? How was he able to get away with those acts of violence?'

'His mother is a distant cousin of my father's. Before Father died, I hardly knew them. And afterwards . . . well, they came to look after me, at least that was what they said, and . . . I don't want to talk about it, Magnus.'

Magnus was frowning. 'The situation sounds irregular at the very least, Caitrin. Why don't you have a word with Rioghan? He knows all about the law. Explain it to him and ask what he thinks. Sounds like something's wrong to me.'

I would never go back to Market Cross. Never. So it didn't matter what advice Rioghan had, since I would not be acting on it. 'I'll talk to him some time,' I said. 'Not today. After yesterday's disruptions, I need to spend all day in the library.'

So early in the morning, the light was barely adequate for writing. I busied myself preparing a broad-tipped goose-feather quill and scoring a fresh sheet of parchment. As the sun rose higher and the chamber grew brighter, I set these items aside – they were not for my use. I got out my own quill and ink, and took up the task of copying my most recent document listing from wax tablet to parchment. I had filled the tablet five times over now, transcribing each list in turn when the wax surface was covered, then erasing and beginning again. It was a thankless, tedious task. All I wanted to do was plunge frantically into the Latin documents in the quest for spells and charms. Common sense prevailed. I must maintain the catalogue as I progressed, or as soon as I left Whistling Tor the library would descend into its old chaos. I wrote quickly, using a common hand. There was no need for this work to be finely executed; it just had to be legible.

From time to time I was aware of a whisper of feet on the flagstoned floor, a shadowy movement at the corner of my eye, but when I glanced up there was nobody to be seen. I knew they were there watching me. 'I'm working as fast as I can,' I muttered, acutely aware that the real work still lay before me. If the truth about Nechtan's sorcery lay in this library, it would be in those Latin documents. I glanced at the chest that held the obsidian mirror. From within the squat form of the box I could feel the malign power of the artefact. *Use me. If you want the answers, use me.*

I completed the pen and ink list, wondering if I would see Anluan at all today. Yesterday had felt like a turning point, and I wished I had not upset him at supper. I remembered his fingers against my arm, when I had thought to leave him and Muirne in the kitchen, and the way I had responded as a harp string does to the touch of a bard.

I used the wooden handle of my stylus to erase the markings on the wax tablet, rubbing hard enough to melt the wax slightly, then smoothing over the surface. When it was done, I set stylus and tablet beside the quill I had readied earlier. The library felt very empty. I wished I had borrowed Fianchu for the day as well as the night. The big hound's company would have been welcome.

I walked over to the window and peered out. Irial's garden was deserted save for the usual bevy of small birds in the stone bowl. A stroll once around the path would get my thoughts under control, then I'd go back to work.

The day had warmed and the garden was full of soft colours: grey-green, muted violet, blushing rose, palest cream. It seemed to me that the man who had created this sanctuary with such care had left something of himself behind in its quiet corners. As I walked I felt tranquillity seeping into my bones. And yet, Irial himself had given in to despair. It didn't seem right.

'Why would you do it?' I murmured. 'Couldn't you see what you still had?' His young son; his most loyal of friends; his adoring household; this garden where lovely things still grew and flourished, even though Emer was gone. Could a man love a woman so much that, without her, everything else in his world ceased to have meaning? That was extreme. How cruel to leave Anluan all alone to deal with everything, the Tor, the host, the curse . . .

As if I had summoned him with my thoughts, the chieftain of Whistling Tor walked in through the garden archway and halted when he spotted me under the birch tree. He was freshly shaven and his hair had been combed, perhaps washed. The light caught the red of it, a dark flame amid the muted shades of the garden. He'd changed his clothes, too; the shirt he had on was one I had mended recently, using a thread that did not match.

'You were talking to someone.' Anluan glanced around the empty garden.

'Only to myself. Not that there haven't been folk about, both last night and this morning. Folk from the forest, I mean.'

Anluan limped towards me, pausing by the clump of heart's blood. 'It's put on new growth,' he observed, glancing down. 'Caitrin, if you wish them to leave you alone, just tell me.'

'No, it's fine. I made them an undertaking and it's fair that they should keep an eye on me to be sure I carry it out as best I can. They don't seem particularly monstrous. There was a child last night, no more than five years old . . . Could you stay in the library awhile this morning? I need your help with something.'

'I'm at your disposal. After my abrupt departure last night, I can hardly offer less.'

'You are chieftain here,' I said. 'You can do what you like. And last night was partly my fault. I spoke without thinking, and I'm sorry. I'm glad you came this morning. Shall we go in?'

There was a certain awkwardness when he saw the writing materials set out on one of the cleared tables. I saw a familiar tightening of the jaw, a flinty look in the eyes. I spoke before he could. 'All you need to do is try something for me. Just a slightly different way of holding your quill. It's not much to ask.' But it was; that was quite plain on his face.

'There is no need for me to write, poorly or otherwise,' he said, an edge in his voice. 'You are the scribe; you are at Whistling Tor to do what I cannot.'

'Perhaps I can do what's required here by the end of summer and perhaps I can't,' I said quietly. 'But after I'm gone you'll still keep on studying, as it's clear you've been doing for years. You'll still need to make notes, to transcribe things, to prepare documents of your own. Think of this as an experiment, as much for my own interest as anything. Please sit down. It will help if you take off your cloak.'

He removed it awkwardly, fumbling with the clasp one-handed. I did not help him.

'I've seen left-handed scribes before,' I told him as he sat at the work table. 'They all hold the pen the way you do, with the hand curved around. I've been wanting to try something like this. You need not change from your usual script, but we're going to hold the stylus differently, like this.'

'But . . .' Anluan began a protest, then fell silent as I moved to stand close behind him, leaning over his left shoulder to guide his arm and hand into the correct position. Teaching a person to write is a very particular task; it cannot be done without a high degree of physical closeness. This is especially so when the tutor is a small person like me and the student a tall, well-built one. The stance required to control the movement of Anluan's arm and hand brought my cheek close to his and pressed my body against his back. The sensation that swept through me, warm and heady, was not at all appropriate to the situation of teacher and pupil. I felt the blood rush to my face, and was glad Anluan's attention was on the tablet and stylus.

'It seems wrong, I know,' I told him. 'But it feels more comfortable, doesn't it? Now you're holding the stylus just as I would with my right hand.'

'I cannot write this way. How can I form the letters?'

'Ah. Here's where the simple trick comes in. We're going to turn the tablet sideways.' I moved the wax tablet so that what would have been the top left-hand corner was now at the bottom left, nearest to his writing hand. 'I hope you'll prove my theory correct, Anluan. I want you to try writing from the bottom of the page to the top, instead of left to right. It will require some concentration. Write the letters o, t and g while I'm guiding your hand, and then I'll leave you to experiment while I do some of my own work.'

Anluan clutched the stylus as if it might attack him.

'Gentler.' I eased his cramped fingers. 'Looser. Imagine you're touching something soft, a cat's fur, a baby's fine shawl. That's it. Form the letters exactly as you usually do. See, your hand is out of the way, and there will be no smudging when you move on to pen and ink. Good! Try a whole word.'

'What should I write?' His jaw was clenched tight. There was a pink flush in his cheeks.

'Whatever you like.' I straightened up and moved back a step. My heart was thumping. That had felt altogether too pleasurable. 'Keep practising. Later you can try it on parchment.'

'That would be a waste of expensive materials.' He glanced at the sheet I had prepared for him, the new quill, the ink pot.

'Don't tell me you never learned how to scrape down your parchment for reuse.'

'I know how. But –'

'I've given you a diluted ink.'

'All the same –'

'Please,' I said.

Out of the corner of my eye I saw his uneven mouth curve into a smile. 'Very well,' he said. 'I accept your challenge.' He applied himself to his work, but the smile hovered, softening his features.

Time passed. I translated a document in which Nechtan did nothing but rant about his neighbour, Maenach, and another in which he methodically listed the number of lambs, calves and piglets born on his home farm that spring. Then I spotted the name Aislinn.

A trying day. All Hallows draws close and time is short. Our preparations are almost in place. Aislinn came in with her apron full of goldenwood, which she had cut in the ritual manner required. No sooner had we begun the next stage when a hammering on the door disturbed our labours.

The dark mirror called me. I glanced at Anluan; he had set down the stylus and was trying ink and parchment, using the new quill to write from bottom to top along the lines I had scored for him. His hair fell forward, the deep red strands emphasising the pallor of his face. The blue eyes were intent on his work, and he was using his weak right hand to hold the parchment steady. The angle of the quill was good; not perfect, but good. I saw purpose and hope in every part of him, and for a moment it made my breath falter. What had I done here? How had I dared awaken something so fragile in this place of overwhelming sadness?

I turned Nechtan's document face down without reading any further. I pushed it over to the far edge of my work table, beyond easy reach, then took up the next sheet of ancient parchment.

They have slain the cattle that were Whistling Tor's livelihood. They have taken lives in the settlement and set fires. Why do they refuse to heed me beyond the border of the Tor? They should be obedient to my will. I revisit the procedure endlessly in my mind, but can find no fault in it. There was no error in the preparations, no omission, no deviation from the form of words. All was carried out exactly as required. But it is wrong. Unleashed, this is no powerful army but a wayward rabble. If I can command their obedience only while I remain on the Tor, I will be set apart from all the world.

And, further down the page, this:

Folk are saying that I am cursed. I will prove them wrong. I will learn how to harness this monster.

'But you didn't,' I murmured, setting that leaf on top of the other. 'You couldn't.'

'What was that?' Anluan set his quill down and flexed the fingers of his writing hand.

'Nothing. May I look at your work?'

'Of course. You are the teacher.'

I did not insult him with exaggerated praise, though my heart lifted when I saw how well he had absorbed the lesson. As for the fact that he had chosen to practise his script by writing my name – it was on the page three times, each version slightly more regular – that set a warm glow in my heart quite out of proportion to its cause. 'Does this feel easier?' I asked. 'It's much more pleasing to the eye.'

'It is better, yes, and my hand hurts less.'

There was something in his tone that made me look at him more closely, seeing what I had missed a moment ago: the smudges under his eyes, the pallor, the droop of the shoulders. 'Good work,' I said, keeping my tone light. 'That's enough for now. Ideally, you'd write a page a day with this method, until it came to you without thinking.'

'I must go,' Anluan said abruptly, rising to his feet. 'Since I've sent Magnus down the hill for the morning, I'll need to help Olcan with some work on the farm.' He hesitated on the threshold, cloak over his arm. 'You look astonished, Caitrin. Cripple as I am, I am not entirely incapable.' Before I could frame a reply, he was gone.

I worked on until hunger drew me to the kitchen, where I assembled a meal of bread and cheese and ate it at the table. I remembered a stray dog Maraid had taken in once, a cowering, wary animal whose past had obviously not been a happy one. My sister had befriended it, using food, warmth and kind words. After a little, the dog took to following her about slavishly; it plainly adored her. But it was never quite at ease. It would cringe at the sound of a spoon dropped on the floor or a sudden sneeze. It would burst into frenzied barking when strangers came to the door. After some months the creature fell foul of a passing cart and was killed; we never knew how long it might have taken to learn trust. If too much harm has been done, perhaps that lesson becomes impossible. Remembering, I saw something of both Anluan and myself in that sad creature.

My simple meal over, I took my cup, platter and knife out to the pump to wash them. As I bent over the bucket, cloth in hand, a familiar voice spoke from behind me.

'Caitrin?'

I straightened, turning to look at Muirne. She had Emer's violet gown in her hands, the skirt draggling onto the muddy ground by the pump. I saw at a glance that it was in shreds.

'The child,' she said. 'I suppose you tried to befriend her. Do not be fooled by what you see. The little one is outwardly angelic. Inside is pure malevolence. No doubt she tugged at your heartstrings as she did with those of Emer, and of Líoch before her. I expect she spoke of her mother, or of being cold. You were kind to her, and look how she's rewarded you. I'm afraid this gown is fit only to be ripped up for cleaning cloths.'

'No!' I almost snatched the garment from her. 'I'm sorry,' I added, forcing my voice to be calm, though my heart was beating fast. 'Perhaps I can salvage it.' The child, so small and frail, so innocent . . . But she had done her ill work on Róise. 'Where did you find this, Muirne?' I was certain I had left my door closed.

'On the gallery, in a heap. Doors and walls will not keep out the host, Caitrin.' She moved closer, putting a hand on my shoulder. 'May I offer you some advice?'

'Of course.' Her touch made me uncomfortable.

'You are blundering into a situation you will soon be unable to control. Each day it becomes more risky. I cannot understand you, Caitrin. You see the host rampaging down the hill; straight afterwards you speak to them as if they were your friends. You witness Anluan's near collapse, brought about by his efforts on *your* behalf, because of a man who came here in search of *you*, and instead of allowing him the rest he so desperately needs, you ask him for explanations, then demand that he summons the host again. You are a skilled craftswoman, a person of some intelligence, I must assume. And yet you put yourself at risk. You put Anluan at risk. These are the actions of a fool. Forgive me if I am too blunt for you. Someone must speak. Do you care nothing for him?'

I took a few careful breaths, trying not to hug Emer's gown too tightly to my breast. I would not lie to her. Nor could I tell her what I realised was the truth: that I was coming to care more than I had ever intended. As for the host, all I had done was try to understand, try to help those I thought were in trouble. All I had done was see them as real men and women. With the tatters of the violet gown in my hands, and the memory of Anluan's waxen pallor and exhausted eyes fresh in my mind, I felt a chill deep inside me. 'Of course I care,' I said. 'I don't want to hurt anyone.'

'Nothing is as it seems here,' Muirne said quietly. 'I ask you, as a woman and an equal, to leave Anluan alone. You think to change him, perhaps; to mould him into a form that is more acceptable to you. Men do not change. They cannot.'

I struggled for an appropriate answer. 'That's true of some, I'm sure.' Cillian, for instance. 'But not all. Muirne, I'm not trying to change Anluan, I just . . .' This was impossible. Anything I said, she would take as a criticism of herself. 'I think he could do more,' I said. 'Be more. He's so weighed down by all of this,' I waved an arm vaguely, 'he can't see a way forwards. But he's perfectly capable of being a proper chieftain; he is not lacking in intelligence, and the fact that he can never excel at hunting, riding or swordsmanship doesn't mean he can't be a leader. He's brave. He's perceptive. He could do wonders if only he could believe in himself.'

'This is not an ordinary man, Caitrin. You cannot apply the rules of the outside world to Anluan. He is the chieftain of Whistling Tor.'

'He's an ordinary man as well,' I felt obliged to point out. 'To be a chieftain one must first be a man. What he needs is purpose.'

'This is nonsense!' Muirne said, losing some of her customary calm. 'You endanger him and you cannot see it! You should have left this place when you had the opportunity.'

I was slow to understand. 'What opportunity? You mean I should have gone down the hill with Magnus this morning?'

She made no reply, simply waited until I should summon the wit to grasp her meaning. When I did so I felt cold.

'You're not telling me I should have let Cillian carry me away, trussed up with a gag over my mouth? You, a woman, think I should have accepted that?'

'At least that man wants you,' she said quietly.

Cold fury took hold of me. 'I can't believe you would condone what Cillian did yesterday. That sickens me. I understand your argument about Anluan, and I regret tiring him. I will be more careful in future. But I'm not leaving Whistling Tor, Muirne; not until I finish the job I was hired for. I don't believe my presence is dangerous to anyone.'

'Scribing is one thing.' She was angry too, but it showed only in her eyes. 'I have some admiration for a woman who can do it with sufficient skill to earn her living. But you seek to do far more here than the transcription of a few documents.'

I had no answer to this, since she was right. I had made an

undertaking to the host. I had promised to look for a counter spell. And what about Anluan, with his odd little smile, like a sudden burst of sunlight in a place full of shadows? This could not be neatly finished by the end of summer.

'You stirred up the host,' Muirne said, folding her arms. 'The host is dangerous. Eventually, inevitably, it will turn against you.'

'How can you say that when you are part of the host yourself?' I asked, not caring whether I had overstepped the mark. 'As for that little girl . . .' My fingers stroked the damaged cloth of the violet gown. 'She's too young to be fully responsible for her actions.'

Muirne's eyes were cold. 'You're wrong,' she said. 'You expose all of us to danger. Do your work if you must; write your copies. But Anluan should have nothing to do with the documents. Tell him you do not want his help.' She turned on her heel and was gone before I could say any more.

My mind was spinning. For a moment I could not remember why I was in the yard. I thought of Anluan, so relaxed, so happy after his success with the pen. I remembered the feeling of his body against mine as I guided his hand; the curious sense of loss as I stepped away, setting space between us. It was not the first time touching him had sent a flood of warmth through my body. Muirne had been right to warn me. I was letting myself feel too much. I was allowing natural sympathy to grow into something else, something with the power to cause real harm.

With a sigh, I finished rinsing the dishes then poured out the washing water by the kitchen steps. Muirne had said Anluan should have nothing to do with the documents. But Anluan had hired me to translate the Latin so he could find out what Nechtan had written. He wanted to read the documents. Why was this dangerous? I could think of no reason but the one I had already considered myself: that Anluan might be inspired to attempt the same kind of work his great-grandfather had tried to such disastrous effect. He might believe that the only way the host could be banished was by sorcery. In walking down that path, he risked becoming Nechtan all over again. Muirne, who loved him, was quite reasonably taking steps to avoid what she knew would be catastrophic.

Back in the kitchen, I dried the dishes and set them in their places. I found myself wiping down the tabletop for the third time. I gathered Emer's gown and went up to my quarters, expecting the worst. The door was ajar but nothing seemed to be out of place except for Róise. I had put her away in the storage chest this morning, but she was on the bed now, propped against my pillow with her torn skirt spread out around her. The child had ripped out far more of the silken hair than I had realised: one side of the doll's head was almost completely bald.

I took a few deep breaths. There was work to be done; Nechtan's documents awaited me in the library. But the encounter with Muirne had unsettled me, and the knowledge that someone had been in this chamber, tampering with my belongings even as I sat with Anluan in the library, set unease in my bones. Before I went back to work, I needed to put right the damaged memories of family.

I assembled my sewing materials and rolled Róise up in Emer's gown. I stepped out of the bedchamber and almost walked into the young man in the bloody shirt. I gasped in shock; he took a step back as if equally disturbed.

'Oh – forgive me –' I fumbled for the right words.

'I mean no harm – I wish only to –'

Perhaps it was his hesitancy that put the strange idea into my head. 'I need your help,' I said. 'I need someone to guard my chamber for a while. I don't want anyone to go in there before I return. Would you do this for me?' Foolish, perhaps; Muirne would most certainly have thought so. But I had not seen a host of evil presences, ready to turn on me at the least excuse. I had seen folk adrift without a purpose. I had seen men, women and children all together, yet each alone. They had nothing to do, nowhere to go. They were not wanted. They were not needed. They had nobody to touch them, to love them, to reassure them. They had lost themselves.

'What will you pay?' His voice was like the rattling of dry stalks in an autumn field.

'I will pay in work. While you keep watch, I will be searching for what I spoke of before, the key to setting you free. But I have other work to do first. Something has been broken, something precious.'

The young man sighed, reaching out a hand whose fingers were little more than bare bone. He touched the fabric of the tattered gown. 'Hers . . .'

Startled, I asked, 'You knew her? Emer?'

'I cannot remember,' he said, but the memory was in those haunted eyes. They had changed when I spoke her name. I could have sworn there were tears glittering there.

'Will you keep watch for me? I will return before dusk.'

He bowed his head, a courteous indication of assent, and took up a position before the bedchamber door. His back was straight, his shoulders square, his booted feet planted apart. So stern was his expression, so formidable his stance that surely no one would dare challenge him.

'Thank you,' I said. 'What is your name?'

There was a long pause, as if he had to dig deep to find the memory. 'Catháir, lady.'

'It is a fine name for a warrior. Farewell for now, Catháir.'

I sat in Irial's garden, under the birch tree, and stitched a new skirt for the doll, using remnants of Emer's gown. I tried to weigh up hope against risk, purpose against peril. If it was too dangerous for Anluan to be exposed to Nechtan's records – and Muirne had made a convincing case – I must reach the truth on my own. It must be done before summer's end. Nobody had said what would happen if I failed to complete the job by then. Perhaps Anluan would let me stay on. But I could not assume so. That meant I must use whatever tools were at my disposal in the search for a counter spell. And there was one very powerful tool shut in a box by my work table, waiting to reveal more dark stories. Was I brave enough to set more of Nechtan's writings on the table and look in the obsidian mirror again? Alone, without Anluan? I had given my word to the host. Perhaps I was already committed to this.

There was no way to fix Róise's hair, not without a supply of silk thread. I made a little veil for her, using the same violet fabric, and sewed it securely to her head, concealing the damage. I murmured to the doll as I mended her, comforting stories of home and

157

family: the warm kitchen, the orderly workroom, my sister singing as she cooked supper. When I came to Father, my voice faltered to a stop. One particular memory would stay with me always, no matter where I went. Blundering downstairs half-asleep, intending an early start on the important commission we were undertaking. Opening the workroom door. Finding that Father had risen even earlier than I had. He had begun work already; he had completed two lines before he died. The tall stool was tipped over. Father lay on his back on the floor, arms outstretched, eyes staring. The quill had fallen just beyond his reach; ink drops made a delicate pattern across the boards. His fingers, a craftsman's long, graceful fingers, were open, relaxed, like those of a child sleeping. He was already gone.

'It was a good place, Róise,' I whispered, making a last neat stitch in her head-cloth and biting off the thread. 'Until that day, it was the best place in the world. Then everything changed. Ita and Cillian came, and almost as soon as Father was buried, Maraid went away with Shea. I hope she's all right. I hope they're happy.' This thought surprised me. At the time, sorrow had claimed me so completely that I had hardly been capable of understanding that my sister was gone. Later, when I had begun to claw my way out of despair, I had felt bitter and angry towards her. Now, regarding the mended Róise and recalling the day of my seventh birthday, when Maraid had presented me with her creation and told me that since our mother was no longer in this world, Róise would keep an eye on me in her place, I realised that my resentment was fading at last. Perhaps Maraid had had no choice. Perhaps she had run away for the same reason I had: to save herself.

The violet gown was beyond repair. There was not enough of the skirt intact to furnish anything save this outfit for Róise. Perhaps I was foolishly sentimental to want to save it. I had not known Anluan's mother, and she was long gone. But people had loved her. I rolled the gown up. Later, I would find a way to use it.

The sun was warm. The garden was peaceful. I could happily have stayed here all afternoon, doing nothing in particular. But the library door stood open and my work lay ready within. *Practise being brave a little at a time*, Anluan had suggested. This was not a little; it was almost overwhelming. But I must do it. If I were to have a chance of fulfilling the promise I had made to the host, I must go into the library and turn over those pages. I must open the box and take out the obsidian mirror. I must look into the darkness.

chapter seven

o sooner had we begun the next stage when a hammering on the door disturbed our labours.

There's a hammering on the door. Nechtan feels his blood boil and makes himself take several slow breaths. The preparations must be perfect; he cannot afford any loss of control. He strides over, slides the bolt and whips the door open. 'What?' he barks, glaring into the pasty features of his temporary steward, a man whose name he cannot quite recall.

'My lord, I very much regret the interruption, but –'

'Out with it! What is so important that you break my specific orders not to disturb me?'

'Lord Maenach is here, my lord. Not with a raiding party; he's come with a group of councillors and kinsmen. There's a priest with them, and Lord Maenach's wife. They want to talk about an agreement, a treaty. Lady Mella said I must disturb you, since this is –'

'Go,' says Nechtan. 'You've done as you were instructed.' He shuts the door in his servant's face.

Aislinn is making the wreath. A lamp burns on the shelf above her workbench, its warm light transforming the soft mass of her hair to a glinting veil of gold. He wants to run his fingers through it, to gather the silken strands, to tug and make her cry out. Observing the neat, meticulous movement of her hands as she threads this most magical of herbs into the garland of winter greenery, eyeing the pleasing curves of her young body beneath the plain working clothes, he wants more than that. But he's learned to suppress the stirrings of his body. To ruin his great work for the sake of such fleeting pleasure would be the act of an ordinary man, a weak man.

He turns his back on Aislinn. On his side of the workroom, three grimoires lie on the table, each open at a familiar page. The first: *For the conjuration of spirits.* The second: *To call the servants of a darker realm.* The third: *Demons, imps, wraiths and visitants: touching on their true nature.* Nechtan sighs.

'My lord, you need not read those again.' It seems Aislinn has eyes in the back of her head. 'You'll be using the other spell, the one you got from the monastery. The writers of those books have it wrong. I would wager none of them has put his theories to the test. They claim to be expert, but their writings are those of men who lack the courage to make their dreams reality.'

Nechtan smiles without turning. Aislinn is devoted; she's giving him back his own arguments. 'Quite true,' he tells her. 'But we could have missed some small detail. This must be flawless, Aislinn.'

'It will be.' Her voice is shaking with emotion. Briefly, this perturbs him. He suspects that even if he had told her everything, instead of only the information she needs, she would still be prepared to comply with his wishes. She would do anything for him. Yet his little assistant is no dumb animal, following its owner out of blind instinct. Aislinn is quick, apt, quite a scholar in her limited way. Clever, but not too clever, Nechtan reflects, turning to watch her again as she weaves a white cord through the wreath then ties the ends in a complex, particular knot. The ritual object resembles a headdress for a bride.

'All Hallows' Eve.' Aislinn's voice trembles as she hangs the wreath on a peg, next to the other items they will be using. 'I can hardly believe it. My lord, I'll never be able to thank you enough for letting me be a part of this great work.'

Another knock at the door.

'By all the powers,' Nechtan roars, 'what have I done to deserve this? My house is full of fools!'

'Shall I answer, my lord?'

'No, Aislinn.' He opens the door. This time it's his wife standing there like a skinny scarecrow in her drab grey, hands clasped nervously together, hair scraped back, jaw tight with nerves. The years haven't been kind to Mella. She was never a beauty, not even when he wed her, and soon, very soon, she'll be a hag. Bearing his son is the one good thing she's ever done for him and for Whistling Tor. The dowry was useful, of course, but that's long gone.

'Maenach is here.' She speaks without preliminaries. 'He wants to treat for peace, Nechtan. He's ready to talk to you, despite everything. You must come and speak with him.'

'Must?' The word hangs between them as Nechtan begins slowly to close the door. He sees the look in his wife's eyes, the fear, then the sudden resolve. He's surprised; he didn't think the dreary creature had any spark left in her.

Mella puts her foot out, arresting the door's movement. She looks past him, her eyes wintry as they pass over Aislinn. 'Nechtan, don't shut the door. This is our future, yours, mine and our son's.'

'I have no interest in treaties,' he tells her, not that there's any point; he knows from long experience that the patterns of his mind are beyond his wife's comprehension. 'They're irrelevant. Sooner than you can imagine, all will change. Maenach will be less than a speck of dust under my boot. I will crush him.'

'Nechtan, listen to me, please. I'm begging you.' Mella's face is creased with anxiety. He can see the wrinkles she'll have as an old woman, if she lives that long. 'This is a chance to stop the fighting, to make peace, to resolve the situation once and for all. I've never understood what it is you're doing down here and I don't especially want to, but neither your little village whore nor your so-called experiment is worth sacrificing your whole life for. The future of Whistling Tor, the future of your family and your people, lies in the balance. Come out, my lord, and sit at the council table. You are chieftain here. Be the man you should be.'

He lifts his hand and strikes his wife across the face, hard enough to send her reeling backwards. He closes the door; slides the bolt home.

'How deep need I go,' he mutters, 'to keep the world out?'

My head dizzy, my vision blurring, for a little I did no more than sit quite still at the work table as the images in the obsidian mirror faded away to nothing and Nechtan's thoughts slipped one by one out of my mind. Outside in the garden a thrush was singing. The sun had moved to the west, sending a stream of light through the library window. When I could move again, I wrapped the dark mirror in its cloth and stowed it away in the chest. There was another leaf of Nechtan's writings on the table, another part of this story to be visited, belonging to the time after the experiment: the time of the wayward host. I would not look at it now.

When I felt strong enough I went outside again. I stood in the sunlight and spoke the words of a prayer, a simple one from childhood, asking the angels to watch over me. This vision had been less dark than the first. It was not so much what I had seen that was troubling; it was the way the mirror had drawn me into Nechtan's mind. How many times had Cillian hit me in just the way Nechtan had struck Mella? And yet, watching that, my thoughts had been not hers but his, all violence and fury. Even now his anger flamed red in my mind. It sickened me.

Would it be like this from now on if I continued to use the mirror? Would a little of Nechtan's evil rub off on me each time, turning me into a person who cared nothing for compassion, forgiveness, kindness, but only lived for power? I understood exactly what Muirne had been talking about. If doing this made me feel so wretched, what would it do to Anluan, with Nechtan's own blood running in his veins? The chieftain of Whistling Tor was in many ways an innocent. He might be able to summon a host of spectres to see off intruders, but this insidious evil could consume him from within. He must not be exposed to it.

'Caitrin?' It was Magnus, standing in the archway. He had a bundle on his shoulder; it looked as if he had only now come back from the settlement, though it was midafternoon. His strong features wore an unusually grim look. 'There's a problem. Where's Anluan?'

'He went down to the farm some time ago. What's wrong?' My mind went to Cillian and I felt cold.

'There's a party of armed Normans on the open ground between the foot of the hill and the settlement, demanding that Anluan come down and speak with them. From what I could understand, they're under orders to pass their message to nobody but him or his chief councillor. They wouldn't tell Tomas what it was all about, and they weren't interested in hearing anything I had to say. They've heard enough about this place to stop them from coming up the hill to deliver this decree or whatever it is. See if you can find the others, will you, Caitrin? I'll fetch Anluan.'

We assembled in the kitchen. The afternoon was passing; there wasn't long to make a decision. Anluan was sheet-white, his features pinched with strain. Nobody sat down. Magnus ran through it all: he had spent some time talking to Tomas about the situation with Cillian – he'd tell me about that later, but I would be happy with the explanation – and had been about to head for home when the Normans had ridden up to the village barrier and demanded admittance. They'd come from Stephen de Courcy.

'The fellow they were using as a translator didn't seem to know a lot of Irish,' Magnus said. 'Took him a long time to convey what it was they wanted. Then they asked about the barrier, and Tomas told them exactly what it was for. After that, they weren't so keen on finding a way up the Tor. Now they're down at the foot of the hill waiting. Tomas is there too, with a couple of the lads from the settlement. Bit of a surprise; you know how mortally frightened they all are of anyone from up here. Tomas was keen to get the iron-shirts away from the women and children. Once Duald and Seamus saw him leading the way, they were more or less shamed into doing the same. Mind you, the three of them are shaking in their boots down there. The sooner we deal with this the better.'

'Deal with it?' Anluan's tone was brittle as glass. 'How can we deal with it? You know I can't set foot beyond the safe margin. If they will not deliver this message to you, Magnus, then we cannot receive it.'

'What do you think the message is?' I asked, not sure if I should take any part in the discussion, but hating that look on Anluan's

164

face and the familiar way he had wrapped his arms one over the other, as if to set a shield between himself and the world.

'It must be something of significance.' Rioghan had his palms together, the tips of his fingers at his lips; I could almost see his mind working. 'Otherwise they'd be quite willing to pass it to Magnus and ask him to deliver it. Whatever it is, you cannot ignore it, Anluan.'

'What do you expect me to do,' Anluan responded furiously, 'send the host out to snatch it from this messenger's hands? I cannot go beyond the boundary!'

'Of course you need not go,' said Muirne, who was standing close to him, her hands demurely folded together, her manner eerily calm. 'There's no need to do anything. These Normans will not wish to be near the Tor after sunset. When night falls, they will go away.'

I stared at her, unable to believe she was serious. Her assessment of the situation was a child's.

'I wish it were so simple,' Eichri said. 'But for once the councillor here is right. Norman lords don't send armed warriors to call on local chieftains just to share a jug of ale and exchange the time of day. They don't insist on delivering messages into the hands of those chieftains if all they want is permission to ride from here to there, or to purchase a cow or two.'

'Should such a message not be delivered because the intended recipient refuses to accept it,' said Rioghan, and he turned his dark eyes on Anluan with a measuring look, 'and should that message contain some kind of warning, the sender might well assume he's been given sanction to proceed with whatever is intended. A move to seize another man's property, for instance. Or an attack.'

'Don't you think I'd go down there if I could?' The words burst out of Anluan. 'What do you think I am, a fool and a coward? If things were different – if I were –' I heard the anguish in his voice, and my heart bled for him. 'One step beyond that line, one single step, and the entire host could descend on the settlement and destroy it.'

'Are you sure?' I ventured. 'They may have changed since Nechtan's time. From what I've seen, there are some amongst them who just want a purpose.'

'It doesn't matter if I'm sure or not!' He turned on me, his voice a snarl. 'The risk is too high, and I won't do it! Keep out of this, Caitrin!'

It felt as if he'd slapped me.

'She's trying to help you,' Magnus said quietly. 'We all are. And time's running short. I'm in agreement with Rioghan: this problem won't go away of itself. There must be a strategy we can put in place.'

'A strategy! There can be no strategy!'

But there was. I had seen it, and I thought some of the others had seen it, too, but were not quite prepared to offer it in the face of Anluan's rage and distress. A challenge; I must be brave. 'You need not go beyond the boundary, Anluan,' I said. 'Didn't these Normans say they were prepared to give the message to your chief councillor?'

'What difference does that make?' Anluan retorted, glowering at me. 'This is not a court with all the trappings: councillors, advisers, lackeys for every purpose. It is a shadowy, ruined, deserted excuse for a chieftain's household. And I am a wretched apology for a chieftain.'

'I don't know about lackeys,' I said shakily, 'but you have a chief councillor right here.' I nodded towards Rioghan. 'He can go. When I first met Rioghan and Eichri we were all beyond the foot of the Tor. If he can walk out there once, he can do it again.'

All eyes turned on me. There was a silence.

'Only one problem, Caitrin,' Eichri said. 'Remember those missiles folk were hurling, the day you arrived? I know *you* thought the two of us were ordinary men. But you were more than a little distracted at the time. No Norman soldier is going to look at my friend here and see anything other than a . . . than something distinctly odd.'

'He can wear a hooded cloak. He can talk to them politely, saying as little as possible. By the time he gets back down there, the light will be fading.'

Rioghan's thin lips curved in one of his rare smiles. He said nothing.

'If it would help,' I added, 'I could go with him. I'm not distinctly odd, as far as I know. And although I don't speak French, I can probably manage Latin.'

'Excellent idea,' Magnus said. 'I'll come along to protect you.'

I saw the bitter denial in Anluan's eyes and flinched before it. He opened his mouth to utter what would no doubt be another furious outburst.

'Of course, it's not our decision,' I said, looking him straight in the eye. 'It's yours. We'll only do it if you think it's best.'

There was a little sound from Magnus, instantly suppressed. In the silence that followed, Fianchu padded over to the hearth, found that nobody had thought to provide a bone, and went back to stand by Olcan, looking hopeful.

'You're not to take Caitrin out of my sight,' Anluan said, tight-lipped. I blinked in astonishment.

'Then you'll need to come down as far as the boundary and wait where you can see us,' said Magnus calmly. I remembered that he was a warrior, accustomed to making decisions and to taking orders.

'I'll wait at the sentinel trees,' said Anluan. 'We'd best do this now. Olcan, I want you and Fianchu to stay up here, just in case.'

'Yes, my lord,' said Olcan, and nobody corrected him.

There were five of them, waiting in a line, seated on their horses. I imagined they were unwilling to dismount so near the forest's edge. Their iron-ring garments were impressive: in addition to the long shirts that covered them to the knee, three of the five wore separate pieces wrapped around forearm and lower leg, and one man wore a kind of hood that protected his neck under his metal helm. They were well armed: I saw daggers, swords, an axe and two spears. One man wore a long robe with a cloak over it; he, too, bore a sword at his belt, but no protective mail. A leather bag by his saddle suggested he was the bearer of the message. The fifth man, by his side, was in simple breeches and tunic under a hooded cape.

At a slight distance stood Tomas, Duald and a third man from the settlement, huddled close together. They looked mightily relieved to see us until they clapped eyes on Rioghan. I thought Duald was close to wetting himself with sheer terror.

We approached, Magnus and I on either side of Rioghan. Our

plan, such as it was, had been put together on the walk down the hill.

Four strides from the Normans, we stopped. Rioghan spoke before anyone else could get in first. 'I am Rioghan of Corraun, Lord Anluan's chief councillor,' he announced in ringing tones. 'What is your business here within his borders? To ride across another man's land armed and without prior agreement flouts the law of trespass. To do so in these parts, close to dusk, is beyond foolhardy.'

The messenger held a muttered consultation with the plainly dressed fellow by his side, and this man then attempted something in Irish. I took it to be a question about my presence among them.

'I am Lord Anluan's scribe,' I said, reminding myself that Magnus was here, and that Anluan was watching from a little way up the hill, and that this had actually been my idea. I switched to Latin. 'If you prefer, we can conduct this conversation in Latin.'

They were taking a good look at Rioghan now, perhaps noting the unusual pallor of his skin, the deep-set eyes, the gaunt features, and assessing them in the light of what Tomas had no doubt told them about the chieftain of Whistling Tor and his household. Their gaze moved from Rioghan to me. A scribe. A woman.

'Lord Anluan's councillor asked you to state your business,' I said in Latin. 'He says your presence here, armed and uninvited, breaks Irish law.'

'Irish law, pah!' The messenger made a gesture of contempt. 'We bear a message from Lord Stephen de Courcy. I thought your man here understood that.' He glanced at Magnus, then looked quickly away.

'What message?' I asked.

'A message for the eyes of Lord Anluan only. It's to be handed to him with Lord Stephen's seal intact. I'd hoped to speak to the chieftain of Whistling Tor in person.'

I translated this for Rioghan and Magnus.

'Tell him Lord Anluan isn't at the beck and call of any poxy foreigner who happens to turn up on his doorstep,' Magnus growled. 'An Irish chieftain can't be summoned the way you'd whistle for a dog. Tell him to give the message to Rioghan and get out of here before I lose my temper and do something foolish.'

'Caitrin, tell him we'll take the letter,' said Rioghan. 'You might point out that no Irish councillor worth his salt would dream of opening a sealed message to his lord. Then say they'd better be out of this district before nightfall or they might meet something that makes them soil those shiny outfits.'

'Please pass your message to Lord Anluan's councillor,' I said in Latin. 'He will deliver it to his lordship with seal intact. This other man who stands with us is Lord Anluan's chief war leader. You will no doubt have heard certain tales about Whistling Tor. Lord Anluan's war leader suggests you depart before the sun goes down.'

'We have heard that the chieftain of Whistling Tor has few retainers.' The Norman messenger glanced at Magnus. 'His war leader, a barbarian oaf.' The man's gaze passed over me. 'His scribe and interpreter, a girl.'

Neither of my companions could understand the Latin, but the sneer in the Norman's voice was unmistakable. 'Arrogant swine!' Magnus snarled, clenching his fists. 'Not content with riding onto our land with your poxy demands, you insult us!'

The Norman interpreter opened his mouth.

'Translate that and you'll be in unimaginable trouble,' I said.

Rioghan moved forward. As he approached the Normans, their horses shivered and lifted their hooves in skittish unease. The messenger had unfastened his leather bag. He brought out a scroll. Rioghan reached up a pale hand to take it; he pushed back his hood and stared straight into the Norman's face. The messenger's eyes widened. The colour drained from his skin. I saw one of the guards make the sign of the cross.

'You!' the messenger called, looking over at Tomas and his two companions, who were every bit as pale as the visitors. He was using Latin, my efforts at translation having evidently been more effective than those of his own man. 'You will ensure Lord Stephen's men are admitted immediately to this settlement next time. There will be no barrier. Do you understand?'

I rendered this into Irish. Tomas muttered something under his breath, but nodded to the visitors. An ordinary innkeeper on foot does not challenge armed and mounted Norman soldiers.

At a snapped command in French, Lord Stephen's party turned

their horses and rode away. It was not yet dusk; just as well, since we had not brought a lantern.

'Home,' muttered Duald. 'It'll be dark soon.'

'Wait,' Tomas said, and came over to me. He was trying hard not to look at Rioghan, who courteously drew the hood back over his head and waited at a slight distance. 'Caitrin,' the innkeeper went on, 'about that fellow who came here looking for you; I heard you had some trouble. Glad to see you're unharmed. If I'd known what would happen, I'd have lied, sent him packing. We argued about it, Orna and me. The man was full of the tale, how he'd been to every inn from his home town to here, spoken to every carter, followed every shred of information – he'd been on the road for a long time, must have been determined, the wretch. It seemed a better solution to send him on up, knowing what generally happens to folk who try the Tor. I feel bad about it, lass. Never meant you to get hurt.' His gaze kept darting to Rioghan. 'Funny how things work out. Never thought to find myself out here with . . .'

'It's all right, Tomas,' I reassured him. 'I understand.' With a jolt I realised that I had just walked down the hill and out onto this open ground without even thinking of Cillian. My mind had been all on the crisis facing Anluan. 'Now you'd best take yourselves back inside the barrier, and we must deliver this message. Thank you for coming out. Thank you for waiting here until we came down the hill.' I glanced at Rioghan and Magnus, wondering whether I could take it upon myself to be Anluan's mouthpiece. 'If Lord Anluan were down here, he would thank you for your bravery and support. I don't suppose this has been easy for you.'

'If that thing has bad news in it,' Tomas said, 'let us know what it is, will you?' He turned away, and the three men headed towards the safety of the settlement.

We walked back up the Tor with dusk turning the forest to a land-scape of purple and violet and shadow grey. Rioghan had passed the scroll to Anluan as we reached the place where our chieftain had been waiting under concealment of the trees. The document was like a weight hanging over us, holding us all silent. I felt the need to know its contents, yet was glad the poor light meant waiting until we reached the house, for this could surely not be good news. I thought it likely Anluan would want to read the message alone.

As we entered the courtyard, I remembered Cathaír, left on guard outside my bedchamber door all this time. Hurriedly I made my excuses and went up to the gallery.

The young warrior still stood at his post, his features stern. His eyes, as ever, moved with restless unease. At a slight distance sat the little girl in her pale garment, cross-legged on the gallery floor, making a pile of dead leaves.

'Thank you, Cathaír,' I said. 'I regret that my errand took so long. Has anyone been here while I was gone?'

'None will pass while I stand guard, lady.'

'Can you come back tomorrow, in the morning?'

'If you have need, I will be here.'

'I am grateful. You have leave to go until then.'

With a solemn inclination of the head he departed, not fading this time, but marching along the gallery and down the stairs as a flesh and blood man might do. I watched him cross the garden towards the trees. Just before he entered their shade he turned to look up at me, raising his hand in a hesitant farewell. I returned the gesture, half wave, half salute, and then he was gone.

The child had moved to stand right beside me. The moment I opened my door she slipped through. Standing in the middle of the chamber, she said, 'Baby's gone.'

I had to think for a moment before I remembered the ruined gown, Muirne, my mending efforts. 'Róise's downstairs, in the kitchen,' I said. 'I had to mend her; she was hurt.'

The little girl stood very still with her hands clasped behind her back and her eyes on the floor. She said nothing.

'I don't want her hurt again,' I said quietly. 'When my things are damaged, it makes me sad. That's why I had a guard on the door.' This child did not seem capable of doing the damage. She looked like something fashioned from twigs and cobwebs. 'I don't mind if people touch Róise very gently, as long as they ask permission first.'

For a moment she simply stood there, then she sank onto the

floor next to the bed, put her head down on her folded arms and began to weep. It was not the full-throated crying of a child who has scraped a knee or lost a battle with a brother or sister, but a forlorn whimper. Without allowing myself to think too much, I picked her up, then sat on the bed with her chilly form in my arms. Her sobs grew wilder, racking through her.

'It's not your fault,' I murmured, stroking the wispy white hair and wondering if I was being utterly foolish. *Inside is pure malevolence.* I could not bring myself to believe it. 'And she's better now, all better. I made her a nice veil. A lovely colour, like violets. It's a memory of a beautiful lady who once lived here.'

After a little the weeping died down. The child nestled against me, sending cold deep into my bones. If she could have slept, perhaps she would have. But like all the folk of the hill, she could not enjoy the peace of slumber. What was her story? How could she, so young, have died with guilt on her soul? *Oh, Nechtan,* I thought, *what kind of warrior is this?*

'Can I stay here with you?' the little voice asked, twisting my heart.

'I'm going downstairs in a moment,' I told her. It was almost dark; I must fetch a candle.

'Your bed is soft,' she said. The statement had a question in it. I imagined sharing my pallet with that chilly little body. I thought of lying awake, wondering when she would creep out and start shredding my possessions.

'Caitrin?'

I started, looking up. Anluan stood in the doorway, a candle in his hand, the unsealed scroll tucked awkwardly under his arm. The light turned his features into a flickering, deceptive mask.

'I need you to translate this,' he said. 'I would prefer to do it in private.'

I should have realised the message might be in Latin. 'Of course.' I rose to my feet, displacing the child, who curled up with her head on my pillow. I hesitated. Anluan seemed to be alone, and it was clear he expected me to do the translation right away. Perhaps he was not worldly enough to realise that a young woman did not invite a man into her bedchamber.

'I need to know what is in this,' he said.

'Of course.' I moved to the doorway. 'If you hold the candle steady, I may be able to see it well enough.'

Steady. It is hard to be steady when you hear ill news. We stood close together, not quite in the bedchamber, not quite out of it, and the ghost girl watched us from the pallet. Draughts from the gallery stirred the candle flame; Anluan brought his weak arm up awkwardly to shield it.

The message was scribed in a bold, decorative hand on the single parchment sheet. It was not very long. 'Do you want a word-for-word translation?' I asked him, my voice cracking.

'Just tell me what it says.'

'It's more of a decree than a request,' I said quietly, wishing with all my heart that I was not the one who had to tell him this, for a glance had shown me the gist of the thing. 'Lord Stephen intends to establish himself on your land, with his stronghold here on the Tor. He states that all surrounding territory as far as the borders of Whiteshore and Silverlake is to become Norman land, under his rule. He claims he has the authority to do so as a knight of the English king.' Although we were not quite touching, I felt Anluan's whole body tighten. I heard his breathing change. 'Then he says he's going to be considerate and give you a choice. He can take your holdings any time he wants. However, he's allowing you the opportunity to discuss the matter with him and reach a mutual agreement, which will spare your land and your people the rigours of armed conflict with its inevitable damage and loss. He believes you will see the wisdom of attending a meeting for this purpose. His chief councillor, with an appropriate escort, will return here on the eve of next full moon to hold this meeting.' Next full moon. By my count, that was around twenty-one days from now. 'Then his signature: Stephen de Courcy.' The message was an insult. His lordship wasn't even planning to attend the meeting in person. Mutual agreement? What chieftain in his right mind would agree to this? 'What will you do?' I asked, my throat tight.

The candle shook in Anluan's hand; wax dripped onto the parchment. 'Do?' he echoed bitterly. 'Do? I suppose I will do just what my people expect of me, Caitrin: absolutely nothing.'

'But –' I began, shocked.

'Don't say it!' It was a furious snarl, and I took a step backwards, my heart thumping. 'Don't tell me I can work a miracle here if only I have hope! You saw those men down the hill – you saw their weapons, their armour, their good horses, the discipline that kept them waiting as dusk drew close and Tomas no doubt regaled them with tales of demons and wraiths. Stephen de Courcy will have a hundred, two hundred such soldiers at his disposal, perhaps more. I have none. He could give me twenty-one days or ten times that: it would make no difference. This is the end for Whistling Tor.'

Deep breath, Caitrin. 'If you decide it is, then I suppose it will be,' I made myself say.

'Oh, so this is all my fault? It's my doing that this poxy foreign lord decides to ride in and take my land for his own? You expect me to pluck solutions from midair, I suppose?' A charged silence as he glared at me, the candle-holder clutched in his white-knuckled fist. My heart knocked in my chest. When a small, chilly hand crept into mine I almost leaped out of my skin.

Anluan looked down at the ghost child, who now stood pressed against my skirt, her thistledown head tucked against my side. His eyes rose to examine my face. 'You're afraid of me,' he said, blue eyes wide. 'Caitrin, I'd never hurt you. Surely you know that.'

I swallowed. There was plenty I wanted to say, but the words wouldn't come.

The chieftain of Whistling Tor looked down at his boots. 'I'm sorry,' he muttered. 'I'm not . . . I can't . . .'

I found my voice. 'People won't blame you for what's happened with Lord Stephen,' I said. 'And I don't blame you. But you'll be judged on what you do next. The Norman messenger said this was a household of few retainers, as if that were something to be sneered at. You are lucky in your retainers, Anluan. They love and trust you. Maybe the next step is to ask their advice.'

'You make it sound so easy.' In his voice I heard the child who had lost his parents all too soon; the boy who had shouldered an impossible burden at nine years old.

I took a step towards him and laid my hand on his arm. He did not shrug me off, though I felt him start at my touch. 'Please don't give up,' I said. 'Please let us help you.'

'Would you number yourself amongst these loyal retainers, Caitrin?' He would not look at me.

'If you'll have me,' I whispered.

'I don't see the point in discussing this,' Anluan said a little later. The household was gathered as usual around the supper table, but nobody was eating the meal Magnus had hastily prepared. 'Even if I were not burdened with the host, too much time has passed since the chieftain of Whistling Tor had the trust of his region and his people. To win that back could take years. I have twenty-one days. It is possible the folk of my settlements would prefer Norman rule to the way things are.'

'Bollocks,' said Rioghan. 'Didn't you notice Tomas and his friends down there, shivering in their boots at the sight of me, yet holding their ground? Those folk may not have a high opinion of you, Anluan, but they know you're the same kind as they are. No Connacht man wants a bunch of mail-shirted foreigners lording it over him.'

'Quite true,' put in Magnus before Anluan could summon a contradictory argument. 'With every step you take to bridge the gap, you'll likely see one taken on the other side. That's my opinion. But you're right in one respect. Time is very short.'

'Too short,' said Anluan.

'As to that,' Eichri said, 'it's clear the Normans expect you to attend this meeting in person. A pity Stephen de Courcy won't be returning that courtesy – we could have seized the opportunity to get rid of the wretch before this came to out-and-out war. I interpret the wording of the message to mean that if you fail to make an appearance when his councillor arrives, Lord Stephen will take it as capitulation. I believe there is one aspect of this we need to clarify, and I offer my assistance.'

'What aspect?' Anluan's tone was not encouraging.

'What is the role of our own high king in the matter? How can such an act of aggression be sanctioned in the very territory of the Uí Conchubhair? Perhaps Ruaridh knows nothing about it. Perhaps, if he did, he might provide some support. We should at least ask.'

In the silence that ensued, I considered how long it might take to get a message to the high king's court and bring back a reply, and which member of our small household might be spared to perform this task.

'You'd be surprised what one can find out at Saint Criodan's,' Eichri said. 'The current abbot, bless his curious heart, has a finger in a great many pies. I can be there and back a great deal quicker than Magnus can. Give me your permission to go, and I'll find out whether an approach to Ruaridh Uí Conchubhair is likely to bear fruit.'

'The high king come to the aid of the chieftain of Whistling Tor?' Anluan's tone was incredulous. 'You'd be wasting your time.'

'There is no need to go.' This was Muirne's first contribution to the discussion; she had sat demurely in her place throughout, expression calm. 'Eichri need not go to Saint Criodan's, and Anluan need not speak to these Normans. Whistling Tor is apart. That has long been the way of things.'

'And when Stephen de Courcy and his well-drilled army come storming up the hill?' asked Magnus.

'They will encounter the host,' said Muirne. It was obvious that, to her, this was the only answer we needed.

A weighty silence.

'Not quite as straightforward as that, is it?' said Olcan.

'She does have a point.' I was reluctant to support Muirne's all-too-simple arguments, but I had seen the way the host drove Cillian off the Tor. I knew what terror it struck in the minds of the local people, a dread that lingered even in those who had never seen the spectral force at first hand. 'Might not an encounter with the host change Lord Stephen's mind about wanting to settle in these parts?'

'We cannot be certain of that,' said Rioghan. 'And because we cannot be certain, the risk of attempting it would be too high.' He looked at Anluan. 'Any appearance by the host would give Lord Stephen his justification for moving into the region by force. He could claim to be ridding the locals of a peril that has threatened them for generations.'

'It is premature to speak of such possibilities.' Anluan's tone brooked no argument. 'We can plan only as far as this meeting or council. I presume they intend to hold it down in the settlement. I cannot go down there. That would endanger the local folk and the people of the wider district. And I will not allow de Courcy's emissaries to come up here.'

'Anluan,' I said, 'you can't let Lord Stephen walk in and take everything.'

'If you have a solution, Caitrin, you should set it out for us,' said Muirne.

I drew a deep, steadying breath. 'Magnus,' I said, 'how long is it since the host was off the hill? How long since they crossed that boundary line?' Nechtan's accounts, and Conan's, were strong in my mind: the destructive rampages, the rending and maiming, the carnage and death. 'It's some time, isn't it? Ten years? Twenty? Fifty?'

'We won't discuss this further,' Anluan said sharply. His face was suddenly ashen; his jaw was set tight.

In the silence that ensued, Magnus looked down at his platter. Eichri and Rioghan pretended to eat. Olcan went over to check the dog. I could feel Muirne's eyes on me.

'But, Anluan –' I began.

'This is irrelevant!' Anluan snapped. 'The host cannot be allowed to leave the hill. Not under any circumstances. That means I don't leave the hill. Didn't you hear me, Caitrin? I said we won't discuss this!'

After a moment, I said, 'You think if you don't talk about a problem it will go away?'

'I could save the Tor and its inhabitants at the price of the settlement and all who dwell there.' His voice was icy; his fingers clenched themselves around a goblet from which he was not drinking. I struggled to see in him the man whose courage and gentleness had so touched me after Cillian's attack. *He's afraid*, I thought suddenly. *He wants to fight this, but he believes he will fail everyone. He believes he will destroy all he cares about.*

'What would your choice be, Caitrin?' he went on. 'Would you preserve the fortress and its wretched chieftain, not to speak of the household of loyal retainers, at the price of a few hundred men, women and children, a few farms, a few cottages? We could save the region from Norman rule. Let the host loose beyond the confines of the Tor and it should send Lord Stephen and his men away screaming. Or he might march in with more men than even the uncanny army of Whistling Tor could combat. Either way, there wouldn't be many folk left alive when it was all over. Which way would your choice lie?'

I rose to my feet. 'It's not my choice,' I said, making myself breathe slowly. 'Excuse me, I'm going to bed.' I touched a taper to the fire and lit a candle. I gathered up the bundle I had left on the bench earlier: the remnants of Emer's gown with Róise tucked inside. 'It seems to me that what's needed here is a display of leadership.'

Anluan stood up. I saw him clasp his hands together to still them, the left hand around the right. All was silence. Even Fianchu's chewing had ceased. As I went out the door, the chieftain of Whistling Tor addressed my back.

'You expect too much of me,' he said, and I heard no anger in his voice now, only bitter sorrow. 'I am no leader.'

You are, I thought as I walked through the empty rooms and deceptive passageways of the fortress, averting my gaze from a mirror in a corner, another on a wall, a third propped at a drunken angle atop a broken stool. *You can be, if only you will believe in yourself.*

I opened my bedchamber door to find the ghost child waiting inside. Her eyes went straight to the bundle I carried.

'All better now?' she asked.

'I'll show you.' I unrolled the ruined gown, took out the mended doll and set her on the pallet. 'I'll make up a bed for you here, on the floor. I think you'll be warm enough.' I busied myself laying out a cloak and a blanket, and rolling up a gown for a pillow. When I turned to look at the child, her little features were full of such longing that tears sprang to my eyes. She was kneeling beside my bed, gazing into Róise's embroidered face. One skinny finger stroked the very edge of the new skirt I had made for the doll.

'If you want, you can hold her.'

She gathered Róise tenderly into her arms; rocked her as gently as any mother might a precious infant. She sang a whispery lullaby. *'Oo-roo, baby mine . . .'*

'We'd have been warmer in the kitchen,' I said, talking mostly to quiet my own restless thoughts. Anluan's bitterness had unnerved me. His mood slipped from sun to shadow with little warning. A chieftain was at a great disadvantage if his capacity to act was at the mercy of such a volatile temper. What if Muirne was right and he could not change? 'At least there's a fire down there.'

The child's eyes went wide, startling me; the little body became rigid. 'No! No fire!'

'It's all right, hush, little one.' I went to her, crouching to embrace her. 'There's no fire up here. And the one in the kitchen is a safe fire, on the hearth. See the nice bed I made for you. Would you like to tuck Róise in?'

She snuggled under the meagre warmth of the blanket, the doll clutched tightly to her breast. 'Sing me a song,' she said.

It was the last thing I felt like doing. 'All right, then. Close your eyes.' I sat down on the floor beside her, hugging my shawl around me and wondering if the others had continued the discussion without me. I made an attempt at the song about the lady and the toad, leaving out the rude parts. The girl lay motionless, lids closed, long pale lashes soft against pearly skin. How cold she was! It was as if winter's breath had touched her deep inside.

I had reached the last chorus when I saw a flickering light out on the gallery and heard footsteps approaching. Magnus appeared in the doorway.

'Just checking that all's well.' His eyes widened. 'Got company, I see.'

'I'm fine, thank you, Magnus. I'm sorry I walked out.'

In the dim light, I could not read his expression clearly. 'No trouble. Olcan said to tell you he'll send Fianchu up. I heard you had a different kind of guard on the door today.'

'Who told you?' As far as I knew, nobody had been here while Cathaír was on duty.

'Word gets about. They all knew about it: Eichri, Ríoghan, Muirne.'

'Magnus, I'm sorry I upset Anluan again. I just wish he would . . .' My voice faded. Anluan had good reason to be angry with me. I wanted things to be different. I wanted him to be the man I had seen in the courtyard facing up to Cillian. Now, in the quiet of the bedchamber, it came to me how unrealistic that was. What he faced now was not a mob of bullies. It was a Norman lord, with all the power and authority that implied. It was the formidable force of men-at-arms such a lord was likely to have at his command. What did I want: that Anluan should perish, taking the folk of forest and settlement with him, simply to prove to me that he could be a man? 'He told us not to discuss it,' I said miserably. 'But I can't think about anything else.'

Magnus folded his well-muscled arms. He had not advanced beyond the doorway. 'We've weathered a lot here, you know. Terrible times; sorrowful times. I never thought I'd say this, Caitrin, but maybe this really is the end. Whistling Tor's got no men-at-arms, it's got no resources, it doesn't even have the trust of its people to fall back on. He knows what he should do, but the risks are high. Step off the hill, even for the time it takes to walk to the settlement and attend a council, and he puts everything he cares about in jeopardy. Suppose he does that, and defies Lord Stephen. Then he's committed to armed conflict. Where's his army?' He waved a hand out towards the forest. 'He's only got *them*, and we know what happened when his ancestors tried to lead them into battle.'

'There must be a new way of looking at this,' I said. 'I refuse to believe there's no solution.' But then, hadn't Anluan accused me of having persistent hope, hope that saw possibilities where there were none? 'Magnus, if Eichri and Rioghan can go beyond the hill without dire consequences, doesn't that mean the others could do the same, given the right conditions? Eichri just offered to go to Criodan's, which is quite a distance from Whistling Tor.'

'Eichri and Rioghan are different.'

'But they weren't always different. If they could change, why can't the rest of them change?'

Magnus looked bemused. 'With enough time and the will to do it, I'm prepared to admit that might be possible. We have less than a turning of the moon.'

I glanced down at the child on her improvised bed. I thought of the look in Cathaír's troubled eyes as he'd marched back to the forest with his head held high. 'All Anluan needs is for them to stay on the Tor while he goes to the settlement for a meeting,' I said.

'And what would you have him do when he gets to this meeting? Threaten the Normans with a fighting force of twenty villagers wielding pitchforks?'

'It sounds foolish, I know. But maybe, if he took that first step, the people down there would think better of him. And it's not as if Lord Stephen himself will be here at full moon, along with his fighting men. Mightn't Anluan have time to rally support in the district?'

Before Magnus could comment, Fianchu came bounding into the bedchamber and went immediately to the child. He turned a few circles, somehow managing not to step on her, then lay down gently beside her. Her uncanny cold did not seem to disturb him, but then, just as she was no ordinary girl, he was no ordinary dog.

'I'll leave you in peace,' Magnus said. It seemed our discussion was over.

'Goodnight, Magnus.'

'Goodnight, lass. In the morning, maybe we'll see this with fresh eyes.'

A fine, persistent rain fell over the towers and gardens of Whistling Tor, pooling in corners, trickling down stone walls, making me shiver as I walked between living quarters and library. The heart's blood plant had put up three flower stems; the oaks were clothed in tender green. I counted the days as they passed: twenty days until the Normans came; nineteen, fifteen . . . Not only was that time looming, but so was the first day of autumn. I had been hired only until then.

The spinning of my mind was unbearable. I tried to keep it at bay with work, plunging into my task with a feverish energy. Anluan spent much of the time shut away in his quarters. I would see him occasionally in sombre conversation with Magnus or Rioghan, but he hardly spared me a glance. He did not come to the library; he did not sit under the birch tree in Irial's garden. Muirne took him his meals on a tray.

At night, when my troubled thoughts kept me awake, I went out onto the gallery and looked across the courtyard. In the dark of the moonless night, Rioghan paced up and down in his nightly ritual. Across the pond and beyond the pear tree, I could see the glow of Anluan's lamp. I whispered to him. 'Why won't you talk to me? I thought we were friends.'

I missed him. I missed the little glances he would turn my way; I missed his awkward conversation; I missed his crooked smile. Even his bouts of ill temper would be better than this absence, this silence. It extended to the rest of the household as well; I deduced that Anluan had ordered them not to discuss the looming crisis with me. I wanted to help him, to talk to him, to be a listening ear. But on the rare occasions when I happened to meet him crossing the courtyard or pass him in a hallway, he looked so grim and distant that I could hardly bring myself to speak.

I needed more time. The documents might still reveal a way of banishing the host forever and freeing Anluan from the curse. If there were no host, he could build ties with his neighbouring chieftains. If there were no host, he could become the leader he was born to be. Then maybe he would have a chance of standing up to the Normans. If only I could find a counter spell. Fifteen days left.

Morning after morning, I was in the library as soon as there was light enough to read by, and stayed there until almost suppertime. In the evenings I worked in my bedchamber, making an Irish version of Irial's margin notes on vellum pages I had cut and sewn into a tiny book. I had pored over everything the library contained in Irial's hand, but this record remained incomplete. If there had indeed been two years between Emer's death and her husband's, some of Irial's writings must be missing. Or he had ceased to keep this record for a season or so before his own demise. He had become too sad to set pen to page, perhaps. His last note read:

Day five hundred and ninety-four. The leaves of the birch, spiralling down, down. A lark's pure notes in the endless sky. Is there a sleep without dreams?

Reading this, I thought not of forlorn Irial but of his son, and I considered the nature of love. I had once watched Anluan in the garden and seen an enchanted prince trapped in a dark net of sorcery. But this was no prince of ancient story. Anluan was a flesh and blood man, with a man's virtues and flaws. The wounds Magnus had once spoken of, the hurts left on him by the past, were as much part of him as the limping leg and uneven shoulders. They made him the man he was.

I imagined the warmth of his body pressed against me, his face close to mine as I leaned over him to guide the quill. I considered how much it hurt to be shut out; more than it should, bearing in mind that I was a scribe hired for a single summer. I knew that whatever happened, leaving this place was going to break my heart.

My translation of Nechtan's documents now covered a sizeable pile of parchment sheets. I stored them between polished oak boards that Olcan had prepared for me, with a leather strap to keep them together. Between the long days of work and my constant anxiety, I grew thinner. My gowns hung loose on me. On the rare occasions when I looked in a mirror – generally by accident – and it gave me back a true reflection, I did not see the rounded, rosy person whom Eichri had called a lovely lady from an old tale, but a pallid creature with dark smudges under her eyes, brow furrowed by a frown, hair scraped back under a practical head-cloth. I recalled Nechtan's cruel assessment of his wife: *Soon, very soon, she'll be a hag.* I wondered what had happened to poor, well-meaning Mella after her husband's great experiment went so disastrously wrong.

I had not expected to be lonely, but I was. Most days the ghost child kept me company, sitting on the floor in the corner where Irial's books were kept, playing mysterious games with Róise. Cathaír had taken it upon himself to guard the entrance to my bedchamber through the daylight hours, and Fianchu kept guard at night.

In the evenings the household still gathered, without its leader and his shadow. But suppertime was not what it had been. We were all despondent and troubled. Olcan and Magnus exchanged a word or two about the work they planned for the next day. Rioghan sat silent, without his usual sparring partner, for Anluan had at last given Eichri permission to visit Saint Criodan's. My appetite was gone. I ate only because I knew I must.

Twelve days until full moon. I entered the library to find an ink pot on its side and a pool of black all over the completed pages I had left on my work table the night before. The transcription was ruined. As I mopped up the spillage, I tried and failed to convince myself that this was some kind of accident. I always corked my ink and put it away before I left the library. Who could have been here? Who would come in at night? With a creeping sense of dread, I recognised this as a warning. But from whom, and why? Was I coming close to the heart of my search? If Nechtan had been so powerful, perhaps he had set some kind of spell on his documents to protect his secrets from curious eyes. If he could make those fell mirrors, he could surely do that. I considered what might be next. It would be something worse than the destruction of a day's hard work, I was sure.

The ghost child was watching me, Róise clutched in her hands. Her big eyes were fearful, as if she had seen into my thoughts.

'It's all right,' I said. 'Just a little spillage. But maybe you should go up and stay with Catháir today. I'm sure he gets lonely all by himself.'

Ten days until full moon. Eichri came back with a supply of excellent vellum and the unfortunate news that one of Lord Stephen's daughters was betrothed to a kinsman of Ruaridh Uí Conchubhair. There was no need to expand on this. It meant the high king would not intervene on Anluan's behalf.

I broke my self-imposed rule about no lamps in the library, and worked through suppertime. I read until my lids were drooping and the patterns of Nechtan's strong script were blurring and bobbing on the page before me. From time to time I sensed presences in the shadows beyond the warm circle of lamplight, shapes moving and shifting: the restless host. My progress was slow. Perhaps they were growing angry.

Eventually I gave up and went to bed. I fell into an exhausted, dreamless sleep, and did not wake until dawn. It was raining outside. Fianchu was already gone, and the door stood slightly ajar. The blanket bed the dog shared with the ghost child lay rumpled on the floor. No sign of the little girl.

I felt it before I saw it: something wrong, something out of place, beyond these absences. A moving shadow. Something above me swinging to and fro, to and fro. I looked up.

Róise was dangling in midair, her limp form suspended by the neck. My heart jolted. I had thought . . . for a moment I had thought . . . but then, people cannot die twice, not even if their ghostly forms have more substance than one might expect. But a ghost can suffer. A ghost can be hurt. I had learned that from Rioghan's anguished retelling of his past, and from Catháir's darting eyes, and from the way the little girl clung to this treasure that had once been mine and had now become hers. I wanted the doll down before she saw it. Now, right now; the sight made me shudder. I glanced at the open door. Perhaps she had already seen it.

Too high to reach. Who had done this? Who could do it brazenly, while I slept only three paces away? Who could get past Fianchu? Only one of the host. But why? They wanted me to succeed, they wanted me to find a way to send them back. These were acts of wanton mischief, serving no purpose at all.

I found the child out on the gallery, squeezed into a corner, weeping. There was nobody else in sight, either up here or down in the courtyard. I went over to the little girl and squatted down beside her. 'Are you all right? I couldn't find you. Where's Fianchu?'

She was curled tightly on herself, her body shaking with sobs, her soft pale hair damp with the rain that blew in through the openings above the courtyard.

'Little one? Where is the dog? What happened in the bedchamber?'

'Baby,' she murmured on a sob, and allowed herself to be gathered onto my knee. 'Baby's gone.'

Perhaps she had not seen it. I rose to my feet, holding her. 'Rioghan?' I called softly. 'Are you down there? I need help.'

At that moment Fianchu came lolloping up the steps to the gallery, tail wagging, expression not in the least contrite. I could hardly blame him. He had probably just seized the opportunity to go out and relieve himself when whoever it was left the door open. Someone he trusted? A member of the household? It didn't bear thinking about.

'Caitrin.' Rioghan was here; I had hardly needed to raise my voice to summon him. 'What is it? You're white as a sheet.'

'There's something in my bedchamber that I would like – adjusted – before we go back in there,' I said, looking down at the child in my arms. 'I woke to find there had been a visitor. Could you attend to it, please, Rioghan?'

He went into the chamber without another word, and I waited, rocking the little girl and murmuring to her. In not much time at all, Rioghan came back out. He was winding the wire into a coil. 'It's all right to take her back in,' he said. 'You'll need to do some mending, Caitrin. The object in question was almost torn in two.'

'Thank you.' For some reason, I was close to tears myself.

'You must tell Anluan about this,' Rioghan said.

'There wouldn't be any point.' I could not keep my voice steady. 'He won't even talk to me these days.'

'There's a reason for that, Caitrin. Your presence here gives him pause. It makes him weigh things up a little differently.'

'It shouldn't stop him from listening when I have something worthwhile to contribute. Anluan knows I'm not stupid. Why can't he trust me?'

'You're upset.'

'Of course I'm upset! He might be about to lose everything, and he won't let me help!'

'He has his reasons. If he wanted to tell you what they are, no doubt he would. Don't think he's shut up in his chamber brooding, Caitrin. He's thinking, planning, working out whether he can take the risk he must take if he's to save this place. Calculating, weighing up arguments. Hesitating, because that risk may simply be impossible for him to bear. What has occurred here this morning is likely to make him even less willing to involve you.'

'Involve . . . you mean he's leaving me out of this to protect me? But –'

'Baby,' whispered the child. 'I want my baby.'

I got to my feet, keeping hold of her hand. 'You're sure it's all right to go in there?'

'The doll is on the bed; the other evidence, I will remove. Caitrin, he should be told.'

'Don't say anything, please. I'll tell him if I get the chance. If he's prepared to see me. And, Rioghan, thank you.'

'Glad to be of service, lovely lady. I know you have a guard up here by day. You might consider asking for another. Under present circumstances, it is possible some elements of the host may find the capacity for . . . mischief. Believe me, that is the last thing any-one would want.'

I shivered. Could he mean that Anluan might be so upset by all this that he would start to lose the control he worked so hard all day, every day, to maintain?

'Don't look like that, Caitrin,' Rioghan said. 'Our boy is strong-hearted, despite appearances. We must have faith in him.'

'I do,' I said. 'Despite everything, I do.'

Róise was seated on my bed, her back against the pillow. At first she seemed undamaged, but when the ghost child ran to gather her up, it became evident that the doll's head had been almost severed from her body by the tightly wrapped wire. A warning. Next time . . .

'She needs a stitch or two, then she'll be fine,' I told the child. 'I'll do it now. Will you pass me that little box with my sewing things? You can be my helper.'

I left the little girl in Cathaír's keeping again. They seemed to get on well, he watching over her with gentle tolerance, she content in his company, though I knew she saw it as second best. I judged that she would be safer with him than with me. There was no doubt in my mind that what had just happened had not been designed to upset the child, but as a warning to me. *Meddle no further, or I will hurt those who are dear to you.*

Nothing out of place in the library this morning, though I had held my breath as I went in, half expecting another unpleasant surprise. All was tranquil; beyond the window, the rain dripped from the trees in Irial's garden.

With a sigh, I settled to the tedious task of rewriting the transcription the ink spill had ruined. As I worked, I consid-ered Nechtan's story, which was making more sense now that I had more of its pieces. In the years leading up to the birth of his

only son he had become increasingly obsessed with his neighbour Maenach, chieftain of Silverlake. It started with a chance
remark Maenach was said to have made about Nechtan, and
grew in gradual steps to a full-blown enmity. Reading between
the lines, I deduced that the ill will was far stronger on Nechtan's side, for the last scene I had watched in the mirror, in which
he struck his wife so cruelly, was not the only time Maenach had
attempted to make peace. There had been messages, attempts
at councils, approaches to the high king to intercede. Each had
been interpreted by the chieftain of Whistling Tor as part of a
devious plot against him. He saw enemies all around him, even
in his own household.

His other neighbour, Farannán of Whiteshore – by my reck-
oning, Emer's grandfather – had been less of an enemy than
Maenach in the early days. As for later, when the host was on the
hill, it was clear that a catastrophic event had occurred. Nechtan
did not waste many words on it; I sensed that even he found the
details too unpleasant to dwell on.

*In their frenzy they set upon Farannán's priest. They tore the man
limb from limb before my eyes. Others perished in like manner, or
worse. I saw a woman reduced to little more than splintered bone. A
clamour of voices from every side:* Call them off! In the name of
God, rein your evil servants in! *I could not make the host obey. All
I could do was ride for home. Where I go, they follow. Behind us we
left a charnel house.*

I sat a long while staring at the wall after reading this passage,
one of the few Nechtan had written after he called forth the host.
I asked myself why it was that in the face of such evidence I still
believed there must be a way for Anluan to cross that invisible
line at the foot of the hill without unleashing complete havoc on
the district. Then I left the library and went in search of Eichri.

Today the green-faced scarecrow was in the garden with summer rain dripping off the dark hood of his cloak. I approached
him. 'I'm looking for Brother Eichri.'

The being pointed towards the east tower, then made his thin
hands into the shape of a cross.

'Thank you for your help.'

The rain was growing heavier; the pond had broken its banks to form a spreading lake in the rank grass. The ducks huddled under a bush. I ran across to the tower, holding up my skirt in a vain attempt to keep the hem dry. My boots were leaking. I squelched up to the tower door, which was ajar, and came to a halt as I heard the singing.

Deep, mellow, like the tolling of a heavy bell or the hum of creatures deep in the sea; that was how it came to my ears. Men's voices in perfect unison, carrying an ebbing, flowing line of melody. The words were Latin. They were singing plainchant.

I stood there awhile, surprised into stillness by the calm beauty of it. When the song came to a halt, I went in. I had not expected to find a chapel at Whistling Tor. But here it was: a plain stone chamber with a narrow glazed window, its altar an unadorned slab supporting a rough-hewn cross of oak wood. A subtle light touched the faces of the five brethren who knelt there, silent now, hands together in prayer. Those hands – so thin, so transparent, pointing to heaven – told their own story. These holy brethren belonged, not to the community of Saint Criodan's or another monastic foundation, but to the host.

The sixth monk was not in pose of penitence. Eichri stood at the back, arms folded. Not a participant, an observer. I was accustomed to the expressions of his bony countenance: cynical, amused, inquisitive, malicious. In the moment before he saw me, I caught something new there. It was a look I had sometimes seen on the ghost child's wan features: the yearning for a home that no longer existed.

'Eichri,' I whispered, moving closer. 'May I talk with you?'

'Shh!' hissed one of the praying monks without turning his head.

Eichri took my arm and we walked out together, pausing by the door. 'It's rather wet,' he observed.

'*Shh!*'

'Oh dear.' Eichri raised his brows. 'Shall we make a run for the kitchen?'

'This needs to be in private.' An idea came to me. 'Could you escort me up to the chamber where the spare clothing is kept, at the top of the north tower? There may be a pair of boots there, something that will keep my feet dry.'

'With pleasure, dear lady.'

We sprinted through the rain, then made a damp progress up the winding stair to the tower room. The key was in the pouch at my belt; the door did not stick. I eased off my sodden boots and used them to prop it open. 'Those monks,' I said. 'They were a surprise.'

'Because they still pray? Because they have retained their faith?'

I struggled for an acceptable way to put this. 'In Whistling Tor's history the host is identified as evil. Demonic. Demons don't sing psalms.'

He shrugged.

'Is this another thing Anluan has ordered you not to talk about? Eichri, I can't bear this! How are we to help him if he won't even discuss the problem? I care about him, I care about all of you! I can't stand by and see everything lost!'

Eichri had settled on the floor, his back against the wall, his legs outstretched. He crossed his sandalled feet. There was no spark of dangerous red in his eyes now, no fearsome grin on his gaunt features. 'Do you have a plan?' he asked.

At last, someone was prepared to listen. 'Not exactly. An idea, that's all. You could help by answering a question or two.'

'I will if I can, Caitrin. I'm bound to Anluan's will, just like the rest of the host. Touch on a topic he's forbidden me to speak of, and I will be unable to answer, even if I'm inclined to do so. You shouldn't lose sight of the fact that I am not an ordinary man. I've learned to pretend, as Rioghan and Muirne have. We play at life so well that we sometimes delude ourselves into believing we are still part of it. That's dangerous. Our nature limits our capacity to act.'

'And yet you are able to travel beyond the Tor without . . .'

'Without running amok? That is true. We've worked on that skill over the years, Rioghan and I. It hasn't been easy.'

I considered this as I took the embroidered slippers from the bigger chest and set them to one side.

'I always liked those,' Eichri said. 'They were Emer's.'

'Unsuitable for the rain. Besides, last time I wore Emer's clothing, someone came into my chamber and slashed it. Perhaps I should leave her things here.'

There was an odd silence. I looked across at the monk. He was frowning. 'Slashed? When was this?'

'A while ago. Other things have happened more recently. Warnings. At least, that's what they seem to be.'

'You should have spoken to Anluan about this, Caitrin.'

'That's what Rioghan said. I do have a guard.'

'One of the host.'

There were no boots in the large chest. I opened the smaller one and began to sort through its contents.

'Caitrin?'

'I trust Cathaír. As I trust you, Eichri. That brings me to my question. When I first saw the host surging out of the forest to terrify Cillian, you were leading the others. If I had not already known you to be a friend, I would have been frightened out of my wits. In life, were you some kind of warrior monk?'

He grinned disarmingly. 'I grew up on a farm. I could ride by the time I was two years old. The other trappings are only for show. The overall effect does strike terror into the enemy.'

'So you wouldn't actually have run anyone through? Made your horse rear up and strike a fatal blow with its hooves?'

'Run a man through?' He sounded deeply shocked. 'Hardly. I can't speak for the horse. I found the creature wandering in the forest some years ago and we took a fancy to each other. What he chooses to do is his business.'

'The host followed you. You led them into battle.'

'Anluan does occasionally call upon us, Rioghan and me, to act as leaders. Only on the hill, of course.'

'Have you ever tried it beyond the boundary?'

'Ah . . .' The monk lifted his hands, palms outward, and shook his head with a little smile.

'If that's a forbidden question, how about this instead: couldn't you and Rioghan keep the host under control while Anluan goes down to the settlement to talk to Lord Stephen's emissaries? He'd only need to be off the hill for a short time. Magnus could go with him. Olcan and Fianchu would be here to help you.'

Eichri said nothing.

'Mightn't there be others among the host who could assist as well? Cathaír for instance, and some of the other warriors, those older ones?' And when he still made no comment, I added, 'If those monks can sing the name of God, they cannot be the devilish creatures folk make them out to be. The little girl who sleeps in my chamber is an innocent child. Cathaír is disturbed by dark memories, but he can still take pride in a day's work. This could be done, Eichri. We could at least suggest it to Anluan. If he'd listen.'

'You don't think this may have occurred to Anluan already, Caitrin?' Eichri's tone was gentle.

'I don't know what to think!' I said somewhat wildly.

'I wager at this moment he's cursing the day he ever let you come up the hill.'

This jolted me. 'Why?'

'Ah, now, don't be upset. I meant he's cursing the day you came here because you won't let him give up. You've filled his mind with possibilities and he's terrified he can't make them real.'

I sorted through the second chest in silence, thinking of Anluan somewhere in the fortress brooding over the unwelcome change I had brought to his life. My folly seemed clear. I had taken on more than I had the capacity to deal with. I had lost sight of what was possible. I had meddled in what was beyond me, and brought nothing but trouble.

'The fact is,' said Eichri, 'if you hadn't come, Stephen de Courcy would still have wanted Whistling Tor. His emissaries would still be coming at full moon, and we still wouldn't be ready for them.'

'Can you read minds?'

'I can read faces, gestures, glances. What you suggest is at least possible. But is it worth the risk if all it can achieve is a defiant statement from the chieftain of Whistling Tor that he won't give up his land without a fight? There's no point in that if Anluan can't follow it up with an armed defence of his territory. He's not going to use the host to wage war. And I don't think he plans to give you the opportunity to present any ideas, even good ones. He doesn't want you drawn into it.'

'I'm translating Nechtan's documents,' I pointed out. 'I'm in it already.'

'Caitrin, there's more to this than you think. I may not be evil. Rioghan and your young guard and your little girl and most of those folk out on the hill may be no more devilish than any man or woman down in the settlement. But there's a force among them with an ill intent: something that can turn the tide if Anluan is not there to counter it. I can't tell you its nature, since I don't know; none of us does. The fact is, if the host escapes the chieftain's control, nobody's spared. Nobody. It is this malign influence that tests Anluan's strength day by day; it is this that exhausts and weakens him. I've felt the tug of this power on me. It's strong. I fear it greatly. Oh, you've found some boots.'

I drew them out of the chest. They were of good leather and looked sturdy enough to cope with the wet and comfortable enough to wear indoors while I worked. I didn't remember them from my last visit. As I sat on the closed chest to try them on, my eye caught the little mirror hanging on the wall.

'I have another question for you,' I said, 'since you've been here since Nechtan's time. Did he make every mirror in the house? Are they all bad?'

'I couldn't tell you. Can an object like that be good or bad? Isn't it more a matter of who's using the thing and how he goes about it?'

Eichri's words hung in the silence between us. They seemed important, as if there were a truth in them that went beyond their immediate meaning.

'There's a mirror in the library so full of Nechtan's sorcery that I can only think of it as evil,' I said slowly. 'The ones in the great hall frightened me. I saw myself as an old woman, and . . . there were other things, bad things. But that one on the wall there feels different. Once before, it gave me useful advice. I would be very surprised if Nechtan had made it.'

Eichri got to his feet and went over for a closer look. 'The frame's old oak,' he said. 'Not much in the reflection; only blue sky. Advice, you say. The thing spoke to you?'

'Not aloud, but I could hear it. This chamber holds memories of the women who've lived at Whistling Tor, women whose lives had more than their share of ill fortune. Maybe the little mirror belonged to one of them.'

'This might be very, very old. Why don't you take it downstairs and show it to Olcan? He's been here longer than any of us.'

I considered this idea as I stood up and tried walking around in the boots. They were a perfectly good fit; perhaps they, too, had been Emer's. I stopped in front of the little mirror and looked straight into it.

Lift me down carefully. And take some other things while you're about it. Don't you have a gown that needs mending? Choose with care. Remember them all.

'Did you hear that?' Despite what had happened last time, I had not expected the artefact to speak again.

'What?' asked Eichri.

'A voice. The mirror.'

'Perhaps it only speaks to females. Ah, you're going to take it. Need a hand?'

It seemed appropriate to carry the mirror myself, but I gave Eichri a pile of other items to bear downstairs for me. *Remember them all.* As far as I knew there had only been three: Mella, Líoch and Emer. There was a girdle of dark grey wool that seemed to match Mella's ancient gowns, and this I passed to Eichri. I took a skirt that had likely been Líoch's – it was much too small for me – thinking I might combine the fabric with that of Emer's ruined gown to make a wearable garment. I folded this and passed it to my companion. 'That's all,' I said, closing the two chests and picking up the mirror again.

'Women's magic?' Eichri queried with a grin.

'I haven't a magical bone in my body, Eichri.'

'You don't know your own power,' he chuckled. 'You've worked some changes here, Caitrin; changes we never thought to see in this lonely old place.'

'What do you mean?'

'I heard you brought a little doll with you to Whistling Tor, a treasure that contains the love of your family. And since you fashioned this poppet's clothing anew, it holds Anluan's family as well.'

'You seem to know rather a lot.' I was sure this was not what he had meant when he spoke of changes.

'As I said once before, word gets around.'

'Whatever it is, magic or only instinct, this feels right. You spoke of dangerous powers within the host, a force with ill intent. I'll use anything I can to counter that. Women have suffered here at Whistling Tor because of Nechtan's wrongdoing. It's time someone remembered their strength. If that's women's magic, then it's long overdue an airing.'

'If I were not so burdened, I would applaud you, Caitrin. Let us hope you can work a miracle.'

'You might ask those brethren of yours to offer up a prayer or two for good measure,' I said as we left the tower room. 'A miracle is what Anluan needs.'

chapter eight

even days until full moon. I was sorely tempted to march over to Anluan's quarters in the south tower, bang on his door and insist that he come out and talk to me. Of course I did nothing of the kind. His difficulties went far beyond any in my own experience, and I would not help him by losing control myself.

The oak-framed mirror hung on my wall now. The child loved it, examining her reflection with eager interest, making faces at herself, even uttering a hesitant laugh at the unaccustomed sight. For her this mirror seemed to function in quite the ordinary way. As for the mirror voice, I had not heard it again, but the artefact felt like a companion, and I was glad I had brought it down to my chamber. It seemed to me that the lonely shades of the departed women were no longer prisoners in the tower, but shared my own space, as if we were sisters.

I encountered Muirne in the kitchen as I was returning from a trip to the privy.

'I hear you have taken a mirror from the tower room, Caitrin.'

'That's right,' I said, keeping my manner polite. Would it be worth trying to enlist her help? She was closer to Anluan than anyone, though of recent times it seemed he was shutting her out as well; on the rare occasions when I had seen her, she had been drifting about the gardens alone. 'I hope you have no objections.'

'You are not free to help yourself to anything you want. That runs perilously close to stealing.'

The look in her eye worried me. In the light of the current crisis, this seemed a trivial matter. 'My boots were leaking,' I said. 'I needed another pair. That was what took me up to the tower. And you did say nobody wanted those old things.'

'Boots were not all you brought away.' She looked me up and down. I had dressed for courage today, in the new skirt I'd made by combining Emer's shredded gown with Líoch's rose-pink garment. It was not an outfit I could have worn in the streets of Market Cross, but I felt I was carrying the other women with me, and that seemed right.

'You'll remember how badly damaged the violet gown was, Muirne. I think I've made good use of materials that would otherwise have mouldered away in the tower. As for the mirror, a woman needs one in her chamber.'

'These are not ordinary mirrors, they are . . .' She gestured vaguely, as if there were no words adequate to describe the power of Nechtan's creations.

'I know that, but this one seems benign. It will be helpful in the mornings when I'm getting dressed.'

'Why would your appearance matter?' She lifted her brows.

'You take a certain pride in yours.' My gaze travelled over the neatly pressed gown, the perfectly folded veil.

'Yes, but . . .' She gave a delicate shrug. *Yes, but you are only a scribe.*

'What I borrowed was taken in a spirit of respect,' I told her. 'Those things in the tower are memories of the women of Whistling Tor. I don't want those women to be forgotten.'

She looked baffled. 'You are not one of the women of Whistling Tor, Caitrin. You're going home at the end of the summer.'

'By the end of the summer we could all be gone,' I said. 'Muirne, the Normans are coming in just a few days to talk to Anluan. I know you're very close to him. Could you ask him if he's prepared to listen to an idea I have?'

'An idea. What idea?'

'An idea for how he might handle this . . . visit. A way it might be safe for him to go.'

'You think to tell Lord Anluan how he should conduct himself?'

I bit back my first response. 'Of course not. He is the chieftain; he must make the decision. It's a suggestion, that's all. A good one, which he should listen to. Will you ask him, please? This threat is real, Muirne. It's not going away.'

She seemed to shrink inside herself, her eyes narrowing, her lips tightening. Maybe she really did understand and was so afraid she denied the truth even to herself. 'You're wrong,' she said. 'Push Anluan into this and you will bring down disaster on him and on all of us at Whistling Tor.'

'Muirne, I do know a little about the Normans, having lived in the outside world before I came here. Further east, they already rule wide stretches of territory. They've built strongholds and moved their own people in. And they have a different way of fighting, a way that is hard for our leaders to combat. They will come to Whistling Tor, and if Anluan doesn't go down and speak to them, they'll be back with an army. Then he really will lose everything. You can't want that to happen.'

She looked me straight in the eye, and I knew I had miscalculated, for the expression I saw was the one that had frosted her features the very first time I met her, when she had tried to dismiss me before I was even hired. 'You are not interested in these Normans, Caitrin. You care only about your own needs. Thanks to your interference, Anluan is exhausted, troubled, racked by doubt. Thanks to your foolish words of hope, he dreams of a future he cannot have. You have wrought untold damage here through sheer ignorance. You must not ask more of him. He has been wise to set himself apart, so he cannot be tempted by your voice, your foolish arguments, your . . . Caitrin, I have lived here for a long time. I know Anluan. I know Whistling Tor. The chieftain must not step off the hill. That is the simple truth. As for your *suggestions,* he is better off without them, believe me. He bears sufficient burdens already.' She turned to go.

'Muirne, wait!'

'Yes, Caitrin?'

'I want the best for him,' I said quietly. 'We all do. I don't believe I'm being selfish.'

She smiled; her eyes remained cool. 'Don't let me keep you from your work,' she said, and walked away.

My work. Just as well she did not know the reason I had worn the motley garment made from women's magic. Just as well she did not know what work awaited me in the library this morning. I needed answers, and time was short. Today I would use the obsidian mirror.

My heart raced. A clammy sweat of dread made my hand slip on the latch as I closed the inner door of the library. Which document to use? Did I really want to see the host unleashed, the bloody mayhem of that attack on Farannán's household, with its rending and devouring? Try that, and I would no doubt learn once and for all that there was no taming the host. If there had been an account of the experiment itself, that would have been my choice, but thus far I had discovered no record of it, only accounts of the time leading up to that fateful All Hallows, the breathless anticipation and tense preparations, then Nechtan's flat observations, set down considerably later, on the aftermath of his failure.

I walked across and shut the other door, the one that opened onto Irial's garden. I stood at the window awhile looking out and trying to steady my breathing. I wanted to stay right where I was, gazing on the lovely place that Irial had made in the centre of his dark world. But there was no time.

Back at the work table, I crouched to open the chest. There was only one item in it: the cloth-wrapped bundle that was Nechtan's mirror. I lifted it out. It did not feel like a dead weight, but alive, vibrant, dangerous. I set it on the table beside me, still shrouded. My fingers refused to choose a document. I closed my eyes, took a leaf and turned it face up before me. I drew back the covering that concealed the dark mirror. In the light from the window, the creatures wrought on its rim blinked and stretched, waking to another revelation.

Something rouses him from his reverie. Not a sound, not a movement. He's alone in the workroom with only the wretched grimoires for company. Nonetheless, his hackles rise; he's alert suddenly, not to danger, to . . . what? Something's wrong; something's happening that he must stop. *He's gone*, a voice whispers in his ear. *She's taken him away.*

He strides across the dim chamber to the door, wrenches uselessly at the handle, remembers the bolt, slams it open, takes the steps three at a time. Along the hallway, out the tower door, across the garden in the gloom of a wet autumn afternoon, slipping on fallen leaves, yelling for his serving people as he goes.

Down the hill, whispers the voice. *Down the path. You may yet stop them.*

He's quick on his feet, fit and strong despite all those years hunched over his books. It helps him now. He spots Mella from a vantage point halfway down. She's moving slowly; she has the boy by the hand, and her maidservant walks in front with a bundle under her arm. Conan is hanging back, dawdling.

'Make haste, Conan! Quickly!' Mella's voice trembles with fear. 'Come, I'll carry you.'

As she stoops to lift the boy, Nechtan gives a little cough. Mella turns, looks back up the hill. Her face blanches; her eyes go wide.

'Not another step,' says Nechtan. 'Release my son's hand. Do it, wife.'

As he hastens towards her down the winding track he clicks his fingers, and in his mind he summons what he needs. The dark forest darkens further. Swirling forms manifest beneath the trees.

Mella's running, the child in her arms. The maidservant is almost out of sight, further down the path.

'Halt!' Nechtan roars, and Conan starts a thin wailing. Why hasn't the boy's mother taught him self-discipline? This is a future chieftain of Whistling Tor. 'I said halt!'

Mella trips; she and Conan go sprawling on the wet path. The cries become shrieks. In a few long strides Nechtan is beside them. He reaches down, seizes his son by one arm, hauls him to his feet. 'Be silent!' he orders, and when Conan does not seem to understand, he gives the child a shake. Conan clenches his jaw; the screams turn to stifled whimpers. The boy has some backbone, after all.

Mella rises to her knees. She clutches her son around the waist, holding on grimly. 'Let him go, Nechtan!'

Nechtan's grip tightens on the child's shoulder. He eyes his wife with displeasure. Now she, too, is crying, ugly red eyes against skin pasty with fear.

'Where were you going?' he enquires.

'Away. Away from this cursed place! Nechtan, let Conan go!'

She seems unaware of the things that are gathering around them, the rustling, shadowy beings that people the woods on either side of the track.

'Answer me, Mella. Were you leaving me? Did you intend to quit your responsibility as lady of Whistling Tor without a backward glance?'

Her lips tighten. 'I'm taking my son to my mother's home in the north. That such a visit seems impossible to you is an indication of how much is wrong here.'

'Ten days' journey. With a single maidservant. On foot.'

Silence from Mella.

'This is no visit,' Nechtan says. 'You're leaving me. You have no intention of coming back. Confess it! Don't lie to me!'

His wife lifts her chin, foolishly defiant. 'No woman in her right mind would come back to this foul place, or to such a husband. God knows, I've done my best to stand by you, to keep things going while you let loose an evil you had no idea how to control, while you left your people and your lands to fall into ruin and made your neighbours one by one into enemies. I won't see my son's future blighted as well.'

'On one point you are correct,' he tells her, exerting considerable effort to make his tone cool. 'You've outlived your usefulness here at Whistling Tor. Go, if that is your wish. I need no wife.' It's been years since he took her to bed, and there are few servants left for her to manage. He'll be glad to see the last of her dreary figure around the place. She can go to her mother's and be done with it. He won't set the host on her. He owes her something; she did give him his son. 'As for Conan,' he adds, wanting to be quite sure she understands, 'he'll do perfectly well without you. It's time I took a hand in his upbringing.'

'No!' Mella breathes. While it's clear she expected him to try to stop her, she has not seen this coming. 'I'm not leaving him here with you! You are not fit to raise a child. Let him go!' Her arms are locked around the boy; she tries to drag him bodily from Nechtan's grasp.

'Take your hands off my son, you're hurting him. He's the future chieftain of Whistling Tor. He's not going anywhere.' Nechtan wrenches the child from her, lifts him to his hip and steps back. 'How could you travel so far with the boy anyway? Where would you lodge? Who would take you in?'

There is a moment's silence, then Mella says, 'Today we go only as far as Silverlake.'

He can't have heard correctly. 'What did you say? You cannot believe that Maenach – *Maenach* – would shelter you.'

Mella gets to her feet. 'I know he will. I'm not the one who is reviled and despised by all our neighbours, Nechtan. Maenach and Téide have offered refuge for me and my son any time we need it. We're leaving now. Give Conan to me.'

He sees it in a flash. His wife is part of the whole thing, the whole outrageous plot to undermine him, to turn his life to ashes and his dreams to darkest nightmares. Somehow she's exchanged messages with accursed Maenach or that mealy-mouthed wife of his. His neighbour, not content with damning Nechtan's name throughout all Connacht, intends to steal his only son.

The fury rises in his heart, a red tide engulfing him. His arm clamps tight around Conan. He backs away, raising his free hand.

'Conan!' Mella's voice is wild now, the harsh call of a crow.

'Mama!' The child starts to struggle. 'I want Mama!'

Nechtan sees only darkness, defiance, betrayal. He gestures, and in his mind he gives the order: *Now*. The host comes forth.

To give her due credit, Mella faces them with courage, stepping away from Nechtan so that her son cannot be caught up in her punishment. She holds the boy's gaze and mouths something to him, perhaps *I love you. Be strong*. The host moves in, rending, tearing, biting, consuming utterly.

Nechtan uses his free hand to shield Conan's eyes as he carries the boy up the hill. 'You'll be chieftain of Whistling Tor one day,' he murmurs to his son. 'Believe me, you'll endure far worse than this. You'll learn how it feels to be alone. All, all alone.'

A little creak from the garden door. I started violently, tearing my gaze from the mirror, where the hideous images were already fading to nothing. Anluan was standing very still just inside the doorway.

'You're using the mirror.' His tone was wounded, incredulous. 'You're using it without me.'

I couldn't stop shaking. 'They killed her,' I whispered. 'Nechtan's wife, Mella. He made them kill her. When she tried to leave with Conan, he . . .' I put my head in my hands.

Footsteps; Anluan came to stand beside me. A faint rustle as he drew the cloth back over the mirror. 'I can't believe you tried this on your own,' he said. 'Why?'

Hysterical laughter welled up in me and turned on an instant to tears. I could not answer. I felt him sit down on the bench beside me. A moment later his good arm came tentatively around my shoulders. In a heartbeat I turned, wrapped my arms around him and buried my head against his chest. I felt a shock run through him, but I was past caring. He lifted his weaker arm to complete the circle. The warmth of his embrace soaked into me, a powerful charm against the dark things. I could have held on forever.

'You weren't here,' I said. 'But I wouldn't have asked you anyway – you said yourself how dangerous it is for you to be close to Nechtan's thoughts. Oh, God . . . Anluan, he tore Conan out of Mella's arms. He ordered them to kill her. That little boy was no bigger than my ghost child, five years old at most.'

'Shh,' said Anluan. His arms had tightened around me; his mouth was against my hair. 'Shh, Caitrin. There's no need to tell it now.'

'I have to tell it, I have to say it. It wasn't just what happened to Mella. I saw them, amongst the host, before they attacked her . . . Anluan, Eichri was there. Rioghan too. Our friends, our trusted friends.' The two of them had stood there with the rest, waiting for Nechtan to give the word, their faces impassive. Waiting to kill. It made a mockery of my hope for the future.

'It was long ago, Caitrin. Nearly a hundred years. Didn't you say they were obeying Nechtan's order? If I ordered them to kill, they would do it. That is the nature of their bond with the chieftain of Whistling Tor.' His fingers were against my neck, under my hair, which had escaped its ribbon and was hanging down my back and over my shoulders. I could feel his heart thumping under my cheek. 'They are not evil men. They are good men trapped by the curse.'

I took a deep breath, then made myself draw back. I could feel how dangerous this embrace was, how wonderful and perilous. Despite my distress, I felt his touch all through my body. 'I've missed you,' I said. 'I needed to talk to you. I want to help you.'

'I've been much occupied.' He too had withdrawn, edging along the bench away from me, but our hands were still clasped. He was avoiding my eyes. 'Not good company. I didn't want you drawn into this, Caitrin. You came here to do a skilled job, and you've done it well. I didn't want you involved in this situation with the Normans.'

'I am involved,' I said, fishing out my handkerchief and wiping my eyes. 'It's all the same thing, the host, the documents, the household at Whistling Tor, the Norman threat. I may only be hired for the summer, but I've made friends here, Anluan. I care about what happens. And . . . well, I suppose you can guess that I've been using the mirror in the hope it may lead me to a counter spell.'

'*Been using?* You've done this more than once since that first day?'

'Only one other time, and it didn't help much. I've been through almost all the documents and I can't find anything about the experiment itself. I'll keep looking, of course. I promised the host, and . . . Anluan, will you tell me what you're planning to do? Can we talk about it?'

He released my hand and got up, moving to stand by the window with his back to me. 'A man isn't supposed to admit to being afraid. I am afraid – afraid for my household, for my people, for all who dwell on the hill and in my wider territories. Afraid for you, Caitrin. There, I've said it. From the day you wrote that you wanted to help me, I've watched you try to do just that. I've seen how hard you work, and I've seen you look for the good in everyone, no matter what their flaws and weaknesses. Even in me. If I speak to you of my fear, I know you will not think ill of me.' He drew a deep breath. 'I owe you an apology. I shouldn't have shut you out. But . . . you'd been hurt when you came here. I hoped the summer would allow you to heal, to become that person you said you'd lost.' He turned; what I saw on his face made my heart turn over. 'I can't let you be hurt again,' Anluan said. 'I can't be responsible for that. I thought, if I dealt with this crisis alone, per-haps . . . But I was wrong, I knew it from the moment I opened that door and saw you with Nechtan's mirror. The look on your face filled me with . . . with feelings I have no names for. So yes, I will talk. But first I want to show you something.' He reached out a hand. 'Will you come?'

'Of course. Where?'

'Not far.'

He led me out through Irial's garden and across the grounds to the south tower. I was shaky on my feet, the mirror vision still clinging close. I sensed the presence of the host, watching, wait-ing. I gripped Anluan's hand tightly and tried to pretend that the ghostly presences of the hill were not all around us. If Rioghan had taken part in that act of slaughter, if Eichri had turned against a woman who wanted nothing for Whistling Tor but a return to peace and rightness, what hope had I that the whole host might change its nature?

'I should never have come here,' I muttered as we reached the steps up to the tower door. At exactly the same time, Anluan said, 'I should never have let you stay here.'

We stopped walking. Our hands still clung.

'I didn't mean that,' I said.

'This is no place for you.'

But you are here, and I want to be with you.

'I and my past are not fit company for anyone,' Anluan said, as if he had read my mind.

'I don't share your opinion,' I told him shakily. 'You are my friend, Anluan. I have nothing but admiration for your strength and the way you have faced your difficulties. You know I wouldn't lie to you. Your past is full of sorrow, yes, but perhaps it's time to change that.' He had said something about change himself – that much changes in a hundred years. Perhaps what I had seen in the mirror did not negate my theory about the nature of the host, but reinforced it.

205

'I didn't like to see you using the mirror, Caitrin. Promise me you won't do it alone again.'

'I promise.' I did not ask for a promise in return, though I dearly wanted one. After this, after the delight of his tender words, the sheer bliss of his touch, I would find it unbearable if he closed himself off again.

'This way,' Anluan said, and led me into the south tower. I hesitated on the threshold, realising the outer door led straight into his sleeping quarters. In the world of Market Cross it was unthinkable for a young woman and an unrelated man to be alone in a private chamber together. There was a bed against the back wall, its covers neatly folded, and a table and bench to one side. The floor was of bare flagstones, swept clean. A tall, narrow window pierced the thick wall to let in light, and winding steps curved up to lose themselves above. I imagined a monk's cell might look somewhat like this, though the assortment of garments flung untidily across the top of a storage chest would not have earned an abbot's approval. A pile of bound books teetered on a corner of the table. The books were old, their covers stained from handling, their binding worn to fragility. I had seen them before.

'Please, sit down.' Anluan released my hand and motioned to the bench, then went back to close the door.

'Nechtan's grimoires,' I whispered, sitting down before them. 'You had them here all the time.' There was a pot of ink on the table, and a jar with quills. His little notebook lay beside them, its covers closed. An extinguished candle had dripped a complex cascade all down its iron holder. The chamber was cold. 'Why didn't you show me these before?'

'I know you're looking for a counter spell.' Anluan stood before me with his arms folded. There was a hardness, a determination in his stance now. 'I know you believe I can banish the host if such a charm is found. These books – I've been aware of their existence for some time. This problem has taxed me since long before I made the decision to hire a scribe. I did not bring them into the light of day until you came to Whistling Tor and I saw that you truly intended to stay. You planted the seed of hope; you know I was afraid of that, afraid of accepting it, then finding it was a lie. I had grave doubts about delving into these books.' For the first time he hesitated. 'I fear that opening my mind to Nechtan's sorcery may awaken a part of me best left sleeping. Reading these seems as perilous as looking into the obsidian mirror. At the very touch of these pages, I hear a voice in my mind, a voice I believe is his. What if my spirit were turned to his will?'

'You are strong enough to withstand that, Anluan.' I trembled as I spoke; I had felt the same malign presence as I gazed into the mirror.

'Perhaps. In fact, I doubted from the first that the counter spell would be here. Nechtan had the grimoires at hand. If such a spell existed, wouldn't he have used it? Conan knew Latin. Where Nechtan might perhaps have held back out of a belief that he could still gain full control of the host and employ it as a tool against his enemies, Conan most certainly would have banished the host if he'd had the means. He was no duplicate of his father.'

'You say you brought them into the light of day . . . but I don't understand why you've waited so long to show me. I could have been working on them all this time. I might have found something by now, something that would help us.' I swallowed, struggling for calm. 'I mean, help you and everyone at Whistling Tor. I know that I am only – I mean –' It wasn't possible to go on. In the silence that followed, I lifted the top book from the pile and placed it on the desk before me. A malign, grimacing face had been worked on the dark leather of the cover. I left the book closed.

Anluan was looking down at the floor. A flush had appeared on his wan cheeks. 'I don't know how to say this,' he murmured. 'I fear I will offend you.'

'Say it, please.'

'What made me bring the grimoires out in the first place also made me reluctant to share them. Your coming here has changed everything, Caitrin. You have opened my mind to possibilities beyond any I had dreamed of. So I fetched the books. I knew you could translate them, but . . . Caitrin, the idea of any action of mine causing you hurt is . . . it's unbearable. You are . . . you're like a beating heart. A glowing lamp. I've never met anyone like you before.'

The words fell into my heart like drops of healing balm. My whole body warmed. Despite everything, I was filled with happiness. 'Nor I you,' I whispered, clasping my hands together lest I do something foolish like jump up and throw my arms around him. His tall form was tense, his features grim; there was more to come.

'I couldn't expose you to these books. They are harmful. Nechtan left his descendants a dark legacy. The key to ending this may well lie in the use of sorcery. I can't ask you to deal with that. The obsidian mirror distresses you; I saw the look on your face today.'

'But –'

'I do know a few words of Latin. My father had begun to teach me. I hoped my scant knowledge of the language would be sufficient for me to recognise the spell if it were within these covers. I've been working on the grimoires since Magnus brought back the bad news about Stephen de Courcy. I've worked long hours, as you have; your candle has burned late into the night. I've watched you growing thinner and paler, Caitrin, and it troubles me deeply.'

A silence.

'But you haven't found a counter spell,' I said eventually. 'And nor have I. And we only have a few days left. Let me borrow these, Anluan. I can work on them in the library.'

'You look exhausted. I have wondered if you should be here at all, with this new threat. If you're harmed I will never forgive myself.'

My heart skipped a beat. 'I want to stay,' I said. The compulsion to reach out and touch him was more powerful with every breath. I wrapped my arms around myself. 'Please let me work on these books. I gave an undertaking to the host. Maybe that was foolish. Maybe I overreached myself. But I want to do the best I can.'

'I don't understand why you would want to stay. I have nothing to offer you, Caitrin. Nothing but shadows and secrets.'

'That isn't true, Anluan.' My voice was not quite steady. 'You've given me a home, and friendship, and work that I love. You've given me . . .' *You've made me look outside myself. You've taught me that I can be strong. You've . . .* 'You've given me more than you know,' I said. 'Let me help. Please.'

He drew a deep breath and released it, then moved to sit on the edge of the bed. 'You understand, I imagine, where my dilemma lies,' he said. 'I have no skills whatever as a leader of fighting men. I have no experience in councils and strategies. If I defy the Normans I risk not only your safety, but also that of Magnus, oldest and most stalwart of friends, and Olcan, who should stand outside all this. I risk all who dwell on the hill. Yes, I include the host – it came to me, that day when you offered them your apology, that they are as much my people as the folk of the settlements are. I may not hold them dear, but I am responsible for their wellbeing. A two-edged sword, since they present the immediate risk, but may also prove the long-term solution if this comes to war. To go ahead with this will require a great deal of faith. It will require the quality you taught me, Caitrin.' He gave his lopsided smile, twisting my heart. 'The quality of persistent hope, hope against the odds. Magnus believes it's time to make a stand. Rioghan agrees that we should act. In their opinion, we must do so or perish. And yet . . . Caitrin, there's no trusting the host. One cannot disregard so many years of violence, so many acts of barbarism here on the hill. Nechtan's shadow still hangs heavy over this place.'

'I have a theory,' I said. 'Eichri and I were talking about the mirrors in this house and what each of them could do. He said perhaps artefacts like those are not good or bad in their own right, but work according to the character of the person who is using them. Mightn't the same theory be applied to the host? All accounts tell us Nechtan was a deeply flawed man, a man with no sense of right and wrong, obsessed by the need for power, cruel to his family, deluded in that he believed everyone was against him. As I understand it, the host is tied to the chieftain of Whistling Tor, whoever that is at any time. Its members are obedient to his will, at least while he remains on the hill.'

'That is true, Caitrin.'

'In the vision I saw today, Nechtan was going to let his wife leave. He was tired of Mella; he didn't want her at Whistling Tor any longer. I know this because the obsidian mirror doesn't only show the vision, it draws me into Nechtan's thoughts.' The memory of it was in my bones, like the deepest frost of winter. 'But Mella made a mistake. She told her husband that Maenach was prepared to take her in; she implied that she had made an escape plan with his arch rival, the man he blamed for all his woes. I felt the change in him, Anluan. There was a boiling, uncontrollable surge of anger, then the command to the host, issued in a moment when all reason was swept away. *Kill her*, he told them. So Mella died.'

'I wish you had not seen that.'

'I hope I never have to witness such a sight again. But I learned something. If Nechtan had not suddenly lost his temper, if Mella had not mentioned Maenach, she would have left the hill, gone to her family and lived the rest of her life in peace. It was not an innate evil in the host that caused her to die so cruelly. All they did was obey Nechtan's order. They had to; they were bound to his will.

'Conan was brought up by Nechtan from an early age. As chieftain he made grievous errors, certainly. Like Nechtan, he tried to make use of the host for war. He neglected his lands and his people as his father had done. But he was not Nechtan all over again. What about his wife and son? We know from Conan's writings that Líoch was concerned about the welfare of the community in time of flood; we know that her husband did make some attempts to help them, though the people's fear of the host made those efforts fruitless. I cannot believe that Irial grew up without love and care; he was such a loving man himself. Anluan, how and when did your grandmother die?' I prayed that he would not tell me that Líoch, too, had been slain by the host. My theory was fragile already; that would shred its last credibility.

In the dim light of the bedchamber, Anluan's eyes did not seem blue now, but stony grey. 'She fell from one of the towers,' he said. 'An accident. She and Conan both lived until my father was a grown man. They died within a season of each other.'

It felt wrong to be delving into such sad memories, but I had no choice. 'So they held on, Conan and Líoch, despite their difficulties. They stayed strong while Irial grew up. They cared about him. And about each other, I would guess, since Líoch did not try to run away as poor Mella did. Conan probably changed somewhat in those later years. Once it became plain that the host could not be led into battle without terrible consequences, he ceased trying to use them in that way. Perhaps the host quieted as a result.'

'There is a flaw in this theory, Caitrin.' Anluan was frowning.

'Please,' I said, 'let me finish before you judge. We know that Irial, as chieftain, followed a completely different path. He had no intention of using the host as an army. He was a peaceable scholar who loved his wife and child. His household retainers worshipped him. Irial was a good man through and through. If my theory is correct, that inner goodness in your father would have meant that in his time the host would have felt no desire to kill, to maim, to perform ill deeds.'

'I wish I could believe this, but I cannot.'

'Didn't your father fight against the family curse? Magnus told me he held a council at Whistling Tor. He let your mother take you to Whiteshore to visit her family. He sent Magnus out to talk to the other chieftains. He tried to make peace. I know how he died, Anluan, and I'm terribly sorry, not only because it is so sad for you, but also because he seems to have been such a lovely man. That's the point. Irial was good. In his time, the host reflected his inner nature. As now they do yours. You want peace; they feel no desire for conflict. You feel burdened by your situation; they despair of ever being released from theirs. If you are able to summon hope, they, too, will see the possibility of a brighter future.'

There was a deep silence. After a long time, Anluan said, 'Can the dead have a future?'

'They can still hope. What they want is rest. A sleep without dreams.'

'It is not within my power to bestow such a precious gift. I cannot even command it for myself.'

I considered this, remembering the nightmares that had plagued me so long: the visions of reaching hands and scratching claws, the images of the dank cell and a monster with Cillian's face. 'Anluan, I know there is a certain power amongst the host that is anything but good. But I believe the rest of them are just like any other group of people, good, bad, in between, with their own aspirations, their own sorrows, their own hopes and fears. Most of them want nothing more than to go back to wherever they came from. Nechtan's spell binds them to you as chieftain. They know that only you can give them what they want. And until that happens, they follow you. That means you control their actions, keeping them in check. It also means they think and act in the way you think and act. You are a good man like your father. Under your leadership, they too can be good.'

'And if I need to fight, they will fight for me.' He was looking at me now; brows up, eyes intent. 'You know, don't you, that once I refuse de Courcy's demands I must follow this through to the end, even if it means leading a rag-tag army into battle against a force of iron-clad Norman men-at-arms?'

The scene he had described painted itself instantly in my mind: Anluan falling to the ground, his clothing all over blood; Magnus fighting a last, lone battle over his chieftain's corpse. I shuddered at the thought. If that came true, it would be partly my doing. 'I don't know anything about fighting. I don't know what the next step should be. I just thought my theory might be helpful.'

'I wish I could believe it true,' Anluan said. 'That would make it possible to carry out my plan with some measure of confidence. I could go down to the settlement and leave the host under the supervision of Rioghan and Eichri, secure in the knowledge that they would not follow me and wreak havoc beyond the hill. There are many warriors in their number. Work to do, meaningful work, might give their long time of waiting some purpose.'

'But?'

'There are parts of this story you don't know, Caitrin, parts I don't talk about, past events my household does not discuss. It isn't true that the host was peaceable and benign throughout Irial's chieftaincy. The last time my father left the hill, he came home to find my mother dead.'

I could find nothing to say. It had been there in Irial's notebook, but I hadn't understood. *Why did I leave them?* A wave of bitter disappointment flowed through me. No doubt my feelings were plain on my face.

'It was not clear whether her death was the work of a malign force or an unfortunate accident,' Anluan said. 'I won't speak of it further. If you wonder why it has taken me so long to make my decision, if you were surprised that I could not speak of this to you earlier, this was the most powerful reason. I could step boldly forth, issue a challenge to Stephen de Courcy, use the host as my personal army. If the old pattern were repeated, I could become

212

instrumental in destroying what I hold most dear. Then I would be Nechtan all over again.'

After a little, I said, 'But you will do it anyway. You said you had made your decision.'

Anluan rose to his feet. I saw him gathering himself. I saw his gaze sharpen, his back straighten, his mouth become resolute. 'The first part of it, at least. I know little of strategy, diplomacy, the conduct of war. My father died before he could teach me how to be a leader. If it were not for Magnus, I would be still more ignorant. But it seems to me that I must hold a council before the Normans come: my own council. I heard how you addressed the host, and I saw how they listened. I learned, that day, that if one speaks to them with respect they will respond as living men and women might. I have delayed this almost too long, thinking I might find a counter spell – that would have changed everything.'

'A council,' I breathed. He really was going to do this.

'The folk of the settlement must also be invited, unthinkable as that seems. If we are all agreed, then I must risk leaving the hill to speak to de Courcy's emissaries. I cannot think much beyond that. I have not yet mastered the art of being brave in large steps. This still frightens me, Caitrin. I must learn not to let it show. I suppose that is part of being a chieftain.' His mouth twisted. Beneath the new Anluan, the one with bright eyes and determined jaw, the uncertain boy still lingered.

'I have faith, Anluan,' I said quietly. 'Faith that this will be for the good. Faith in you.'

He reached out a hand in my direction, not meeting my eye. I got up and slipped my hand in his. 'I hope you're right, Caitrin,' he said. 'Because, from this point on, I must set aside all my doubts. A leader cannot be seen to have misgivings. As for this council, I do have Rioghan. Let us go and speak to him.' For a moment, just a moment, he put his arm around my shoulders. 'Thank you,' he said, and touched his lips awkwardly to my temple. It was the boy who did that; but it was the man whose body brushed against me, setting my pulse racing and sending the blood to my face. 'Without you, I would not have found the courage.'

We met Rioghan in the courtyard; it was not necessary to summon him. He was quick to comprehend the situation. Almost before I had finished explaining my theory to him, he and Anluan were putting plans into place.

'How soon?' Rioghan asked. 'We've only a few days until this delegation from Lord Stephen comes to the settlement. Would tomorrow suit you, my lord?'

Anluan let the formality pass without comment. 'I don't expect anyone will come up from the settlement,' he said, 'no matter how carefully the invitation is worded. We must offer them the opportunity, but we need not allow them a great deal of time. As for the host, they won't be comfortable with a daytime council. We should meet this evening after supper. Can you have everything ready by then?'

If Rioghan thought that not quite long enough for adequate preparation, his doubt showed only momentarily. 'Yes, my lord, if Magnus can be spared to take a message down the hill this morning. You're right, the folk of the settlement will want to be kept abreast of things. They may be afraid of us, but I'd wager they fear the Normans far more. As for the trappings required, you can leave those to me.'

'Trappings?' I asked, thinking that perhaps I should return to the library to work, leaving this to the men. The change in Anluan was startling; I saw it reflected in his councillor. Perhaps my theory really was correct. Perhaps all it took to turn things around was hope.

'This and that,' Rioghan said. He was almost smiling; his eyes had a glint in them. 'I'll deal with it. Someone needs to tell the host. I won't have time for that, and neither will Eichri. I'll be using him as my assistant.'

'Since this is an exercise in trust,' I said, 'what about my guard, Cathaír? So far he's been very willing to help me. I could ask him to let all the folk of the Tor know about this. If you agree, Anluan.'

Anluan frowned. 'I know little about this Cathaír. And who would guard your chamber in his absence?'

'I know the young man.' A memory of past sorrow echoed in Rioghan's tone. 'He is trustworthy, my lord. A warrior who could have been a future leader, a fine one, had his life not been cut brutally short.'

Anluan and I looked at him. Neither of us asked for further explanations.

'Very well,' Anluan said. 'Caitrin, please ask Cathaír if he will help us. Perhaps he will also find you another guard – by all the saints, this requires act after act of blind faith. We can't have the entire host present at our council. That could quickly turn to chaos. What we need are representatives.'

'A sound idea, my lord.' I could almost see Rioghan making a list in his mind and crossing off items one by one. 'Eight or ten would be a good number. They should be aware that they'll be putting forward the opinions of the others. There will be a need for some consultation before this evening. The unpalatable fact is that if this comes to war, the host is the only army Whistling Tor has.'

'We'd best get to work,' Anluan said.

'Of course.' Rioghan's tone was level, controlled. 'Just one more question, my lord. Where should we hold this? The great hall? The library?'

'Out of doors.' I had the impression that Anluan had already made these decisions, perhaps some time ago. 'The host won't be comfortable within four walls. We'll gather in the courtyard. I'll leave the practical arrangements to you, Rioghan. I doubt if they will be taxing to a man of your experience.'

Cathaír responded to the challenge, listening intently as I explained what was planned, though he could not still the restless movement of his eyes. He strode off into the forest, and very shortly afterwards a strapping, shaven-headed warrior appeared on the gallery outside my bedchamber to announce that he would take on Cathaír's duties as guard while the younger man addressed the folk out in the woods.

'Not much of a thinker myself,' the warrior said, planting his legs apart and leaning on his spear. 'The lad can speak for me, and I'll do this job for him. Nobody will get past while Gearróg's on guard, my lady.'

'Thank you, Gearróg. I'm not a lady, I'm a craftswoman. Please call me Caitrin.'

'You're a lady to us.' The big warrior sounded a little awkward, but his tone was warm. 'Young fellow says maybe his lordship's going to take things in hand at last. That true?'

His eyes held the same desperate hope I had seen in Cathaír's when first he came to speak with me. It was important not to lie. 'Anluan will do his best. This is difficult for him. He can't easily shake off the shadows of the past.'

'What about us? They're saying maybe there's something can be found that will let us go. Let us sleep at last. Something to silence that voice, the one that puts bad things in our heads. I'd give anything to make that happen, my lady.'

'Voice? What voice?'

'We don't talk about it.' Gearróg's eyes darted nervously from side to side, as if this entity might appear from nowhere to punish him if he said more. 'It turns us wrong way up and inside out. When it's there we don't know what we're doing. You never know when it'll come.' Then, after a moment, 'I don't suppose it's true, what they're saying. Stands to reason. It's our punishment, being here. If there was a way to stop it, someone would have done it before.'

'There might be a counter spell,' I said cautiously. 'I'm looking for it in the old books. If there is one, Anluan can use it to let you all go. But I can't make any promises about that, only that I'll try my hardest to find it before the end of summer.'

'End of summer? Why then?'

'I was hired for the summer. I assume that when it's over I will . . . leave.' *Go home* did not sound right. Increasingly, I was feeling as if this odd place, the place no person in her right mind wanted to come near, was my real home, and Market Cross an alien place, the stuff of nightmare.

'Leave? You'd leave, just like that?'

The warrior's tone, shocked, sad, perfectly reflected my own feelings on the matter. 'I can't say. It depends on what Anluan does; on the Normans; on all sorts of things.' No matter what happened, I wanted to stay. Even if there was war; even if something went wrong and chaos descended on Whistling Tor. I wanted to be here with my friends. I wanted to stand by Anluan's side as he faced this challenge. 'I hope I won't have to go,' I said. 'But don't tell anyone I said that.'

Gearróg grinned, showing a mouthful of broken teeth, and made a gesture as if he were sealing his lips. 'Best go and find his lordship, my lady. He'll be needing you. Oh, and I'll keep an eye on the wee girl. Catháir says that's part of the job up here. She'll be safe with me.'

I had not even noticed the ghost girl crouched in a corner of the gallery, rocking Róise in her arms.

'I'm good with little ones,' Gearróg said. 'Had a brood of my own once, I seem to remember. Gone. Long gone. Can't quite recall their names.'

'I hope one day you'll see them again.' I blinked back sudden tears.

His smile was sad now. 'Me, go where they've gone? That's not going to happen, my lady. Best I can hope for is the long night of no dreams. Never mind that. Off you go now. I'll keep things safe for you.'

Anluan explained the plan to the rest of his household, with my help and Rioghan's. Magnus's broad features were transformed first with surprise, then with relief that at long last his chieftain had made the decision to act. Olcan listened intently. Muirne came in late. She did not speak until the discussion was finished, and then she said quietly, 'This is insanity. You must know what will happen. Are you all fools, that you give credence to Caitrin's misguided theories? The chieftain of Whistling Tor does not leave the hill. He cannot.'

'You'd best not be present for the council if you're fixed in that opinion,' Rioghan told her. 'Anluan will make a strong state-ment of his intention. As his household, we must be seen to stand behind him. If you can't do that, it's best if those present don't hear from you.'

She turned her chilliest look on him. '*You* think to exclude me?' she asked. 'You, the man whose wise advice sent his leader and all his fellow warriors straight to a bloody slaughter? Are you so car-ried away with this ridiculous plan that you have forgotten your beloved Breacán?'

Rioghan flinched visibly. Eichri got to his feet, putting a skeletal arm around his friend. 'That was a low blow,' the monk said. 'Let us not argue amongst ourselves, or we'll never be ready in time. We're not going to war tonight, only to a council.'

Anluan was seated at the head of the table. Now he got to his feet, his eyes on Muirne, who was in her usual place opposite him. 'If you belong to my household, if you are loyal to me, then you are part of the plan. We do it all together. And we support one another. There are precious few of us. We must work as one.'

In answer, Muirne rose to her feet and left the room. It was the first time I had seen her treat Anluan with anything other than fawning adoration, and I found the change unsettling. The men, however, seemed to think little of it. Magnus was quizzing Anluan about exactly what he should be saying to Tomas and the other villagers during the brief visit that was all he had time for. Eichri was making an effort to divert Rioghan's mind from the unthinkable words Muirne had hurled at him by offering a crew of monks to set things up for the council. I tried not to consider the possibility that Muirne was right, and that we were heading straight into disaster.

Anluan had said the council should take place after supper. With Magnus gone down the hill, there would be no supper unless someone else attempted to cook. Anluan and Rioghan paced together outside, working out exactly what should be said to this evening's gathering. Olcan had gone down to the farm to tend to the animals. I put together a simple repast, vegetables and herbs in a kind of pie with a crust made from stale bread.

Eichri came into the kitchen in search of a cloth to drape over the bare wood of the council table. 'Rioghan tells me this calls for a certain degree of ceremony. I wouldn't know. It's been a long time since there was a council held at Whistling Tor. More years than any of us can remember.'

'Not as long as that, surely.' I lifted the lid of the pie dish to examine my creation. It smelled surprisingly good. 'There was the council where Irial met Emer. Twenty-seven years, thirty; a long while ago, but well within your memory and those of all who were part of Irial's household. Eichri, don't go yet, I need to ask you something.'

The monk hesitated on the threshold, his expression suddenly wary.

'Do you believe it's true, the theory we spoke of earlier?' I wanted to ask him whether he could remember the time of blood, Nechtan's time, and the terrible things the host had done. I wanted to know if he had felt a change in himself with the coming of each new chieftain. But how could I ask something so outrageously personal?

'Maybe.' It was clear this was not the question he had expected.

'Eichri, there's an older warrior, Gearróg, guarding my bed-chamber today. He spoke of a voice. A voice that whispers in the ears of the host all the time, speaking evil, tormenting them. Can you tell me what this voice is? Is it the same force Anluan fears so much, the dark entity that exists within the host?'

Eichri's face closed up before my eyes. 'I know nothing of that,' he said.

'Really?' It was obvious that he was lying to me.

'This fellow you mention should keep his mouth shut.'

'More secrets,' I said.

'Not secrets. Just things best left unsaid. I must go.' Eichri forced a smile. 'That smells good. You'll be taking over Magnus's job next.'

'Nobody could ever do that,' I said as my companion went out. Magnus was the real heart of Whistling Tor. He held every-thing together. What if there was a battle and he was killed? No, I would not think of such things. I seized an onion, stripped off the skin and began to chop with more force than was really necessary.

'Smells tasty.' Olcan was at the door, Fianchu behind him. 'I won't come in, I'm all over dirt. Brought some greens for supper.' He held out a bunch of glossy dark leaves. 'Everything all right? I thought you'd be holding Anluan's hand, advising him about tonight, not in here slaving over the fire.'

'Olcan, may I ask you something?'

He waited, arms folded, bright eyes watchful. Fianchu had

come in, his feet leaving a muddy pattern on the floor, and was busily cleaning up the breadcrumbs under the table.

'You were here in Nechtan's time, weren't you? Even before that.'

A wary nod.

As with Eichri, a question came out that was not the one I had intended to ask. 'How did he die? Nechtan?'

'Peacefully in his bed. He outlived his wife by some years. Funny how things turn out.'

'Olcan, I know you are not part of the host, but something much older. Are there others like you on the Tor?'

A strange smile then, sad, accepting, proud. 'I'm the last of my kind in these parts, Caitrin. I've heard tell of others far to the south, but that might only be a story.'

'That's sad for you. Haven't you been tempted to travel there, to seek them out?' I did not ask if he had ever had a wife and children, a family, or whether he had wanted one. There were so many stories in this place, and most of them sorrowful.

'You'd like to make things right for all of us, wouldn't you, lass? I'm content enough here on the Tor; it's my place, has been for far longer than you can imagine. The host, Nechtan's spell, the whole sorry business, that's only a bump in the road for me. Still, I'd like to see the lad happy. I'd like to see him make something good out of all this.'

'The lad – you mean Anluan?'

'He's got a lot to contend with. We all need to stand by him, help him see this through.'

'I plan to do that, Olcan. Let me ask you –' But there was no asking about the voice Gearróg had mentioned, or about Muirne's strange attitude to the current crisis, or about a number of other things that were exercising my mind, because Anluan was in the inner doorway, leaning against the frame, looking too weary to do so much as sit down at the table, let alone address a formal council in just a few hours.

'Caitrin?'

'I'll be off,' muttered Olcan, and clicked his fingers. Fianchu snatched up a last crust and was away out the door after his master.

Anluan and I gazed at each other across the kitchen. *Don't tell him how tired he looks. And don't tell him one glance brings back the feeling of being in his arms, the lovely, safe feeling, the throbbing, delicious feeling . . .* 'Finished with Rioghan?' I asked as calmly as I could, lifting one of Magnus's herb jars down from its shelf and putting a pair of cups on the table.

'Finished for now, yes.' He came over and sat down on the bench, then put his elbow on the table and rested his brow on his hand. 'He believes I can do this. But hope is such a tenuous quality. To feel it and then to be denied what one most longs for . . . Better, surely, not to hope at all, than to open the heart to a hope that is impossible.'

I had stilled in the middle of putting the herbal mixture into the cups. I set the spoon down. Surely he wouldn't turn back now, change his mind about this, after showing such strength? 'No, Anluan,' I said, my heart thumping. 'That is quite wrong. You must let hope in, then instead of simply waiting for good things to happen, work as hard as you can to achieve them. The goal someone hopes for can be anything: writing a line of perfect script, or baking a pie, or . . . or raising a child well, despite the odds. Or standing up for what is right.'

He had lifted his head. In this light, his eyes were the hue of ultramarine, an ink that rivalled heart's blood for rarity. I could not read his expression. I only knew that from now on I would not look at him without wanting to touch. I wondered whether he could see this on my face. 'I thought I'd make Magnus's favourite restorative draught,' I said, feeling my cheeks flush. 'This seems an appropriate time for it.'

Anluan watched me as I finished preparing the drink. 'Raising a child well,' he mused after a while. 'You mean Magnus?'

'I was thinking of him, yes. He did a good job with you, against quite extreme odds. At least, that's how it seems to me. And my parents raised me and Maraid well, first the two of them together, and later Father on his own. I was luckier than you. I didn't lose him until I was already grown.' I felt my throat close up, reluctant to let the words out. I heard the familiar trembling in my voice, but this time I was determined to say it. 'He collapsed in the workroom one morning. By the time I went down to join him, he was lying on the floor dead. He hadn't even been ill. After that, I . . . I was not myself for some time.'

'Come, sit by me.'

It was easy, then, to move to the bench beside him; natural to sit close enough so that from time to time, not quite accidentally, his thigh touched mine. We sat thus awhile, watching the steam rise from the two cups and listening to the sounds from outside: Eichri arguing amicably with one of his brethren, Rioghan issuing orders, Fianchu barking.

'About hope,' Anluan said. 'There is no point in hoping for what can never be.'

'That's true. But sometimes we do that anyway. I know about impossible hope, Anluan. After Father died, I prayed that time would go backwards. I prayed that I would wake up and find that it had all been a bad dream. I longed for him to be alive again and the others gone.'

'Others?'

'Cillian and his mother. They came to take charge of everything when Father died. Ita – Cillian's mother – told everyone I was out of my wits. Perhaps it was true. It was a mad kind of grief, it took up every part of me. I wanted the whole world to go away. If I could have crawled into a shell and hidden for the rest of my life, that's what I would have done.'

Anluan reached out to lay his fingers against my wrist for a moment. It was the most tentative of caresses, and yet my pulse raced at his touch. 'But you are the bravest person I've ever met, Caitrin,' he said.

'I wasn't brave then. I had to make myself face up to my fears. The hardest step was the first: deciding to run away from Market Cross. The most frightening thing was not my father's death, not Cillian and Ita, but the . . .'

'Tell me,' Anluan said.

I took a deep breath. 'It was me, the way I shrank down after it happened, the way I lost myself . . . Like falling deep into a well.' I had dreamed of that, over and over: the yawning hole, the clutching hands, the long, long way down . . . 'I started believing what they said about me, that I was useless, hopeless, crazy . . . I even believed that when Cillian beat me, it was because I deserved

222

it . . . If people say those things often enough, it starts to feel true.'

'You're shivering,' Anluan said.

'I'm all right.'

'Tell me, what was it made you decide to run away? What made you brave enough to take that step after so long?'

'I got up one morning and looked out my window, and I heard a lark singing. I picked up the little doll my sister had made for me, and I looked at the treasures I had kept from my mother and father, and I found a very small spark of courage. I knew my parents were looking down on me. I didn't want them to be ashamed of me.' I brushed away tears. 'They taught us to stand up for ourselves, Maraid and me. For a while I forgot that.'

'Where was your sister when you were lost in this grief, Caitrin?' Anluan's tone was level.

'Gone. She went away with her sweetheart, Shea. He's a travelling musician.'

'She left you on your own.'

'Don't judge Maraid,' I snapped, though he was only echoing my own thoughts on the matter. 'She loves Shea. And she did offer to take me with her, but they had no money; it was going to be hard enough for them without me to support as well. Besides, Ita said she'd look after me, see that I got the attention of a physician and so on.'

Anluan turned a quizzical look on me, but said nothing.

'I don't suppose you can understand,' I added miserably. 'I was not myself. I was a . . . a husk, a shell. A thing beset by shadows and fears. Father and I . . . He trained me in my craft. We worked side by side, every day. And then, with no warning at all, he was gone. Gone forever. It was as if the centre of my world had collapsed. When Ita and Cillian came, I had no strength to stand up to them. Ita was right, in a way. For a while, I was mad.'

'Where did your sister go with her musician?'

'North. I can't remember the name of the place. His band moves around. They play in the halls of noblemen as well as performing for village dances and weddings. There was no place for me in that kind of life.' Gods, I was crying again. 'I'm sorry, I had no intention of burdening you with this now. I wanted to help you prepare for your council, not talk about my difficulties.'

'Ah,' said Anluan, reaching up as if to wipe away my tears. He drew his fingers back before they touched my face. 'But you have helped. You've demonstrated, again, how to practise courage in small steps. Have you forgotten that I challenged you to speak of this before and that you could not bring yourself to do it? So you have taken a step, and tonight I will take one. I have a favour to ask you, Caitrin.'

'What favour?'

'I want you to stay with me until it's time. I am afraid that if you are not here I will fall back into the old way of thinking. I am so accustomed to that. It's almost as if an inner voice tells me, over and over, that there is no point in trying, that the patterns of the past must inevitably repeat themselves, that because I am not a . . . a real man, I cannot do what is needed here.'

'You are a real man, Anluan.'

'A real man can be a warrior. He can ride out at the head of his troop. He can wield sword or spear in defence of his own. He can summon folk to support him; he can care for those in his responsibility. A real man has a proper home, a calling, a family . . . He can . . .'

What had brought about this sudden waning of confidence? It was as if the voice of despair itself had been whispering in his ear.

'My father was not a warrior, Anluan. He was a real man who loved his family and was dedicated to his craft. Maraid's husband, Shea, would hardly know one end of a sword from the other. My sister loves him; she trusts him to look after her. He, too, is a real man, a man with a calling. It's not any particular ability that makes you a man, it's what is inside.' I laid my hand over his heart. 'You are a leader,' I told him. 'You are a good person. You are the chieftain of Whistling Tor and you're going to change things for the better. If you speak from the heart tonight, these folk will follow you to the death. I know it.'

'To the death,' echoed Anluan, putting his hand over mine. 'It seems likely that is exactly where I will take them. I fear for those who are dear to me, Caitrin. I fear for all my people.'

chapter nine

e waited in the courtyard as the light faded to the half-dusk of summer and the moon slipped out from a veil of cloud, turning the leaves to silver and setting a shimmer on the still water of the pond. The torches were lit. The table stood ready, a rich blue cloth spread across it, candles burning in a pair of ancient iron holders shaped like leaping salmon. Rioghan had unearthed these and the rod that lay beside them, fashioned of dark wood with bands of inlaid bronze. 'To keep order,' he'd explained. 'If things get unruly I'll rap it on the table a couple of times.'

For a while, it seemed there would be nobody here but ourselves: Anluan, pale in the moonlight, with Rioghan next to him; Eichri stationed a few paces to his left with the monk who had been helping earlier; Olcan and Fianchu to the right. Anluan had asked me to stand beside him, but I had said no, for that did not seem at all fitting. Instead, I stood on the steps behind him with Magnus, and Muirne came out to join us. I greeted her, trying to conceal my surprise. She made no response.

Time passed. Cathaír came out from the trees, taking a place on the very edge of the circle, half in shadow. He seemed unable to stand still, but constantly shifted his balance, folding and unfolding his arms, looking back over his shoulder. I wished I had thought to offer him a clean shirt in place of his bloodstained garment, but perhaps wearing that remnant of some long-ago battle was part of the curse; perhaps it symbolised his unfinished business in the world of the living.

'Two,' remarked Rioghan, looking from Cathaír to the ghostly monk by Eichri's side. 'Well, it is early yet.'

'They won't come.' Muirne's voice was a murmur, but in the quiet of the courtyard it carried clearly. I could have hit her.

'Of course they'll come,' I said. 'I'll lay a wager on it. Any takers?'

'Don't be silly, Caitrin.' Muirne's voice registered irritation, but I had made the men of the household smile.

'None of us is prepared to take you on,' Eichri said. 'Of course they'll come. They know what's riding on this.'

'Give 'em time,' said Magnus. 'This is new to everyone.' He had come back from the settlement just before supper. None of the villagers had been prepared to accompany him up the hill, but Tomas and the others had expressed a keen interest in the results of our council. They wanted Magnus to return in the morning with news. Tomas had suggested sending a message to Brión, chieftain of Whiteshore, to keep him abreast of things. Someone else had remembered a cache of old weaponry hidden somewhere down near the river. The thought that there might be a real possibility of mounting a defence against the Normans had sparked something new in the frightened inhabitants of the settlement. Magnus had counselled caution; they must wait for Anluan's decision, he'd told them. They had sent him back up the hill with three loaves of freshly baked bread and a crock of honey, but none of us had been able to eat. That bounty, along with my pie, still lay untouched on the kitchen table.

It grew colder. The moon edged higher. Owls cried; creatures rustled in the bushes.

'There is no point in this,' said Muirne.

'We will wait until they are ready.' Anluan sounded quietly confident. It seemed he had conquered his earlier doubts. 'All night, if need be.'

Muirne said no more. In the hush that followed, I could hear Eichri whistling between his teeth.

A little cough from Rioghan. Muirne tensed beside me.

'Here we go,' muttered Magnus.

Cathaír had been told to specify the number: no more than ten representatives from the host, exclusive of those who lived within the house. They manifested one by one beneath the trees, then moved up to take their places around the circle. Gearróg would not come; he had remained on guard outside my chamber, content to let Cathaír speak for him. But there were other warriors here: a tall man with a pike; an old, bearded one bearing a bow and quiver; a man with one leg, hobbling on a crutch, with a fearsome array of knives at his belt. His battered leather helm and breast-plate and the great slashing scar across his face marked him as a combat veteran. With Cathaír, that made four; with the monk, five.

'Welcome,' Anluan said quietly. None of them spoke, but they acknowledged the greeting with a nod, a jerk of the head, a fist raised in soldierly respect.

A woman came next, her garb a hooded robe, her grey hair in long plaits. On her brow was tattooed a crescent moon. A wise woman, I guessed, perhaps a priestess of an older faith. She hesitated just beyond the circle of torches. Behind her was a younger woman with glittering ornaments around her neck and her hair artfully dressed, the kind of woman to whom men's eyes must go instantly, though this one looked somehow faded, as if the brightness that had been hers in life had slowly leached away over the long years on the Tor, leaving a pale copy of her former self. A third stood by them, a personage of middle years clad in the practical homespun garments of a hardworking village wife. None seemed prepared to step into the circle.

'They are afraid, lady.' It was Cathaír who spoke.

Anluan turned to me. 'Caitrin, will you bid them welcome?' As if I were the lady of the house. As if I were his wife.

I did not look at Muirne, but her voice was in my mind: *You are not one of the women of Whistling Tor.* 'Come forward into the circle, please,' I called, smiling at the three. 'Lord Anluan welcomes you all.'

They moved forward in silence to stand together, a little apart from the warriors. That made eight.

For a while, nothing stirred save the flames of the torches, turned to fiery war banners by the night breeze.

'Are there more?' asked Rioghan eventually, looking at Catháir.

As if in answer another figure came forth from the trees, one who dwarfed even Magnus. His arms were muscular, his chest formidable. His skin was marked by many scars, not combat injuries, I judged, but burns. He was the kind of man whose features are handsome only to his mother. His physical presence, however, would be sure to prevent anyone from telling him this.

'Donn the smith, my lord.' The giant gave the very slightest of bows, and Anluan returned the courtesy gravely. 'Representing the working men of the Tor.'

'I welcome you, Donn. We may have need of your expertise.'

'Likely you will, my lord.' The smith moved into position alongside Eichri and the other monk, and now there were nine.

'Our number is complete, my lord,' said Catháir.

Rioghan frowned at him. 'Only nine?'

As one, the representatives of the host turned their eyes towards a particular place in the circle, a place that seemed deliberately left vacant, the warriors to one side of it, the women, the smith and the clerics to the other.

'We are ten, my lord,' said the grey-haired woman. 'We leave this place for one whom we love and respect; one who, like us, died with unease in his heart. We cannot see or hear him, but we sense his presence. He is not of the host. He watches over the Tor.'

My skin prickled. I heard Muirne hiss softly beside me, as if this frightened her where none of the rest of it had the power to do so. Magnus muttered something under his breath.

'Very well.' Anluan allowed his gaze to move around the circle, taking in everyone present. 'All are welcome here, the seen and the unseen. Each is part of our community of Whistling Tor. You know why I have summoned you. A peril confronts us. I need your help.'

He set the situation out once more. As I listened I watched his audience, and very soon it became apparent to me that the host had not limited its representation to ten after all. Ten stood within the circle of lights, nine of them visible, one mysteriously not so, but in the moonlight beyond that circle were gathered many more. Anluan was surrounded by troubled souls.

He did not spend long on my theory about the host, and that was wise – this was not the time to remind these folk of the ill deeds in their past. He told them that he planned to visit the settlement at full moon. He outlined what he would say to Lord Stephen's emissaries. He asked the spectral folk for an undertaking that they would stay within the boundaries of the hill while he was gone, obey the commands of those he left in charge, do no harm until he returned. Each of them would be given a job, a responsibility to carry out during that time, which would not be long, less than a full morning. As for what happened after that, it depended on Lord Stephen's response. But very likely Anluan would have to ask more of them: a great deal more. His question was, could he trust them? He glanced at me.

'Caitrin has spoken to you before; you know her,' he said. 'Indeed, without her influence it is unlikely we would ever have attempted this. She believes you trustworthy. She assures me that you can do what I ask of you. Caitrin, will you add your voice to mine?' He turned, holding out a hand towards me. I stepped down to stand beside him, facing the host, my heart thumping with a confusion of feelings.

'I greet you all with respect and in friendship,' I said, aware of the eyes watching me from out there under the trees, so many eyes. 'I am not trying to belittle your difficulties when I tell you that I know how it feels to be afraid; to be so afraid that you cannot force yourself to move so much as your little finger. I think sometimes that happens here. And I think sometimes folk do things they don't want to do, because on their own they are not strong enough to stand against . . . whatever it is that compels them to evil deeds. But we're not on our own any more. We're all here together, we're all Lord Anluan's people, the people of the Tor, and there's enough strength in us to do the right things and make the right choices. Tonight, all Lord Anluan asks of you is an undertaking to stay on the hill while he visits the settlement on the eve of full moon, and to do no harm while he is beyond the boundary. That doesn't seem very much to ask, but of course it is – if you achieve it, you'll have done something it seems the host has never done before. You'll have taken control of your own destiny. You'll have taken the first step towards solving all the difficulties that beset Whistling Tor and its chieftain. I know you can do it. That's all I have to say.' I stepped back, and a clamour of voices broke out all around the circle.

A sharp rapping – Rioghan had got the opportunity to try out his rod. 'One at a time!' he ordered, and the hubbub died down. 'Step forth in turn and speak. All will be heard.' After a moment he added, 'Keep it brief.'

Cathaír took two paces forward, his head high. He laid his arm across his chest, clenched fist against his shoulder. 'I will stand strong, my lord,' he said, and his jaw was set firm, though the red of the torches flickered oddly in his eyes. 'My fellow warriors stand with me. We are twice fifty in number, some with full weaponry, some partly armed. Although some bear old injuries that may hamper their fighting skills, all can make a contribution.'

'Good, Cathaír,' Anluan said. 'I commend you for your industry. Have your men questions for me?'

Rioghan appeared ready to interrupt, but Anluan murmured, 'Let him speak, Rioghan,' and the councillor fell silent.

'The same question is on everyone's lips, my lord,' said Cathaír. 'It concerns payment for services rendered. You know what we want, all of us. We know the lady's looking for it, looking as hard as anyone can. But she might not find it. She said she's leaving at the end of summer. It might take longer to find. It might not be here at all. I told them to set that aside, my lord. I told them we should do what needs doing and forget about what we might get out of it. I said it was worth doing just because you believe in us. But those ones out there, they want an answer. They've been waiting a long time for all this to end.'

I saw Anluan draw in a long breath, then let it slowly out. He spoke quietly. 'I will not give you a false promise. I do not know if we will find the means to release you from your long time of imprisonment on the Tor. We will continue to try our best.'

The wise woman stepped forward, her long hair gleaming

silver in the torchlight. 'What if your best falls short of what is required, my lord?' she asked.

'Then I will have shown myself unworthy to be your chieftain. I do not know exactly what is required yet, only that I will put all that I am into defending Whistling Tor and my people, and into doing what is right.'

'Defending's only part of it,' said the one-legged warrior. 'You'll want an attacking strategy for good measure. You'll want barriers, traps, diversions. We need to think ahead.'

'You're straying from the point,' said the tall man with the pike. 'There's three steps in this: challenge, fight, reward. What we're talking about here is reward. We do the job, we get sent back where we came from. Simple. If his lordship here can't send us back, we don't do the job. Even simpler.'

Rioghan cleared his throat.

'If all goes to plan at full moon,' Anluan said, 'we will hold another council, a bigger one, with representatives from further afield. Should an armed resistance be required, we must somehow involve the local populace and perhaps the neighbouring chieftains as well. There are many challenges: challenges beyond anything we've ever dreamed. Caitrin and I will continue to search for the means to help you, I promise that. She believes there must be a way. I . . . I believe in her hope. Be quite clear on this: if we don't manage to stand up against these invaders, it's the end for all of us. Without us to help you, you'll never be free of the curse. Without you to help us, we cannot save Whistling Tor.'

'By all means work on strategies for attack and defence,' Rioghan said to the warriors. 'We'll take all your ideas into consideration, but they can wait for a council of war. What Lord Anluan needs now is your assurance that you will submit to the control of his designated leaders at full moon. He wants an undertaking from the ten of you on behalf of the entire host.'

'You putting yourself forward as war leader here?' asked the ancient bearded fighter, scowling at Rioghan. 'After what you did last time you got the chance?'

'Hold your tongue!' Eichri had taken three steps out into the centre of the circle; the flickering torches made his eyes glow red, and I was reminded of his fearsome arrival on the day Cillian

231

had nearly stolen me away from Whistling Tor. 'Lord Anluan just asked us to work together, dolt, not to stir up suspicion and distrust amongst our own ranks. He needs a simple answer: yes or no. The rest of it can wait.'

The old man grimaced at him, but there was no real malice in it.

'Does anyone else wish to be heard?' Rioghan was fighting for calm; I heard the struggle in his voice.

'I'll have a word.' Magnus stepped down to stand at one end of the table. He positioned himself so that he was facing neither Anluan nor the host directly. I thought he was trying to establish that he was neither leader nor follower here, but his own man. If anything, he was looking toward the gap in the circle, the place occupied by the invisible tenth. 'First, I should tell you all that I've been down to the settlement today, and I've asked the folk there for their opinions. They're wary, and that's no surprise; they've had good cause for that over the years. They don't trust any of the folk of the Tor, human, spectral or otherwise.' A nod towards Olcan and Fianchu with this last. 'But they understand that there's a new danger coming, and that we need to break old habits if we're to have any chance of standing up to it. It's vital that we get this next part right. If anything untoward happens while Lord Anluan is off the hill, if the people down there are given any cause for alarm, we'll have lost all chance of winning their trust. And we need it.' Magnus squared his shoulders, looking out now towards the shadowy folk gathered under the trees, beyond the light from the torches. 'I'm a fighter,' he said. 'I haven't used those skills much in recent times, but believe me, I still have them. I'm not a strategist like Rioghan here, but I know how to lead men. I know how to keep them going when the blood and the carnage and the misery seem fit to break the bravest and best. Chances are we'll be fighting together before long. When we do, we'll do it properly. You've got worthy warriors amongst you, leaders too, no doubt, and we'll all work together. But not until the right time, and only if Lord Anluan bids us do it. He's our chieftain. He gives the orders. And Rioghan's his councillor. Anyone who wants to make comments about his fitness for the position can make them to me when we're finished here.'

There was a brief, charged silence.

'That's it.' Magnus turned and inclined his head to Anluan. 'Thank you, my lord.' He walked back up to stand beside me.

'If others would express an opinion, now is the time,' Anluan said. Nobody responded. 'Very well,' he went on. 'I will ask for a formal declaration of your support. If you are prepared to provide that, I will speak to you again before full moon with further details of the plan. I believe that the control I exercise over certain elements amongst you will wane when I leave the confines of the hill. That is what has occurred with each chieftain in turn since my great-grandfather's time. If I go to the settlement for this meeting, I must be confident that you will obey those I leave in charge. Those ten of you who represent the others, I ask you to raise a hand as indication of agreement to this.'

Cathaír's hand went up straight away, fist clenched. A moment later, those of each of the warriors standing beside him followed. Donn the smith lifted his brawny arm high. The women and the monk seemed hesitant.

'If you need time to consult those for whom you speak, we will wait now while you do so,' Anluan added. His tone had lost something of its confidence; I knew he was bone weary. 'We must have a decision tonight.'

The monk raised his hand. It would have taken a brave man not to do so with Eichri at his side, baring those teeth.

'The will of the host is to support you, my lord,' said the wise woman. 'But there is disquiet. Memories stir, memories some had hoped gone forever.'

'Most of it's vanished into shreds and tatters,' put in the woman clad in homespun. 'Most of us can't recall much about our lives before, nor about the time you mention, my lord, when your antecedents were chieftains here. But some of it won't go away. The best and the worst, those cling even in the minds of folk such as we are, in-between folk, neither one thing nor the other. Dark deeds, terrible deeds we'd give much to wipe from our memories. Our own deeds. If . . .' She faltered and fell silent, unwilling to give voice to the next part of her thought.

The third woman raised a hand to adjust her glinting neck-piece. 'Lord Anluan,' she said, 'there can be no certainty in our promise, no matter how strong our will to help you. A darkness hangs over each one of us, from the innocent child to the battle-scarred warrior; a force that tampers with our minds and leads us into evil-doing. Without your guidance, we may be unable to resist it.'

Anluan looked down at his hands, clasped on the table before him. 'It was my ancestor who began this,' he said. 'I am that man's flesh and blood. I have borne the weight of his ill deed every day of my life, and every night it robs me of sleep. It was the same for my father, and for his father before him. Under that burden it is all too easy to give in to despair. The history of my family makes that painfully clear.' He drew a shuddering breath and looked up, facing the circle of wan faces and shadowy eyes. 'Enough of this. I have learned, this summer, that the most powerful weapon is hope. I understand the nature of your concern. Neither your promise nor mine can be made without reservations. Our bargain should be this: that each of us does the very best he can to be true to his word. I will be content with that. Will you?'

A rustling around the circle, not speech but restless movement, as of a trembling passing through the insubstantial forms of the host. 'We will,' said the woman, and she and her companions raised their hands. Out in the darkness, a forest of pale arms arose in unison.

'I thank you,' said Anluan. His voice was a thread, but it was nonetheless the voice of a chieftain. I glanced at Magnus, and he smiled; I knew we felt the same pride.

'What of the tenth amongst you,' Rioghan asked, 'the one whose voice we cannot hear? Is this entity in agreement with the rest of the host?'

All eyes turned towards the empty space in the circle. 'Yes, my lord,' said the wise woman. 'If there is a single certainty tonight, it is that.'

'Very well,' Rioghan said. 'Our council is concluded and you are all free to go. Be sure you will be called again, for there are plans to make for full moon, and likely a great deal of work after that. For now, we bid you goodnight.'

'Again, thank you,' Anluan said. 'Trust can be a hard lesson; hope still more difficult. We are all learning.'

When the host had dispersed and the torches were extinguished, we retreated to the warmth of the kitchen fire. Nobody had much to say. Magnus poured ale; I divided one of the loaves he had brought back and served up the cold pie. Anluan looked utterly spent. I had cut him only a small slice: his appetite was poor at the best of times. To my surprise, he worked his way steadily through it.

'Not a bad effort for a woman who reckons she can't cook,' Magnus observed, reaching for a second helping. 'Fancy another job, Caitrin?'

I managed a smile. 'I have more than enough work already,' I told him. Tomorrow I would ask Anluan again if I could move those grimoires into the library. I must go through their contents, if only to prove they did not contain the counter spell. 'But I'm glad you like the pie.'

'Makes a big difference, not having to do it all myself.' Magnus passed the bread down the table. 'A little bit of help goes a long way.' He glanced at Anluan. 'Sounds as if we've got a big job on our hands. We'd best put some strategies in place for this meeting of yours first; who goes where, who does what while you and I are off the hill. If we've got to find jobs for all of that lot, we'll need to start working on it right away.'

'It's late,' Anluan said. 'I have no heart for more tonight. In the morning we will speak of it. I should thank you. All of you. It is not necessary that you continue to stand by me. It is a mystery to me why you do so. But Magnus is right. Each act of support, each gesture of friendship makes it easier to take one more step; to face one more sunrise. I'm tired. I'll bid you goodnight now.'

As he stood up, all of us did the same. Anluan looked bemused, but the shadow of a smile touched his lips as he went out. A moment later Muirne, too, was gone.

'She still doesn't like this,' I observed. 'What is it that makes her so sure things will go wrong?'

'She's worried for him,' Magnus said. 'Not that the rest of us aren't, but Muirne has more cause than most to be troubled. She spent a lot of time with Irial during those dark years after Emer's death. Losing him broke her heart. I suppose she fears she may lose Anluan if this comes to war.'

'What is her story? She's never talked to me about what her life was . . . before.'

'Nor to me, Caitrin. Muirne doesn't talk much to anyone, except him.'

'Rioghan? Eichri? What do you know about her?'

Eichri ran a finger around the rim of his goblet, frowning. 'We're used to her always being about, but she keeps herself apart. She did tell me her story once. Nothing especially interesting. Born and brought up in one of the settlements, betrothed to a miller, died of a winter ague before they could be wed. Sad little tale. Don't know what happened to the fellow.'

'Olcan, what about you?' I asked. He was finishing up the last of the pie, one bite for himself, one bite slipped to Fianchu, who was waiting just behind him, small eyes following every mouthful from platter to lips. 'You've been here longer than anyone.'

'Never gave her much thought, to tell you the truth. She looks after Anluan, makes sure he's not too much alone. That has to be a good thing. And as Magnus said, she did the same for his father.'

I felt a creeping sensation, a sudden inexplicable unease. 'And for Conan before him?' I asked.

'She was around the place then, I seem to recall. It's a long while ago, Caitrin.'

'One thing's certain,' Magnus said. 'She doesn't much care for you.'

Rioghan sighed. 'Nobody can criticise the girl for that. She wants what she can't have: another life, a real one. In that she's no different from me or from Eichri here. She's hostile to you, Caitrin, because you're what she can never be: a real woman. She fears you, with your rosy cheeks and red lips, your tumbling dark hair, your . . . well, you get my drift. Anluan will never look at her the way he looks at you.'

These words hung in silence for the space of three breaths. I did not know what to say in this roomful of men.

'Don't let it trouble you,' said Magnus. 'Muirne has her little oddities, but she's a good soul underneath.'

'Mm,' I said, neither agreeing nor disagreeing. It troubled me that Muirne remained hostile to what Anluan was doing, but I did feel some sympathy for her. To die on the threshold of marriage was particularly sad.

'I'm going to bed now,' I said. 'Poor Gearróg has been on guard for hours. May I have Fianchu again tonight, Olcan?'

The dog was up as soon as I spoke his name, ready to accompany me.

'Of course. Sleep well, Caitrin.'

Although he had seemed weary to death, Anluan's lamps burned long into the night. I stood on the gallery in the moonlight, looking across the garden towards that faint glow and wishing I could break all the rules. He should not be by himself in that bare chamber with only Nechtan's grimoires for company. I sighed, hugging my shawl around my shoulders. It seemed so simple, the idea of going down the stairs, running across the garden, tapping on his door, telling him I was lonely, cold, worried. Suggesting . . . what, exactly? If a young woman were to act in such a way, a man would put only one interpretation on it. Of course I would not go into his bedchamber at night, alone. The very idea was outrageous.

My body felt strange tonight, different. I was not so naïve as to be ignorant of what it meant, even though such feelings were new to me. I had known, when Anluan put his arms around me for comfort earlier today, that a profound change had happened in me since I had come to Whistling Tor. It wasn't only the relief of finding safe haven, the pride of doing a job well, the pleasure of good companionship, the delight of respect and friendship. I had learned how it felt to want more than the sweet touch of hand to cheek or lips to palm, more than a kiss, more than an embrace. I was starting to discover that it is not only the mind that understands love, but also the body.

Lust, came a whispering voice in my ear, freezing me where I stood. *Crude animal lust. You couldn't feel it before. Once you looked in the obsidian mirror, once you shared that man's memories, his desire inhabited you like a hot flood, trembling and quivering and throbbing through that lush body. You know Nechtan's mind; you feel his needs. No wonder your face goes hot when Anluan brushes close to you. No wonder you look at him as if he were a stallion and you a brood mare in heat.*

Don't fool yourself that this is love, Caitrin. You don't want Anluan, you just want that lust slaked, and he happens to be the only young man around. That hungry body of yours is full of Nechtan's passion and Nechtan's cruelty.

'Baby's cold.'

I started violently. I had been transfixed by that voice, a voice that must have come from my own mind, for the gallery held only me, the ghost child now standing very close to me with the doll in her arms, and Fianchu waiting patiently by the bedchamber door for me to go back in so he could settle to guard the entry. If someone had been standing by me, taunting me as I stared down towards Anluan's lonely lamp, that presence was nowhere to be seen.

'She's cold because you got out of bed,' I said, taking the girl's chilly hand and leading her back into my chamber. 'Let's tuck you in, shall we?'

I stayed long awake on my pallet, a candle flickering beside me, while the girl lay with eyes obediently shut and the big dog at her back. Fianchu could never warm her, but perhaps his body helped her remember how good that had once felt. As for me, I breathed every breath with Anluan; in my imagination I fitted the curves of my body to the straight, strong planes of his. I imagined his hands on my flesh, his fingers tangled in my hair. I touched the irregularities of his features tenderly, exploring that surprising landscape with wonder and delight. I felt our two hearts pressed close together, two drums keeping time to the same haunting melody. My body was full of unanswered pleas.

I blew out the candle before the sky began to lighten. In the dark, my body aching with need, I remembered Nechtan's desire for his young assistant, his cruel dismissal of his wife, the pride and the obsessive fear that had overridden all. 'It's not true,' I whispered, as if the owner of that disembodied voice could hear me. 'I'm not like him. What I feel is not selfish desire, it's quite different from that, it's . . .'

Fianchu stirred. He would be up at first light, wanting to be let out into the garden. The little voice of the ghost girl came in the semi-dark. 'You sad, Catty?'

I had told her my name, but this was the first time she had

attempted it. 'No, not sad.' It was hard to say just what I felt. There was too much stirring in me, yet there was only one image before my closed eyes, and that was Anluan's.

Three days passed in a blur. I read my way through page after crumbling page of unlikely sounding spells and incantations, while beyond the library doors Anluan and the others put in place their arrangements for the eve of full moon. I read until my back ached; until my eyes hurt; until my neck felt like a stick of dried-up firewood. I saw nothing of Anluan in the library, but several times when I went outside to stretch my cramped limbs I observed him in sombre-faced conversation with Magnus and Rioghan. Once or twice it seemed to me their talk hushed as I came closer, as if what they were discussing must be kept from my ears, and that surprised me. But the need to get through the grimoires drove me hard, and I did not trouble the men with questions.

I learned how to put a spell on a rival that would make her hair fall out overnight, leaving her as bald as an onion. I discovered the means to turn a perfectly ordinary garment into one that would burn and torment anyone unfortunate enough to put it on. I read three different ways to find out if a person was lying and five theories on turning base metals into gold. I ploughed through a dissertation on the distinction between leprechauns and clurichauns. There were guides for the use of scrying vessels. There were instructions for making fire without smoke and smoke without fire. There were incantations to assist with the transfer of special qualities to mirrors of bronze or silver or obsidian – I did not read those in full, for it chilled me to be so close to the heart of Nechtan's power. I stayed at my desk until I was almost weeping with exhaustion, but I found no charm for the release of unquiet spirits.

On the second day, I waylaid Eichri in the courtyard as dusk was falling. Since the council, much had changed at Whistling Tor. Warriors of the host patrolled the high walkways atop the fortress walls, in plain sight. Torches burned in iron sockets; I saw here a spear point, there an axe blade glinting in the uneven light. Down in the courtyard, knots of spectral folk gathered, muttering among themselves. A nervous anticipation filled the air, the scent of change.

'Caitrin,' Eichri said, halting as I put a hand on his sleeve. 'You look tired.'

'Too long at the books. I have a question for you, Eichri.'

'Ask it, then. These days, everything's questions. Pity there aren't more answers.'

'I understand you can go in and out of the monastery at Saint Criodan's without anyone noticing.'

The monk nodded. 'You need more supplies?'

'I don't need you to steal for me. Not exactly. Can you go into any part of that building, even if there's a locked door? I'm thinking of the secret part of the library, the place where it seems Nechtan obtained his incantation to summon the host.'

'Perhaps.'

'If the counter spell is to be found in writing anywhere, it might perhaps be there, alongside the original charm. I thought maybe you could . . .'

'Slip in, find it, memorise it, come quietly back? If only it were so simple, Caitrin. You forget one critical detail. I cannot read. Even if I were to take a little sharp knife with which to sever a page from a book and slip it under my habit, how would I know which page to choose?'

I felt more than a little foolish. 'Can any of your brethren here at Whistling Tor read?'

'Never asked. I will if you like. It's immaterial, really – they can't go off the hill.'

'Wouldn't it be safe, provided you went too? Those monks seem so peaceable.' But then, Eichri himself had been in that mob that came to Nechtan's call, the day Mella died.

'We're none of us safe.' He fiddled with his peculiar necklace, moving the little bones along the cord that held them. 'The greatest fear for all of us, holy brothers included, is that we'll be let off the hill and perform some deed there's no forgiving, not if we wait an eternity of years. You heard what that woman said, the night of the council. Memories fade in time, and that makes it possible to bear each day as it comes. But some memories linger; some you can't wipe away completely. We've all got our share of those, and we're not keen to make new ones.'

I wanted to ask him what his own sin was, what deed had condemned him to become part of the host, but I couldn't get the words out. It felt like asking a man to whip himself for my entertainment. If Eichri decided to tell me his story one day, as Rioghan had his, I would listen without judgement.

'I'm a sinner unrepentant,' Eichri said, shrewd eyes fixed on me. 'What I did, I did purely for my own gain. I can't in all sincerity say I'm sorry. If I'm not sorry, I can't atone for my sins, supposing that's why I find myself back in this world. If there's no atonement, what choice have I but a return to that nothing place I was in before Nechtan performed his cursed experiment? I can't face that, Caitrin. I want to stay here; I want to go on living the life I have at Whistling Tor. It'd suit me very well if you never found a counter spell.'

'A sinner unrepentant?' I echoed. 'But you seem such a good person.'

'Ah, but you see good in everyone.'

After a moment, I said, 'There *is* good in everyone.'

'Even in that fellow who trussed you up and tried to haul you away off down the hill?'

I grimaced. 'It may be a long time before I learn to see the good in Cillian,' I told him. 'If it's there, it's buried deep.'

The eve of full moon, and a chill morning. Atop the wall, men-at-arms from the host moved through shreds of mist, dark figures appearing and disappearing as they kept their watch. If this was summer, Whistling Tor must be a bitter place when winter sank its teeth into the land. I walked to the pump huddled in shawl and cloak, and instead of carrying a bucket upstairs in my usual fashion, I made do with a brief splash of face and hands before heading for the warmth of the kitchen fire. Fianchu went off into the garden on business of his own.

A sound of voices as I approached the kitchen door. I was not the only one up early.

'If it'll set his mind at ease, I'll stay up here with her.' Olcan's voice. 'Me and Fianchu both.'

'You're needed down on the boundary.' Rioghan this time. I hesitated at the foot of the steps. 'If anything goes wrong, you must be in position to call Anluan and Magnus back.'

'Maybe so,' Olcan said, 'but if he doesn't think Gearróg can do the job on his own, Anluan's going to insist on one of us staying. If it's not me, it has to be Magnus. And if Magnus stays, Anluan goes down there on his own. That's not right.'

I walked up the steps and through the doorway. 'If you're talking about who's supposed to watch over me this morning,' I said, 'I don't see why anyone need do so. I'll do what I usually do, sit in the library and work. The inner door can be bolted and Gearróg can guard the other.'

'Anluan says Gearróg on his own isn't enough,' Magnus said. 'Cathaír's been given the job of controlling the guards up on the wall. We've made various other suggestions, but Anluan doesn't like any of them. Bit of a sticking point.'

I glanced from one man to another. Magnus had on the field armour he had worn the day I first saw him in the settlement, a protective chest-piece of old leather, padded clothing beneath it, and buckled leather strips bracing his forearms. His grey locks flowed over his broad shoulders. He looked every bit the warrior. There was a frown on his brow, and it was mirrored on Olcan's features. Rioghan was tapping on the table with his long fingers. Time was getting short.

'I'll be perfectly safe with Gearróg,' I said. 'But if Anluan has doubts, why can't Eichri stay?'

'Eichri's required out on the hill, as am I,' Rioghan said. 'Everyone has a job for the morning.'

'Well,' said Magnus, lifting the porridge pot from hearth to table, 'whatever happens, I suppose we still have to eat. Might almost be simpler if you came down to the settlement with us, Caitrin. I think that's what he wants.'

'That wouldn't be right. These are councillors, not ordinary messengers. If they can't speak Irish, they'll bring a capable interpreter.' The idea of accompanying Anluan on his mission felt completely wrong. Whatever I might wish I could be to him, I was only a hired helper, one of the ordinary folk. 'I'll talk to him,' I said.

'Now might be a good time.' Magnus jerked his head towards the open doorway. Looking out, I saw the chieftain of Whistling Tor standing by the pump, gazing up towards the half-visible guards on the high walkway. His hair, neatly tied back with a cord, made a single bright note in the misty grey of the morning. He wore his long cloak over a sombre outfit that matched the stone wall behind him.

I went out. As I approached he turned towards me and I saw the look on his face, tight-jawed, grim, apprehensive.

'It will be all right.' I reached to take his hands, heedless of who might be watching, and his mouth softened slightly. 'We all have faith in you. You should have faith in us.'

'Faith,' he echoed. 'It's an elusive thing. I can't believe I'm about to do this.'

'You wouldn't step back now, would you, right at the end?'

'No, Caitrin. I've set this in motion, and now I must be the leader it seems folk need here. It's not the end, of course; today's meeting is the beginning of something so big I can hardly bring myself to think of it. Caitrin, I spoke to you before about the risks, not just that I may lose my control of the host once I cross the boundary, but . . . You know what happened in the past. I'm worried about you. There are too many elements of this that we cannot predict.'

'I'll be fine in the library. I'll have Gearróg.' After a moment I added, 'And Muirne, if she's prepared to sit with me.'

'You mustn't be in the library.' His tone was adamant. 'Stay out of doors, but close to the house. The safest place for you is Irial's garden. I'll ask Olcan to leave Fianchu with you. Even so, this troubles me.'

He was thinking of what had happened to his mother, perhaps. But the situation was not at all the same. Besides, he'd said himself that Emer's death might have been accidental. 'I'm sure I'll be safe,' I told him. 'How soon are you going?'

He glanced up at the walkway again; the pacing forms of the guards flickered, dreamlike, amongst the shrouds of mist. 'We've men on watch who will alert us when the Norman party rides into view,' he said. 'That's if anything can be seen through this mist. Magnus says we'll have time to get down to the settlement before them, if they use the Whiteshore road.'

Magnus chose that moment to appear in the kitchen doorway. 'Breakfast,' he said. 'You can't be a hero on an empty stomach.'

'Not much of a hero,' murmured Anluan. 'But perhaps I can learn. Shall we go in, Caitrin?' He held out his arm. The gesture was formal, but as I slipped my arm through his, I had the curious feeling that each of us was incomplete without the other. Apart, we would always be wanting; together, we were whole.

Since I could not tell him this, I said, 'Come home safely,' my voice so quiet that I might have been speaking to myself.

The sun rose higher and the mist dissipated. A call came from the sentries atop the wall, and Anluan and Magnus set off down the hill. With Fianchu following me, I went to Irial's garden as Eichri, Rioghan and Olcan headed for their various positions. Everything had been planned to the last detail.

I settled on the bench with a basket of mending, needing an occupation for my hands. My stomach was tying itself in knots. I would not be at ease until I saw Anluan walk back in through that archway, smiling his crooked smile and telling me all had gone to plan.

Muirne had not been present at breakfast, but she joined me in the garden soon after the men left. She did not offer to help with the mending, simply sat at the other end of the bench and watched me, features grave, hands folded in her lap. Gearróg was stationed just inside the archway, spear in hand. Neither of them had much conversation today.

Time passed. A little breeze rustled the leaves of the birch tree. I patched the knee on a pair of Magnus's trousers and repaired a seam on a grey tunic of Anluan's. With my eyes on the plain linen, I saw instead his wan face, his troubled eyes, a lock of his hair escaping its cord to tumble down over his pale brow, frost and flame. I imagined him standing as straight as he could, facing Lord Stephen's emissaries; in my mind, I heard his deep voice speaking with such authority that everyone sat up to listen. He could do it. Of course he could.

The tunic was done. I folded it neatly and put it back in the basket. I got up and stretched, glancing at the sky and trying to judge how much time had passed. I walked around the pathway, stooping to examine the heart's blood plant. Buds were developing, their tight-furled forms barely hinting at the brilliant colour to come. Within a turning of the moon, the blooms would be ready for harvest. There was a lean-to building against the garden wall, a low stone structure that I assumed might hold tools, including perhaps equipment for distillation and decoction; a herbalist like Irial must have had such paraphernalia. I'd never seen the place open; the door was bolted. Perhaps nobody had used it since his time. I entertained a brief vision of myself in there, making a perfect batch of heart's blood ink. Then I walked around the pathway again, thinking how long ago that day seemed when Anluan had accepted my wager.

'You appear agitated, Caitrin.' Muirne's voice was calm as a millpond. 'Are you having second thoughts about this plan?'

'Of course not!' I snapped, my fraying nerves getting the better of me. 'The plan makes good sense. Everyone agreed to it.' *Except you.* I sat and fished in the basket for more mending, something to stop me from getting into an argument with Muirne, which would achieve nothing beyond upsetting me further. 'I'm sorry,' I made myself say. 'I am a little edgy.' It seemed I'd even upset Fianchu. He'd been lying at my feet, but now his head was up, his ears were pricked, and a subterranean growling was issuing from his throat. 'Be calm, Fianchu, lie down, good boy.'

The dog ignored me, scrambling up to stand alert, the warning growls becoming barks of challenge. Alerted by the sound, Gearróg came along the path towards us. 'What is it – aaaghh!' His words were lost in a groan of pain as he crumpled to his knees, his spear falling with a metallic clang to the stones of the path. He doubled up, shielding his head with his hands. His chest heaved; a powerful shaking possessed his body.

I jumped to my feet, mending forgotten. 'Gearróg, what's the matter, what's wrong?' He was in terrible pain, hunched over and moaning. Fianchu began to whine, as if he, too, was in agony. A moment later, as I was crouched beside Gearróg, trying to get him to kneel up, the big dog bolted out through the archway and off into the forest. 'Muirne, help me!' My guard's body was seized by retching spasms; he fought for breath. 'Fetch someone, quickly! We need help!'

No answer. I glanced frantically over towards the seat, but nobody was there. During the commotion, it seemed Muirne had slipped away from the garden.

'Gearróg, I'll get help. Try to lift your head, here . . .'

Gearróg swung out suddenly, catching me across the arm and chest. I went sprawling backwards onto the flagstones, jarring hip and elbow. 'Stop, make it stop!' he yelled. 'Keep away! No! No!' The arm swung again. I ducked my head to avoid it. His eyes were wild. Whatever he was seeing, it surely wasn't me.

My heart hammering, I got onto one knee. Try to help him or run away as fast as I could? He swiped the air, then clapped his hands over his ears. His features were twisted in a grimace of agony. 'Make it stop!' he screamed.

Somewhere out in the forest Fianchu was barking. I crouched just out of Gearróg's reach.

'Gearróg, it's Caitrin.' I hardly knew my own voice, it was shaking so much. 'Caitrin, you remember? I'm trying to help you. Just hold on a little longer. I'm going to fetch someone –'

Shouts broke out on the walkway, not warnings of coming danger but cries of pain. I looked up. Men were staggering, falling, clutching onto whatever they could find to stop themselves from a long drop to the courtyard. Weapons clattered down as hands lost their grip. Two men were at each other's throats, fingers squeezing, legs braced, eyes bulging. Another snatched up a fallen knife and charged along the narrow way, screaming.

'Muirne!' I yelled. 'Muirne, where are you? I need help!' A warrior leaped up onto the parapet, spreading his arms as if to launch himself into flight, and there was Catháir, seizing the man's leg, shouting, 'No, you fool! Hold fast! Hold fast, all of you!' One of the monks was cowering in a corner, trying to fend off a big fellow with an axe. Dear God, what was this?

A sudden chill by my right side. The ghost child was there, Róise clutched in one hand, the other slipping into mine. 'Catty,' she whispered, 'my head hurts.' And then, sharp and distinct, there came to my nostrils the smell of smoke. I whipped around, the child's hand still in mine, Gearróg huddled on the pathway in front of me, and saw it seeping out under the library door, an insidious grey blanket. Through the glazed window something flickered, golden, deadly. The library was on fire. The manuscripts. The books. The grimoires – the ancient pages would go up like a torch. A burst of light, a flare of heat and the history of Whistling Tor would be gone. With it would go any chance of finding the counter spell.

'No!' shrieked Gearróg, rolling over, booted feet kicking, arms threshing. 'Make it stop! Leave me be!'

Cold sweat broke out on my skin. From behind the library door I thought I could hear the crackling of hungry flames. I stood frozen as the child clutched at my skirt and began a piercing wail, 'No fire! No fire!' Gearróg had come up onto his knees and was groping for his spear, which had rolled out of reach. His arm was twitching so violently that for now he had little chance of grasping the weapon. The smoke thickened around us. Blind panic was only a breath away.

'I need you to help me,' I said, squatting down beside the ghost child. 'Take Róise up to my bedchamber right now. Run as fast as you can. You can get into my bed if you want. Stay there until I come, however long it takes.'

She obeyed, silent now, running across Irial's garden through the drifting smoke and out through the archway. I turned back to find Gearróg on his feet with the spear in his hand, four paces away and facing me. His eyes were desperate. He would kill me without hesitation if he believed that would silence the voice in his head. Behind him the library burned.

'Gearróg,' I said shakily, 'you're a good man. You're a warrior. Anluan needs you. He needs you to stand guard until he comes back up the hill. It won't be long.'

The warrior shifted from foot to foot, his fingers clenching and unclenching on the spear shaft. His eyes darted from me to the walkway, where men still fought and yelled and fell. 'Anluan doesn't want me hurt,' I said. 'I'm his friend. I'm your friend. Gearróg, the library is on fire. Please let me pass so I can save the books.' I edged forward; he stood immobile, blocking the way. God help me, if I didn't get in there soon it would all be gone. 'Gearróg, let me pass! Please!'

Gearróg lurched to one side, striking his temple with a clenched fist. 'Stop your wretched ravings,' he muttered. This time he wasn't talking to me. 'Hush your poisonous prattling! Let a man do his work!'

Up on the walkway, someone started to sing. It was a ragged, desperate sort of song, dredged from old memory, the kind of tune a man reaches for when there is nothing else to keep the mind from tumbling right over into madness. *Stand up and fight, men of the hill* . . . A creaky old voice, not quite in tune, but raised high enough to cut through the mayhem of shouts and screams, scuffling and cursing:

'Stand up and fight, men of the hill
Dauntless in courage, united in will
Swing your swords proudly, hold your heads high . . .'

Gearróg was staring up towards the walkway as new voices joined in, first one, then another, then more and more in an uncertain chorus. *'Brothers together,'* he muttered, *'we live and we die . . .'*

I dashed past him, along the path, up the steps, pausing for a moment to snatch my handkerchief from my belt and press it over my nose and mouth before I pushed open the library door. In my mind a desperate list of priorities was forming itself: Irial's notebooks, which were nearest to the door and might not yet be damaged. The grimoires, left in a stack beside my work table. Nechtan's documents and the transcriptions I had already completed. The box with the obsidian mirror . . .

The place was thick with smoke. I couldn't see an arm's length before my eyes. Choking, coughing, I groped my way over to the shelves where Irial's notebooks were stored, ready to grab an armful and flee out into the garden with them. I had no chance of putting out the fire. By the time I fetched even one bucket of water, everything could be gone, and Gearróg was in no fit state to help. My arm swept along the shelf, but Irial's records were not there – someone had moved them. Or was I in the wrong place? The smoke was stinging my eyes, making my nose run, creeping into my throat. My breath rasping, I screamed, 'Muirne! Anyone! Help!'

No books on the floor beneath the shelf; nothing at all of Irial's. Smoke wrapped me in a clinging shawl; I could no longer see the open doorway. I fumbled blindly towards the place where I had piled up the grimoires. My head felt odd. I could see patterns in the smoke, faces with gaping mouths, hands with rending claws . . . 'Muirne,' I whispered, or maybe I only spoke in my mind. *Someone come . . .*

I fell to my knees and crept forwards. Every instinct told me not to breathe, but I had to, and with every breath my chest hurt more. *Keep going, Caitrin.* The grimoires . . . I couldn't let the counter spell be burned to nothing . . . *You can do it, Caitrin. This way . . . this way . . .*

I reached the stack of books and collapsed beside it, eyes stinging, chest heaving. Dimly, I registered surprise that I could see no flames in the library, only the dense, choking cloud of smoke. My hands fastened around a book; one seemed to be all I had the strength to lift. Now out, out into the garden and fresh air . . . Which way? I turned my head, but the place was full of the suffocating blanket. Where was the door? My head reeled; the smoke swirled around me. I couldn't seem to catch my breath. *You're going to die, Caitrin. You're going to die for a book full of ridiculous love potions and improbable straw-to-gold charms.*

I dropped the grimoire and began to crawl, trying to feel my way out. The leg of a table. A box – the chest holding Nechtan's wretched mirror. My head struck something hard: the bench. A chair. A smaller table. Not far now.

The door slammed shut. The air seemed to tremble around me. The smoke thickened. I covered the last distance on my belly, retching, feeling the poison seep into my lungs. I clawed my way up the wall, clutching for the iron bar that held the door closed. I wrenched at it. Why wouldn't it move? Why were my hands so weak? Around me everything dimmed, as if the day was already over. My fingers could not hold on to the latch. *Help*, I mouthed. *Someone help me.* But all that came was the dark.

chapter ten

rifting. Dizzy. Sounds coming and going, lancing through my head. Voices, muffled. A clanking of metal. Trying to swim up . . . A heaviness holding me down.

'Don't move, Caitrin. You're safe. Lie still.'

His voice. Tears running down my face. Every breath a little mountain to be climbed, a new test of courage.

'You're safe, Caitrin. Don't try to move.'

No breath to speak. There was something I had to say, but all that came out was a croak. 'Books . . .'

His hand against my cheek, warm, strong. 'As if the books mattered,' he said.

'Tell . . .'

'The books are safe. Don't try to talk. If you can, take a sip of water. Here.'

A cup at my lips. Sip, swallow. Fire. Pain. Something wrong with me.

'Lie back, Caitrin. I'm here, and so is Magnus. Rest now.'

'. . . hold . . .'

His fingers laced themselves through mine. I turned my head against the pillow and fell back into the dark.

Swimming up again, not so slow this time. Eyes open. Beams, stones, spider webs. A man in a blue cloak riding into battle; a hound at the horse's heels. A little draught stirred the embroidered panel. Dust danced in lantern light. My own chamber, and late in the day. Nobody holding my hand, but someone in the room with me. I turned my head. Magnus was sitting on a stool a few paces away, a big sword across his knees. He had a cloth in his hand, and was polishing the blade. A blood-red glint in the shining metal. Signs of war.

'Magnus.' My voice crackled like an old woman's. 'Can I have some water?' It still hurt to breathe, but maybe not so much as before.

His hand lightly against my back, steadying me as he reorganised the pillows. The cup at my lips again. I drank deep, relishing the coolness. My throat felt as if it had been scraped raw.

'It'll hurt for a while.' The big man's tone was matter-of-fact. 'Smoke does that. You've been lucky, Caitrin. Seems you somehow locked yourself in. Gearróg broke the door down. We got back just as he was carrying you out.' It was clear to me that Magnus did not believe this fairly simple account of what had happened.

'Anluan?' Why wasn't he here? Had I imagined those soft words, that gentle touch?

'You've had quite a few folk anxious over your state of health, and him more than anyone. I packed him off to rest. He didn't go willingly.'

'Magnus, what . . .' It seemed an immense effort to ask; there was so much I needed to know.

'All in good time.' His gaze was the calmly assessing one of a person who has cared for more than his share of the sick and wounded. 'Drink some more of that water first, and we'll get you a bowl of broth.' He went to the door, stuck his head out and said, 'Caitrin's awake. Send someone down to the kitchen for supplies, will you, lad? Broth is all she can take right now. There's a pot beside the fire.'

'Who's out there?' I asked. In my head was the image of men from the host up on the walkway, striking out at random as if the whole world was their enemy. I saw Gearróg writhing, his eyes

251

full of demons. My arm was sore. When I rolled back the sleeve of my gown, it was to reveal a deep purple bruise.

'The first thing he's going to ask you is who gave you that.' Magnus pulled the stool up beside my bed and sat down. He had placed the sword atop a chest, his hands careful.

'It was an accident. Magnus, are they all safe? The men of the host, I mean? There was a . . . they seemed to . . .'

His mouth formed a grim smile. 'We've had an account of it; there's been no reason to doubt that story. Safe? If you mean, has anyone died twice over, I don't think that's possible. As for the fire, that was an odd thing, very odd. Some of your documents sustained a bit of damage from the smoke, but nothing was burned. The whole thing seemed . . . conjured; not quite real.'

'The smoke was perfectly real,' I said, my skin prickling with unease. 'What are you suggesting, Magnus? That it was all just . . .' I couldn't bring myself to say it. *It was devised with the sole purpose of getting rid of me.* I remembered Róise swinging, swinging from the wire.

'I'm not suggesting anything,' he said, but he was avoiding my eye. 'Caitrin, this has shocked Anluan badly. Both of us, to tell the truth. When Olcan called out to us from the barrier, and we came out and saw the smoke, it was . . . It brought back some very unwelcome memories. I've never run so fast.'

I scrutinised my companion more closely, seeing what I had not taken in before: the pallor of his strong features, the frown between the bushy grey brows, the set of his shoulders, not as square as was customary. 'Fianchu raised the alarm?'

'He raced down to where Olcan was on guard, and Olcan came to fetch us. We ran back up the hill. Anluan couldn't keep up; he made me go on ahead. God, Caitrin, I expected to find the same thing as last time, the very same, the house half burned away and you lying dead in the embers.'

'What are you saying?' My voice was a whisper.

'Emer died in a fire. The circumstances were much the same. Perhaps you've thought Anluan weak or cowardly for his reluctance to leave the hill, especially when there was such a need. You might have wondered why I didn't encourage him to try it earlier.'

'I never thought him weak, Magnus. Will you tell me the whole story?'

He got up and began to pace, as if the chamber were too small to contain what he was feeling. 'It was in the time when Emer's brother was chieftain. As I told you before, he had a low opinion of Irial; couldn't forgive his sister for marrying Nechtan's kin. Irial recognised the need to forge new links, since Whiteshore was no longer the ally it had been. We discussed it at length, and when he got an unexpected invitation to attend a council at Silverlake, to the southeast, he decided to risk going. I went with him, since he had to have a personal guard. Emer was expecting another child; she didn't want to undertake a long ride. She insisted she'd be safe here with Olcan and Fianchu and the small number of other folk we had working at Whistling Tor in those days. It was a sort of test. If the visit went well, Irial planned to hold a council of his own involving a much wider group of local chieftains. He had hopes that Whistling Tor could regain the status it had before Nechtan's time. An ambitious plan. Risky, of course, but the host had been quiet in Irial's time, and like you he was prepared to trust them. Emer was so proud of him, Caitrin. It shone in her eyes as she bid us farewell.

'The council went well. Irial spoke with conviction; folk listened to him. We rode home with high hearts. What we found was the great hall blackened and burned, Emer dead, young Anluan shrunk to a little shadow with his eyes full of death and terror. He wouldn't say exactly what he'd seen, and none of the others had witnessed it – everyone had been elsewhere, busy, only realising that there was a fire and that she was trapped when it was far too late to save her. Anluan wasn't hurt, not physically, but . . . he wasn't the same. There was some damage in him, deep down.'

The woman in the mirror, screaming . . . Oh, God . . . No wonder Anluan had struggled so hard with the decision to risk going off the hill. No wonder he'd had that look on his face this morning.

'When we saw the smoke today, both of us expected the same thing,' Magnus said. 'That run up the hill was . . . I've never seen him so angry with himself, cursing his lame leg, cursing his own poor judgement, cursing the host . . . We were sure we'd find you dead. Me, I was looking ahead, seeing him the way his father was when he gathered up what was left of Emer . . . Sitting on the ground, cradling her poor burned body to him, specks of ash floating around them like dark snow . . . I've seen a lot, Caitrin, and I've heard a lot. War is my calling, and a warrior gets his fair share of blood and sorrow. I'd never heard a man make the sort of sounds Irial made that day. I took Anluan away; tended to him in my own quarters. Olcan looked after the farm. The others helped with what had to be done. Muirne was the only one Irial would take any heed of. He had nothing left for his son. He was consumed by grief and guilt. Such a loss can make a person selfish. Don't get me wrong, I loved the man like a brother. But Anluan had sorrow of his own to bear, and so did I.'

'You never found out who was responsible for that fire?'

He shook his head. 'There were no witnesses, save possibly Anluan, and he wouldn't talk, or couldn't. I found no clues. But Irial was convinced the host was responsible; that by leaving the Tor, he had brought down this fate on Emer. It seemed to me that fire might just as likely have started with a draught and a candle. After today, I'm not so sure.'

'Why would the host, or anyone else for that matter, want to harm me? I'm nobody.'

'You're somebody to us,' Magnus said quietly. 'Caitrin, I've talked too long. You're not well, you should be resting.'

A tap at the open door. There stood Cathaír, holding a laden tray. Beside him, her hair turned to a pale nimbus by the sunlight behind her, was the ghost child, clasping a little jug in careful hands.

'Bring it in,' Magnus said, but Cathaír did not move beyond the doorway. The child came in, stepping over to set the jug on the storage chest. She crept to the foot of my bed and stood there, eyes downcast, fingers pleating little folds in the blanket. There was something in her stance, and in that of Cathaír, that troubled me greatly.

'How long was I unconscious?' I asked as Magnus retrieved the tray. The moment he took it from Cathaír, the young warrior backed off and vanished along the gallery.

'A while. Don't trouble yourself with all this now, Caitrin. Eat and rest. We'll keep you safe.'

I drank the broth in cautious sips. My throat felt as rough as dry leather. It hurt to breathe, but the warm liquid was soothing. 'Where is everyone?' I asked. 'Rioghan and Eichri? Olcan and Fianchu?' I realised that I had forgotten the most important question of all. 'The Normans! What happened down at the settlement?'

'Funny the way things play out sometimes. It went well. The host stayed within the boundaries of the hill. Anluan made his speech, the Normans listened, they said their piece, he stood up to them. They were just getting into the next part, about how foolish we'd be to build this into an armed conflict, since they'd be sure to make mincemeat of us all, when we heard Olcan bellowing from beyond the barrier, and the fellows they'd left on guard yelling back at him. Then we came outside and saw the smoke.'

'Anluan defied Lord Stephen's emissaries? He refused to give in to their demands?'

Magnus turned a very level look on me. I wondered that I had not noticed before how like his eyes were to my father's. 'What else did you expect?' he said simply.

'So it's war.'

'When he thought he'd lost you, it seemed to me for a bit that he'd give up the fight. I was wrong. He won't step back from this now, Caitrin, not after rallying the host, not after making that speech of defiance to the Norman councillors. If war comes to Whistling Tor, we'll fight and fall under the banner of a true leader.'

The afternoon passed. I coaxed the ghost child to perch on the end of my bed, with my shawl wrapped around her. Magnus raised his brows but made no comment. I wondered that he did not go off to attend to his usual work, but I did not ask. His strong, quiet presence made me feel safe, and I wanted him to stay.

Olcan came up to see me, Fianchu by his side and apparently none the worse for wear. The forest man had a long look at the mirror on my wall, the one I had brought down from the tower, but he made no comment on it, merely nodded sagely as if its presence in my bedchamber was exactly what he would have expected.

At a certain point I heard Rioghan calling from down in the garden, and Catháir came to the door again.

'I'm wanted down there.' The young warrior had his eyes down-turned, his head tilted away, as if he didn't want me to notice him. 'Permission to leave my post?'

'Go,' Magnus said. 'You'll be asked to give your account of what happened, no doubt, along with the rest of them. Tell the truth; that's all you need do.'

'Catháir,' I put in, 'is all well with you? How is Gearróg?' The image of my guard writhing in pain, hands pressed over his ears, was strong in my mind. It hardly seemed consistent with the story that he had broken down a locked door to save me not long afterwards.

Catháir gazed fixedly at the wall. 'We're not worthy of your interest, lady. Nor your compassion. We failed.'

A moment's silence. 'Because a voice tormented you, gave you intolerable pain, made the men crazy?' I asked him quietly. 'I saw you doing your very best to control them up there, Catháir. I saw how Gearróg wrestled with it. From what Magnus tells me, no lasting harm was done. I did think I heard singing, as if you men were making an effort to hold together against difficult odds.'

'That was the old fellow, Broc. He pulled us out of it. Fact remains, when the frenzy came on us the men broke ranks, lost their discipline.'

The frenzy. Nechtan had used the same word, describing the host running amok in its bloody attack on Farannán's people. Whatever this was, it had been here a long time. 'You kept to the hill and nobody was hurt,' I said. 'You achieved what you agreed to at the council.'

'You were hurt.' Still he would not look at me. 'We couldn't help you; couldn't see or hear straight. We can't put the blame on the frenzy. If a man loses his courage in battle, if he doesn't stick to his post, he's got nobody to blame but himself.'

Magnus cleared his throat. 'Go and account for yourself to Rioghan, lad. He's a councillor of long experience, he'll weigh things up fairly. Lord Anluan was angry before. He said things he may possibly regret later. He'll realise in time that he took a calculated risk, as we all did, Caitrin included. If things didn't turn out quite as he hoped, at least part of the responsibility is his. Go on, now. As for the future, our chieftain's just committed us to war, and if we're not to repeat today's errors, we need to put all our strength and skill into working out how.'

'My lady,' Cathaír muttered, then turned on his heel and was gone.

'Anluan was angry? What exactly did he say to them?'

'You know how he can be,' said Magnus. 'Tore into them for not coming to your aid; told them they were worthless and way-ward, and a lot more of the same. They just stood there and took it. This frenzy, I've heard them talk of it before. *The voice*, some of them call it. Either it gives you a blinding headache, or it fills your mind with bad things from your own past. Or both at once. It'd be hard work staying at your post and keeping alert while that was playing havoc in your head.'

'Where do you think it comes from, this voice?' Snippets from the documents started to come back to me. *Sweet whispers; I must not heed them*. A voice, yes, but it hardly sounded like the same phenomenon. *Night by night a whispering in my ear. It tempts me to despair*. 'It must be very powerful if it can disable the entire host all at once.' I wondered, not for the first time, if Nechtan could have left an enchantment that continued its fell work long after his death. 'Were Rioghan and Eichri stricken by it?'

'Only to the extent of a headache. Muirne was more badly affected. A pain that drove out all reason, that was how she described it.'

Muirne had suffered the same pain as Gearróg? That was not what my memory told me. But then, she had been behind me when he fell, and then she'd disappeared. I should give her the benefit of the doubt, at least. 'I would like to speak to Muirne, Magnus. Do you think she would come up here?'

'She was looking a bit shaken. Leave it till later, that's my advice. You shouldn't be doing anything but resting, Caitrin. Lie down again.' He glanced at the ghost girl, huddled under the shawl with not much more showing than wisps of white hair and frightened eyes. 'I don't suppose *she* saw how the fire started?'

'I sent her away. The voice drove Gearróg a little mad. I was afraid for her; she's so small.'

Magnus folded his arms and gave me a shrewd look. 'So Gearróg did hit you,' he said.

'Not me. He struck out at something he thought was there. He had a kind of convulsion, a fit. I happened to be in the way.'

'Mm-hm.'

'It's true, Magnus. I saw how all the men were behaving, Gearróg included. This thing is powerful.' I lay back on the pillows, considering what I had learned. Nechtan had been so sure he had got things right. He'd been so careful in his preparations. But somehow the great experiment had gone awry. I saw the aftermath, the wayward host, the battles, the slaughter, the blood and hatred that had flowed from one man's obsession. I saw the accidents, the errors, the fire and flood and careless cruelty. 'Magnus,' I said, 'this voice, the one that wreaks havoc within the host – that alone could have caused almost everything that has gone wrong since Nechtan brought them forth. Whoever's doing it would wait until Nechtan or Conan was out in the field, in the midst of a battle, and then it would speak to the host, and they'd go into what they call the frenzy. Gearróg said it turns them upside down and inside out, so they don't know what they're doing. The frenzy could make people light fires. It could . . .' It could send people into such despair that they would kill themselves. I would not say that. But it seemed to me the voice that caused this frenzy could also speak to the living. Indeed, perhaps I had heard it myself, telling me I had been corrupted by Nechtan's fleshly desires. It was not only cruel, it was clever. 'Is that the family curse?' I asked him. 'The ever-present voice, meddling with people's attempts to set this right? Does Anluan hear it?'

'You'd need to ask him that. It doesn't speak to me, nor to Olcan. Is it the curse? I can't say. Nobody knows who laid the curse on Whistling Tor, or what exactly was meant by it. The way I see it, there's one brighter note in this. Folk always said it was a hundred-year thing, Whistling Tor condemned to a hundred years of ill luck or failure or sheep diseases or whatever interpretation people decided to put on it. Seems to me the hundred years must be nearly up. That's a powerful reason for Anluan to follow through on his defiant statement to Lord Stephen. If you take such things as curses seriously.'

I thought about this awhile. 'You mean this might all come to an end even without the counter spell?'

'Maybe. The way Anluan was speaking not so long ago, he's seeing things a bit differently since you nearly got yourself killed. I doubt if he'll want you to go on looking through those books of spells. What happened just now has shaken him badly.'

'I should talk to him,' I said. 'I have to get up anyway, I must go to the privy. Besides, you shouldn't be spending your time watching over me.'

'You'll have a hard time convincing him it's safe to leave you on your own.'

'Maybe if he sees me walking around . . .' I swung my legs over the side of the bed, smoothed down my skirt and rose to my feet. The chamber spun; my knees buckled. Magnus caught me before I fell.

'Then again,' he said, 'if he sees you like this he might order you back to bed for a few days and stand guard over you himself. I'll carry you.'

Down in the courtyard the warriors of the Tor were assembled in all their strange variety, listening to Rioghan as he paced up and down before them.

'. . . techniques for dealing with this kind of thing. It can be something quite simple – counting in your head, repeating a rhyme, concentrating on a pattern you've remembered, anything to block out the distraction.'

'Distraction. Is that what you call it?' That was the tallest of the men-at-arms, the one who usually carried a pike.

'That's the way you have to treat it, even if it hurts fit to blow your head apart.' Rioghan's tone was measured; if I had been one of the men, I would have found it reassuring. 'That's what Broc knew and the rest of you didn't. You've him to thank for getting you out of this mess, him and the fact that he's seen more battles than Donn here's seen iron nails.'

A ripple of appreciative laughter. Then Cathaír spotted Magnus walking towards the main door with me in his arms. Heads turned towards us, and a sudden hush fell over the courtyard. Rioghan nodded respectfully in my direction, then resumed his address. 'You see what can result if you lose concentration. You were lucky this didn't turn out any worse. Next time around, we won't just be manning the defences and keeping ourselves out of trouble, we'll be fighting a battle. If the frenzy comes on you just as you're about to run a Norman through with your spear, are your bowels going to turn to water? Are you going to attack the comrade standing next to you? You are not. And I'll tell you why not. Because every day, between now and the time we march down there to defend Whistling Tor, you'll all be working so hard you won't have time to listen to anything but your leaders' orders. If you didn't like what Lord Anluan had to say to you before, make sure you don't give him cause to say it again.'

'Magnus,' I murmured as he manoeuvred me inside and out of view, 'I didn't see Gearróg there.'

'He may have saved your life, but he wasn't looking happy when we first came up the hill. Off somewhere on his own having a think, that's my guess. Same as Anluan.'

'I thought you said Anluan was resting.'

'I said that's what I told him to do. You know and I know how likely it is that he followed my advice.'

After a visit to the privy and a wash, I felt strong enough to walk on my own, though it was still an effort to catch my breath. Magnus was all for taking me straight back to my chamber, but I persuaded him that one of his herbal draughts would be good for me. I sat at the kitchen table to drink it while he chopped vegetables for a soup. He worked with one eye on me, as if he expected me to collapse the moment he looked away. I wondered whether I would have died if Gearróg had not broken the library door down, and who would have taken the news to my sister. There was a sudden powerful need in me to see Maraid again, to tell her I forgave her for deserting me. I was coming to understand that people make extreme choices, for good or ill, and that there are sometimes good reasons for them. I wanted to know that she and Shea were happy. I was by no means sure the life of a travelling musician would suit Maraid, a woman whose home hearth was precious to her.

'Do you have sisters or brothers, Magnus?'

The big man paused, knife in hand. 'A couple of brothers. I haven't seen them in long years; don't even know if they're still alive. Both fishermen, back home in the isles. The sea's a hard mistress; she doesn't discriminate.'

'Haven't you thought of going home, at least for a while?'

His smile was resigned rather than bitter. 'I can't, Caitrin. I left that life behind when I joined the *gallóglaigh*. I told my mother to count me gone for good; didn't want her spending her days in hope of a sight of me and being constantly disappointed. Anluan needs me here.'

'You must have been proud of him this morning.'

'I was.' He resumed cutting up the onions.

'And he's going to need you even more now he's committed Whistling Tor to standing up against a Norman attack. He'll need all of us.'

'As to that,' Magnus said, 'there might be a few hard choices ahead.'

'What do you mean?'

'Talk to Anluan, lass. He's going to go through with this, but he's not happy with what it means. I expect he'll come to find you again later, explain it all to you.'

'I'll talk to him now.' I got to my feet, steadying myself with one hand on the table. 'Where do you think he is?'

'You're not going anywhere on your own,' Magnus said.

A slight form appeared in the outer doorway: Muirne, with purple marks like bruises under her eyes. She hadn't been lying when she spoke of a debilitating headache.

'You are recovered, Caitrin.'

'I'm feeling somewhat better, thank you. Is your headache gone?'

A wintry smile. 'It will pass.'

'You left the garden rather quickly, earlier.'

'You could not understand. The pain is such that one does not act sensibly. I was unable to help you.'

Magnus was concentrating on his cookery, leaving the awkward conversation up to the two of us.

'Muirne, do you know where Anluan is?'

She took a step into the kitchen, then turned to adjust some cups on a shelf so they were perfectly in line. 'Yes,' she said.

'I need to talk to him. Will you walk there with me?' I glanced at Magnus, expecting him to order me straight back to bed.

'Where is he, Muirne?' the big man asked.

'Through there.' Muirne waved a hand vaguely towards the inner doorway. 'Close by.'

'I suppose it's all right, provided Caitrin doesn't go on her own,' Magnus said. 'He'll likely have words with me for letting you get out of bed so soon, Caitrin. Muirne, make sure you look after her.' He was lifting the ham down from the hook where I had hung it.

'Of course.' Muirne's brows went up, as if it were ridiculous to suggest she would be anything other than the most caring of companions. She took my arm – her touch chilled me – and we went through the inner doorway into the maze of chambers and hallways beyond.

I was foolish, perhaps. Once before, up in the tower, I had imagined her pushing me over the edge and down to oblivion. I had suspected her of shutting me in. I had even wondered if she was responsible for the damage to my belongings, though it was hard to imagine such a self-possessed creature shredding a gown or ripping out a doll's hair. As for her sudden disappearance earlier, just before I noticed the fire, she had a perfectly plausible explanation for that. I had seen how the frenzy affected the host, causing those men on the walkway to turn on one another, sending the steady Gearróg suddenly mad. I should be grateful to Muirne. If she had not removed herself from Irial's garden, she might have been driven to attack me.

'Something amuses you, Caitrin?'

'Not really. This has been a difficult day. I thought the whole library would be lost.'

'That would indeed be bad, since you seem to believe the host can be dismissed if only you find the right page. If the records were gone, you would have no reason to stay.'

After a moment I said, 'Fortunately, it seems nothing was burned. Some smoke damage, that was all. Not a real fire. Something else.'

'This is Whistling Tor. It is not like the outside world.' She stopped in front of a tall bronze mirror, hung flush with the stone wall. Verdigris crept across its surface like a spreading canker.

'In many ways that is true,' I said. 'But Whistling Tor exists in the outside world; it cannot be forever isolated, keeping only to its own rules. Without Magnus's trips down to the settlement and the readiness of those folk to send supplies back with him, this place could not keep going. Now the Normans are coming, and Anluan is going to put up a fight for his lands. He has gone into that outside world, Muirne, and he's made a pledge that he'll confront the threat bravely, he and the host together. Times are changing.'

Muirne had her hand flat on the wall beside the bronze panel. There was a small frown between her neat, pale brows. 'You've never really understood, have you?' she said, and the mirror swung away from the wall to reveal a shadowy space within, and steps going down. 'Anluan is down there. Come quietly.'

The hairs on my neck rose in unease. There was something deeply unsettling about this hidden entry, a menace, a wrongness. I hesitated, warning bells ringing loud in my head.

'Afraid?' Muirne said softly, her hand on my sleeve. 'It's quite safe. Come, I will show you.'

Something in her eyes led me down the steps after her. At the bottom a heavy iron-bound door stood ajar. We halted. Lamplight shone from within. The chamber was deep in the ground; there would be no windows here.

I took a breath to ask what the place was, but Muirne's cold fingers were suddenly against my lips, rendering me silent and still. Her eyes moved from me to the gap in the doorway, and when I followed her gaze I saw that Anluan was within the chamber. He sat on a bench, quite still, his back to us. He was staring into a mirror. I wondered why he had not immediately seen our reflections and turned. Then I glimpsed a swirl of movement and colour on the surface before him and realised that this was another of Nechtan's artefacts, showing something quite different from what stood before it. I should not be here watching. I should retreat or make a sound to alert him to my presence. But I couldn't. The images that held Anluan there were plainly visible, and they gripped me as it seemed they had him. Beside me, Muirne stood quiet as a shadow.

This was a mirror of glass with a reflective surface behind it, an object such as one would find only in the wealthiest of homes.

The images within it were as clear as if seen through a window on a sunny day. There was Anluan astride a tall black horse, riding fast along a dappled forest pathway. He sat straight, his shoulders square, his head high and his flame of hair streaming out behind him. A sword hung at his belt, a bow was slung over his shoulder. Two sleek hounds ran at the horse's feet. Behind him a company of men-at-arms rode two by two, one of them bearing a banner: a golden sun on a field the hue of a summer sky.

The image wavered and changed. I saw the same group of men, dismounted and at ease in a forest clearing, with the horses grazing nearby. While some of the warriors tended a camp fire and others rested under the trees, most stood in a circle watching a wrestling match – Anluan and another young man, half naked and locked in a tight bout, strength against strength. I saw at a glance that the Anluan of the vision had two strong arms, two strong legs, a stance that was straight and even, a perfect balance. He was in every respect a fine example of healthy manhood. For a moment he seemed to look straight out into the subterranean chamber, and I saw that his features were quite regular, with no trace of the odd lopsidedness that afflicted the real Anluan. It was so well balanced a face that it was completely lacking in character.

This was wrong. I should not be spying on the man I cared about most in all the world. I made to turn away, and Muirne put her hand on my shoulder. I started; I had forgotten she was there. There was a powerful, silent message in her touch: *Not yet, Caitrin.*

And then, ah, then came the third vision. Pale flesh in graceful rise and fall, dark hair curling down over a body all curves and softness, bright locks spilling across strong male shoulders. Hands stroking, caressing, tender at first, then more urgent as desire mounted fast. A confusion of limbs, a cascade of discarded garments. Lips touching, parting, touching again, clinging, tasting; tongues exploring. A body lifting; another plunging deep. I felt my face flame with heat. That was me in the vision, me naked and exposed, opening myself to him, straining him to me, giving him everything I had with joyous abandonment. The finely made man who tangled and tumbled in intimate embrace with me was Anluan; not the Anluan I knew and loved, the man of sun and shadows, my friend, my companion, whose oddities and troubles had shaped both his form and his character, but the perfect Anluan, the first among warriors, the one who could do all the things a true chieftain should do: ride, fight, lead. Make love to a woman.

The real Anluan drew a deep, ragged breath, then punched forward violently with his good left fist. The mirror shattered into a thousand pieces. There was blood on his hand; he looked at it as if he scarcely knew what it was. In the moment before I turned and fled, I glanced about the chamber and saw that it was indeed familiar. Shelves lined the walls; on them stood dusty paraphernalia: books, scrolls, jars, crucibles, strange instruments whose uses one could only guess at. A clever chimney to vent smoke; a row of pegs for the hanging of garments; a table big enough to hold a person, lying down. A pallet in a corner. I had seen this before. It was Nechtan's workroom.

I ran. I did not stop until I was almost back at the kitchen door, and even then I only halted because I knew I would faint if I didn't take time to catch my breath. The hallway spun around me. I forced myself to breathe slowly, leaning on the wall for support.

'The mirror of might-have-been.' Muirne had followed close behind me and now stood opposite, her hands behind her back, her face quite calm. She spoke in an undertone. 'One of Nechtan's cruellest. Anluan sees himself as he would be had the palsy not struck him: a man straight and tall, a handsome man, the kind others follow. The kind who can make his mark in that outside world you think so important, Caitrin. Of course, Anluan can never be such a man. Before you came here, he had accepted that.'

I had to stop myself from grabbing her shoulders and giving her a good shaking. 'Why did you show me this? He'd be mortified if he knew we were watching! I only want to help him, Muirne. I care about him. I thought you did, too.'

'Oh, Caitrin. No matter how much I care, I cannot change the way things are, and nor can you. Anluan will never be that fine man in the mirror. He will always have crooked shoulders and a hobbling leg. His right hand cannot hold a quill, let alone a sword. The palsy ruined him. He has nothing to offer a woman like you. Do you understand what I mean? A real woman wants children.

265

She wants to be . . . satisfied. If you want a real man, Caitrin, don't look here.'

Her careless cruelty was as brutal as a blow. I found words, perhaps not wise ones, but they came from my heart. 'I thought you loved him,' I said quietly. 'I see now that I was wrong. I pity you, Muirne. You don't seem to understand what love is.' I turned my back on her and walked away.

I hadn't wanted to trouble Magnus further, but when I went into the kitchen, my mind still reeling from what had happened, he took one look at me, scooped me up in his arms and carried me back to my bedchamber, muttering that he should never have let me out of his sight.

'You weren't gone long,' he observed once I was lying down under the covers. 'Did you speak to Anluan?'

'No, I couldn't find him. Magnus, you don't need to stay. I'll be fine. I just want to sleep now.' A lie twice over. I was far from fine and I would not sleep. But I did need to be alone so I could try to come to terms with this. How could I so much as look at Anluan now? My new-found knowledge must be painted all over my face. How could I speak to him? The simplest *good morning* must surely tremble with pent-up emotion. The vision still burned bright in me, and the bitter aftermath had lodged itself deep in my heart.

Magnus gave me a penetrating look, but evidently decided further questioning was not in order. 'You can't be left on your own, lass. It may not be strictly proper, the men of the house tending to you up here, but Muirne's the only female amongst the inner circle and I don't think she'd excel at this job. I'll call Rioghan. I do need to finish what I started in the kitchen.'

A piercing whistle from the doorway brought Rioghan, who seemed quite happy to sit with me now that he had finished briefing his unlikely army. He told me he'd sent the men of the host off to discuss matters amongst themselves. They were to return tomorrow with a preliminary plan for dealing with the frenzy next time around. It all sounded quite practical; oversimple, perhaps, but I did not say so. He was the strategist, after all, and right now I was a tired and sorry mess.

'Since I'm here,' Rioghan drew the stool closer to the bed and settled himself on it, his cloak making a carpet of crimson around him, 'we might talk further about your home situation, Caitrin, with these distant relatives who apparently believe themselves entitled to take control of your affairs. I feel that matter needs clarification.'

Why was he raising this now, out of the blue? Ita and Cillian seemed far away, hardly worth considering any longer. My heart was full of Anluan. 'I may not have much to contribute,' I said, managing a weak smile.

'All you need do is listen,' Rioghan said. 'And perhaps answer a small question or two.'

'All right.'

The ghost girl was at the door, looking out. I wondered if she was expecting Gearróg, who had been kind to her. Where was he?

'Now, Caitrin,' Rioghan said, 'I understand you and your sister were your father's only children, is that correct?'

'Yes.'

'The house where you were living was not tied in any way to your father's employment? It belonged to him outright?'

'It did. He never attached himself to a particular patron, though there were many who would have liked his exclusive services. We worked independently. That was what Father preferred. It gave us more control.'

'And the unpleasant Cillian and his mother are not close kin? What is the connection, exactly?'

This was more than a small question or two. 'Ita is a distant cousin of Father's. But she said that because Cillian was the only male kinsman, he had control of Father's property. There wasn't much. Really just the house. And the tools and materials in the workroom. She sold most of those.'

Rioghan turned his dark eyes on me. He clasped his long hands together, elbows on knees. 'This Ita lied to you, Caitrin,' he said.

'About Father's assets? How can you know that?'

'Where the assets are concerned, I cannot be certain, but I think it likely a skilled craftsman such as your father would possess far greater resources than you suggest, unless he was a heavy drinker, a lover of games of chance, or had some other vice on which to squander his earnings.'

If I'd had the energy I would have laughed at this. 'None of those. Father was a clean-living, hard-working man. Even if he'd wanted to do those things, he never had time.'

Rioghan nodded. 'I thought as much. You would not speak of him with such love and pride if he were anything else. Now let me tell you a fact or two. There is an established law on inheritance, and it still holds in all parts of Erin not under Norman rule. If a man has no sons, his daughters inherit, at the very least, a lifetime share in his estate. Your father's house, his land and all the chattels within should be yours and your sister's, in equal share. A distant cousin has no claim on your family home, Caitrin, nor on the tools of your father's craft, nor on stock or furniture or anything else your father owned. The fact that Cillian is a man makes no difference.'

So Ita had told me barefaced lies. This would once have been a stunning revelation, for the news held out the wonderful gift of independence, an entitlement to go on living in the house where we had once been the happiest of families. Perhaps, in time, I might have established myself as a scribe in my own right, earning a good living. Some part of my mind knew it was welcome news, but that life seemed so distant now. I tried to imagine myself returning to Market Cross to present the facts to Ita. I tried to picture her and Cillian being removed from the house they had taken under false pretences. But all I could see was Anluan's fist striking forward, and shards of glass flying through the air in that underground chamber. All I could hear was Muirne's precise little voice saying: *If you want a real man, Caitrin, don't look here.*

'Caitrin?'

I glanced over at Rioghan. He deserved a better response from me. 'I'm sorry,' I said. 'It's hard for me to concentrate, I feel so weak still. It's a pity I didn't know this before. But it doesn't matter now, since I don't intend to go back to Market Cross.'

He did not reply at first, and there was something awkward in the silence. Then he said, 'I'm tiring you; I should let you rest. Think about this, at least. When such a wrong has taken place, it seems to me one should try to see justice done. What about your sister, who has also been deprived of her entitlement and is, I presume, unaware of that? Wouldn't you confront these wrongdoers for her sake, if not for your own?'

Suddenly I felt so weary I couldn't lift my head from the pillow. A tear rolled down my cheek and I hadn't the strength to wipe it away. 'Some time. Maybe,' I murmured, but I knew I would never go back. Not for Maraid. Not for anything.

I closed my eyes and pretended to be asleep. The daylight faded; Eichri came and replaced Rioghan. Magnus came to the door with a tray of supper for me and left it in the chamber to go cold. Eichri departed and was replaced by Olcan. Fianchu settled on the floor. Beneath lowered lids I watched the ghost child creep over to curl up beside the massive hound. Outside, it was night.

At some point there was a quiet conversation out on the gallery: Olcan and Magnus discussing whether Fianchu would provide adequate security for me overnight. A belated fit of propriety had come over them, it seemed. They were still trying to decide which of them would spend the night outside my door when a deeper voice spoke.

'I'll stay up here. You both need your sleep.'

Anluan. My heart gave a wrenching leap and subsided, thumping painfully. He had come back at last. The maelstrom of feelings surged in me again.

'What about you?' I heard Magnus protest, not steward to chieftain but father to son. 'You need rest far more than either of us. Besides, this isn't your job.'

'No arguments, Magnus. Is Caitrin awake? Has she eaten supper?'

'She's been sleeping since before I brought her tray up. Upset, I think, as well as hurt. Anluan, this is not . . .' Magnus hesitated.

'Not proper? Not correct according to the rules of that world out there, the one we don't live in?' I hated it when Anluan used that sharp, antagonistic voice. That he would address the loyal Magnus thus was terribly wrong.

'It might seem improper to Caitrin, lad,' said Magnus quietly. 'She didn't grow up at Whistling Tor.'

'Magnus,' Anluan said, 'you can go.'

With my eyes shut, I heard two sets of footsteps retreating, Magnus's long stride, Olcan's steady pace, and then silence save for the slight whistle of Fianchu's breathing. The door closed. Anluan moved about the chamber for a little; I could not tell what he was doing. Eventually he drew the stool up to the bedside and sat down. In the silence that followed I counted my heartbeats and wondered what he was thinking. After what seemed a very long time, he took my hand, lifted it to his lips, then set it down again. I heard him let out a long breath, like a sigh.

I opened my eyes and looked up into his. Summer lake blue; I could drown in that colour. There was a difference in his face, as if the day's events had stripped away a layer. He looked a new man. He had been strong at the council. Now he seemed . . . formidable. Before, we had spoken easily, like close friends. Now the gap between us yawned wide and deep, and in it lay the splintered vision of what could never be. I could think of nothing at all to say.

'You're awake.' His voice cracked on the simple statement. He cleared his throat and tried again. 'Water. Let me get you some water, Caitrin.'

As he went to fill a cup I reached for my shawl, then realised the ghost child was wrapped up in it. The chamber was full of little draughts.

'You're cold.' He was beside the bed, holding the cup. 'You should be in a chamber with a fire, not up here.' He put the cup in my hand, then took off his cloak and laid it around my shoulders. His arm did not linger.

'Thank you, Anluan. You must be tired. Magnus said it went well this morning, with the Norman emissaries.' My words sounded awkward, artificial, as if I were making polite conversation with someone I hardly knew.

'So they're telling me.' He moved to stand awkwardly by the wall. He looked as if he wanted to be somewhere else. 'Caitrin, there's something I must say to you. I need to do it before I . . .' He glanced at the sleeping Fianchu and the little spirit curled up beside him. 'I need to do it right now.'

Now I was really cold; chill to the bone. 'Go on, then,' I said.

'This morning I spoke words of challenge down in the settlement. I vowed that I would lead my people against anyone who tried to take our land and our independence. I committed myself and my household to action. Most likely that means armed conflict. I did what you challenged me to do, Caitrin. I acted like a chieftain.'

'I know how much courage that took,' I said, but my voice

was small amid the shadows of the chamber. The image in my mind, his hand smashing the mirror, his cruel visions of the man he could never be, did not fit with this grim-jawed stranger. There was a core of iron in his voice. 'I always knew you could do it, Anluan. They will follow you, I'm sure of it – not only the host, but your people all over your territory. We'll stand by you, whatever happens . . .' I faltered to a halt. He had turned to look at me, and what I saw in his eyes made it impossible to go on. 'What?' I croaked. 'What's wrong? What is it you need to tell me?'

'Caitrin, you can't stay here. I want you to leave.'

I couldn't have heard right. 'What did you say?' I whispered.

'Your work is done here at Whistling Tor. You cannot stay any longer.'

'But –' In my visions of the future, some less realistic than others, I had not once considered the possibility that I might leave before summer's end.

'You wanted me to be a leader. A leader makes decisions, and this one is made. There's no point in arguing about it. I regret the inconvenience, but you must go as soon as possible. It will take a day or two to make some arrangements for you.'

This was a bad dream, it couldn't be happening. It made no sense at all. 'What about the grimoires? What about the counter spell?' Even as I spoke, it dawned on me that he had been working up to this for some time. Magnus had said, *There might be a few hard choices ahead.* Rioghan had made a point of explaining my legal rights and taxing me with the idea of going home. They'd known, the two of them. Perhaps even Muirne had known. 'I haven't finished the job you hired me for!' I protested. 'You said I had until the end of summer!' *I love you; please don't send me away.*

'We won't discuss this any further, Caitrin. The search for a counter spell has been overtaken by the probability of war. The grimoires must be set aside until the question of Stephen de Courcy is resolved one way or another. There's no longer any work for you at Whistling Tor. There's no reason for you to be here.'

'But, Anluan, even if there is no work, even if –'

'No.' The word cut off my hopes with brutal sharpness. 'I hired you for a job, Caitrin, and the job is done, as far as is possible. There is nothing else for you here.'

271

'But . . . I had thought . . . I had hoped . . .' With the images from the shattered mirror in my mind, I struggled for a response. 'Anluan, why –'

'Don't press me on this, Caitrin.' The tone was a warning.

I sat motionless. This was no well-meaning attempt to send me out of harm's way until the conflict was over. I would not be coming back in time of peace. He was banishing me forever.

'You will be paid for the whole summer, of course,' he said, almost as an afterthought. 'You'll need funds to travel home.'

'Home,' I said blankly. 'Home.' Cillian slamming my head into the door frame, making my teeth rattle; Ita pinching the tender flesh of my breast, setting her own mark on me as she hissed vile insults. Myself cringing, trembling, silent. Helpless, voiceless, cowardly Caitrin. I drew a deep, steadying breath and felt anger come alight inside me, a small, hot flame. *'Home?'* I said, getting to my feet. 'How dare you order me to go back to Market Cross, knowing Cillian is there? How dare you give me your trust and your friendship, and let me help you, and tell me . . .' Remembering the tender words, the gentle touches, I almost lost that fire. *I've never met anyone like you,* he'd said. His eyes had been soft then, soft with what I had foolishly thought might be the same feelings that had throbbed through my body as he held me. All I could see in those eyes now was cold determination.

The flame flared up, hot and indignant, and with it came a flood of words, words that, before tonight, I would never have believed I could say to him. 'How dare you! How dare you offer me payment, as if all I needed was a bag of silver to take away from here and a pat on the head for a job well done! How dare you take that arrogant tone with me, when you made me a friend! Is this the way you treat your friends, sending them back to a place where they'll be beaten and abused and terrified? What kind of man does that?'

His eyes darkened. His mouth tightened. He took a step towards me, bunching his left hand into a fist. I forced myself to keep still, holding his gaze. *I will stand my ground. I will not flinch. I will never be cowardly Caitrin again.*

'There's more of Nechtan in you than I thought,' I said.

It was as if I had slapped him. The blood drained from his face, leaving him pale as winter. A single lock of fiery hair was hanging down over his brow; he pushed it back with some violence, then turned on his heel and strode to the door, where he paused with a hand against the frame, as if to steady himself. 'You believe that of me.' He spoke with his back to me, his tone incredulous. 'You think I would despatch you back to Market Cross, into the arms of that – that vile oaf. Since your opinion of me is so low, you'll be relieved that it's Magnus making the arrangements: an escort to Whiteshore initially, then safe carriage to the place where your sister and her husband are staying. You are too free with your challenges, Caitrin. You ask much of me. And yet, you are afraid to face your own greatest challenge, the one that sent you running up Whistling Tor and into my garden.'

I opened my mouth to answer, but Anluan was gone into the night. He did not shut the door behind him; where the gallery was open to the outside I could see the dark field of the sky, sown with bright stars. Fianchu had lifted his head while we argued; now he gave a token growl and settled again. By his side the ghost child lay with eyes wide open, staring into the dark.

chapter eleven

After the careful watch that had been kept over me since the fire, the plan that had seen one friend after another come up to sit with me, now Anluan had left me alone save for the child and the hound. He had completely flouted his own rules. I was alone to sleep; alone to dream of Cillian and of demons. And then I must wait out a day, two days, an endless time until the so-called arrangements had been made for me. I had become a piece of baggage to be despatched.

It would be easy to give way to sorrow. I could wrap myself up in the blanket, howl my anguish, dream of what might have been. I could cling to every last moment I had at Whistling Tor, I could stay until the bitter end so I might drink in every last glimpse of the man I loved. That way lay madness. I would not go down that path a second time.

I would not wait for anyone's arrangements. Anluan wanted me to go. I would go, then. There was no guard on duty. The household was quiet. I would pack up my things and head off down the hill. At least that way I would not have to say goodbye to all my friends and have what was left of my heart shredded into little pieces.

I did not weep. As Fianchu slept on and the ghost child lay preternaturally still, watching me between slitted lids, I slipped Anluan's cloak off my shoulders and hung it neatly on a peg. I changed into the gown I had worn the day I first came to Whistling Tor. I folded the skirt made from the garments of Líoch and Emer and laid it on the foot of the bed. I rolled up Mella's grey belt and set it on top. I'd have to keep the boots. There was no knowing how far I might need to walk. I packed my spare shift, my nightrobe, my second gown, my small personal items. A cold calm had come over me. Somewhere underneath it a wild creature raged, a hair-tearing, screaming banshee of a woman, but I would not release her until I was gone from here.

No sign of Mother's embroidered kerchief, though I knew it had been in the oak chest with a sprig of dried lavender between its folds. I looked for it under my pillow, under the pallet, amidst the bedding, on the shelf, but it was nowhere to be seen. I glanced at the ghost child, wondering if she had squirrelled the pretty item away somewhere, but her narrowed eyes told me nothing save that she knew I was leaving her. I tucked Róise down the side of my bag. Emer's russet gown joined the pile on the bed.

My writing box stood next to the tray of untouched food. Anluan must have brought it up from the library. Already planning my departure. Before those visions in the mirror or after? I would not think of that. I lifted the box to fasten the strap more securely. It felt unusually heavy. I slipped off the strap and opened the lid.

A small bag of kidskin lay on top of my carefully stowed materials. When I picked it up there was a jingling, metallic sound that made Fianchu prick up his ears. I carried the bag over to the lamp, loosened the drawstring, peered inside. Silver pieces. My earnings for a summer's expert scribing. Enough to get me across country and support me while I found Maraid. Enough to ensure I need not sleep under haystacks and in the shelter of bridges; enough to stop men from thinking me easy prey as I travelled. Now, at last, tears stung my eyes: tears of humiliation. I wanted to scatter Anluan's silver on the floor. I wanted to trample it under my feet. Common sense told me I must take it. The turbulent season at Whistling Tor had not driven out the memory of my flight from Market Cross. I never wanted to be that frightened, helpless woman again.

The bag was packed. The box was fastened tight. The silver was hidden away in my pouch. I sat on the pallet listening to the night sounds from outside: an owl calling, another replying, a whisper of leaves, and perhaps a muttering voice from the courtyard as Rioghan made his nightly rounds, not going over the details of his old betrayal now, but planning ahead, devising ways to make the host into a workable fighting force. How could I slip away unseen if he was there? How could I get out without Fianchu raising the alarm? Doubts crowded into my mind, and with them came the pain. *You're like a beating heart . . . a glowing lamp . . .* Why had his wretched mirror of might-have-been shown us together, as if that were one of his fondest dreams, if he'd already decided to send me away?

Don't forget me.

I started. The mirror; the odd little mirror I had brought down from the north tower. I had heard its voice as if it had spoken aloud, though Fianchu had not stirred. I moved to the wall, peering into the tarnished surface, but all I saw was my shadowy reflection: a woman with red eyes and pasty skin, her dark hair rumpled, her brows creased in a frown.

Take me. You'll need me.

I unhooked the mirror, lifted it down, opened the bag again. There was just enough room to slip it in. As I did so, I saw that there was another item I had forgotten: the little book I had made, with the translations of Irial's sad marginal notes scribed in neat half-uncial. It lay on the shelf beside the lamp. I couldn't take it away. It belonged at Whistling Tor; it was part of the sorry record of Anluan's family and the curse that lay over them. I set the little notebook beside the lamp, its covers closed.

How long should I wait? I must be well away before Magnus or Olcan or Anluan himself realised I was gone and came after me wanting to impose *arrangements* on me. If I had to go, I would do it by myself. But I must not go too soon or I might come to grief in the dark before I reached the invisible boundary that marked the end of the Tor. I must wait until the pre-dawn light made it possible to go without a lantern. Any artificial light would be spotted quickly by Rioghan or by one of the sentries on the wall. Suddenly, waiting seemed the hardest thing in the world to do.

In my mind I wrote Anluan a letter along the lines of the sample I had made for him on my first day at Whistling Tor. *I love you. I'm proud of what you're doing. But you've hurt me. I don't understand.* That would be honest. Or I could write, *In less than a turning of the moon it will be time to gather heart's blood. But I will not be here. Goodbye, Anluan. We both lost the wager.*

I had not expected to get away without some challenges. First was the ghost child, who never slept. She had lain quite still watching my preparations, but when I finally judged the light was good enough and made for the door, my bag over my shoulder, my writing box under my arm, she was suddenly there by my side, clinging to my skirt, shadowy eyes turned on me.

'I come with you.'

Fianchu woke at the tiny sound, lifting his head.

'Hush,' I whispered. 'You must stay here; you can't come with me.'

'I come!' Louder this time. The dog, still slow from sleep, began to get up.

I put down the box, took off the bag, dipped my hand down inside. I pulled out Róise. 'I have to go away for a while,' I murmured, crouching beside the little girl. 'I need you to stay here and look after her. Can you do that for me?' The deception was cruel, but I could see no other way.

The ghost child took the doll in her arms, cradling her. She said nothing more, but the question was written on her face: *When are you coming back?*

'I might be gone a long time,' I said. 'I know you'll do a good job with Róise. She needs someone to love her, just like all of us. Goodbye, little one.'

Fianchu was on his feet now, ears pricked, stance alert. Very possibly, he understood enough to go bounding off and wake his master the moment I went out the door.

'Fianchu,' I said, making sure I had his full attention. 'Guard her.' I pointed to the ghost girl. 'Stay here and guard her!'

Fianchu sat. His little eyes, fixed on me, were entirely knowing. But he was a dog and it was his job to obey.

'Good boy. Stay here until the sun's up. You too,' I told the girl. 'He will look after you.'

I crept out the door, along the gallery, down the steps. Shades of grey inhabited the garden; eyes watched me from under the dark trees. Across the courtyard, a lamp still burned in Anluan's quarters. The mad woman inside me stirred – *go to him, run to him, now, now* – but I quashed her pleas. I walked down the path, out the gap in the fortress wall, into the forest.

Nobody came after me. I pictured the ghost child in the bedchamber, the doll pressed to her skinny chest. I imagined I could see in her eyes the pain of yet another betrayal, another abandonment.

My thoughts showed me Anluan, alone in his quarters, staring empty-eyed at the wall, or seated on his bed with his head in his hands, long fingers threaded through his fiery locks. Foolish imaginings. More likely he was working out how to form an army from wayward spectres, untrained villagers and reluctant neighbours. Perhaps, now that he had dealt with me, he had put me right out of his mind.

My foot hit a stone. My hands tightened on the writing box. I teetered a moment then regained my balance. It was not yet light; the woods were full of shifting shadows. As I went on down the track, I felt a tug on my left arm; a tweak at my right shoulder. A whisper in my ear: *Wrong, all wrong . . . Poor silly girl, what were you thinking?* And on the other side: *Wretched Caitrin, sorrowful girl . . . Who wants you? Where can you go? Where can you be safe now?*

A pox on the wretched creatures, whatever they were. I *would* leave. I *would* find somewhere to go. I did not belong at Whistling Tor. I should never have let myself see it as home. A fool. A cursed fool of a woman.

Oh yes, a cursed fool . . . You cannot stay here. You cannot go home. He's there, the one who turns you into a helpless child. Poor lonely Caitrin. Nowhere to go, no one to love you . . .

I swatted at the unseen presence by my right ear. The other spoke by my left.

Come this way, down this little winding path . . .

Come with us! Follow us . . . You will be safe forever . . .

Invisible hands clutched onto my skirt and my cloak. They gripped my bag, tugging backwards, almost toppling me. I opened my mouth to cry out a protest, then shut it again. Make a noise and I'd alert Rioghan or one of the others to my solitary departure. Box wedged under my arm, I managed to form the shape of a cross with my fingers. '*Kyrie eleison; Christe eleison,*' I muttered.

There was a momentary slackening of the uncanny grip, then it tightened again. So much for the efficacy of a Christian prayer. I forced down a powerful urge to scream.

A violent push. I fell. The writing box crashed to the path. Something was hauling on my bag again, trying to rip it from my back. 'Stop it,' I whispered, struggling to draw air into my lungs. 'Leave me alone . . .'

'Leave her alone!'

The voice was Gearróg's, and it was Gearróg's hands that lifted me to a sitting position, then retrieved the box and set it safely down by me. For a while, all I did was try to breathe. The insidious whispers had ceased; I sensed the two of us were alone.

Gearróg squatted down beside me, his plain features creased with worry. From time to time he reached out to pat me awkwardly on the shoulder, but he seemed reluctant to do more.

'Thank you,' I gasped eventually. 'You saved me again. Gearróg, I'm going away. Will you walk to the foot of the hill with me? I need you to keep me safe.'

'Me?'

There was a lot in that little word: *I hurt you. Aren't you afraid of me? I failed at my job, and Anluan was angry. I betrayed your trust.*

'Please.'

He helped me up, his big hands gentle. I gave him the bag to carry; I took the writing box. We walked down the path together.

'Why would you go away, my lady?' Gearróg asked after a while. He held his voice to a murmur, and his tone was diffident.

'He said I had to leave. Anluan.' Despite my best efforts, my voice shook. 'He doesn't want me.' It hurt to speak this bleak truth aloud.

Gearróg kept walking, steady and quiet at my side. We had

gone some distance before he spoke again. 'That can't be right,' he said.

'It is right. He told me, just now.'

A lengthier silence, full of things unspoken.

'He'd be sending you away to keep you safe.'

'No. Well, that's probably part of it. But he meant forever.'

'Then he's less of a man than we all thought.' Gearróg's tone was blunt. 'Only a fool gives up his one treasure.'

Tears stung my eyes. I could not let him go down this road. I must be strong. 'Where did you go, Gearróg?' I asked. 'Rioghan held a meeting. All the men of the host were there, or so it seemed. But Cathaír said he couldn't find you.'

He held his silence to him like a shield. We walked on.

'You can't fight the frenzy on your own,' I said after a time. 'But perhaps all of you together will find the strength to hold firm against it. Rioghan has ideas about that; he's clever where these things are concerned. I expect Cathaír and the others will have their own techniques for mastering it. Gearróg, I want you to go back up there and face them. I heard that Anluan spoke harsh words to you earlier. He was upset. Troubled. The fire awoke dark memories for him. I hope you will understand why he was angry with you, even though you had just saved my life.'

'I did a bad thing.'

'You hurt me by accident. I was simply in the way. That wasn't you flailing around, it was something else using you. Promise me you'll go back up and join the others, Gearróg. Anluan needs you. You have a special strength in you. You proved it by saving me even when the frenzy was on you. You've just proved it again by making those creatures go away. I can't imagine how you did that.'

'They haven't gone far.' The words were dismissive, but warmth was creeping back into his voice. 'My lady, you're the one Lord Anluan needs most. And what about us? You changed everything. What's going to happen if you go away? How can you not come back?'

My eyes were brimming. I bowed my head; I did not want him to see how badly this was hurting me. 'I said something terrible to Anluan. Something so cruel and hurtful that it shames me to think of it. Something so bad that he's never going to want me back. And he . . .' There was no describing how I had felt when I had thought, for just an instant, that Anluan might strike me. Now, I recalled that when sudden anger seized him he would often clench his left hand into a fist in that way. I'd seen him use it to break the mirror. I'd never seen him hit anyone.

'Gearróg, the little girl will need friends once I'm gone,' I said. 'She trusts you.'

We were at the boundary. It still lacked some time until dawn, but I could see the shadowy outline of the settlement through the deceptive light, a huddle of dark shapes, the line of the make-shift defensive wall, the flickering points of torches set around the perimeter. Tomas and the others kept them burning all night, fearful of the host.

'Promise me,' I said as the sky lightened towards the true rising of the sun. A bird gave a summons, an upward call of two notes: *Come forth! Come forth!*

Gearróg held his silence.

'I must go now,' I said. 'I don't want to see any of them from up there; I wouldn't be able to bear it. Will you promise, Gearróg?'

'Say you'll come back. Later, when this is all over. Say you'll come.'

'I can't. Not if he says no.' I must move on, I must run now, before the sun rose and they found me missing. I must flee before I lost the will for it.

'You say, go up and face the others. But you're running away.'

I lifted my chin and squared my shoulders. 'I have to go and find my sister. I have to face up to my own others, people who wronged me. And afterwards . . .'

'You'll come back to Whistling Tor?'

Naked hope trembled in Gearróg's voice. It shone in his eyes and transformed his features, forbidding a refusal.

'If Anluan truly wanted me, if he needed me, nothing in the world would keep me away,' I said, and as the words left my lips I heard a great sigh, not from my companion, but from a dozen, fifty, a hundred ghostly voices out in the forest. The host was watching. The folk of the Tor knew I would not be there in the library tomorrow seeking out answers for them. They knew I would not be working through the grimoires in a quest to end their suffering. I had let them down. I had broken my promise. Yet I sensed that they understood; that the words I had just spoken were enough for now. 'Be strong, Gearróg. Watch over him for me.' I looked out under the trees, unable to see the others, but acknowledging their presence. 'Be strong. Help him.'

'Farewell, my lady. You have my promise.' Gearróg placed a fist over his heart. He had halted right on the border of the hill, between the guardian trees.

'Farewell, Gearróg.' I turned my back, and as the sky brightened I walked steadily downhill and away.

As if to mock me, the day I left Whistling Tor the weather turned fair, with sunny skies and gentle breezes. It was enough to make me wonder if this was a different world, in which summer had followed its natural course through all the time of my stay in Anluan's fortress, while mist, rain and bitter cold had clung steadfastly to the Tor.

I held fast to the decision I had made as I packed to leave, that I would not give in to the helplessness that had befallen me after my father's death. If I had learned anything over the strange summer at Whistling Tor, it was that I must not become the lost soul of last winter again. Never mind that the man I loved had sent me away forever. Never mind that I had been forced to break the deepest promise I had ever made, and abandon my friends in their time of greatest trial. If Anluan didn't want me, he didn't want me. It was as simple as that. I would grit my teeth, summon my courage and get on with what must be done.

I did not go to Whiteshore. I did not even go to the settlement at the foot of Whistling Tor. I walked the other way, up to that crossroads where I'd been unceremoniously dumped on a day of mist and shadows. There was no point in waiting for a cart to happen by. I set my feet forwards, making lists of colours in my head to keep out thoughts of Anluan.

It was so early in the morning, nobody was astir. Birds chorused in the woods by the cart track, and somewhere down under the elders I could hear the voices of frogs. Everything seemed swept clean, open to light, full of promise. It felt wrong. Part of me wanted to protest that such a lovely day ill fitted the catastrophe facing the folk of Whistling Tor. Another part of me whispered, *You never belonged here, Caitrin. Forget these folk. Forget Anluan. If he loved you, he would never have done this.*

For half the morning I walked without seeing a soul. I grew thirsty and stopped to drink from a stream a little way off the track. I grew hungry. My precipitate departure had left me ill equipped to travel far without help. Memories of my flight to the west returned. I suppressed them, making myself move on. My feet were hurting; Emer's boots were not such a perfect fit after all. The day grew warmer. I took off my shawl and stuffed it into my bag.

A rumbling, squeaking sound and the thump of hooves sent me down under the bushes to the side, wary of carters travelling alone. A pair of stocky horses came into view, pulling a well-kept cart laden with bundles. A man and a woman sat on the bench seat; she had a child on her knee.

I stepped out and waved a hand. A little later I was perched on a sack of grain in the back, on my way eastward. I imagined the mist-clad slopes of the Tor behind me, slowly diminishing until they could no longer be distinguished from the ordinary landscape of fields and woodland. As the cart moved further and further to the east, I did not once look back.

It made a difference having funds. I spent two nights in a village inn, with my own chamber and a lock on the door. I got directions and arranged lifts. I read a letter for a local trader in return for a place on a conveyance that was going all the way to Stony Ford, a settlement about three days' travel north of Market Cross. Father and I had executed commissions for the chieftain there, and I was fairly sure Shea and his fellow musicians would be known in that house.

My fellow passengers on this somewhat larger and grander cart must have thought me dour and uncommunicative. They could not know the whirl of thoughts that filled my mind every moment of the day, those I fought to banish and those I tried to concentrate on, in particular how to track down Maraid and Shea without going too near Market Cross. If Stony Ford did not provide any clues I must try other places Shea had mentioned when telling us of his travelling life, but those were few and far between. I thought I could recall a town called Hideaway or Holdaway, where the band had regularly played to entertain people at a big weekly market. Lean enough pickings, Shea had said with good humour, but if they stayed on for the evening's dancing there would generally be a few extra coins tossed their way.

Failing that, I could look for Shea's family. That would mean a far longer journey, as they lived somewhere well to the northeast, close to Norman-ruled territories. His father's name I had forgotten, but he had been a master harp-maker before his hands were afflicted by tremors, and such craftsmen would be few in any part of the land. I had a good chance of finding him eventually. Eventually. How long would it take?

As the cart rolled steadily on and my fellow passengers chatted about the weather or how long it might be until the next stop, I pictured Anluan, Magnus, Rioghan and the rest of them in pitched battle against Lord Stephen's army. I imagined the spectral voice filling the ears of the host with poison and sending them into howling, tortured disarray. I thought of Anluan cut down, wounded, dying, while I went from village to village asking about a band of musicians who might or might not have passed by some time earlier. I saw the Latin words of the counter spell clean on a parchment page, useless without me there to translate them. Often I came close to tears, and it was necessary to remind myself that if Anluan had really loved me, he would not have sent me away forever. That worked for a little, until my mind began to tell me that perhaps Anluan had banished me because he thought there was no chance of defeating Stephen de Courcy, and that he and Magnus and Olcan were all going to die, leaving the host leaderless and adrift. Once this perfectly logical idea had come to me, I couldn't shake it off. It made me cold all through. I sat on the cart's padded seat with my shawl hugged around me and my gaze set straight ahead, seeing nothing but Anluan's pale face, his bright hair, his lovely crooked features. Over and over I thought of the unforgivable words I had said to him, and of how he had looked when he heard them.

The journey to Stony Ford took several days. We stopped one night in a hostelry that was a cut above the others. Two of my fellow travellers, Brendan, a physician, and his wife, Fidelma, had shown me particular kindness on the way. They and I sat down to supper to find the other folk at the inn table in spirited discussion about the Normans.

'They say there's been a treaty signed,' said an old man nursing a mug of ale between knotted fingers.

'If you can call it that,' said another man, grim-faced. 'More or less gives away all the lands of the east, and a lot besides, to this King Henry. May the Uí Conchubhair break out in a rash of blisters, every one of them from the high king downwards. That man's handed our birthright to a bunch of grey-shirted foreigners, as ready to burn a good Irish town to ashes as they are to listen to their own folk.'

'You'd want to watch your mouth,' a third man said, voice lowered.

'War's not over.' This from an ancient in the corner, who had seemed fast asleep.

'Ruaridh Uí Conchubhair's not the only leader we've got, though he may see himself that way,' said a brawny man at the far end of the table. 'We'll keep on fighting till the last of us lies on the sward with his blood soaking into the breast of the earth. Uí Conchubhair's gone weak in his old age, if you ask me. He was something of a leader, once, a man almost worthy to be called high king. He's fallen far.'

'No king lasts forever.' Brendan spoke quietly. 'As for Henry of England, I know of this agreement, and you're right – under the terms of it the high king keeps sovereignty here in Connacht, and in other places where the Normans haven't yet set their mark. But the fact is, Henry can't keep effective reins on his own lords – they've got used to taking what they want, by force if necessary, from us and from each other. They'll still be jostling for territorial advantage, treaty or no treaty.'

'They've proven themselves no respecters of boundaries,' said Fidelma.

I cleared my throat, regretting deeply that I had not taken much interest in such matters when I lived in Market Cross. I had always believed that Connacht, at least, was safe from invasion. That was what everyone said. So far west, with much of the land too barren for farming, it had not seemed a place the English would want. King Henry's treaty sounded quite true to that theory.

'Has any of you heard of an English lord called Stephen de Courcy?' I asked. 'He – I heard that he threatened to take an Irish chieftain's holding, quite some way to the west of here. I was told there's a tie of kinship by marriage between Lord Stephen's family and that of the high king. That means Ruaridh Uí Conchubhair won't step in to help this chieftain.'

All eyes turned to me.

'Never heard of the fellow you mention,' said the old man. 'But it happens. Place up north, can't remember the name, they rode in and cut down the chieftain's men-at-arms; a rout, it was. Put their heads up on pikes afterwards, Northmen-style, as a warning to other leaders not to stand up for what was rightfully theirs. Burned the settlement; killed women and children as if they were less than human. That's what they think, of course. That we're no better than dumb beasts of the field. It sickens me.'

'You believe something like that could happen right on the coast of Connacht?' I felt a lead weight in my belly. 'It makes a mockery of Ruaridh's title. A high king should protect his own, surely.'

'Ruaridh's always done what was expedient,' someone said, lowering his voice and glancing around the room. 'That's why he's lasted so long. His sons are better men.'

There was a short silence, during which nobody met anyone else's eyes. Then Brendan said, 'I believe I've heard the name de Courcy before. I can't remember in what connection. He's a youngish man, I think, and ambitious. My brother would know more. He's very well informed on such matters; his line of work demands it. Why do you ask, Caitrin?'

'My father always said the far west would hold out against the Norman advance. But it seems this treaty is a sham, if our own high king can step back and allow someone like Stephen de Courcy to take territory from one of his own chieftains. It's wrong that we have no protectors, no leaders of our own who can stand up for us.'

A weightier silence this time.

'Do you have kinsfolk in the far west, Caitrin?' asked Fidelma, concern written all over her kindly features. 'Perhaps in the territory of this threatened chieftain?'

'Just friends.' I offered no more. Start to discuss Anluan's situation in any detail and I would lose my hard-won self-control.

'Give it time,' said the man who had mentioned the high king's sons. 'Connacht will stand, that's my opinion. There will be new leaders, men with stiffer spines and bolder hearts. Men I'd take up arms for myself, if the call came.'

'You?' queried someone with a chuckle. 'That leg of yours can't even walk straight behind a plough, let alone charge into battle against a line of mounted grey-shirts. But maybe you fancy a quick and bloody death.'

'I suppose a man with a damaged leg can still use a bow,' I said with somewhat more emphasis than I had intended. 'Or throw stones. Or perform a hundred other essential tasks.' I looked the would-be warrior in the eye. 'I commend your courage,' I said.

Now everyone was staring at me, not as if they believed my speech odd, but as if they were interested in why I had made it; as if they wanted to hear my story. But I could not tell it. I picked up my ale and took a mouthful, eyes downcast, cheeks burning.

'Well, Caitrin,' said Fidelma quietly, 'if you want more information about this Stephen de Courcy, you couldn't do better than Brendan's brother Donal. When we reach Stony Ford, why don't you stay with us a few nights? You can talk to him and enjoy some good hospitality at the same time. Unless you must move on straight away, of course.'

'Isn't it Donal who's getting married?' I'd heard them talking about it: how Brendan's brother, a confirmed bachelor close to forty years old, had astonished everyone by deciding to wed a widow with three little girls. 'I'd be in the way, surely.'

'Not at all. The place will be full of guests; one more will make no difference. And Donal carries out his legal practice in a separate area of the house. Think about it, at least.'

So Donal was a lawman. This was not simply an opportunity to rest and recover before setting off to find Maraid. It was a chance to begin putting my affairs and hers to rights; the next step in facing my own hardest challenge. My belly crawled at the thought. I did not know if I could be brave enough. Speaking to this man of the law would set me on course for a confrontation with Ita and Cillian. Sooner or later this road must lead me back to Market Cross.

By the time we reached the township of Stony Ford I had seen the sense in accepting Fidelma's invitation, at least for as long as it took me to get an idea of where Maraid and Shea might be. The purse of silver was not bottomless, and I might have to travel quite some way further. An offer of hospitality in a safe house among good people was not to be refused.

Brendan's brother proved to be not at all the austere, strict kind of man I had expected, but small and cheery, with sparse mousy hair and twinkling eyes. He delighted in teasing Brendan about anything and everything – the bond of love between them was plain, and it reminded me sharply of Rioghan and Eichri, whose jibes and jests had so unsettled me until I had realised it was all in a spirit of friendship.

The widow and her children were already living in Donal's house, which was a fine sprawling place of mud and thatch, with a well-tended garden and stabling for three horses. But softly spoken Maeve was not sharing Donal's chamber at night; she slept in her daughters' room. This was not from any lack of enthusiasm for the marriage bed, I thought, noting the way Donal reached to touch her plump arm as she served his breakfast porridge, her quick blush as he caught her eye in passing, the sweetness in their voices as they spoke to each other. They would be wed on the fifth day after our arrival; either they were waiting for their wedding night, or the presence of so many guests in the house had made discretion necessary until then. Two of Maeve's sisters were there with their husbands and a total of seven children, as well as various other kinsfolk. Maeve's mother, who lived nearby, came over every day with pies or puddings to complement her daughter's cookery. It was a busy, happy home.

I found myself sharing a bedchamber with a pair of nieces a few years my junior. Watching them put finishing touches to gowns, dress each other's hair or run outdoors to be children again for a while, I felt a hundred years old.

Donal's clients kept coming. He and Brendan had both chosen professions in which there was no such thing as a rest, Fidelma pointed out dryly. Despite the steady stream of folk going in to see the lawman each morning, he found time for me on the second day. His study was a haven of quiet after the bustle and noise. He sat at a big desk, on which there were two bound books, a sheet of parchment and a pot of ink. A single quill lay beside this, with a little dish of sand for drying. The walls of the chamber were lined with shelves on which rested numerous documents, set out so tidily that I was quite certain the lawman knew exactly where to find any given item. There was a smaller desk in a corner, today untenanted. On the window sill an earthenware pot held freshly picked wildflowers, purple, pink and blue – the widow's touch.

'Come in, Caitrin. Please, take a seat. I am a little behind – I've given my assistant leave of absence until after the wedding, and I find myself less able to keep abreast of things than I expected. So many distractions . . .' Donal grinned suddenly; it gave him the look of a leprechaun. 'But welcome ones, of course. No doubt I'll catch up in time. What can I do for you, Caitrin? Fidelma tells me it's about the law of property – not my first area of expertise, I must confess. And, of course, under Norman law, which extends across all areas where Henry's barons have established them-selves, our own legal system no longer holds any weight at all. Mention Brehon law and its long traditions, and a Norman lord or cleric will look down his nose as if you're an ignorant savage. Such are the times we live in.' He was watching me closely, his eyes shrewd. 'I don't imagine that is what you want to hear.'

'I had believed Connacht safe. It seems that isn't so. How would matters stand, then, if an Irish chieftain fought for his land and managed to drive back the Normans?' I hesitated. 'This chieftain has been told that if it comes to armed conflict, the high king will not support him. There's an alliance through marriage between the Uí Conchubhair and the Norman lord who wants the land. Which law applies to such a situation, Norman or Brehon?'

Donal's gaze had sharpened. 'This is a specific case, I take it.'

'It is. I'm telling you in confidence.'

'That's understood. Nothing leaves this chamber without a client's consent. There are various learned answers I could give you, Caitrin, weighing up treaties, verbal agreements, precedents. But the most honest answer is that in such a situation control of the land goes to the man with the best trained army, the sharpest weapons and the strongest will. I never thought I'd make such a statement; I've been trained to trust good Irish law for fairness and justice. It's served us well for hundreds of years. But there it is. I'm sorry I cannot answer differently, but I have been honest.'

'I see.' I had known the answer already in my heart, just as Anluan and Magnus had. It all came down to one factor: the host. The irony was stunning. The one weapon Anluan had that might, just might, allow him to hold on to his land and turn his people's situation to the good was the accursed army called forth by his evil ancestor, the very thing that had made Anluan himself an outcast, isolated and powerless. 'Thank you.'

'May I ask whether this individual, the chieftain whose lands are under threat, has the wherewithal to make a stand?' Donal's tone was diffident.

'The situation is . . . unusual. So unusual that folk would not believe me if I set it all out. Donal, there's another matter on which I need to consult you.'

'Brendan did mention that you were looking for your sister. I can certainly assist you with that, if you wish. It would be a simple matter to send messages of enquiry. That could save you a great deal of time.'

'I'd welcome your help, Donal. But finding Maraid is not the only challenge. Once I do find her, it may lead to something else, something very serious. I believe discussing that would take up quite a lot of your time, and I lack sufficient resources to pay a professional fee.' I glanced at the empty desk in the corner. 'It did occur to me that I could pay in another way. As I explained, I'm a trained scribe, and I have brought the tools of my trade with me. I could copy, reckon, make notes for you, write letters and so on.'

He beamed. 'Excellent! And since we're on that track, I should say I believe I met your father some years back – Berach, was that his name? Fine man, did lovely work. I heard of his death. Very sad.'

'He was a fine man, yes.'

'There's a question I must ask, Caitrin. If your family home is in Market Cross, why not make that the first point of your enquiries about your sister? Fidelma did explain to me that Maraid is married to a musician and has no fixed place of residence. All the same . . .' He lifted his brows.

'May I tell you about our situation at home?' *Be brave, Caitrin.* 'It's complicated.'

Donal leaned back in his chair and crossed his arms. His eyes remained alert. 'Start at the beginning, Caitrin,' he said. 'Don't leave anything out. We have plenty of time, especially if you are prepared to deal with some letters for me later today. I don't suppose you read Latin?'

'I do.' Suddenly, when least expected, tears stung the back of my eyes. If I had found this courteous, capable man before . . . If I had thought to ask for a lawman's help as soon as Ita and Cillian began to take control . . . But no. My flight to the west had led me to Anluan and the household at Whistling Tor. Even if I had been banished from that place forever, I could not wish that I had not met the man I loved, nor the odd folk who had become my dear friends. This summer had healed me, freed me, opened me up. And, in the end, broken my heart. 'I'm happy to write letters, transcribe documents, read and translate – anything you need doing.'

'Excellent. Would you be prepared to stay until my assistant returns? He'll be back a day or two after the wedding. I think it likely I can track down your sister in that time through my existing contacts. That should be more efficient than your travelling about looking for her. Now let us hear this story.'

I hesitated, wondering how to start.

'You like mead, Caitrin?' Donal had produced a flask and two cups from a shelf. 'This is a particularly fine one; Maeve brews it, one of her many talents. She's planning to keep bees here in the garden, she tells me. Take a few sips before you begin your account. And don't be afraid of shocking me. In my line of work one hears everything. That's it, my dear. Take your time.'

Donal was an expert listener; no doubt he had acquired the skill over years and years of hearing the tales of folk in trouble.

From time to time he interrupted, gently, to ask for clarification. Here and there he waited in comfortable silence while I composed myself. Once or twice his expression revealed some emotion: shock, pity, surprise. At certain points he made notes on his parchment in a quick, precise hand.

'And so, finally, I ran away. I headed west, thinking perhaps I might find someone who had known my mother when she was a girl, but mostly just wanting to – to be somewhere else, somewhere Cillian could not reach me. I found a place to stay and work to do. I can't talk about that. But Cillian came. He tried to abduct me. He was . . . driven off. He didn't come back. I think it likely that if I went to Market Cross, he and Ita would try to convince folk that I was mad, just as they did after Father's death. They are good at that. Even I believed it.'

Donal had refilled my glass. From outside came the sound of the children at play in the garden, shrieks of excitement, a dog barking, Maeve's calm voice restoring order. I sat quietly, letting the sweet honey taste of the mead calm me, while the lawman studied his notes, the slightest of furrows between his brows. He no longer looked in the least like a leprechaun. His eyes, sharp and intent, were those of a man who would make the most formidable of adversaries.

'Very well, Caitrin,' he said, sounding almost abstracted. 'Without studying this further, I can tell you that it appears the law has been broken not only in relation to your inheritance, but in several other matters. I'll need a little time to consider the best course of action.'

'I am afraid to return to Market Cross and confront them. I'm not sure I can do it. They . . . they have such a capacity to change me, to make me lose sight of my courage.'

'No need to consider that now, my dear. I do have a question.'

'Yes?'

'Why didn't you go straight to the lawman in Market Cross once you had summoned the will to leave the house?'

'I wasn't thinking clearly. I wasn't myself. All I could manage was to run. Besides, the lawman at Market Cross would have believed me out of my wits, as everyone else did. I had been acting like a madwoman; it was reasonable enough, I suppose.'

Donal's mouth went into a grim line. 'Reasonable? Hardly. No lawman worth his salt would make such a judgement solely on the advice of a woman who stood to gain from your incapacity, Caitrin. He should, at the very least, have sought an independent opinion on your ability to understand your situation and make decisions about your father's property. Besides, I gather nobody was suggesting your sister was also out of her wits – why didn't they send for her? You've been lied to, swindled, duped most mercilessly, not to speak of the personal indignities this Cillian fellow has visited on you, seemingly with his mother's complicity. They must both be brought to justice.'

I felt an inner part of me shrinking down. The sensation was all too familiar, and I fought against it. 'I want to find my sister first,' I said. 'I don't want Cillian and Ita told where I am. I know I must go back and confront them eventually, Donal. But I'm not sure I'm ready yet.'

'You do want to see justice done.' There was no reproof in this; it was simply a statement of fact.

'I know that is what should happen, yes.' I had heard this already from Rioghan, from Magnus, from Anluan himself. 'But I'm afraid.'

Donal put down his quill. 'You're in a safe place here, Caitrin. No need to look beyond that at this point. The situation is complex; I must consider it further before we decide how this should unfold. I'd like your permission to write to a friend of mine named Colum, a senior practitioner of the law, who presides over the district around Market Cross. In strictest confidence, of course.' When I made to protest, he added, 'No matter what occurred during that time when you were at the mercy of these kinsfolk of yours, the law will treat you fairly. While not the warmest of men, Colum is absolutely rigorous in his pursuit of justice. That should reassure you. Nobody's going to suggest that you confront these miscreants on your own. It also occurs to me that we have a physician in the house. Brendan is well qualified to report on your state of mind, Caitrin, and to provide a written opinion that you are perfectly competent to make your own decisions.'

Holy Saint Brighid. I had not even thought of this. It was all moving so fast.

'Have I your permission to write this letter? Or perhaps you should write it for me. That way we can be sure we concur on the wording before anything goes beyond these four walls. Do you agree?'

'I can see it's the right thing to do. I'd like a little time to think before I say yes, Donal. If you have some work for me, I'll do that first. It will help clarify my mind.' I longed for the balance of the pen in my hand, the orderly lines of script flowing onto the page, the tranquil silence that attended the exercise of my craft. The children might still be laughing and shouting on the other side of that window, but once I began writing I would not hear them.

'By all means. I will act straight away on the other matter, finding Maraid for you. The sooner a message leaves here, the sooner you'll be reunited with your sister. Ideally, we should advise her of the situation concerning the inheritance before we proceed with action.'

'I'll fetch my writing things – that's if you are happy for me to start work now.'

Donal grimaced. 'There's plenty of it waiting. I'll give you some copying to be getting on with, then I'll leave you awhile. I promised Maeve I'd try on my wedding finery. I imagine I will resemble a small rotund bird that sprouts colourful feathers in the mating season, but if it pleases her . . .'

Some time later I settled myself at the assistant's desk with the small pile of documents Donal had given me for copying. It was an easy job, which was just as well, for my conversation with the lawman had given me altogether too much to think about.

I opened my writing box. Donal had a supply of quills, but I preferred to use my own and to trim them with Father's special knife. That, at least, I had brought safely away from Whistling Tor. I wondered what the ghost child was doing, and whether Róise had been any comfort to her. I hoped that Gearróg would watch over her and be kind to her. Perhaps she had already forgotten me.

I had not needed to look in the box since the day I left Whistling Tor, when I had discovered Anluan's bag of silver and removed it

294

for safekeeping. Now, reaching deeper to find the padded roll of quills, my fingers encountered something else that did not belong there, something flat and smooth. I lifted out the quills; removed the ink pots each in turn. There beside them, tucked in neatly, was a notebook whose tooled calfskin covers were familiar to me. My heart turned over. Anluan's book. My hands were shaking as I drew it out and laid it on the desk. My breathing was unsteady as I opened it to see his wayward script wandering across the first page. *This is thankless, pointless. It dulls my mind and wearies my body. Muirne is right; it is a road that leads nowhere. Yet I continue with these wretched documents. What else is there but utter despair?*

I turned a page, another. More words of despond, scrawled in writing that was near illegible. How could I bear to read this? Why had he given it to me? I turned more pages and came to a leaf that stood out, for most of it was blank. Only, right in the centre, was written in the same scrambling script these words: *So bright, so perfect, so alive. You do not belong in this place of shadows. What do you want of me?*

And, as I recognised without a shred of doubt that Anluan had recorded here my own arrival at Whistling Tor, I put my head down on the desk and wept.

chapter twelve

ach morning I awoke while the two girls who shared my chamber were still rolled in their blankets, fast asleep. I had long been an early riser, and now, in the quiet time before the household began to stir, I allowed myself to read Anluan's record of my summer at Whistling Tor, the summer that had changed my life and his. One page a day; I would not let myself read faster. I savoured each surprising entry, feeling with him each moment of doubt, each little spark of hope. The longer it took me to reach the end, the better. While there were still pages unseen, I could pretend the link between us remained unbroken. I was not sure I wanted to read the last page, which must surely tell of his decision to shut me out of his future, the choice that made less and less sense the more I read.

Before the girls were astir, I would close the covers softly and slip the little book back into the pouch at my belt. I carried it everywhere. I thought of him constantly. *There is a change in some inward part of me*, he had written. *I cannot tell if I welcome it or fear it. Muirne calls me foolish; she says nothing can change at Whistling Tor, not even its poor excuse for a chieftain. But you have changed me already. My heart beats more quickly. My blood runs more swiftly. Light*

bathes everything when you are near me, dazzling, terrifying. It is as if you have called me awake after a hundred years of sleep.

With Anluan's voice beating in my heart, I sat at the desk by day, calming myself with the exercise of my craft. None of the tasks Donal gave me was taxing in any way. I was pleased that I could carry them out to his satisfaction, and happy that I need not spend my day keeping up cheerful conversation with the ladies of the household, pleasant women as they all were. Alone or in Donal's silent company, I could hold Anluan's memory close. I could contemplate this morning's fresh page and dream of tomorrow's.

I had agreed that Donal could send his letter to the senior lawman in Market Cross, questioning the matter of my father's legacy and, in particular, the tenancy of the family home. In the end, the missive he dictated was somewhat more detailed than I had expected, setting out certain sensitive matters including Cillian's assaults on my person and the false stories his mother had put about.

'I trust Colum completely, Caitrin,' Donal had said. 'He taught me much of what I know. He'll be discreet in his enquiries. I do want him fully apprised of the serious nature of this, especially if it turns out the local lawman has been derelict in his duty. Someone should have stepped in to assist you, or at the very least to ensure that you were being properly looked after.'

So I let him send it, and at the same time he despatched messengers to seek out Maraid and Shea, folk who would visit market squares and grand houses, the kinds of places where musicians might play. Donal was confident that Maraid would be found by the time his assistant returned to work. And if it took a little longer, he said, I must stay on, of course. He would discuss the situation with all of us together, Maraid and Shea and me, and help us make whatever decisions were required. When I protested that I should not stay on after the wedding, both Donal and Maeve insisted that I would not be at all in the way. Indeed, Donal said, it seemed he had sufficient work to keep two assistants busy. If I wished to continue helping him, he would pay me for my efforts.

The sun rose on Donal and Maeve's wedding day. The sky was a tranquil blue with not a cloud to be seen. After a substantial and noisy breakfast, everyone changed into their best apparel and set off on foot for the local church, where a simple but touching ceremony was enacted. I had feared my presence would set a blight on my host's day of happiness, but I was swept up in the joy of the occasion and almost forgot my own problems until the moment we arrived back at Donal's house to find a messenger waiting.

'I'd best speak to you alone, Master Donal.' Under his broad-brimmed hat, the man's face was very serious. A frisson of unease ran through me.

'Is it about my sister? Maraid?'

An awkward pause as folk chattered and laughed, going in the door behind us.

'We'll go to the study,' Donal said, glancing at his new wife. 'I'm sorry, my dear.'

'Go on,' said Maeve with a smile. No doubt she had known what it would mean to marry a lawman. 'If there's news, Caitrin needs to hear it straight away.'

Then we were in the study, Donal, the messenger and I, and still the man seemed reluctant to speak.

'Come on, out with it,' Donal said. 'You can speak in front of Caitrin; she's the one who is seeking information in this particular instance.'

The man cleared his throat. 'I have news, yes, but it's not the best sort of news. Maybe the young lady should be sitting down.'

I felt the blood drain from my face. 'Tell me!' My voice was shaking. 'What's happened? Is my sister all right?' For although I had known we might not find Maraid and Shea immediately, I had never thought that something might be badly amiss with them.

The messenger glanced at Donal, and Donal nodded assent.

'They were staying at the big house in Five Birches, that's quite some distance north, when an illness struck the household,' the man said. 'Many folk fell sick and some died of it, including the chieftain's own son. And . . . well, the musician, Shea, was one of the unlucky ones. Vomiting and purging one day, gone the next.'

'Gone?' My mind was not making sense of this. 'Gone where?' Then, as both men regarded me with sombre faces, 'You mean . . . you mean Shea is dead?'

'Sit down, Caitrin.' Donal came across and took my arm. 'Come, now, sit here.' He turned back towards the messenger. 'These are ill tidings. How long ago did this occur?'

'Some while ago, I was told. The widow, Maraid, she's gone home to her folk in Market Cross, her and the child. There was nobody to take them in up at Five Birches. That household lost many of its own, and for a while it was all at sixes and sevens.'

I knew that if I tried to stand up my legs would not hold me. My head reeled; my stomach lurched. *Be strong, Caitrin.* 'Child?' I croaked. 'What child?' Perhaps the messenger had got things confused, and this sad tale was not Maraid's but someone else's.

'You didn't know? The young woman, Maraid, had an infant; it wasn't more than a couple of months old when her man passed away. Your sister was lucky she and the baby weren't struck by the sickness, and that they had somewhere to go.'

Lucky. Her husband dead before he was five-and-twenty, her child fatherless, and me, her only sister, away in the west where she could not reach me. And now Maraid was in Market Cross, in that house, with her baby. The two of them were at the mercy of Ita and Cillian.

'Caitrin.' Donal crouched down beside me in his wedding clothes and held out a cup of mead. 'Take a few deep breaths. You're among friends here, and we will help you.' He dismissed the messenger, telling him to wait outside, then came back in and quietly shut the study door. 'This is sad news indeed,' he said. 'A terrible shock for you. Weep all you want, my dear.'

But I couldn't weep. That was too much of a self-indulgence; a waste of precious time. Every moment I spent in this hospitable place was another moment of sorrow, of fear, of crushing loneliness for Maraid and her child. I saw her in the house at Market Cross, weighed down by grief, and I saw myself as I had been after Father's death, an empty shell, all alone in the world.

'I have to go there,' I said, getting to my feet. The chamber rocked and swayed; I drew a deep breath and stiffened my spine. 'Now. Today. Maraid's there with *them*. I must go to her.'

To his credit, Donal did not remind me that this was his wedding day. He did not tell me I was being ridiculous. Instead he called in Fidelma and Brendan. Fidelma settled herself beside me, her arm around my shoulders. The men sat opposite. A discussion ensued and a plan was devised. I would leave Stony Ford in the morning, accompanied by Brendan and Fidelma, along with the very large young man who looked after Donal's horses and performed heavy duties about the place. Aengus happened to be the district wrestling champion.

'I'll be far happier if you have some brawn to back you up, Caitrin,' Donal said. 'Aengus can drive the cart and help to procure lodgings on the way. Make sure he's there when you first confront your kinsfolk. You should go to see Colum as soon as you arrive in Market Cross, and before you make any attempt to go to the family home. He should have received my letter and read it, but of course he won't know you are on your way. We cannot be sure what reception your kinsfolk will give you.'

'I'm frightened for Maraid. Cillian may be cruel to her. And the baby – anything could happen –'

'And you would rather be off right now, yes, I understand that,' Donal said. 'But you do need the rest of today to prepare, Caitrin. Brendan can write his report on your state of health and take it with him, to produce if anyone should query your capacity to make your own decisions. You and I need to sit down and discuss inheritance law. You must be able to set out your argument clearly. These kinsfolk may attempt to convince you that they were within their rights when they took over your father's house.'

'But –'

'You don't go into battle without preparing your weapons. Believe me, not to take this time would be a grave error. Maraid has managed without you thus far; one more day can make little difference.'

I knew he was speaking sense, though my mind and body were gripped by the urge to act. Maraid must not be hurt as I had been. I could not let it happen.

'We'd best put in an appearance out there,' Fidelma said, 'just to reassure Maeve.'

I came abruptly back to the here and now. The wedding day; Maeve; the house full of guests. 'Donal, I can't expect you to do this today. And how can I ask Fidelma and Brendan to leave so soon? Poor Maeve. I've spoiled everything.'

'Not at all,' said Donal. 'Maeve knows how things are likely to be from now on. It's my great good fortune that she's taken me on in spite of that. As for these two, if they didn't want to go with you they'd say so, believe me.'

'Nonetheless,' put in Fidelma, 'we should all go out and join in the festivities, if only for a little. And you, Donal, might reassure your wife that you'll set aside only an hour or so before supper to explain these legal matters to Caitrin. Maeve will want you to be present for supper, and for dancing afterwards. You mustn't disappoint her.'

The lawman gave his leprechaun grin. 'You're a paragon of practicality and tact, Fidelma. I quite understand why my brother wed you. And I won't disappoint Maeve in any way at all, I trust.' He became suddenly serious. 'Caitrin, you've had bad news and you've a great deal to think about. I imagine you'll be wanting quiet and solitude.'

'All in good time,' Fidelma said. 'Some food and drink first, I think, and you might have a little word with Maeve yourself, Caitrin. She may well understand what being a lawman's wife means, but there's a limit to the tolerance even of a saint.'

We were three days on the road. Two nights we spent in the houses of folk known to Donal. Aengus soon proved his worth, smoothing the way for us with his quietly insistent manner. What that did not achieve, his intimidating bulk did. Fidelma and Brendan kept me company without asking too many questions. I could not sleep. As the miles passed, I thought of the house at Market Cross, and the long time of darkness I had spent there seemed to outweigh the happy years that had gone before. I should be brave. I had a guard. I had friends. I had a doctor who would vouch for my competence and a lawyer whom I could call upon for help. But Cillian had hurt me, and his shadow was a long one. When I thought of Ita, I remembered weeping before her, pleading with her, and I heard her saying, *My son would not punish you unless you deserved it, ungrateful girl.* At night, when weariness finally overtook me, my dreams were full of dark wells and rending claws. I woke exhausted, wondering if I were not, after all, the same fearful woman who had fled Market Cross a season ago.

I was still rationing myself to one page of Anluan's book each morning. On the day when we expected to reach Market Cross, I read these lines:

Can a split quill write fair script?
Can a blunt axe cut wood for the fire?
Can a cripple please a lady?

That shocked me so much I broke my self-imposed rule and turned to the next page. There, so familiar I thought I could remember every word of the conversation Anluan and I had shared that morning, was a scrap cut from the parchment sheet on which he'd first attempted the new method of writing. *Caitrin*, it read. *Caitrin. Caitrin.* Tears stung my eyes. I wanted to turn another page, and another, to devour the whole book, for it seemed a feast after famine. But I did not. It was too precious to squander thus; I would savour each morsel in turn.

A cripple. I had never thought of him in that way, except perhaps on that very first day when he had lurched across the garden and frightened me. I could swear that none of his household even saw the disability any more. 'You would please me,' I murmured, remembering the mirror of might-have-been, the rise of my body, the thrust of his, the power and rhythm of it. 'I know you would.' But perhaps that was foolish. Muirne had more or less told me Anluan was incapable of the act of love. How she had learned this, I could not imagine, but I was becoming convinced this was his main reason for sending me away so abruptly. I could not doubt his feelings for me, not after reading this book with its tenderness, its passion, its confusion.

With a sigh I put the book away and began to dress. Aengus had said that if we started off straight after breakfast we would reach Market Cross in the afternoon, all being well. As I took off my nightrobe and donned shift, stockings and gown, I tried to imagine what might happen when I walked in through the door of my childhood home. I did not like any of the variations my mind showed me. *I won't be afraid of them, I won't*, I told myself, but the churning feeling did not leave my belly. Sheer panic was not far away, the kind of fear that would send me fleeing inside myself. *This is foolish. You must help Maraid. And you don't have to do this alone.* But perhaps I did have to do it on my own, or I would never conquer the terror that lurked deep inside me, threatening to cripple me when I most needed to be strong and whole.

One step at a time. If I looked neat and tidy, I might feel a little more in control. I would plait my hair and pin it up, then tie on a scarf. At least that would keep out the dust of the journey.

There was no mirror in the chamber where I was lodged. I reached into my bag and took out the little old one I had brought from Whistling Tor, propping it on a shelf. I laid the hairpins ready beside it, then put my hair into a single long braid. When I was ready to coil it atop my head, I glanced into the mirror. My heart leapt. There he was, standing in his bedchamber, clad in warrior's garments, a leather breast-piece, wrist and arm braces. He was staring down at something held in one long-fingered hand, something small and glinting – a fragment, a shard of glass?

'Anluan,' I whispered, but he could not hear me. As I stared, not daring to move lest I cause the image to vanish, he turned the item one way then another, as if changing the angle of it might make a difference, and I saw that it was a jagged piece of mirror. It caught the light from his lamp, now shining like a star, now, when he turned it, dark as night. The mirror of might-have-been; the broken mirror. Did I only imagine that I saw his crooked mouth form the name *Caitrin* as he struggled to make the shattered glass show him once more the image that had made him smash it to pieces?

'I'm here,' I breathed. 'I'm here, beloved, dearest one . . .'

He straightened; looked up and around, almost as if he had sensed my call. But it was another summons he had heard. I saw him slip the piece of glass under the pillow on his bed, then go to the door. He paused to scrub a hand across his cheeks. He straightened his shoulders and lifted his chin. He drew a deep breath and let it out slowly. Then he opened the door, and there was Magnus, clad in similar garb, with a sword by his side. Anluan stepped out; the door closed, and the scene was lost. A moment later, there in the mirror was the chamber that had been mine. It seemed much as I had left it: neat, bare, empty. The place was a study in greys, shadow on shadow. The door stood slightly ajar. The only light was from the gallery openings beyond. It seemed to be dusk, or a stormy day.

One shadow caught my eye: a neat figure sitting cross-legged in the centre of the floor with the little doll, Róise, in her hands. Not the ghost child. Muirne. Her eyes stared straight ahead; her expression was perfectly calm. Her hands worked in spite of that, pulling, tearing, ripping every remaining shred of hair from the doll's linen scalp. Such strength in those hands; such violence that it sent a tremor of sheer horror into my bones. The little scarf I had made to cover the earlier damage lay on the floor beside Muirne's outspread skirt, torn into pieces. Muirne's face told me nothing, but now that I had seen Anluan's notebook, I thought I could guess what was in her mind. *She's gone at last, gone forever, far, far away, and still she consumes your thoughts. She came here, you let her in, and she changed you. She changed everything.*

'Caitrin? Are you ready for breakfast?'

The image fled. The mirror showed me my own face, eyes wide with shock, cheeks stained with tears. I was as white as Róise: linen pale. 'I won't be long,' I called to Fidelma through the closed door. I rolled the mirror in my nightrobe and thrust it back in my bag. My plait had unwound itself; I braided it again with my mind on Muirne's detached gaze and her furious, destructive hands. That scene made no sense. I was gone from Whistling Tor. What could she hope to achieve by destroying my possessions? Was the woman simply unhinged?

And Anluan . . . I had seen him racked with regret and uncertainty, just as I was. I had seen him dash the tears from his cheeks and walk through his doorway to greet what faced him – another day as leader, another day of preparation for an impossible battle. He had found the courage hidden deep inside him.

He had been cruel to me that last night, taxing me with my cowardice over Cillian. But I had been crueller; what I had said was indefensible. Despite that, he had moved on bravely. Today, I recognised that he had been right to challenge me. I would not conquer my particular monster unless I could walk into that house in Market Cross and confront Ita and Cillian alone.

The day was sunny and bright, but not everything in this part of Connacht was so fair. We saw a troop of Norman men-at-arms riding to the north, the sun glinting on their shirts of chain links and glancing off their weapons. They bore long shields and wore helms of metal with nose guards. They looked formidable. Aengus pulled the cart into a byway and we sat there quietly as they passed.

Later, we saw a house and barn that had been burned. A thread of smoke still rose from the scorched remnants of the place, and something dangled from a tree, like a broken doll. A dog was barking hysterically, running to and fro on its rope, hurling its defiance at an enemy long gone. The men made Fidelma and me wait on the cart while they went to see if there was anyone who could still be helped. I saw Aengus release the dog; it bolted. The men came back and, in silence, we rode on.

I could have done with a councillor, someone like Rioghan, to make a plan and help me execute it. As it was, I made my own plan, which I explained to my companions as we neared the settlement. Confronting my enemy all alone would be foolhardy. It would put not just my safety but that of Maraid and her child – Holy Saint Brighid, I hadn't even asked if it was a boy or a girl – in danger. That I would not do. So I explained how the plan would work, and the part each of us should play in it, and was pleasantly surprised when all three of them agreed without demur. Rioghan would have been proud of me.

My heart was beating fast and my skin was clammy with nervous sweat, but there was a purpose in me now, a will to succeed that was growing every moment. My strength was building with every turn of the corner, with every creak of the cartwheels, with every step that took me closer to my destination.

We reached Market Cross in midafternoon. Outside the home of the senior lawman, a substantial house shielded by a tall fence of woven wattles, we dropped off Fidelma, after sending Aengus in to make sure Colum was at home. Then Aengus drove us on until we were at the town square. He drew the cart to a halt beside the patch of well-trampled grass that housed the weekly market from which the town had got its name. On the far side of the square my childhood home could be seen: a comfortable dwelling of modest mud bricks, whose thatched roof was decorated with owls fashioned from straw. I got down, making myself breathe slowly. I squared my shoulders just as I had seen Anluan do, then walked across the grass to the front door. Aengus came behind me, while Brendan stayed with the cart and horses. By now, one or two passers-by had noticed our arrival, and there was some talk and gesturing. I could imagine what they were saying: *Oh, there's poor Caitrin home again! You know, Berach's daughter, the one who lost her wits and ran away.*

With my head held high, I stepped up to the door and knocked sharply. *Anluan*, I said silently to myself, making his name a charm against faint-heartedness. I knocked again. 'Ita, open the door!' I called out. Still no response. They were home. The kitchen fire was smoking and I could hear someone out in the yard, raking or sweeping. The thready squalling of a small baby added itself to the mix, sharpening my courage. It was my house, after all. I gave the door a push, but it did not budge. I glanced at Aengus.

He put his shoulder to the wood and shoved. The door fell open with a crash. Following the instructions I had given him, Aengus took up a post against the wall just outside the doorway, where he could not be seen from within the house. I walked in.

The noise brought Ita to the kitchen doorway, where she stood with hands on hips, surveying me, a tall, thin figure with her hair scraped back tightly under a cloth. A curious sequence of expressions crossed her face. Whoever she had thought might be making a violent entry into the house, it was certainly not me.

'Caitrin!' She summoned a smile. It was as convincing as a grin painted onto a scowling gargoyle. 'You're safe!'

I almost asked her to explain; almost gave her the opportunity to tell me how fortunate it was that I had not been slain, or worse, by the evil sorcerer whose lair I had foolishly stumbled into – Cillian would have brought back his own version of events, I was sure. But no, I would not ask Ita for anything. I had several things to say, and I would not let her stop me, not this time, not ever again.

'Where is my sister?' I heard the iron in my own voice. Within the house somewhere, the baby was still crying.

Ita moved to take my arm; to usher me into the kitchen that had once been Maraid's pride and joy, the warm heart of our home. Forcing myself not to wrench away, I allowed her to seat me at the table. The chamber was no longer bright and welcoming. Maraid's weavings, the flowers she used to set here and there in jugs, the strings of onions and bunches of dried herbs were absent. Yet Maraid was here; had been for some time. With a chill in my bones, I waited for Ita to answer my question.

'Maraid is resting. She's been quite ill. The baby is sickly. She's always crying, crying – it's enough to try anyone's patience to breaking point. But we took them in, your sister and the child, since Maraid had nowhere else to go. And now you're here, Caitrin.'

'How burdensome for you,' I said grimly, holding on to calm. 'A grieving widow, a crying baby and now a madwoman as well – it really is too much for you to shoulder. I think you and Cillian would be best to move back home.'

Her eyes darted to me then, and quickly away again. I saw her draw a deep breath and compose herself. 'This is our home now, Caitrin, you know that; it came to Cillian on your father's death. As for the burden, the obligations of kinship can be onerous, that is true, but we accept them. It is our duty.' She took a jug from a shelf, then stood holding it as if she had forgotten what she was doing. 'I must call Cillian,' she said.

'If you wish. When you call him, please call Maraid as well.'

'I said she's resting. If you're home for good, Caitrin, and I take it that is so, you will have plenty of time to see her.' Ita had set the jug down. 'You must be tired yourself after such a long journey. Cillian said you were far to the west, almost on the coast.' Her gaze sharpened suddenly. 'Are you with child to this cripple you were lodged with? Is that what brings you back here? There are limits to our generosity, Caitrin – what Berach left will only stretch so far.'

'Call my sister,' I said. 'And call Cillian. I have something to say to you and it won't wait.'

Cillian had been out in the yard. At his mother's call, he came to the doorway where he leaned, staring at me. For a moment the old panic gripped me. I felt his hands on me; my skin ached with the memory of bruise on bruise. His smell was in my nostrils, bringing the dark time sharply back. 'Cripple throw you out, did he?' he queried, grinning.

And then, in the opposite doorway, the one that led into the sleeping quarters, there appeared a wan figure, her clothing disarranged, her complexion blotched, her eyes reddened. She was a shadow of herself, her generous curves shrunk to nothing. She raised a hand to brush her hair from her brow, and the wrist was all bones.

'Caitrin,' she whispered. 'Is it really you?'

A moment later we were in each other's arms, Ita and Cillian quite forgotten. 'Maraid! I've missed you so much! I'm sorry, oh, I'm so sorry about Shea!'

Maraid said something, but her face was pressed against my shoulder, and I could not understand her. She was shaking with sobs. She felt so frail that she might break apart. My lovely sister, buxom, rosy and full of life, had been reduced to this. It was not solely down to grief, of that I was certain, for Maraid had always been strong, resilient, a survivor. As I helped her to sit at the table – she seemed too weak, or too distracted, to do even that by herself – a cold strength entered my heart. I turned to face the two people I had feared most in the world; the two who had almost destroyed me.

'Listen carefully,' I said. 'I've consulted a senior lawman in the matter of our legal situation, mine and Maraid's. As Father's only two children, Maraid and I became joint owners, on his death, of this house and all his worldly goods for our lifetime. You have no entitlement to any of it, Cillian, and nor does your mother.' And, when Ita made to interrupt, 'Wait! Don't try to tell me that I'm crazy, that won't help you. I have a document from a physician testifying that I am entirely in my right mind. In the absence of sons, daughters inherit a life interest in their father's property. This is set out under Brehon law, and I suspect you both knew that all along – why else would you intend to marry a woman you clearly despise, Cillian, save that you realised you had no legal entitlement to Father's property? You probably expected to gain control of it through your children, those you imagined I would bear for you. Perhaps you hoped that I would conveniently die young, or that my mind would remain so confused that you and your mother must make all the decisions for me.'

For a little, the two of them simply stared at me. Then Cillian looked at his mother, raising his brows. 'That's not true, is it?' he said. 'It can't be.'

'Of course it isn't.' Ita had folded her arms and set her jaw in a manner that was all too familiar to me. 'Delusions, that's what it is, brought about by these adventures Caitrin's been having among God knows what kind of disreputable folk. Caitrin, you need rest; you need peace and quiet, my dear. I'll have someone get your bedchamber ready . . .'

I saw it in her eyes, a realisation that the comfortable world she had created for herself and her son was about to collapse, and the determination to stop me before I could make it happen. She'd rendered me powerless before; all she'd needed to do was lie.

'Oh, dear, what are we to do with you girls?' Ita's voice was suddenly dripping honey as she came over to us, putting one hand on my shoulder and one on Maraid's. 'Let Maraid go, Caitrin. You're upsetting her. Come, my dear, let's get you off to your chamber –'

'Take your hand off me, Ita.' My voice was cold and calm; I had not realised I had such power in me. 'I'm not finished yet.' I looked at Cillian, who was rolling up his sleeves. Perhaps he planned to move me forcibly if I would not obey his mother's wishes and retreat into seclusion. 'By all means challenge me under the law – that's your entitlement. You should be aware that Maraid and I intend to follow due legal process to ensure we get our rights.'

'What are you talking about, foolish girl?' Ita's tone had a new edge. 'Legal process, entitlements . . . You're not in your right mind and haven't been since the day your father died. Indeed, even before that I always believed you somewhat . . . flighty. As for more recent times, the wild stories Cillian brought home from the west made it quite plain that you'd never be capable of living a normal life again.'

'Old ruin full of freaks and monsters,' Cillian rumbled. 'Never seen anything like it. Nobody could stay long in a place like that without running mad. You've got even less wit than your sister, Caitrin. At least she saw the sense in coming home.'

I saw Maraid flinch.

'How dare you!' I could have struck him for his thoughtless

cruelty. I put my arm around my sister's shoulders. 'Maraid came back here because she lost her beloved husband. She came because she and her child had nowhere else to go. And now that I'm here, we're going to make this house into a proper home again, not the travesty it's become since you moved in and took what was rightly ours. Now listen to me, and listen well. You will be out of this house before dusk. The two of you will not show your faces to me or to my sister ever again.'

A wrenching sob from Maraid; it made my heart sick to hear her.

'Where's the baby, Maraid?' I asked quietly, my hand on her shoulder. 'Is she safe?'

My sister nodded. 'She's in the bedchamber with Fianait.' Fianait had been an indispensable member of our household when Father was alive. A sturdy, good-natured girl, she had done everything from killing and plucking chickens to polishing fine silverware. Ita had dismissed her. If Fianait had come back, it meant Maraid had not been entirely friendless. 'Caitrin, is this really true?' my sister said now. 'I can't believe it . . .'

'Nor should you.' Ita was struggling for calm now. 'As I said, it's a pack of nonsense. When did Caitrin ever become an expert in legal matters? Cillian, I think Caitrin may be a danger to herself. You'd best help her to her chamber . . .'

Cillian moved towards me, arms outstretched. Memory welled up in me; sudden panic held me motionless, a rabbit under the fox's stare.

Maraid rose to her feet. 'Don't you dare lay your hands on my sister,' she said, and though her voice was faint, her courage blazed in her eyes. As she slipped her arm through mine, I remembered that I had a plan, and that I had friends, and that I was not the same woman who had fled this house a season ago.

'I'm not here alone,' I said quietly. 'I referred to a physician. He's waiting just outside. As for the legal situation, I think you'll find I have the backing of the administrator for the district. His name is Colum, and you can expect a visit from him very soon. I want you packed up and ready to leave within an hour, Ita, and Cillian with you. If anyone sets a hand on me, or on Maraid, or on the child or Fianait, that will be added to the charges you already face. Think carefully before you resort to physical violence. Colum knows all about what Cillian did to me, both here and at Whistling Tor.'

'This is outrageous!' Ita had gone pale. 'A – a conspiracy! How dare you circulate foul lies about my son, how dare you poison folk's minds . . . Don't think you can get away with this, Caitrin. We have witnesses, reliable folk who will support us –'

Cillian had not understood quite as well as his mother had. 'You can't order us out of the house!' he shouted. 'We live here! It's ours by right!' He reached for me again.

'Aengus!' I called. 'You can come in now!'

The wrestling champion of Stony Ford was quick for such a big man. He appeared, all sweet smile and bulging muscles, and behind him came Brendan in his physician's robe, looking as if he wouldn't mind a sparring match himself. Cillian took a step backwards. His hands fell to his sides.

'Shall I throw him out?' enquired Aengus.

I felt a profound desire to say yes, but that would be to reduce myself to Cillian's level. 'Not yet,' I said. 'My kinsfolk need a little time to pack up their things and arrange a lift back to their home settlement. A little time, not a lot. I want the packing supervised; they're to take only their personal belongings. We don't know yet the full extent of what Father left, but if there's a store of silver or anything else of value in the house, these people must not be given the opportunity to take it with them.'

'This is ridiculous!' spat Ita. 'You can't forbid me to take my own things –'

A discreet knock at the door.

'That will be the lawman, Colum,' I said. 'I think he may have some bailiffs with him. No doubt he'll be wanting a word with you both before you go. I can't be sure when the hearing will be, but I am quite certain Colum will expect all of Father's goods to remain in the keeping of Maraid and myself until due legal process has been carried out. Brendan, will you let him in, please?'

'I feel so hopeless, Caitrin,' my sister said. 'I've tried to be brave, for Etain's sake, but sometimes . . .' She sighed, as if her thoughts were too sad to be put into words.

311

'Tell me, Maraid.'

The two of us were at the kitchen table alone. It was night. An oil lamp hung from a hook; beyond the circle of warm light, the chamber seemed full of shadows. Maraid had made an effort at suppertime, appearing with her hair combed and her face washed, but she was not herself.

The lawman, Colum, and his bailiffs had seen Ita and Cillian off the premises after stern words. My kinsfolk would be subject to the full force of the law. Colum had been working on our behalf since Donal's letter first reached him, and he had news for me: there were indeed funds available to us, silver carefully set away for the purpose of providing for Maraid and me on our father's death. There was no need for me to earn a living, at least not right away. There would be time to set our house in order; time to come to terms with our losses.

I had offered the hospitality of the house to Brendan, Fidelma and Aengus. After a happy reunion, Fianait had helped me prepare beds while Fidelma cooked supper. Now our guests were all abed; it had been a long day. I had seen the look on Fidelma's face as she watched my sister push her food around her platter, eating almost nothing. I had noticed Brendan scrutinising little Etain. Even to my inexpert gaze, my niece looked scrawny and pallid.

'I can't tell you,' Maraid said now. 'You'll despise me, Caitrin.'

'I won't,' I told her. 'I'm your sister and I'm here to help make things better. Ita and Cillian are gone. We have the house; we have resources, Maraid. We have our self-respect. Those things can't bring Shea back, I know. But . . .' I stopped myself. I knew all too well how it felt, that empty, blank hopelessness. 'You need to tell someone,' I said. 'Please, Maraid.'

'Etain,' she whispered. 'Sometimes I don't even like her very much, Caitrin. Sometimes I wish she wasn't here. She cries all the time, as if she hates me. I'm no good as a mother. I should never have had a child.'

Silently I cursed Ita, for her influence was written all over this. 'Is that all?' I asked.

Maraid turned bleak eyes on me. 'Isn't it enough?'

'I'm not shocked.' But I was, just a little. Etain was so small and innocent, so fragile. 'Maraid, you should let Brendan examine you in the morning. You look ill, not just sad and tired, but . . . to be honest, you look half-starved. And although I don't know much about these things, people do say that if you're nursing an infant you should eat more than usual, not less. Etain doesn't hate you. A little baby isn't capable of hate. She's probably just hungry.'

'Ita said I should stop trying to feed her. She said goat's milk would be better. But I do want to nurse her, Caitrin. I always thought I'd be a good mother. I don't want to be a failure.'

'Well, then.' My attempt at brisk confidence fell something short. Maraid was crying and so was I. 'Let's make a sisters' pact right now.' I headed for the pantry, where I filled a small bowl with suppertime leftovers – a little pease pudding, a scoop of soft cheese, a handful of dried plums.

'What are you doing, Caitrin?'

I set the bowl before her, then poured two cups of ale. 'This is the agreement. You eat, and while you're eating – I mean properly, not just playing with your food – I'll tell you a story. Tomorrow, the same, but I'll tell some of the story each time you feed Etain too.' Fianait had taken the baby away to settle her for the night. I would enlist Fianait's help in the morning.

'A story? What story?' Maraid eyed the little meal without enthusiasm.

'An exciting one about a girl who runs away from home and goes to . . . you'll have to start eating to find out where.'

'All right.' She picked up a single dried plum; I did not speak until she put it in her mouth and began to chew. A fleeting smile crossed her face. 'You never used to be so bossy, Caitrin. What happened to you?'

'This girl,' I said, holding my ale cup between my hands, 'had been very frightened; so frightened that she had lost sight of what was real and what wasn't. So frightened that people thought she was out of her wits. She felt all alone in the world; she thought everyone she loved had deserted her. Then one day, out of the blue, she found the courage to flee. She ran, she walked, she took rides, she slept under hedges and in the shelter of haystacks, until the day a carter dropped her off in the middle of nowhere and drove away without a word.'

Intent on the story, my sister had stopped eating. I waited, eyes on the bowl.

'Bully,' Maraid said, getting up to fetch herself a spoon. 'And then what?'

I told her how the girl had met two friendly strangers who had vanished when they were most needed; how she had prayed her way into a fortified village; how she had raced off up a hill in pursuit of a man named Magnus, and had been helped by a gnome-like person and a giant hound.

'And then,' I said as my sister put a piece of cheese in her mouth, 'she wandered into a lovely little garden, all overgrown but full of bright flowers and singing birds, with a birch tree in the centre, and a bench on which lay a book. Nobody was in sight. She wandered about, seeing how cleverly the plants had been chosen, and there, in a corner under a comfrey bush, she saw a clump of heart's blood.'

Maraid made a little sound; she knew what a treasure that herb was.

'She stooped to admire it, and at that moment a commanding voice rang out behind her: *Don't touch that!*' I stopped to take a mouthful of my ale, Anluan's image strong in my mind: pale as snow, red as fire, blue as speedwell, sad as a broken heart.

'Who was it?'

'That must wait until next time.' I wanted to be sure I had captured her or this experiment might be short-lived. Her grief was deep; it would not be easily healed.

'Was it an ogre? A beast? A handsome prince?'

I smiled. 'Not exactly.'

'Is this a true story, Caitrin?' Maraid had eaten almost everything I had given her; now she was sipping her ale.

'I'll let you make your own judgement. I haven't told it to anyone else. If I did, most folk would think I really was mad.'

'That's what Ita told me, Caitrin. She said that after I left here, you became completely unhinged. She said you couldn't even keep yourself clean. She told me you bolted with only the clothes on your back. She said you were never coming home.'

'I don't suppose she told you that Cillian came after me, and found me, and tried to force me back here.'

Her eyes went round. 'He *found* you and they didn't tell me? How could they do that? What happened, Caitrin?'

'Tomorrow,' I said. 'It's a long story.'

As summer became autumn my sister began to mend, along with the house in which we had been raised with such love and hope. The milestones were small but each was cherished: the first time Maraid smiled; the first time she offered to help prepare a meal; the day when Fidelma and Brendan decided we could cope without them and returned home. They told us we would be welcome in their house any time we wished to pay them a visit, and I offered the same invitation. Their kindness had been a remarkable gift.

Fianait and I scrubbed the house from top to toe. We aired bedding and set flowers on windowsills. We baked bread, brewed ale and made preserves. I hired a boy to help with the outside work, and he whistled as he replenished the wood pile and dug over the vegetable patch. Slowly our old home began to get its heart back, and my sister hers.

As Maraid's cheeks regained their rosy blush and her body began to fill out, Etain blossomed, turning before our eyes from a pale waif to a bonny, healthy babe. The fretful crying ceased. She bellowed for her meals, drank with enthusiasm, then slept in blissful silence. I liked to set her free of her swaddling cloths and see her kick her legs and stretch her arms as if eager for what the world might have to offer. I loved to watch her sleeping, for there was a tender mystery in the little face in repose, closed lids concealing secret thoughts beyond the comprehension of all but an infant new-minted. Looking at Etain, I longed for a child of my own.

There came a day when I passed the open doorway of the bedchamber and heard my sister talking to the baby as she fed her.

'He made the most beautiful music, Etain; he had a voice that would melt the heart of a stone statue, and his fingers on the harp were as light as swallows in the sky. He was the best papa you could ever have had, my love, the best in all the world. His eyes were just like yours, green as grass and bright as dewdrops. Never say he's gone. Only that he's nearby, and watching over us every moment of the day.'

I tiptoed away, eyes streaming, knowing a far greater milestone had been passed. As I stood in the courtyard trying to compose myself, the longing for Anluan stabbed sharp as glass in my breast. I would never hold his child in my arms; I would never lie with him and experience the joy Maraid had had in Shea. My body ached for that loss. My heart bled for it.

Maraid had heard my story in small instalments. Fianait, too, had listened with rapt attention as it gradually unfolded. I told of the dear, odd friends I had made at Whistling Tor, the folk I had had to leave behind. I described every part of that strange and eventful summer. Almost every part. I did not show Maraid Anluan's book, though I had long ago turned the final page to find, not a grim decision to banish me, but this perfect reflection of my own feelings:

At last I begin to understand why my father acted as he did. To lose you is to spill my heart's blood. I do not know if I can bear the pain.

He must have written this before he came to see me that night; before he told me we must part forever. I had read it over and over. I kept the little book under my pillow and looked at it late at night by candlelight, or first thing in the morning, when even Etain still slept. I tried to understand why he had been so cold that night if his heart had been breaking, just like mine. Perhaps that had been the only way he could bring himself to utter the decree of banishment.

The mirror was my link with him, a frustrating, unreliable guide to what was happening at Whistling Tor in my absence. I looked in it often, but not while the others were about, for while such eldritch phenomena were part and parcel of life in Anluan's household, they did not belong in Market Cross.

Sometimes the mirror showed me the blue sky of an imaginary summer, and sometimes my own reflection, dark curls neat, features composed, eyes a little desperate. But sometimes I saw Whistling Tor, and Anluan in the garden with Muirne, his tall figure stooping to listen, her smaller one gesturing as she tried to convince him of something. I pondered all I had learned of her, putting together a chance remark here, another there, and imagined her whispering in Anluan's ear: *You cannot win this. There is no hope.*

And yet, he did not give way to despair. On a day when autumn was well advanced, and gusty winds sent dead leaves dancing in the courtyard, I closed the bedchamber door, took the mirror down from the shelf where I kept it and sat down to look for answers. What I saw warmed me; it made me want to shout for joy. Men were gathered in the settlement, Tomas, Duald, a good number of them. They had makeshift weapons over their shoulders. Anluan and Magnus were there, too, and Anluan was addressing the assembled crowd, his head held high, his manner both calm and authoritative.

This vision dissolved to make way for another: a party of riders, not Normans, but Irish. They were waiting at the foot of the Tor. The brawny figure of Magnus came down the path, greeted them, then turned and led them up. The horses were restless as they traversed the winding way through the forest. No sign of the host, though I sensed their presence, watching. In the courtyard, Anluan stood on the steps before the main door with Rioghan beside him and Cathaír on guard behind. The riders dismounted, and Olcan came to lead the horses away. The chieftain of Whistling Tor stepped forward to greet the visitors, as any nobleman might do. There were white faces and nervous glances aplenty, but the visitors stood their ground, and their leader put his hands on Anluan's shoulders as if they were friends, or perhaps kin. Brión of Whiteshore? Had Anluan somehow made peace with his mother's family, despite the wrongs of the past? No sign of Muirne. I gazed at the man I loved, willing the mirror to show me more, but the image faded, leaving me looking into my own eyes. My heart was racing. He was doing it. He was bringing them all together. Maybe, just maybe, Anluan could beat the odds and win his unlikely war.

Autumn was passing quickly. Fianait set her hand to spinning and fashioned a warm shawl to cocoon the baby in. Phadraig, the boy who did our heavy work, brought a supply of firewood indoors and stacked it against the wall near the stove. The days grew shorter.

Our legal hearing came and went. I, who had once been turned by fear into a silent, shivering apology for a woman, stood up and answered the judge's questions with calm competence. I had told my kinsfolk that I never wanted to see them again, but on that day I faced them across the court without flinching. I no longer felt anger. Maraid's recovery had moderated the harsh feelings that had arisen in me when I first saw her again. I almost felt pity; pity that folk could be so eaten up by selfish greed that they lost all sight of humanity. Cillian was incoherent under questioning. Ita was shrill and bitter, unable to understand how she had erred. They brought one or two witnesses, folk of my acquaintance who gave accounts of how distracted I had been after my father's death, how distant and odd my manner. We had witnesses, too – those who could testify to Ita's refusal to let anyone visit me in that dark time, those who remembered her turning down an offer of a physician's services, those who had known me since I was a child and believed all that had ailed me was grief. In addition, Brendan travelled all the way to Market Cross from his home town in the west to testify in person as to my sanity. When it was over, and reparations determined at a level likely to see Ita and Cillian lose not only our property but their own as well, I thanked Colum and the other lawmen, came home with my family and closed the door on the past.

The days grew shorter still. Fianait baked spice cakes, Maraid brewed mulled ale, and we invited Colum and his wife to visit us and admire the baby. Some of Father's friends came too, people who had stepped back while Ita ruled the house. If I did not quite forgive them for once believing her story of my madness, I knew I must make peace with them.

When everyone was gone, and a yawning Fianait had retired to bed, Maraid and I sat awhile before the fire, she with Etain at the breast, I staring into the flames. I no longer had to tell a story to encourage my sister to eat or tend to her child. She was well now, and if sadness still lingered in her, she did not let it swallow up her love for Etain or her hope for the future.

'Caitrin?'

'Mm?'

'When are you going to start scribing again? We have funds

now, plenty to be going on with. You could buy inks, parchment, all the things you need to restock the workroom.'

I had hardly stepped inside the workroom since I came home. I had not even considered beginning again. But Maraid was right; what Father had left us would not keep us for the rest of our lives. Sooner or later I must seek out new commissions. It would be hard. Few of our former clients had known how large a part I had played in the execution of the fine documents in which we had specialised. They might be reluctant to give me a trial. Still, it wasn't impossible. Colum might be prepared to recommend me locally. If I was not bold enough to seek commissions, I could always go and work for Donal in Stony Ford, performing the relatively simple tasks of copying and letter-writing. I could summon little enthusiasm for any of it.

'Caitrin?' Maraid's gaze was shrewd.

'It's a sensible suggestion. I will do it. Some time.'

'Why not now? This is what you love. You used to spend all day over it, so engrossed in the next stroke of the pen that you forgot the rest of the world existed while there was a job to be done.'

I said nothing. The truth was, the future I had always wanted, the long days of peace and tranquillity, the perfect manuscripts evolving under my hands, the satisfaction of putting my craft into practice and earning a living at it, no longer seemed significant. And yet, I had a life here; I had my sister and my niece, I had a home and resources, I had the opportunity to go back to something resembling the old existence I had so cherished. But it was no longer enough.

'I see you don't want to tell me, so I'm going to guess, Caitrin. No, don't stop me, you made me talk about my troubles. You love this Anluan of yours, the monster in the garden. Even with the Normans at his gate, you're longing to go back. That household, and one member of it in particular, is more important to you than anything else in the world.'

'Not more important than you and Etain! Don't ever think that!'

Maraid smiled. 'Maybe not, but important in a different way. Caitrin, it's written all over you when you speak of him. Why are you so determined to put it behind you?'

'Anluan sent me away. Whatever his reasons were, he meant it to be forever.'

'Of course he wanted you to be somewhere safe when the Normans came. But it seemed to me from the way you told your story that he loves you as deeply as you love him. And he doesn't sound like a man who would care much about the sort of convention that says a chieftain doesn't marry a craftswoman. Why can't you go back when the Normans are gone? Whether he wins or loses, he'll need you.'

Tears stung my eyes. 'That was what Gearróg said, the morning I left. *You're the one Anluan needs most.* And maybe that's true. But he won't marry me.'

Maraid frowned. 'Did he say why not?'

'It's a bit awkward . . .'

'I'm your sister, Caitrin. If you don't tell me, who can you tell? Come on now.'

I looked down at my hands, clasped on my lap. 'He never said it plainly, only hinted at something amiss. He was concerned for my safety, I know that. But there was . . .' How could I possibly tell her about that vision, the one that had made Anluan smash a mirror with his bare fist? 'He said . . . he implied that the palsy affected more than just his arm and leg, Maraid. And Muirne said Anluan would never . . . She said he would not be able to satisfy me. Or any woman. That if I wanted children, I must look elsewhere.' My cheeks were flaming.

Maraid did not speak for a while, but sat thinking, her arm curled around Etain, who had fallen asleep on the breast. 'That's very sad,' she said eventually. 'If it's true. Caitrin, does Anluan feel physical desire for you?'

My cheeks grew hotter still. 'Yes,' I muttered. 'I told you about the mirror of might-have-been, the one that showed him images of himself without the disability, riding, wrestling, enjoying the activities of a fit young leader. I didn't mention that one of the images had me in it.' This was hard to get out, even to my own sister. 'Anluan and me, together, doing what husbands and wives do. It was . . . it was quite clear that he felt desire, Maraid. Perfectly clear.'

'And the mirror showed what might have been. What he could

320

have done, if he had not been stricken by the palsy. Caitrin, there are other ways a man can satisfy a woman, you know, without performing the act of love itself. Using his mouth, his hands.'

'But . . . I don't think Anluan would be incapable . . . I know he can . . . can manifest the physical symptoms of desire.'

'Oh?' Maraid was smiling now.

I had not thought this could become any more embarrassing, but I was wrong. 'I don't mean that he and I . . . there was only one time we were close enough to tell . . . but . . . it was plain enough that he wanted me.'

'So the palsy may have weakened his right arm and leg, and altered his face, but it hasn't had the same effect on his manhood? He has the equipment he needs, and it seems to be in working order?' Maraid's voice was gentle; she understood me all too well.

I nodded. 'He doesn't seem to believe he can do it,' I said. 'Muirne implied the same. *If you want a real man, Caitrin, don't look here.* That was what she said.'

'Does that woman love Anluan or hate him?'

I could only grimace; I had no answer for that.

'Let's take this one step at a time,' Maraid said. 'If he wanted you back, but you could never have children with him, would you go?'

'Yes,' I said without hesitation. 'But . . . it's not simple, is it? I'd marry him even if I knew we would be childless. I'd live with him even if we couldn't marry. But I do want children of my own, Maraid. I want his children. The absence of them would be hard to set aside. In that, perhaps a little of the family curse would linger on. He would always feel that he had failed me. That's the kind of man he is. I would always feel that there was something missing from my life.'

'It's a pity you didn't fall in love with Magnus instead,' my sister said dryly. 'He sounds the kind of man who would father as many little *gallóglaigh* as you wanted, and look after you as well as any woman might need.'

'Not to speak of cooking supper every night,' I said, managing a smile. 'Maraid, how could Anluan know whether he was able to father children or not? He's hardly been off the hill since he was seven years old.'

'A man only knows something like that if he's tried over a long time and failed,' Maraid said. 'Perhaps it's all in Anluan's mind. When would he have had the opportunity to lie with a woman?'

I considered what I knew of Anluan's past: Magnus nursing him back to health after the palsy, when Anluan was thirteen years old; the isolation of the household; the reluctance to leave the hill; the difficulty in getting folk to help. 'He wouldn't have had much opportunity at all,' I said. 'I suppose there would have been serving girls up there for short periods. Or Magnus might have arranged . . .' This was so far beyond what I knew, I could hardly begin to imagine how it might have been.

'You know,' Maraid said, 'for a boy with his past, and his disability, it might only take one bad experience to convince him that he was a complete failure. He does sound unduly prone to despair. Could it be only that, do you think?'

We considered that awhile, and I thought how impossible it would be, even if I did some day manage to return to Whistling Tor, to broach such a subject with Anluan.

'A boy might feel pretty awkward making love,' said my sister, 'if he had limited use of an arm and a leg. If it was his first time and he was unsure of himself, and the woman didn't understand his difficulty, it's easy to see how it might go wrong. With the right woman, one who could help him a bit, that same man might find the experience quite different. As for children, they don't come along if folk don't try to make them.'

After a moment I said, 'I've never lain with a man in my life.' My heart was thudding.

'He loves you,' said Maraid. 'You love him. Who else will he manage this with, if not you?'

chapter thirteen

It was the first time I had seriously considered that I might return to Whistling Tor in defiance of Anluan's decree of banishment. The idea sat uneasily with me, though my heart would have winged there like a homing swallow if it could. It was easy enough for Maraid to say these things. She could not understand the layers of history that sat so heavily over the place. Beside Nechtan's dark legacy, the question of whether Anluan had been unmanned by the palsy or was merely beset by self-doubt dwindled into insignificance.

Unable to make a decision, I distracted myself by obtaining a fresh supply of materials for the workroom – not a great quantity, just sufficient to produce some samples that might be shown to potential customers. I could see that Maraid was pleased, though she made no comment.

I set out parchment, quills and ink on the familiar table. I would make three samples and I'd keep them simple. Time enough for embellishments, complicated scripts, gold leaf and rare inks once I'd established myself. First would be a passage of poetry rendered in minuscule, the kind of piece a noblewoman would appreciate as a courting gift. I began to score up the page, using the plummet and straight-edge from my writing box.

The empty desk beside me was eloquent. I found myself glancing across as if to check how Father was progressing with his own work. I recalled the gleam of his bald head under the light from the window; his habit of sucking in his bottom lip when particularly engrossed; his neat, square-tipped fingers placed precisely so, holding the parchment steady.

I had never said goodbye, not properly. On the day of his death I had been disbelieving, unable to accept that he was gone. At the burial rite I had been numb.

I set down the plummet and moved to kneel on the flagstoned floor, in the place where he had fallen. In this precise spot I had cradled him in my arms, begging death to change its mind, willing time to turn backwards. Here I had uttered the full-throated sobs of an abandoned child.

'Father,' I said now, 'you have a beautiful new granddaughter. Maraid and I are together again, and the house is . . . cleansed. We're making it a good place, as it was before. I hope you're watching over us, you and Mother and Shea. That's what Maraid believes. Father, I haven't done very well since we lost you. I haven't always been as brave as I wanted to be. But I'm trying. I want to make you proud of me. I want to use everything you taught me.'

I knelt awhile, and it seemed to me that beyond the window the sky grew a little brighter. The chamber was as quiet as a sleeping babe. 'Goodbye, Father,' I whispered. Then I got up and went back to work.

I completed the poem, finishing it with a border of vines. The piece looked pleasing, if unadventurous. My eyes needed a rest. The next piece I planned, a legal document rendered in a common hand, must wait until the afternoon.

A shriek from somewhere in the house; something fell with a crash. I ran out into the passageway and almost bumped into Maraid, who was hastening towards our bedchamber. We reached the doorway together. Inside stood Fianait, linen-pale, with a shattered jug at her feet and water pooling. She was staring at the shelf before her as if it housed a demon. 'That mirror,' she gasped. 'There are things in it, things moving –'

I had forgotten to put the mirror away. 'It's all right,' I murmured, stepping across the debris to remove the artefact while Maraid went about reassuring the frightened girl. As I picked up the mirror, something dark and shadowy shifted within it: a chamber, the moon through a tall window, a face . . .

'Caitrin?' Maraid's voice was a murmur. 'What is it? What did she see?' And, when the silence drew out, 'Caitrin? Are you all right?'

I stood frozen, the mirror clutched in my hands. There was Anluan in his chamber at Whistling Tor, lying on the pallet as still as death. His eyes were closed; his chest showed no rise and fall; his skin was a sickly grey. There was I, my face a mask of anguish, cradling him in my arms. 'No,' I breathed, and 'No!' I screamed.

'What is it, Caitrin? What can you see? Caitrin, speak to me!'

'He can't be dead! He can't be!'

My sister was peering over my shoulder at the polished metal. 'Is that Anluan?' she asked. 'Oh, God . . .'

Caitrin in the mirror laid her hand against Anluan's cheek; she bent to kiss his pallid brow. Just for a moment, before the image faded, I saw a figure in the doorway of Anluan's chamber: a slight, neat person in a demure gown and veil, her lustrous eyes fixed on the grieving woman, the motionless man. Her features showed not a trace of emotion.

'I must go to him,' I said. 'Now, straight away. Something's terribly wrong, not this, since I was in the vision with him, but something . . . It's a warning . . . I need to be there, Maraid.' I knew that whether or not Anluan could ever love me as a husband loves his wife, and whether or not I could ever bear his children, I was bound to him as tree is to earth or stars to sky, bound in a love that would transcend all obstacles. I must go. I would go. Nothing in the world was going to stop me.

I left next morning, my sister having prevailed upon me to wait while she arranged a ride with a reputable carter, and to get a good night's sleep before I started off. We had talked things through after supper, more openly than before. For all my need to be on the road and heading towards Whistling Tor as quickly as possible,

I'd felt torn. 'I hate leaving you on your own,' I'd said. 'It seems too soon.'

'I'll be fine.' Maraid's calm manner had reassured me. 'I'm hardly on my own, with Fianait and Phadraig in the house, not to speak of Etain. Caitrin, I wasn't here when you needed me after Father died. I was so desperate to get away, I didn't think about what it would mean for you. I owe you the opportunity to do this. Don't feel any guilt about leaving us. But please do send me a message, if you can. I'll worry about you. Caitrin, I hope Anluan is all right. I hope you get there in time.'

Thank God for my sister's readiness to accept even the strangest parts of my story, I thought as the cart rumbled along the road towards Stony Ford, where I would change conveyances for the westward part of the journey. I'd given her a full description of my visions in the obsidian mirror, and told her the dark details of the host's past activities, including Mella's death. I'd even shown her one or two pages of Anluan's notebook. She had asked many questions; the curious mixture of folk making up Anluan's inner circle clearly intrigued her. I wished she could have come with me.

As my various rides took me slowly, oh so painfully slowly, towards Whistling Tor, I considered what might await me there and prayed that I would find Anluan alive and well. The mirror came with me. I looked often into its dimly shining surface, to meet my own worried eyes gazing back. The weather was bleak. We travelled on under lowering skies, down tracks treacherous with mud, across flat lands where the wind whistled keenly, sharp and salty as we neared the western sea.

The further we went, the less ready carters were to linger. When each reached his destination he dropped off his load, left me at the nearest inn, then headed straight back. The inns were full of talk, and it set a new fear in me. A force of Norman soldiers had been spotted heading west. Rumour had it that they'd been sent to seize the territory of a local chieftain and establish one of their own in his place. Nobody was quite sure where this was happening, but they thought it was near the holding of a chieftain named Brión. I asked how many soldiers and was told too many for any Irish lord to prevail over. I asked how long ago they had passed and was told ten days or more. Nobody had heard of Stephen de Courcy, but they had no other name to offer in its place. As the men-at-arms had gone by on their fine warhorses, with their chain-link garments and their carts loaded with supplies, folk had withdrawn silently into their houses and barred the doors.

Near the territory of Silverlake we saw something lying across the road ahead. The man who was transporting me along with three protesting pigs drew his cart to a halt. 'I don't much like the look of that,' he muttered. 'Couple of fellows off to the side there, in the bushes. Could be anyone.' His hand went to his belt, where a worn leather sheath held some kind of weapon. There would be no turning around silently and retreating unobserved, not with pigs on board.

'Halt!' someone called out, and a man stepped onto the track beside the barrier. Peering through the rain that had accompanied us for some time now, I saw that the obstacle was a solid length of wood, the trunk of a small tree that had perhaps been brought down by a storm, then dragged across to bar the way. The man wore woollen breeches and tunic, both garments saturated. He did not look dangerous. 'Where are you headed?'

'Three Trees Farm,' said the carter, both hands back on the reins. The fellow on the road was a Connacht man. 'Five miles down this track, but how I'm to get the cart around that thing I don't know. What's the trouble?'

'Who's your passenger?' There were two men on the track now, both of them giving me the once-over. My clothing and my general demeanour must have made it plain I was no carter's wife.

'I have friends at Whistling Tor, near Whiteshore,' I said. 'I'm going to visit them, and I'm in a hurry. Someone may be gravely ill.' Let that not be true.

'Whistling Tor? Isn't that the place –' one said to the other.

'You'd best go no further,' said the second man. 'There's a fight brewing; anyone on these roads is asking for trouble. You should take this young lady back to the last inn, and the pigs with her. That's my advice.'

The carter stared at him, and so did I, wondering if I could ask whose pay he was in, for it was obvious the barrier had been placed across the way, rather than falling there in an entirely convenient manner. The carter spoke before I could frame a question.

'Don't know a lot about pigs, do you? What do you expect me to do, ask the innkeeper to put them up for the night in his best bedroom, with a pint of ale apiece thrown in? Move that thing for us, will you? If I don't get them to Three Trees soon I won't be home before nightfall.'

'The lady heading to Three Trees as well?'

'I told you,' I said, 'I'm going to Whistling Tor. This man is taking me as far as Three Trees, then I'll get another lift. Will you do as he asks and let us through, please? We have to get on.'

'You won't get to Whistling Tor,' said the second man. 'There's an army of Normans camped all around the place, waiting to starve the local chieftain out. You wouldn't even want to go near. Apart from Normans on the road, there are . . . *things* about.'

'Things?' I queried, my heart cold with the thought that I might be too late. How could I reach Anluan in the middle of a siege? How could I change the future if I couldn't even let him know I was here?

'Strange things. Things that shouldn't rightly exist. A horse all bones; a dog as big as an ox. Shadows and voices. You wouldn't want to go any further than Three Trees.'

It seemed they'd decided to let us through. The carter got down to help the two men shift the log. When they had eased it far enough to let us slip by on the hard-packed earth of the road, I asked, 'Who arranged for you to be here? One of the local chieftains?'

'You're foolish if you expect an answer to that,' said the first man. 'Be glad we were here or you'd have driven straight into trouble. Take my advice, lass, and go back where you came from as soon as this fellow's dropped off his swine.' Seeing my expression, he added, 'Maybe your friend got out before the Normans laid siege to the place.' His tone did not inspire confidence.

We drove on to Three Trees Farm, which lay within the border of Silverlake, southeast of Whistling Tor. In this region Maenach had once been chieftain, Maenach whom Nechtan had viewed as a bitter enemy. Pigs unloaded, the farmer offered us mead and oatcakes and a chance to warm ourselves before his fire. It was plain that the carter intended to start straight back as soon as the simple meal was over.

'I'm not going with you,' I told him. 'I must get to Whistling Tor as soon as possible. If there's nobody who can take me, I'll walk.'

The farmer, his wife and the carter all turned their heads to the half-open door, beyond which the rain was falling steadily.

'You're crazy,' the farmer said.

'We could give you a bed for the night.' His wife sounded dubious. 'But you won't find anyone to take you to Whistling Tor today, tomorrow or any time soon. It's not just the Normans. Nobody goes to that place. You know what they say about it.'

'That the chieftain is a misshapen good-for-nothing and that the hill is swarming with monsters and giant dogs?' I said, fighting to stay calm. 'Yes, I know that; I lived at Whistling Tor all summer. I must get there. Isn't anyone using the roads?'

They looked at each other, and I thought there was something they were not saying, or had been forbidden to say.

'What? What is it?'

'Nothing,' said the farmer. 'We know nothing, except that if you head for Whistling Tor, you take your life in your hands. Fair warning. You're not really planning to walk all the way?'

'I have no choice. How long do you think it will it take me?'

If they believed me out of my wits, it did not stop them from offering help, and I blessed them for that. I set out from the farm with a thick felt cloak on top of my damp clothing. They gave me a strip of leather to tie around my writing box so I could sling it over my shoulder along with my pack, leaving my hands free. They gave me a walking stick and a packet of food. Best gift of all was a crude map of the path I must take, with landmarks scrawled in charcoal on a piece of birch bark. I sheltered it under my cloak against the rain. The farmer advised me to stop at one of the farms along the way and go on in the morning, since I had no chance of reaching Whistling Tor by nightfall. The moon would be near full, but with heavy cloud covering the sky it would not light my path. I did not say that I had no intention of stopping before I reached my destination. Never mind if night fell; never mind if there was no moonlight. Somehow I would find the way. *Anluan.* His name was a talisman against the dark, against fear, against giving up. *Anluan, I'm nearly home. Wait for me.*

I walked through the afternoon and into the dusk. I walked on the road and, when I heard a body of horsemen approaching in the fading light, down beside it, under the cover of trees. I could not see the riders well, but as they passed I heard the jingle of metal and voices speaking a tongue unfamiliar to me. Reinforcements for the besieging army, perhaps. How could Anluan prevail against so many? I set my jaw and walked on. It grew dark. I followed the paler ribbon of the earth road; on either side, in the gloom, there might have been anything. Sudden steep rises; abrupt, perilous drops. Cattle, sheep, monsters. Old stories swirled in my mind, full of the menace of what lurked in the shadows beyond the light of hearth fires. I kept on walking. I would get there in time. I must get there in time. Why would the mirror show me what it had chosen to show, if only to draw me back to Whistling Tor after Anluan was dead?

When my feet ached and my back hurt, when the layers of damp clothing and the chill night air had begun to leach away my courage, when I could no longer pretend that I need not rest, I sank down in the shelter of a crumbling stone wall. The moment I stopped moving my knees began to shake. My head was dizzy. My fingers were so cramped I struggled to unfasten my bag. The clouds had thinned, and there was a suggestion of moonlight. I ate some bread and cheese from the package I'd been given and drank some water from my flask. It was too dark to tell if I was on the right track. It was too dark to read my birch-bark map.

I packed the remains of the food into the bag, my hands touching the edge of the mirror as I did so. 'Now would be a good time to show me something useful,' I muttered. 'A lamp, for instance, or a candle; something to light my way.' But I did not draw it out. That last vision was strong in my mind: Anluan's grey face, his limp form; my bending, sorrowful figure holding him; and Muirne standing in the doorway with that odd, impassive look on her face. That look made my skin crawl. It was as if she had no understanding of right or wrong . . .

330

In a moment of insight it came to me. Aislinn. Aislinn in the obsidian mirror, watching as Nechtan performed his acts of torture. Aislinn who had learned so much from the man who had taken her under his wing: to help him in his work, to keep meticulous records, to gather and prepare the materials for ritual magic, to set aside the suffering of human and animal if that suffering could provide vital knowledge. Aislinn, whose face I had never seen, for those visions had shown her hands scrubbing, her form bending over the table, her fall of wheaten hair, but never the features that no doubt had gazed on her patron with nothing but admiration as he had taught her how to set aside her conscience.

My heart raced. Could it be? Could Aislinn have come back after death to join the host that she and Nechtan had unleashed with their flawed experiment? After that fateful All Hallows, the girl had vanished completely from Nechtan's writings. I could not remember a single reference to her after the description of their preparations: the herbs, the wreath, the white gown, the incantation. Where had she gone? Had she perhaps thought better of the path down which Nechtan was leading her, and moved away from Whistling Tor? Or did she linger still? Muirne. Oh, God, Muirne who was as devoted to Anluan as Aislinn had been to Nechtan, Muirne who had been companion to each chieftain in turn . . . Images teased at me: Muirne adjusting cups on a shelf so they were perfectly aligned. Aislinn clearing away the debris of torture, fastidious, detached. Muirne's veil, covering every strand of her hair – if she removed that covering, would a cascade of golden locks tumble over her shoulders and down her back? Aislinn and Muirne. It could be. And if it was, that meant Muirne had a talent nobody at Whistling Tor knew about. She could read.

The moon made a gradual appearance, revealing a landscape in many shades of grey, the path winding on, stony hillsides to either side, pale forms that might have been rocks or sheep. I must go on. The new blisters stinging my feet must wait for attention until I reached Whistling Tor. Anluan needed me. He might even now be lying sick, wounded, despairing. And if my suspicion about Muirne was right, I didn't want her anywhere near him.

I came down a small hill and saw in the distance a bigger rise, dark on dark, with what might perhaps be a high wall at the top.

Nearly there. And now, here was a side road. I took out my map and squinted at it in the moonlight. Yes, there was a grove of oaks nearby, and a single tall pine to the north. I must get off the main track here and go by this lesser way, still wide enough to accommodate a cart or a troop of mounted men-at-arms, but not well travelled. It was the way I had first come here, when I had been running so hard from my demons that I had ventured where no person in her right mind would go. When I reached the marker stone I would be following in my own footsteps.

Before I got close, the mist began to rise. In shreds and ribbons, in twisting tendrils that wrapped themselves around me as I passed, it crept up to obscure the way, turning a moonlit track into a deceptive tapestry of shifting patterns. Curse this place! Even the elements conspired to keep folk out. The memory of that day in the library returned: the blinding clouds of smoke, the panic, the struggle for breath. I willed it away. If I stayed on the edge of the track I could keep going, finding my way step by step.

Time passed; my progress was painfully slow. I held to the side where the marker stone for Whistling Tor had been and prayed that I had not gone past it unknowing. Sounds came to me through the curtains of mist, the call of an owl, something creaking, a shiver in the undergrowth as a small creature passed nearby. And then, not so very far off, I heard men's voices, foreign voices, and a sliding, metallic noise, perhaps a weapon being stealthily drawn. Somewhere ahead of me I could see a glow, as of a cooking fire. I took two steps forward and blundered into the marker stone, cursing as I bruised my knees. A moment later, someone shouted what was unmistakably a challenge, and there came the sound of booted feet approaching.

Nowhere to hide; only the mist to conceal me. If I fled blindly off the path I would soon come to grief. If I stood here I'd be taken by the Normans. I slid the bag off my back, ripped open the fastening, grabbed the mirror. *Help me. Help me now.* I stared into the polished surface, seeking I knew not what. *Quick!*

Within the metal something stirred. Before I could see what it was, a tall form loomed up, a man clad in the garment of woven metal rings that was the Norman form of armour, with a helm on his head and a spear held ready to thrust. He shouted something, and two more warriors appeared through the mist behind him. I stood there immobile, writing box on my back, mirror in my hand, staring at them. Tossing his spear to one of the others, the first man stepped up and grabbed my arm, hard enough to bruise me. The mirror fell to the ground. Bile rose in my throat; my heart knocked in terror. I would not scream. The more attention I drew, the harder it would be to get away.

The three of them were having a conversation, the gist of which was clear: *It's only a woman. Should we let her go her own way? No, take her down there.* This couldn't happen. It mustn't happen. Find out that I was connected to Anluan and these Normans could use me to force his capitulation. Let them do that and I'd be making a mockery of his sacrifice in sending me away. I'd be the one responsible for his downfall.

'Let me go!' I said sharply, trying to seize the initiative. 'You can't do this! Release me right now!'

The fellow responded by tightening his grip on me. One of the others had a look in his eye that made my stomach clench with unease. They might take me to their leader and interrogate me. Or they might decide they'd like a little quick entertainment with no questions asked. The mist would provide perfect concealment.

'Let go of me!' I snarled, pulling against my captor's hold, and one of the others cuffed me across the mouth, hard enough to rattle the teeth in my jaw. He hurled a comment at me, and they began to drag me off the road. Through the thickening vapour I caught glimpses of tents and tethered horses, neat stacks of bags that might hold supplies, poles stuck into the ground that might be for flags or pennants. Faint glows here and there suggested there was more than one fire. This was an encampment of many warriors, a substantial besieging force. Whether it encircled the Tor fully, there was no telling. At the very least, I suspected there would be guards posted at strategic points all the way around, preventing Anluan's forces from breaking out.

We were heading for a larger tent, more of a pavilion, within which a light still burned. One of the men went ahead, stepping up to the bigger tent, calling out to someone within. *A spy. A spy in the camp. Will you question her?* Four more strides and I'd be inside the place, completely at their mercy. I had to do something.

I sank my teeth into my captor's hand. He cursed, his grip slackening momentarily, and I turned to bolt into the mist and out of sight. One of the others reached to grab me, and then there came a strange sound, a clattering, a rattling, an eldritch whinnying. The men froze, their faces paling, as the sound became a shape and out of the obscuring curtain came a tall horse, a creature all bones, its lips stretched in a hideous grin, and on its back a red-eyed rider in a monk's robe, his head a skull's, his smile fearsome as death itself. My companions scattered in all directions as horse and rider came up beside me and halted. I balanced my writing box with one hand and reached up with the other. Eichri bent, hooked an arm around me and lifted me to the saddle before him as if I were no heavier than a child. We backed up a little.

'Hold tight, Caitrin,' the monk said, and wrapped his bony arm around me. The skeleton horse bunched itself up, then launched itself in a mighty leap. I screwed my eyes shut. I did not dare to look until I felt the uncanny steed come to ground. We were on the other side of the Norman lines. The horse raced ahead along the path and up the hill into the forest. 'Did they harm you?' Eichri asked.

Slowly my heart returned to its usual rhythm. 'A bruise or two, that's all,' I said. 'How did you know to come?'

'We saw you in a mirror. All right? Not going too fast for you?'

It was like racing on a pile of sticks, precarious and uncomfortable. Never mind that; I was safe. I was home. Now I must ask the question. 'Eichri, is Anluan still alive?'

'Alive? Very much so. You've come back right in the middle of things. We have a surprise for the poxy grey-shirts in the morning. At first light we'll be down on them with everything we have. My old friend Rioghan made the battle plan, and a good one it seems to be, though the fellow won't admit as much until it's all over and the Normans are gone from Anluan's land.'

Holy Saint Patrick, I had arrived on the very day of the battle. 'He'll be angry,' I said. 'Anluan. He didn't want me here. But . . .' I was becoming aware that we were no longer alone. As the horse made its way up the hill path in a shivering dance of bones, figures were appearing from under the trees, men, women and children, watching us pass. I saw the look in their eyes, proud, vindicated, full of hope and excitement, and I heard their shadowy voices. *She's back. The lady's back. It's her, come home again.*

'Angry?' Eichri queried. 'If he's angry, I'll eat my sandals. Of course, you didn't see him when I told him you were down at the foot of the hill. He would have rushed off to fetch you himself, straight through the Norman camp, if Rioghan hadn't made him see sense.'

'Oh.' As we clattered into the courtyard followed by a whispering crowd of spectral folk, my heart soared.

'Been a few changes since you left,' Eichri said, as his formidable mount halted. The monk swung down, then reached to lift me to the ground.

A few changes. That was somewhat of an understatement. There were people everywhere, not just the fighting men of the host, but men from the settlement, ordinary men who were working alongside the uncanny inhabitants of Whistling Tor. There was Cathaír, still in his bloody shirt, looking my way in wonder as he helped a young fellow, perhaps a farmhand, to string a bow. There were Eichri's clerical colleagues, going in and out of the east tower, where the chapel was, with piles of folded cloths, basins and bottles. The chapel had become an infirmary; they anticipated casualties of war. There was Tomas's wife, Orna, crossing the courtyard with a ghostly woman by her side. The moon illuminated this nocturnal activity. A single torch burned outside the main entry to the house. Despite the unusually large number of folk about, there was a hush over the place.

'I can hardly believe this,' I said, looking one way then another. 'To get them all working together . . . to break down so many barriers . . . How has he done it, Eichri?'

'Cooperation. Planning. Sheer persistence. We've all helped him. He sent Magnus to talk to Brión straight away, soon after you left. It turned out the local chieftains were far more worried about the Norman threat than they were about the host. Everyone had come to believe Anluan had no will to lead. When opinions were sought, they'd become used to leaving him out. Once they learned things had changed, we worked on persuading them that the host was under control now.'

The host did seem to be under control. The quiet cooperation I saw between living villagers and spectral folk made my spine tingle. 'Is it true?' I asked. 'Does he really have control even beyond the hill? What about the frenzy?'

'We've been working on that,' Eichri said. 'Rioghan's taught them ways to keep strong; so has Magnus. Of course, it hasn't been fully tested.'

My heart sank. At dawn they would head out to confront the Norman army. The risk did not bear thinking about. 'Where is Anluan?' I asked. It was the only thing that mattered right now.

'In his own quarters; he's waiting for you there. Caitrin, you won't have a lot of time alone. We attack before dawn. Anluan's got work to do. And he needs rest, too. He'll carry a heavy burden once the host leaves the hill.' Perhaps I looked surprised, for Eichri added, 'Rioghan's plan has half of the host moving down beyond the boundary to manifest within the Norman lines. Anluan must go down there with them. If the frenzy comes upon our fighting forces, he's the only one who can hold them together. Don't look like that, Caitrin. You have a little time. Gearróg's on guard; he'll make sure nobody interrupts you.'

As we walked towards the south tower and Anluan's private quarters, my mind was full of the dark vision: Anluan lying on his pallet, I grieving, and Muirne . . . What if I walked in that door and Anluan was stretched out stone dead? 'Where is Muirne?' I asked.

'She'll be here somewhere. We haven't seen so much of her since the folk from the settlement came up the hill, when we knew the Normans were on the way. I've spotted her once or twice, up in the north tower or in Irial's garden. And she's been in the library. Doesn't come to meals any more, since the household suddenly expanded. And Magnus isn't here.'

I looked at Eichri, astonished. Surely the loyal Magnus would not desert Anluan at such a time of crisis. 'What happened?'

'All part of the plan. Anluan can tell you. If this goes as expected, we'll be seeing Magnus again in the morning. That woman, Orna, has been doing the cooking, with a whole bevy of assistants. Olcan's looking after the farm.' We were nearly at the tower. 'Ah, look at that,' Eichri said as a small form hurtled towards me. I knelt and caught her, feeling her ice-cold arms around my neck. I stroked her wispy white hair. She was clinging, crying. 'I'm back now,' I murmured. 'It's all right. But I have to talk to Anluan. You wait here with Gearróg. I'll see you soon.' I rose to my feet and met the eyes of the man who had saved me from the fire; the man who had called me Anluan's dearest treasure. He stood in guard position outside the door to the north tower, spear in hand.

'I kept my word,' Gearróg said. 'I kept him safe for you.'

'And I kept mine. I'm home.'

Gearróg was a man of few words. 'You'd best go in, then,' he said. 'Not so long until first light.' After a moment, he added, 'Found your sister, did you?'

It seemed typical that he would remember such a thing. He was the kind of man who would never put himself first.

'I did, and she's . . .' The door of the south tower opened, and there stood Anluan, hair a river of flame across his shoulders, one hand against the doorframe, the other holding a lantern whose warm glow spilled forth, making a path for my weary feet, lighting the way home. Anluan's face was white as winter. But his smile was all summer.

The rest of the world disappeared. He reached out his hand; I took it and was drawn inside. Anluan set the lantern down and closed the door behind us, sliding the bolt across. Then we were in each other's arms, words tumbling out of us, none of it making much sense, for there was a tide rising that swept away all reason. I had not thought that I might be putting my sister's words of advice into practice so soon, but all of a sudden it seemed to me I should perhaps be trying to recall them.

'You need rest, refreshment,' muttered Anluan, releasing me and stepping back. 'You're hurt, your feet –'

'It's nothing.' I sat down and discarded the boots, wincing. 'But my clothes are wet. And I lost my bag when Eichri came to fetch me.' Thank God I had kept Anluan's book in the pouch at my belt. 'Can you give me something to wear? We have so little time, I don't want to go out and ask –'

Anluan said nothing at all. He moved to take a garment from the untidy heap that lay atop his storage chest, but did not give it to me. Instead, he stood with it in his hands, three paces away from where I sat on the edge of the bed.

I can do this, I told myself. *I love him. He loves me. He wants me. I can do it.* Then I stood up and, one by one, removed each article of clothing. I kept my eyes on his, watching him watch, seeing the changes in his face as cloak, shawl, bodice, skirt, stockings, fell each in its turn to the floor. I knew my cheeks were red as ripe apples, but I cared nothing for that. All that mattered was the look on Anluan's face, and the throbbing excitement building in my body. I slipped my fine lawn shift over my head; dropped it slowly. I stood facing him, clothed only in the fall of my hair. 'It's not exactly warm in here,' I said. 'Eichri told me you need rest before the morning. Will you lie down with me awhile?'

Anluan had not moved. 'Caitrin –' he said, then cleared his throat. 'Caitrin, I will disappoint you – I can't –'

'You couldn't disappoint me,' I said, pulling back the blanket and lying down on the bed as my heart performed a wild dance of terrified excitement. 'Don't even think of that. If rest is what you need, then rest beside me and keep me warm. I've missed you more than I can put into words, Anluan. I want to hold you close.'

And then we stopped talking, and I helped Anluan to take off his own clothing so we could lie skin to skin, and very soon the two of us warmed each other very well, but we did not rest. Maraid's wise words were in the back of my mind somewhere, helping me as my hands showed his where to touch, as my mouth grew bolder and his followed the example. I made my body accommodate his, finding ways to move and hold, to slide and twine, within the boundaries of what his weaker limbs could do. Once or twice it was awkward, a little; but not so awkward that it made him draw back, fearful of failure. We had already moved past that point, and when at last our bodies came together, it was like the vision in the mirror of might-have-been, lovely, powerful, overwhelming, a giving and receiving, a meeting and parting, a congress that was both desperate and tender, until a wave of sensation crashed over us and left us drained and spent, hearts hammering, bodies entwined.

It was some time before either of us spoke. I lay tucked against his side, his arm around me, my head against his shoulder. My body touched his in a hundred, a thousand points of skin against skin; I felt each one of them. I never wanted to move from this spot.

'By all the saints,' murmured Anluan. There was a note of utter wonder in his voice. 'I feel as if I could do anything. Anything.'

'You can,' I said. 'I always knew that.' I did not ask him why he had believed this was a thing he could not do. If he wanted to tell me, in time he would.

'Caitrin?'

'Mm?'

'Will you stay this time? Stay and be my wife?'

For a moment my heart was too full to let me speak. 'I'd be honoured,' I whispered. 'I never want to leave you again.' And it came to me that this had not, in fact, been like the vision in the mirror, where Anluan had seen a perfect version of himself making love to me. That had been a fantasy, an embodiment of what could not be. This had been real: real in its flaws and uncertainties, real in its small triumphs, real in its compromises and understanding. 'Anluan, will you forgive me for what I said to you the night we quarrelled? I didn't mean it. It hurt so much that you didn't want me, I think a sort of madness must have come over me . . .'

'Shh,' he said, touching his fingers to my lips. 'There's no need to speak of that. Besides, I was as cruel as you. I banished you in the unkindest way possible. If I had allowed myself to soften, I could not have spoken the words. I feared for your safety.' His cheeks flushed. 'That was not the only reason. I suppose you know that I have just surprised myself somewhat. Caitrin, I longed to keep you by my side; I longed to have you in my bed. But I did not believe I could ever be . . . adequate.'

'I have little experience in these matters,' I said, blushing in my turn. 'But it seemed to me you were a great deal more than adequate. Anluan, I read your little book over and over. When I left here, I thought you didn't love me; not as I loved you. The book told me how wrong I was.'

'How could you not know?' His voice was full of wonderment. 'You changed me utterly. You were like a . . . like a bright,

339

wonderful bloom in a garden full of weeds. Like a graceful capital on a page of plain script, a letter decorated with the deepest, finest colours in all Erin. Like a flame, Caitrin. Like a song.'

I held these words to me as we lay there together, at rest but not asleep. Beyond the closed door of the south tower the full moon crossed the sky and the night wore on towards dawn. So little time. And then he must march out to a battle so uneven, so unpredictable that the thought of it made my heart clench tight with fear. I said nothing of this. Anluan's newfound belief in himself might be his best weapon.

Inevitably, there came a tap on the door.

'My lord?' Gearróg's voice. 'There's food and drink here. Orna brought it over. Rioghan said I should wake you; you need something before you march out.'

Anluan sighed. 'Thank you, Gearróg,' he called.

'I'm hungry,' I said, realising it was rather a long time since that uncomfortable meal eaten by the roadside. 'I'll fetch it, shall I?'

'Not like that.' Anluan regarded me from the bed as I wriggled out to stand stark naked in the centre of the room. 'Put the shirt on, at least. Even so, you'll shock that devoted guard of yours. He's done a fine job, Caitrin. Rewarded your trust a hundredfold. I've asked him to stay with you when we go down the hill today.'

At the door, I took the tray from Gearróg. There was a smile on his blunt features. Orna had assembled a tasty meal for two, some kind of cold roast meat, slabs of dark bread, eggs cooked with herbs. A little jug held ale. It seemed to me the whole household must be awake, and doubtless the whole household had worked out what Anluan and I were doing alone together in his chamber, but I did not really care. The Tor was full of hope tonight. Hearts were high. I had found the treasure I had believed lost forever, and a little embarrassment was neither here nor there.

I poured two cups of ale, then passed one to Anluan, who was sitting up on the bed with the blanket across his lap. I was cold in the borrowed shirt. I moved to the storage chest, rummaging through the heap of garments for a tunic or cloak. Later I would see if any of the clothing I had left was still in the house.

A sound from behind me, like a faint cough or clearing of the throat; then a thud as something fell to the floor. I turned. Anluan had dropped the cup. He had both hands at his throat and his face was grey.

'What?' I was by his side, my heart pounding. 'What is it, what's wrong?'

He tried to speak, but he couldn't seem to catch his breath. He gestured frantically, trying to convey some message to me, but I could not understand what he meant. As I reached to support him he fell back onto the bed, his eyes rolling up.

'*Gearróg!*' I screamed. Oh, God, it was true, it had happened after all. I had asked too much of him, drained his energy . . . There had been something wrong that he hadn't told me, some illness . . .

Gearróg burst in, uttered an oath, then strode back outside to yell for help. As I fought for calm, laying a hand on Anluan's chest to feel if his heart was still beating, putting my fingers to his neck in the place where the blood pulsed, the chamber filled up with people: Olcan, Eichri, Orna and Tomas. And just after them, Rioghan, who took one look and said, 'Dear God, it's Irial all over again.'

'*What –*' I began, outraged that anyone would believe Anluan, beloved Anluan who had held me and lain with me and made magic with me, might want to kill himself. Then I realised what he meant. The cup. The sudden collapse. The blue-grey pallor, the loss of speech, the laboured breathing . . . 'He's been poisoned,' I said. 'The ale – that was all he took – who prepared this tray?' *Do something, save him, now, now!* screamed my inner voice, edging me closer to complete panic.

'Sionnach prepared the food,' Orna said. She kept glancing sideways, as if the close presence of uncanny folk still made her nervous. 'Tomas got the ale for us and I brought the tray across to Gearróg. I was halfway back to the house when I heard you scream. It's the same food and drink all of us had for supper, and nobody else is sick.'

A silence, though everyone was busy, Olcan supporting Anluan, Eichri at the door giving terse instructions to Gearróg, Orna dabbing a damp cloth to the stricken man's brow. Anluan's breathing was shallow and uneven. His skin was a corpse's, all shadows.

'Did anyone else come into the kitchen when Sionnach was preparing the food?'

'Who else would be there in the middle of the night?' Orna frowned. 'Oh, that strange creature did come by; the girl in the veil. Slipped in and out in that way she has, gives me the creeps. She was only there for a moment.'

A moment was long enough. Long enough to put a drop of poison in a jug. Long enough to kill a man. 'There must be an antidote – we just have to work out what the poison is – who knows about herbs?'

'Only Magnus,' Rioghan said. 'And he's not here. Besides, if it's the same thing that killed Irial, we never found out what it was. Nobody knew.'

I wanted to scream, to rend my garments and wail like a madwoman. I summoned the same chill purpose that had helped me once before, when I had walked into the house to confront Ita and Cillian. 'Someone does know,' I said. 'Find Muirne. Bring her here right now. This is her doing.' Aislinn was expert in herb lore. Aislinn knew all about potions. She loved Anluan, but perhaps she hated him too; hated him for loving me, hated him for changing everything on the hill. Maybe she hadn't cared which of us drank first. 'Hurry,' I said, but Rioghan was already gone.

'Caitrin.' Eichri spoke quietly. 'If it's the same thing Irial took, we don't have very long. An hour, maybe. We can't wait for Muirne, even if you're right.' I heard in his voice that he could not believe Muirne would turn on the object of her lifelong devotion. 'We must do something now or we'll lose him while they're still trying to find her.'

'Irial,' I said, as a new idea came to me. If Muirne was prepared to kill her beloved Anluan out of jealousy, might she not have done the same thing to Irial, to whom it seemed she had been as devoted a companion? 'Irial would have known the antidote. He wrote notes on everything he discovered; he'll have recorded every plant that grew on the Tor, I'm sure of it. It will be in one of those little books. He'll have written down the symptoms, every detail – we need to find the poison first, and he should have noted the antidote underneath.' An hour. A little less than an hour. And I was the only one in the house who could read, apart from *her*. If there had been a better scholar among them, perhaps Irial could have been saved.

I took Anluan's limp hand and brought it to my lips. He seemed already gone, but I had felt the blood still moving in his veins, weakly; I had felt the halting heartbeat. To release his hand and walk away was a little death. 'I'm going to the library,' I said over my shoulder. 'I need a safe lantern and a man to guard each door. If anyone finds Muirne, I want to see her straight away. Gearróg, don't let her anywhere near Anluan.'

I ran across the courtyard in my bare feet, with Gearróg's cloak slung over the borrowed shirt. The news was spreading fast. By the time I reached Irial's garden, folk of the host and folk from the settlement were gathering in huddled groups, faces sombre. Cathaír came running into Irial's garden before I entered the house, a lantern in one hand, a long dagger in the other.

'I'll take this door, my lady. Broc's on the other, with the dog. Let me open up for you.' He pushed the library door and it swung open; the inner bolt had not been fastened. 'Where do you want this light?'

'On the shelf, here in the corner. If Muirne comes into the garden, call me straight away. She has the answer, I'm certain of it.'

'Muirne?' Cathaír sounded less dubious than Eichri. 'She did come in here a lot, while you were gone. Dusted shelves. Moved things about. Looked at the books.'

My heart was as cold as the grave. I swept an armful of Irial's notebooks from their shelf and set them on a nearby table. Fumbling in my haste, I began to turn pages, not taking time to read anything fully, for there was no time – *stay alive, please, please* – but scanning them for words that might jump out at me: sudden onset, breathing, speech, grey-blue, poison, antidote . . .

One book, two books, three . . . There were poisons here, but not the one I wanted. There was blue-grey, but that was only the description of a leaf. My hands were sweating with fear; my body was clammy. My heart was knocking about in my breast. My stomach had tied itself in knots. Irial's spidery writing blurred before my eyes. Five books, seven, nine . . .

'Any good?' Cathaír had stepped inside the door. When I glanced up, pain lanced through my neck. I had barely moved for . . . how long? Too long.

'I can't find it!' My voice cracked. 'I can't find anything! And it's not just finding it, it's making the cure and giving it to him, and I'm running out of time!' I seized another book, started to flick through the pages, knew I was close to losing the ability to understand the words before me.

'My lady,' Cathaír said, his tone diffident, 'they're saying you think Muirne did this. Gave Lord Anluan the poison.'

'That's what I think, yes. That she can read. That she knows plants and their uses. That she gave it to him, and that she's hiding so I can't make her tell me the antidote before he dies.' Herb of grace; comfrey; wormwood. Meadowsweet, mugwort, thyme. This was useless, useless. I should go back and hold him, cradle him. At least I would be there to say goodbye.

'It's just that . . .' Cathaír hesitated.

'Go on.'

'If it's her, Muirne, you might want to look in the stillroom – you know, that little place next to the garden wall. That's where she goes at night. Irial used to do his work in there, his brewing and concoction. Since he died, nobody's gone in; nobody but her. And she loves those little books, the ones you have there. Those are the ones she looks at when she comes to the library. Holds them against her heart as if they were children.'

I was out in Irial's garden before he had finished speaking. The door to the low stone outbuilding was bolted, as always. That would be no barrier to Muirne. She could probably walk through walls. 'I need you to open this for me,' I said. 'Quickly. And I need you to help me search. It'll be a small book like those others.' Irial's sad margin notes had been numbered up to five hundred and ninety-four. But he had outlived his wife by two years, and that was more than seven hundred days. Unless he had stopped writing them, unless he had lost the will to write at all, somewhere there was another journal.

Cathaír set his boot to the stillroom door. The timbers parted, the chain fell loose, the bolt came tumbling out of the stone wall. I peered into the dim interior. 'Hold up the lantern,' I said, stepping inside. There was a wrong feeling about the place, something I could not quite identify. I had expected old, musty things, tools stored and forgotten or the crumbling remnants of Irial's long-ago botanical work. But the stillroom was perfectly tidy. A millet broom stood in a corner; a duster hung on a wall. Candles were ranked on a shelf. There was a workbench with crucibles and jars, some holding objects I could not identify. A mortar and pestle stood beside a rack of knives and other implements that gleamed darkly in the lantern light. Bunches of herbs hung from the roof. At one end of the immaculate room was a pallet, and on it lay a small lidded box.

No books in sight. 'She must have it here somewhere,' I muttered. 'Look everywhere, Catháir. It's here, I know it. Here but hidden.' I grabbed the blanket that lay bunched at the end of the pallet, the only untidy note in the whole room. I shook it out; nothing there. I reached down the back of the bed. Nothing at all. I crouched to look underneath, while Catháir worked his way along the shelves, picking things up and setting them down. A bundle of rags lay on the floor, under the bed; I drew them out. Familiar somehow, but what were they?

'Baby!' The little voice spoke from the doorway, and a moment later the ghost girl was crouched beside me, gathering up the pathetic heap, trying to hold the pieces together, pieces that were white, like Róise's face, and violet, like the little veil I had made to cover the doll's ruined hair, and brown, like the skirt that had been shredded and destroyed in the quiet of my bedchamber. Threads of woollen hair; tattered fragments of a smiling mouth embroidered with love. The child stood clutching her violated treasure to her breast. 'All right now, baby,' she whispered.

Catháir squatted down beside the girl, and while his eyes were as wild and shifting as always, there was something gentle in his manner. 'Little sister,' he said, 'have you come in here before?'

'Mm,' she murmured, but did not look at him. Her head was bent over her ruined baby.

'Is there a book here?' the young warrior asked. 'Does the lady in the veil have a special book hidden away?'

A silence.

'Please,' I said, trying to keep my voice as calm and kindly as Catháir's, though a scream was welling up in me. 'If you know where it is, please show us.'

A little hand rose; a finger pointed to the box on the bed. It was much too small to hold a book, even a tiny one, and my heart sank anew, but I lifted it and unfastened the catch. I opened the lid to see my mother's embroidered kerchief, folded precisely. Under this was a strange assortment of little items: a strip of bright weaving in shades of violet and purple; a decorative buckle from a lady's shoe; a striking cloak-fastener of silver and amber. *She's kept a trophy from each of us*, I thought. *From each of those she hated and thought to kill. From each who took a beloved chieftain from her.*

'What's that at the bottom?' Catháir asked.

'It's a key.' A thin thread of hope at last. 'What does this open?'

The child shrank into herself, perhaps frightened by my desperation.

'Please,' I said more quietly. 'Please help me. Lord Anluan is very sick; we have to save him. Do you know what the key is for?' I lifted the embroidered kerchief and spread it out on the bed. 'You can put the baby in this and wrap her up safely.'

The child placed her pile of scraps in the middle of the kerchief and watched while I tied the corners together, two and two, making a neat bundle. 'The mirror,' she murmured.

'Mirror?' There was an odd note in Catháir's voice, and when I looked up I saw him put a hand to his brow as if in pain. 'What mirror?'

Abruptly, the girl began to cry. 'My head hurts,' she whispered, picking up the kerchief bundle and holding it against her breast.

Not this; not now, oh please . . . 'Hold fast, Catháir,' I said. 'I need you. We must find this book.' From outside, in the garden, came sounds of folk cursing, wailing, shouting.

The young warrior staggered, thrust out a hand, gripped the bench and straightened. He pursed his lips and whistled a few desperate notes: *Stand up and fight . . . men of the hill . . .*

'*That* mirror,' sobbed the ghost child, and pointed.

It was old, corroded, revealing nothing at all save the crusted debris of long neglect. It stood against the wall at the back of the workbench, screened by a row of jars. As I moved them aside their contents stirred in an unsettling semblance of life. I lifted the ancient mirror away and there, behind it, was a wooden hatch with a keyhole.

'*Dauntless in courage . . . united in will,*' sang Catháir, and other

346

voices joined in from outside the stillroom, men's deep tones, women's higher ones. *'Swing your swords proudly, hold your heads high . . .'*

I turned the key; I opened the door.

'Books,' said Catháir, breaking off his song. 'Here, let me shine the light for you.'

Two books, one the same as Irial's notebooks, the other even smaller. I opened up the first on the workbench and saw the familiar spidery script and delicately rendered illustrations. 'This is it,' I said, slipping the other book into a pocket of Gearróg's cloak. *Quickly, quickly . . .* I began to turn the pages. Some kind of journal entry, not related to herbs at all; a poultice for earache in children; a discussion of various herbs that might be used to alleviate grief . . .

I found it about halfway through. The poison brewed with precise quantities of dragon-claw berries, ground and steeped in a strong mead, then strained through gauze and left to stand for seven days. *The onset is rapid,* Irial had written. *First comes a greying of the skin, followed by shortness of breath, loss of speech, then unconsciousness leading to death in little more than an hour. The antidote is . . .*

'Heart's blood,' I muttered as I ran across the garden with the book in one hand. Folk dodged out of my way – many had been waiting as I searched. 'I should have guessed. Curse Muirne! Catháir, I need someone who can help me brew this.'

I reached the corner where the herb grew. I fell to my knees; Catháir held up the lantern. The circle of light bathed the soft grey-green leaves of the comfrey bush and showed, beneath it, the dried and withered remnants of the heart's blood flowers. Only two. *One handful of finely chopped petals,* Irial had written. *As fresh as possible.*

'It has to work, this must be enough,' I muttered, reaching across to pluck my pathetic harvest. Around the garden the song rang out, more confident now: *'Brothers together, we live and we die!'* Rioghan had tutored them well. He had taught them hope in the face of despair.

'I will help you.' It was the wise woman of the host, she with the moon tattoo on her brow. Her features were calm, but I saw pain in her eyes; the frenzy, it seemed, touched each and every one of them. 'You need other herbs?'

'Dried flowers of lavender – there's a bunch hanging in the stillroom. I'll run ahead to the kitchen.' Back into the library, the quicker way, through the darkened space and out the other door, surprising the old warrior, Broc, who stood roaring out the song with his hands gripped tight as ancient ivy around his spear. Fianchu barking, racing ahead of me as if he knew just what had to be done. Catháir coming behind me, desperate to keep me safe, fighting the pain. The kitchen full of folk, the fire glowing, Orna's friend Sionnach lifting a steaming kettle. Orna herself in the doorway, and coming in after her the wise woman, a sheaf of dried lavender in her hands. She had been quick.

'One of you chop this as finely as you can. One of you shred the lavender blooms. Orna, we need . . .' The look on her face halted me.

'He's still alive,' Orna said quickly. 'But we haven't long. What is it we're brewing?'

'Life, I hope. It's an antidote to what I think he was given – simple enough, just these two plants made into a tea.'

'Have you a precise measure for this?' asked the woman of the host. 'Heart's blood is a perilous herb. Give him too much and it will carry him off forever.'

'Two cups of water, just off the boil.' The remedy was burned into my mind; I could see every stroke of Irial's writing. 'One handful of finely chopped heart's blood petals. Two handfuls of lavender.' I looked at the scant harvest of heart's blood. 'I don't know if this is enough.' Terror welled up in me. That Anluan should die for want of a single flower . . .

'Half quantities,' said Orna, taking a knife from the bench and coming up to the table. 'You can't expect a man barely conscious to swallow two whole cups of this stuff. It should be enough, don't you think?' She glanced at the spectral woman.

'It will suffice, I believe.'

'Let's do this, then. Sionnach, don't put that kettle back on, didn't you hear what Caitrin said? Just *off* the boil.'

'Did Muirne come?' I asked shakily, realising the task had been taken out of my hands. Orna chopped; the wise woman measured;

348

Sionnach poured the hot water into the jug. Outside the singing went on. I hoped the sound would not carry as far as the Norman encampment, or the surprise attack would be no surprise at all.

'Wretched tune,' muttered Orna, but her tone was good-natured. 'I'll be hearing it in my sleep. I can even hear Tomas singing. Fair enough, I suppose; we're one and the same now. Men of the hill. And women.'

'She did not come,' the ghostly woman said. 'The girl in the veil. If you achieve this, if you cure him, she will fear you more than ever.'

'Fear?' I echoed, started. 'Muirne fear *me*?' But there was no time to ask more. Eichri was at the door.

'They're saying you found it. The antidote. Is it true?' He sounded desperate; a faint rattling sound told me he was trembling.

'We're bringing it now,' I said. 'He only has to hold on a few moments more.' *Dear God, don't take him from me . . .*

'You'd want to make haste,' Eichri said.

The wise woman passed the jug into my hands, carefully. It was so hot I almost dropped it. Orna snatched a cleaning cloth from a peg and helped me wrap it around the jug. 'By the time we reach the tower,' she said, 'it will be cool enough for him to drink.'

Sionnach had fetched a clean cup. We walked out of the house and across the courtyard, and as we passed the song dwindled and faltered and ceased. Eyes were on us from all around, the stricken eyes of those who still battled the enemy that sought to poison their thoughts; the frightened eyes of ordinary folk whose world had changed forever. I wanted to run, to fly, to be at Anluan's side this moment, but I held the jug, his salvation within, and I walked as if on eggshells, step by careful step.

At the entry to the south tower, Gearróg stood strong, though I saw the tension in his body and the strain of resistance on his face. The frenzy tried him hard, as before. He was muttering to himself, and as I passed him I heard him say: 'God, don't let Lord Anluan die. They say you'll listen to a sinner's prayer. Hear mine tonight, will you? We're all in the balance here.'

Then I was in the chamber and by Anluan's bedside. He lay in Olcan's steady arms, his mouth slightly open, his lids closed, his breath whistling like the wind in reeds. Alive; by all the saints, still alive. My hands were shaking so hard I could not pour the infusion from jug to cup, so Orna did it for me, but I was the one who held the vessel to his lips.

'Anluan,' I said with tears running down my cheeks, 'you must drink this. Just a sip is enough to start with. Anluan, please try.' It was plain that he could not hear me. The precious draught would spill from his unconscious mouth to soak into the blankets and be lost.

'Dip the cloth.' The calm voice was that of the wise woman. 'Squeeze a little into his mouth. Feed him as you would a motherless babe.'

I soaked up a little of the infusion in the cloth she had given me; brought it carefully up. To waste even a drop might be to lose this battle. Olcan tipped Anluan's head back slightly and I squeezed the tea into his mouth. *Drink it. Drink it.*

He swallowed. I released the breath I had been holding and dipped the cloth again. And again. The chamber was so still I thought I could hear my heart beating. Another few drops; Anluan's eyelids flickered. He gasped for air, tensed, turned his head.

'Use the cup now,' said the wise woman. 'He'll soon come back to full awareness. Go slowly.'

'Drink, dear one,' I said, laying one hand on Anluan's neck and tilting the cup against his lips.

He drank; stopped to suck in air; drank again, thirstily. His eyes opened, blue as the sky on the loveliest day of summer and utterly confused. 'What . . .' he managed, then ran out of breath.

'Hush, don't try to talk.' I set down the empty cup, turning my head away so he would not see the tears pouring down my cheeks. 'It's all right, you're all right now. Take your time.'

'Caitrin – Olcan – what –?' Anluan turned his head one way and the other; he put a hand to his brow, tried to sit up, collapsed back against Olcan's supporting arm. 'What happened to me? Did I dream . . .' A silence, then I felt his hand brush against me where I sat bent over on the edge of the bed. 'Caitrin, you're crying. What . . . what is this?' His voice was a little stronger, and when I turned to look, there was a slight flush of colour in his wan cheeks.

'Who'd have imagined it?' said Orna. 'Heart's blood. Thought it was only good for rich folk's ink. My lord,' she was suddenly shy, her tone diffident, 'you've been terribly sick. Near death. Caitrin brought you back.'

'Sick?' Anluan frowned, his eyes moving over the empty cup in my hand and the empty jug the wise woman was holding. 'But . . .' He cleared his throat. 'I dreamed . . . Caitrin, are you really here?'

'Yes,' I said, a blush rising to my face.

'That was real . . . you and I . . .'

The blush deepened; my cheeks were on fire. 'It was,' I said. 'And so am I. Anluan, you must lie down and rest; you've been very ill.'

'No . . .' He was trying to sit up again, his breathing laboured. 'No, there's no time for this . . . I must . . . God, I can't catch my breath . . . Tell me what happened . . .'

I explained it as calmly as I could, while he worked on his breathing, and Olcan supported him until at last he could manage to sit on his own. I said nothing of Muirne, only told him about the poison, and that it was the same one that had killed his father. I explained that we had found the antidote, but not where. I did not speak of the little hoard of trophies I had found.

'Poison,' Anluan said, his tone flat. 'Now, on the brink of the battle, poison . . .'

Before I could say anything more, the tall, red-cloaked figure of Rioghan appeared in the doorway with Cathaír behind him. 'God be praised,' the councillor breathed, his dark eyes on Anluan. He turned to face the courtyard, and no doubt he wanted to shout in a voice like a war trumpet, but he held his jubilant announcement quiet: 'He's safe! Lord Anluan is well again!'

Well? Hardly that, I thought, clutching Anluan's hand in mine. I glanced over at Rioghan, guessing what was coming.

'My lord,' Rioghan said, walking in and falling onto one knee beside the bed in courtly fashion, 'it's close to first light. We can't do this without you.'

'He can't go now!' I protested. 'You can't ask this of him!' A few heartbeats ago Anluan had been lying there close to death. He looked barely able to stand up on his own. He couldn't possibly lead an army into battle. 'Can't the venture be delayed until tomorrow?'

'It must be today, Caitrin,' Rioghan said. 'The plan is in place. We go down the hill before dawn. Half of our force manifests in the Norman camp and engages them. The other half waits under the concealment of the trees. When we've created general chaos in the enemy ranks, Magnus brings in the war bands from Silverlake and Whiteshore, under their own leaders. The Normans are driven back up into the woods and into the waiting trap. It's too late to withdraw Magnus's reinforcements now; they've ridden out from their own territories to take this risk for us, and we can't send out a messenger without alerting the enemy. We're hoping Eichri's sudden dramatic appearance to rescue you didn't do that. The mist will have helped; he doesn't think many saw him. With luck, those who did may still be arguing about whether you really were carried off by a spectral rider or whether they imagined the whole thing. My lord, you have time to put on your battle gear. No more than that. Cathaír and I will help you.'

Anluan rose to his feet. He swayed, then straightened. 'I can do this, Caitrin,' he said, setting his jaw.

I struggled to find the strength to match him. 'I know you can. I'll leave you to get ready now.' I glanced around the chamber, where all of them stood quiet: stalwart Olcan; Rioghan with his jaw tight, battling the memory of failure; Eichri in his brown robe; Orna and Sionnach; the woman with the graven moon on her calm brow. Cathaír moved to the storage chest to take out various items of clothing: a leather breast-piece like the one Magnus wore, a helm, a silver-buckled belt. 'I'm proud of you, so proud it breaks my heart. Come back safely.' I wanted to kiss Anluan properly, but this was not the time. At this moment, standing there a little crooked and clutching a sheet awkwardly in front of him to conceal his nakedness, he was every bit a chieftain. I stood on tiptoe, put my hands on his shoulders and laid my cheek against his. 'I love you,' I whispered.

'I love you, Caitrin.' Anluan's was no whisper, but a declaration, strong and proud. 'Gearróg must stay with you until I return. Several of the men from the settlement will be up here as well, and we have a small force posted atop the wall. Take no risks.' He was shrugging on a shirt Cathaír held ready. 'Caitrin, who could have put poison in the cup?'

As Anluan bent over to pull on a pair of trousers, Rioghan caught my eye. He gave the slightest shake of his head, and I swallowed the words I had been about to say. This was not the time to speak of Aislinn, and of what now seemed not suspicion, but reality. 'We can talk about it later,' I said. 'May God watch over you and shield you from harm.'

chapter fourteen

hey assembled in the courtyard not long after. Still clad in my borrowed shirt and cloak, I stood on the steps with Orna on one side and a watchful Gearróg on the other. Around us were gathered the women and children of the host, and the women and children of the settlement, a far smaller group, along with a few very old men, those too frail to march into battle. Above us on the walkways were stationed men of the host, bows and quivers ready, eyes on the hillside beyond the wall. A hush lay over all; in the semi-dark of very early morning, a single bird could be heard uttering a sleepy chirp, more question than statement. *Is it time yet?*

It was an extraordinary army, the stuff of mad dreams. Anluan cut a sombre figure. He wore black under his protective garments, and his bright hair was concealed by the leather helm. The only weapon he bore was a long knife at his belt. He looked pale. The lines around nose and mouth, those that had once made me believe him far older than his five-and-twenty years, were all too visible this morning. I made sure my anxiety did not show on my face.

By his side was Catháir in his bloody shirt. He had a sword sheathed at his hip and a thrusting spear in his hand. It seemed to me his eyes were calmer today; indeed, there was a purpose about all this motley band that stilled my heart, letting hope in. Perhaps they could do it. Perhaps, even beyond the boundaries of the hill, they could hold strong against the frenzy if it came, and follow their chieftain to victory.

Olcan was on Anluan's other side with Fianchu on a rope leash. They were formidable, the two of them, all harnessed strength. It was hard to believe this fearsome war hound had slept curled around a little child, warm against her eternal cold. Close by them was Rioghan, grim as death.

A rattling of bones preceded the appearance, from among the trees, of the skeletal horse and its monkish rider. Eichri looked in my direction, and he and his mount grinned. On the edges of the assembled force stood men of Whistling Tor settlement, Tomas among them. They had perhaps sufficient armour for half their number, but the pieces had been shared: one man had only a helm, another mismatched wrist guards, a third, luckier individual a worn breast-piece. Some bore round shields, chipped and worn but freshly painted with the emblem of a golden sun on a field of blue. I recalled the mirror of might-have-been and the image of Anluan riding out with a band of fit young warriors under a banner with just such colours. The men from the settlement looked decidedly nervous. They had grown up on stories of the host, dark stories of murder and mayhem. To reach this point must have required a remarkable degree of leadership by both Anluan and Rioghan, and a great deal of courage from these ordinary folk.

'It's time,' said Anluan, turning to include the entire assembly in his gaze. 'You know the plan. Keep to it and we'll drive these invaders off our land and into oblivion. Men of the settlement, you know what rides on this. We fight for our land, for our families, for the future. Men of the host, for you the stakes are still higher. Win today and you win us time to seek out the counter spell. Win me this battle and I swear to you that I will find it, if it takes all the years of my life.

'Men, you know what you must do. The first wave goes beyond the boundary of the hill, and beyond the line where I am certain I can keep you in check, whatever comes. If the frenzy touches your mind, you won't be able to sing to hold it off, not until the moment of attack. Once outside the fortress walls we must maintain total silence or the enemy will be alerted. I will be there to lead you. I am your chieftain. If the frenzy comes, remember that mine is the only voice you must obey. If madness threatens to drive you off course, cling to that. You are my men; you are the men of the hill. We march to victory. When every last Norman soldier is gone from our territory, when Whistling Tor is ours again, we'll march up here with our hearts high, singing fit to rattle the walls of this fortress.'

The urge to give this speech the resounding cheer it deserved showed on every face. That nobody uttered a word was testament to the transformation of this extraordinary band of frightened villagers and wayward spectres into a disciplined fighting force. Anluan turned his head toward me. He smiled, and in that smile I saw his love for me, and his fear. I found a smile of my own and hoped it was full of confidence.

'Forward, men!' Anluan said, and they moved away, out through the gap in the wall and down into the dark forest. The men of the hill: young and old, dead and living, monk, councillor, warrior, craftsman, innkeeper, farmer. Hope shone in their eyes; pride held their bodies straight and tall. Above the trees the sky held the faintest hint of dawn.

'Well, then,' said Orna when the last in the line had vanished from sight. She wiped a hand across her cheek. 'You'd best not stand about in your bare feet any longer, Caitrin, not to speak of that shirt that shows half your legs. Let's see if we can find you a gown somewhere. Coming in?' This last was addressed to the wise woman.

'We will wait out of doors.' The woman with the moon tattoo had been joined by the others I had seen on the night of Anluan's council, the village wife and the elegant creature with glittering jewellery and features of faded beauty. 'Be wary, Caitrin,' the wise woman added. 'If poison was in the jug, you, too, were an intended victim. If you are right, and the girl in the veil has done this, she is cleverer and more devious than any of us believed. We thought her harmless. Her devotion to the chieftains of Whistling Tor seemed of little consequence. She may have the ability to make others see in the way she wishes them to see. She is still here. She still watches you. Take care.'

I nodded, a frisson of unease passing through me. This rang true. It could explain the surprising blindness of all the men of the inner circle to just how odd Muirne's behaviour was. They thought her well meaning and harmless. Often they hardly seemed to notice her. And perhaps that was just the way she wanted it. How convenient to be so invisible that when bad things happened, nobody gave any thought to the possibility that she might be the one responsible.

Some time later, clad in a borrowed gown, shawl and slippers, I sat at the kitchen table with a group of women from the settlement. Gearróg stood guard at the outer door. At the inner one were stationed two village boys no more than thirteen years old, a sharpened stick apiece.

'I've a good carving knife within reach,' Orna murmured, following my dubious gaze. 'And there are three pokers in the fire, red-hot every one. We won't be sitting back and letting the Normans take this place, Caitrin. Whistling Tor is our home. Nobody's going to drive us out.'

I hoped it would not come to that, since the enemy would only reach the fortress if Rioghan's bold strategy failed and Anluan's army was cut down. Or if that army was touched by the frenzy and turned on its own. 'I wish we could see what's happening,' I said, hugging the shawl around me and trying not to imagine the worst. They would be at the foot of the hill by now, dividing into their two groups, one to go forward across the boundary, one to wait under concealment of the trees. What I had not asked, because I did not want to think about it, was where Anluan planned to be when the first group manifested in the centre of the Norman encampment. To keep them strong beyond the boundary, he would need to be close to them, to lead them. They were spectral in nature and could not be killed. Anluan was a living man.

'Cold out there,' commented Orna, speaking to fill the nervous silence.

I realised that I had left Gearróg's cloak lying across a bench when I changed my clothes. I picked it up, intending to take it to him, and realised there was something in the pocket: the little book I had taken from Muirne's secret hoard. I drew it out.

'What's that?' Orna asked. And, when I did not answer, 'Caitrin?'

I stood very still, the book in my hands, its front cover slightly open to reveal, scribed in neat minuscule, the name *Aislinn*. 'She used a crow quill,' I murmured absently, turning the first page with fingers that were less than steady. 'Orna, I must read this. Will you take the cloak to Gearróg, please?'

I set the book on the table beside Irial's notebook. I could understand why the smaller book had been hidden away; not only did that name reveal Muirne's identity, but I could see from a glance that the pages contained personal notes, formulas, diagrams suggesting this might be the very same work book in which she had been scribbling when I had first set eyes on her in the obsidian mirror. A diary of cruelty, of sorcery, of grand ambition gone terribly askew. But why had she put Irial's notebook with it? That was just one of many. She might have wanted to stop me finding the antidote, but that book had been missing since I had first read Irial's records: long before her jealousy had led Muirne to today's evil act. Was there some further evidence of wrong-doing in Irial's book? I leafed through the pages, looking for anything unusual, and glimpsed a heading: *For the preparation of heart's blood ink*. The components and method were set out below. There was not a shred of excitement in me, only disappointment at yet another page with nothing I could use, no key, no clue.

Wait a moment. There *was* an essential difference here, something that made this particular volume stand out from Irial's other notebooks. I leafed back to the beginning; checked the middle again; examined the last pages. There were no margin notes in this book, no record of Irial's long time of sorrow. On the very first page, in Irish, not Latin, Anluan's father had written this:

Farewell, my sunshine and my moonlight, my sweet rose, my love. Six hundred days have passed since I lost you, and I will shed no more tears, though my heart will mourn until we meet again in the place beyond death. Our son lives and grows. While I have been so sunk in grief I hardly knew myself, Magnus has nurtured him with such wisdom and tenderness that he might be a second father. In our boy I see all your good gifts, Emer: courage, wit, steadfastness, hope. Today, in the garden, Anluan fell and hurt his arm. It was not to me that he ran for reassurance, but to Magnus. I must start afresh. I must shut my ears to the voice of sorrow and despair if I would help our son grow to be a man. Though I write no more of my sadness, never believe I have forgotten you, beloved. Every day, you live on in him.

Mother of God. How cruel, how needlessly cruel to hide this book away so that Anluan would never know how much his father loved him; to keep it from Magnus, who bore a weight of guilt that he had not recognised the depth of his friend's despair. These were not the thoughts of a man about to kill himself from grief. In my mind, I saw Muirne with the sorrowing Irial, the man whose garden she haunted, the man whose workroom she had made her own, her secret place. I saw her watching him with Emer; I saw the look on her face, twin to the one she had sometimes turned on me. I imagined her lighting the fire that took her rival's life. I had no difficulty at all in believing that she had poisoned her beloved Irial solely because he loved his wife and son too much and had nothing left for her. She had believed Emer's death would make him hers. She had been wrong. So she had killed him as well. And today she had almost killed his son.

With shaking hands I opened Aislinn's little book. She was here in the house somewhere. She would come back, and when she did I must be ready for her. What to do – read from beginning to end, which would take some time, as there was Latin here as well as Irish, or skim through the book quickly? I began to turn the pages, glancing at numbers and figures that meant little to me, a pentagram within a perfect circle, the latter drawn in the form of a snake devouring its own tail. A list of unusual herbs, with notes as to precisely how each should be gathered. Goldenwood to be cut only on the sixth day of the moon, and with a sickle of bone; the harvest not to be allowed to touch the earth, but to be conveyed with great care to the place of preparation. Preparation for what? Here and there, observations that were not related to her work: *Nechtan is a paragon of learning and courage. I can never hope to match him.* And a few pages later: *He watches me when he believes I am not looking. He confides his deepest secrets. He loves me. I am filled with happiness.*

It made my skin crawl, and yet I felt a trace of pity for her, remembering Nechtan in the obsidian mirror, and how easily he set aside his lust for the girl in the interests of the work ahead. Love? Never that. Such an idea had been only in Aislinn's mind.

Only three days until All Hallows' night. My gown is almost ready; I will fashion the wreath on the last day, so it will be fresh. I can scarcely believe that he has entrusted me with the most vital task of all. When he has marked out the secret pattern, I will stand in its centre. As he speaks the words of the invocation the beings will emerge, drawn by my essence. The army will form around me, between the points of the pentagram. I know the words of the charm; he rehearses them endlessly, muttering to himself as he attends to the tasks of preparation. I asked him to describe precisely how it works, but he will not tell me. To know more is to be at risk, Aislinn, *he said,* and I will not risk you, my dear. *He tells me I will be like a priestess; like a queen.*

And on another page:

He has not touched me yet. But he looks; oh, how he looks. He has said nothing of afterwards, yet I see a promise in his eyes. When this is over and Mella is gone, we will be together.

And then, at the foot of an untidy page on which various nonsense words – *erappa, sinigilac, egruser* – had been scrawled, crossed out, combined in various ways as if she were solving a puzzle, she wrote:

I have it at last. The secret. The key. I have it. So simple, too simple for a mind like his that seeks always for higher ground, for challenges beyond the limits of ordinary men. He scoffs at the very thought that we might ever need this; and perhaps he is right. After the great work is done, I will tell him that I have discovered what he could not. I cannot wait to see his look of pride.

'What is it?' Orna was staring at me. 'What are you reading?'

'*Sinigilac oigel,*' I muttered, feverishly turning pages. '*Legio caliginis* . . . army of darkness . . .' I sprang to my feet, clutching Aislinn's book in my hand. The other women stared. 'I have to go to the library,' I said. 'Now. I need the obsidian mirror. Gearróg!'

He came racing in, then halted abruptly, his hand halfway to his sword hilt.

'We're going to the library. Bring a light.' My eyes fell on the two lads guarding the inner door, both of whom looked half asleep. They'd have trouble fending off anything bigger than a stray dog.

'I'll come.' Orna was taking a lantern from a hook, picking up her warm shawl. I would feel far safer with her and her big carving knife next to me than these boys trying to be men. 'Sionnach, keep an eye on this door. The rest of you, be ready to snatch one of those pokers and use it if need be. Lead the way, Gearróg.'

We ran, the three of us, through the house to the library door, unguarded now since Broc had left his post to join the march down the hill. Trembling from head to foot, I went to the desk where I had spent long hours with quill and inks restoring order to the chaos of Anluan's collection. I drew a deep breath, reached down and opened the chest that had held Nechtan's personal papers. I drew out the cloth-wrapped bundle; set it on the table; unveiled the obsidian mirror. Gearróg had stationed himself by the door to Irial's garden, alert for danger. After placing the lantern for me, Orna had gone to stand just inside the other door. For all her pallor, there was a grim and capable look about her, and I knew I owed her a great debt for her courage.

I opened Aislinn's notebook to the page where she had begun to describe the ritual: the secret pattern, the invocation, her role as a sort of conduit for the spirits. There was a chance, slight but real, that what had worked with Nechtan's writings might also work with those of his devoted assistant. I must try, at least. A creeping dread was coming over me, a dark misgiving. I hoped very much that I was wrong. It seemed Aislinn had believed her scrambled Latin was a charm of power. A counter spell: she must have believed that, for why would one reverse the words in an invocation – *warriors of darkness, come forth* – save for the purpose of sending those demons back where they came from?

361

Aislinn had probably got it wrong. It did seem far too simple, something Nechtan must surely have tried once he discovered he could not make the host obey. Still, my heart was racing with fearful anticipation. If what she had written in her book was indeed the counter spell, Anluan possessed the means to banish the host. He could undo the family curse and end a hundred years of suffering. I had to know more; I must see the ritual to find out how they had done it and what had gone wrong. This must be more complicated than speaking a few Latin words backwards. 'Show me,' I muttered, my gaze moving from mirror to book and back again. 'Show me quickly.' When Muirne found her book missing, she would come after me to get it back. She would not lightly give up its hidden treasure, the tool of immense power she had kept to herself all these years. I must find out how to use the spell before Muirne found me.

Aislinn's neat script looked up at me, its rows perfectly spaced, its letters round and careful, not a stroke out of place. *I will be like a priestess; like a queen.* The face of the obsidian mirror gleamed in the lantern light. Through the open door to Irial's garden I thought I could hear a clamour down the hill, shouting, screaming, the clash of weaponry, the high, hysterical neighing of horses.

'It's started,' said Gearróg. 'Stand strong, lads.'

'God keep them,' murmured Orna. 'You finding what you need, Caitrin?'

I did not reply, for the mirror's surface had begun to swirl, to change, to darken and lighten and open up, and there before me was the courtyard within the fortress wall, not overgrown as now, but bare and open. The cold light of a full moon bathed the central space, but under the trees lay a profound darkness. At the foot of the steps stood Nechtan, clad in black. The light from a brazier transformed his bony features into a mask of fire and shadow. 'The herbs, Aislinn,' he said.

'The herbs, Aislinn,' he says, and she passes over her small harvest, dry leaves reduced to powder, a mixture designed to aid the transition between worlds, to open portals. Tonight, of all nights, such doors may swing wide. At All Hallows, she muses, one would be a fool to expect anything but the unexpected. There is a tingling in her body, a sharp anticipation that makes her restless as she stands there waiting, knowing that if ever she was beautiful, it is now. The gown is of whitest linen, finer than any she has worn before, its borders embroidered with delicate flowers and vines. Nechtan has bade her wear her hair loose, and it cloaks her in pale silk. Aislinn can feel every thread of it against her skin. She can feel the weight of Nechtan's gaze. His eyes devour her. *Later*, those eyes promise. *Later*.

He has marked out the pentagram in sand, its points touching the circle that encloses it, a circle fashioned in the form of a serpent, its tail between its jaws. Now he casts the herbs into the brazier. The fragrant smoke begins to pass across the place of ritual. There is a great magic afoot tonight, but Nechtan will keep her safe. He loves her. When this is over, she will be his wife. Mella does not deserve him. She is not fit for him. Mella understands nothing of this work; her mind is too small to encompass it. Mella has never been beautiful.

The moon hides behind a cloud; a shiver of wind crosses the courtyard. The brazier flares strangely, sparks dancing upward. 'It's time, Aislinn,' Nechtan says, his voice deep and soft. He comes towards her, an imposing figure in his ritual robe; he extends a hand. Aislinn takes it in hers. Ah, his touch! She feels it deep inside her; the secret parts of her body quiver and throb. *Later . . . later*. He leads her to the centre. They have rehearsed this until it is perfect in every detail; not a grain of sand stirs as their careful feet pass over. Now they are in the middle of the pattern. Nechtan places her just so, arms by her sides, her face towards the place where he will stand for the invocation, on the second step leading to the main entry. He will be outside the circle.

The house is in darkness. If Mella knows what is unfolding here, she has closed herself off from it. Perhaps she's putting cold compresses on her bruised face, or tending to her whining brat. More likely she's abed. She'll sleep alone. From this night forward, she'll always sleep alone.

Nechtan bends to kiss Aislinn on the brow, a chaste touch. He makes his way across the circle to the foot of the steps. She sees him take several deep breaths, readying himself, summoning his strength.

Aislinn knows the rules she must obey tonight. *Keep silent; do not speak. Stand as still as stone. Whatever you feel, whatever you see, remain in the centre. Do not be afraid. I will control them; they cannot harm you.* She can do it. She's practised standing still for far longer than she'll need to tonight; she's learned to conquer the dizziness. No need to practise being quiet. Often she and Nechtan work from dawn to dusk with scarcely a word between them, content in their silent companionship. That he has chosen *her*, that *she* is so honoured . . . It makes her heart swell. It is a miracle, a wonder, a blessing.

She thinks of her secret, the charm she has discovered all by herself, with no need for Nechtan's tutoring. She cannot wait to share it with him. As soon as this is over, she'll tell him of the study she's been doing in her own time, the things she's learned, oh, many things, the secret knowledge she's gained. Perhaps when they have lain together at last, and she has satisfied him, and he lies back to rest, she'll say, quite casually, *Guess what I discovered?*

The capricious wind stirs dead leaves across the flagstones. The moon emerges, a pale, blank face staring down at them. Nechtan begins a solemn progress around the circle, starting in the north.

'By the enduring power of earth, I call you!' He walks to the east. 'By the invisible power of air, I call you!' He moves sunwise, since this is a ritual of manifestation. 'By the transformative power of fire, I call you!' And to the west: 'By the fluid power of water, I call you!' He has cast the circle, and now begins a measured walk along the lines of the pentagram, making sure his feet do not disturb the pattern.

When the figure is complete he stands at the north point, closest to the steps. He turns to face the centre. 'By the all-ruling power of spirit, which knows neither beginning nor ending, I summon you! I call you out of shadow! Out of boundless darkness I conjure you!'

His voice is deep and powerful. It rings around the moonlit courtyard, making the trees shiver. The ancient words tug and pull, coax and beckon, cajole and command. Who could resist such a call?

A trembling courses through Aislinn's body, a premonition of change, and for the first time she is anxious. *What if . . .?* No; look at Nechtan, his dark eyes blazing with confidence, his pose triumphal. He is a master of this craft and he cannot fail.

Now comes the charm proper, the Latin words of power. Once, twice, three times he intones the spell: '*Legio caliginis appare! Appare mihi statim! Resurge! Resurge!*'

All is silence. As she waits, still as a statue in pale marble, Aislinn hardly dares breathe.

Around the circle, in the spaces between the star's five points, wisps of vapour begin to rise. As she watches, her heart pounding, the threads and shreds form into shapes, figures of men in the clothing of ancient days, with weapons in hand and helms on their heads. There is a giant warrior with a club in his fist; there a young one with his shirt all bloody, clutching a spear, with his eyes darting to and fro, as if he is astonished to find himself here. Here a dark-skinned man with bow and quiver, there a thin fellow with a belt full of knives . . . They are but half-formed, these spirit warriors, still more of mist than substance, their figures wavering as if inclined to vanish back to the realm of shadows from whence they have been summoned. Not strong enough yet . . .

'*Resurge!*' Nechtan calls again, a great shout.

Aislinn's legs feel odd, numb and weak suddenly, as if she might collapse. She must not faint; she must not let him down. *Stand still as stone.* She takes a deep breath, fighting the weakness. But something's wrong there too; she can't seem to catch her breath properly. *Remain in the centre.* She gasps, struggles, tries to suck in air, but her lungs aren't working as they should. Her limbs feel leaden.

The figures are clearer now, manifesting in what seems almost fleshly form; there are colours, the blue of an ancient shield, the red of the bloody shirt, a man's fair hair shining in the moonlight. *Stand still . . . in the centre . . .* Aislinn's head feels strange. She snatches a shallow breath. She must not faint. She will not fail him. More spectral forms appear, a dozen, twenty, fifty. The spaces between the points are full of them, packed shoulder to shoulder, their eyes fixed on Nechtan where he stands on the steps, his face incandescent with triumph.

It's done. He has his army. Waves of nausea sweep through Aislinn, but now she can't seem to move at all. Her head is swimming, she feels as if there's an iron band around her chest. *I can't breathe*, she wants to say, but her voice won't work. Not just the lack of air, something else. The heavy stillness is creeping up her body, she cannot move so much as a finger. She tries again to speak but her tongue is frozen, her jaw stiff, her throat rigid. She tries desperately to show Nechtan with her eyes that something has gone wrong. *Help me. Nechtan, help me.*

At last Nechtan's eyes meet hers. Thank God, now he will undo whatever fell charm has fallen on her, and save her. *Help. Help.*

He looks at her, and his face shows only the triumph of the experiment, the grand plan executed without flaw, the tool of his future greatness delivered into his hands. In a sudden moment of chill insight, Aislinn understands. *Your essence will bring them forth*, he told her. Her essence . . . her life . . . this is the price of the power he craves. The white robe, the wreath, his reluctance to touch her . . . A sacrificial victim, young, beautiful and pure. Her body still as if encased in stone, her laboured breath rasping in her chest, Aislinn looks into Nechtan's eyes and sees the bitter truth. He has known all along that she would die, and he doesn't care. He has used her, and now he will discard her without a second thought.

But wait, the charm, the counter spell . . . she has it, she knows it, all she need do is speak the words and this can be undone . . . Through the fog fast filling her mind, Aislinn struggles to find what she needs, to whisper on a faltering breath the words that can save her: . . . *sinigil . . . mitat . . .* She almost has it . . . *sigilin . . . oileg . . .* The fell warriors are becoming brighter, heavier, more solid: a formidable army. They stretch, regard their own limbs, stare at one another, perplexed. *Erap . . . sinigla . . . egur . . . egrus . . .* Too late. The charm has slipped away. Fixing her dying eyes on the man she has loved, the man she has worshipped with every fibre of her being, Aislinn speaks in her mind words her lips cannot form: *I curse you! One hundred years of ill luck attend you, one hundred years of sorrow, one hundred years of failure! You think to discard me like rubbish to the midden, but you will not be rid of me. I will haunt you. I will shadow your steps and those of all you hold dear, I will torment your family for generation on generation. Let the army you so desired be a burden and a misery to you and yours! With my last breath I curse you!*

As everything blurs and fades around her, as the last shreds of clarity leave her mind, Aislinn sees Nechtan's expression change, his transcendent triumph muted by the first trace of doubt. *Something . . . something wrong . . .*

A scream, a crash, and I came back to myself. I dragged my gaze from the mirror, lifted my head, looked straight into her eyes. She stood facing me across the table, her veil slightly askew, her gown a touch less than immaculate.

'Give me my book.' Her voice was precise and clear; each word rang a warning bell.

Gearróg. Orna. Where were they? What had happened while I was absorbed in the vision? The chamber was bright with morning light. How long had I sat here, staring into the mirror, while down the hill the battle raged?

A moan from near the doorway. Out of the corner of my eye I saw Gearróg curled up on the floor, his arms tight over his head. Just like last time; just like the day when Anluan left the hill, and the host went mad, and I nearly died. I looked the other way, and there was Orna, sprawled motionless on the flagstones near the inner door, one arm outstretched, the fingers limp. My mind filled with terror, for the three of us and for Anluan's army, even now out beyond the safe boundary. I rose to my feet, clutching the little book against my breast.

'Give me my book.'

When I did not reply, Muirne turned toward the cowering Gearróg and lifted her hand, pointing. His whole body jerked, and a febrile trembling gripped him. 'You killed them,' she said. So changed was her voice it might have been a different person's, for the tone was that of a sorcerer pronouncing a fell charm. 'Your wife, your children, you killed them in a fit of jealous rage, all gone, all drowned, your little boy, your baby, all gone under the water . . .'

'Nooo!' moaned Gearróg. 'Lies, those are lies!'

'You did it.' Muirne was calm, calm and cold. 'Why do you

think you're here with the rest of them? The stain of it's on you forever. You'll never –'

'Stop it!' I found my courage. 'Leave him alone!' A moment later, the true significance of what I had just witnessed dawned on me and for a moment left me wordless with shock. 'It's you,' I breathed. 'The whole thing, all of it, the voice, the frenzy . . . you used what he taught you, and then . . . Aislinn, this is truly evil!'

'Give me my book or I'll break the host as I've broken your guard here. I'll snap their minds like twigs! I can do it! Give me my book or I'll make sure your precious Anluan never walks back up this hill. They'll be carrying him home on a board, as dead as that woman on the floor there.'

My heart was cold. Orna dead, for the sole misdemeanour of standing up to this twisted spirit?

'You love Anluan,' I said. 'Why would you want to kill him? Why would you kill Irial? Isn't a hundred years of vengeance enough for you, Aislinn?'

Her eyes narrowed. 'Give me what is mine, Caitrin,' she said. 'You are a fool to doubt me. I can wreak utter havoc among the host. I've done it before. Clever reader that you are, you should know that already.'

Though I still stood frozen, my mind had begun to work very quickly indeed. With Gearróg crouched helpless on the floor, why didn't she snatch the book from me? *Stall for time*, said the voice of common sense. *Make her talk.* I must distract her, delay the moment when she would set the frenzy on the host. Anluan must win his battle. This must not end, yet again, in mayhem, chaos, retreat, failure. Once Anluan stepped back within the boundary of the Tor, she would lose her ability to wreak such havoc. In Nechtan's writings, in Conan's, that had always been the pattern of it.

'How do you do it?' I asked, my voice shaking. 'The – the frenzy, the voice? How can you control so many of them at once? Was it your doing every time the host disobeyed Nechtan, every time they ran amok under Conan's leadership? How could you become so powerful, Aislinn?'

That little smile passed over her lips, the smile of superiority, of entitlement. 'I've had a long time to perfect my craft,' she said, and I saw that I had chosen just the right turn of conversation to keep her talking. 'I was always apt, quick, clever. He loved me for that.' The smile vanished. 'He did not love me as he should have done.'

'But how can you speak to all of them at once, telling each one something different? You seem to know just what memories will most torment folk. Even I felt the touch of it, and I am a living woman.' I selected my words carefully. 'It seems to me that you are as powerful as Nechtan was.'

Her lips curved again. 'More powerful. Believe me, Caitrin, there is a way into any mind, if only one knows how to look for it. Here on the Tor, all bend to my will.'

Not quite all, I thought. While Anluan was within the boundary and in control of the host, his power outweighed hers. There was not a shred of doubt in my mind that if he had not been here to keep me safe she would long ago have ensured I was sent away, or worse. She would have pushed me from the tower, to die as Líoch had done. She would have left me shut in the library, to perish by fire as poor Emer had.

'Give me the book, Caitrin. Don't keep me waiting.' Her voice had acquired a new edge; she was no longer calm and controlled. She lifted a hand, and in it was Orna's carving knife.

My heart juddered in panic. I ran through the words of Nechtan's invocation in my mind: *Legio caliginis appare! Appare mihi statim! Resurge!* I was fairly sure I could remember it correctly. I knew the image of the pentagram within its snake-formed circle. I could remember the words Nechtan had used at the beginning, addressing the elemental spirits. Even without the book, I might be able to give Anluan what he needed to end this. If I could stay alive long enough. 'I don't understand why you tried to kill Anluan,' I said, 'but I do know I could just as easily have been the one who drank the poison first. There'd have been nobody to find Irial's notebook and read the antidote if I'd been lying there unable to speak. I can't give you back your book without a promise of good faith.'

I backed away from the table that stood between us, but I could not go far, for a set of shelves stood behind, effectively boxing me in. Chances were she'd still stick the knife into me, even if I gave up her treasure. What to do, with Orna lying there, perhaps dead, perhaps needing my help, and Gearróg now ominously silent? From down the hill noises still came to my ears, a great roaring as of many voices raised together in a war cry or perhaps a song; the thunder of hooves. 'The Tor!' someone shouted, and *'The Tor!'* screamed a hundred voices in response. Cry of comradeship or call to retreat, I did not know which it might be.

I held Aislinn's eye and spoke as calmly as my hammering heart would allow. I must keep her attention off the host. 'You were cruelly wronged, I saw that in the mirror just now. Nechtan failed to recognise your strength, your ability, your potential. I understand why you punished him so. But Irial . . . he was a good man. He never sought to use the host for ill, and I don't believe he was unkind to you. Why would you kill him? Why would you kill Anluan, who wants only the best for Whistling Tor? I thought you loved him.'

'Love, hate,' Aislinn said, and as she moved around the table towards me, knife in hand, she held my eyes with hers, 'little divides them. Nechtan's heirs are weak. They cannot match his lofty aspirations, his genius, his . . . his beauty.'

Holy Saint Patrick, after everything, after the callous betrayal, after the long, long time of suffering, she still had tender feelings for him. Even as she worked to perpetrate the curse she had laid on him and his, she cared for him. It was a notion of love so warped that it sickened me, and I could find nothing to say.

'I had hopes for Irial,' Aislinn said, taking another step towards me. The point of the knife was an arm's length from my heart, and shaking. That icy calm was deserting her. 'I learned much from him, and taught him in my turn – don't look so startled, Caitrin, I know far more of herb lore than one man could learn in his lifetime. But in the end, Irial disappointed me. He loved unwisely. He dared to be happy. Irial wanted a future for Whistling Tor that was . . . not allowable. As for Anluan . . .' Her eyes softened, then as quickly turned to flint. 'You sealed his fate when you opened his mind to hope,' she said. 'At Whistling Tor, there can be no hope. The curse forbids it. He will lose his battle. He will know despair again. As for you, meddling scribe, you thought to change what had been sealed with a dying breath. Why should you survive?'

The slightest of sounds from the garden doorway. I looked past

Aislinn and saw the ghost child standing there, her hair thistle-down pale in the sunlight from beyond. Her eyes were wide with fright as she glanced from me to Aislinn to the prone Gearróg. She clutched her small bundle with both hands. 'Catty?' The little voice wobbled with uncertainty.

Aislinn turned towards the child. I saw her freeze. *'Where did you get that?'* There was such venom in her tone that I shrank back as if from a blow. It was the embroidered kerchief that had done it, one of her trophies, taken from the secret place. The next leap of logic was lightning quick. 'You, you puny wretch, you abomination, you told her where it was! I'll make you sorry –'

'Here, take your book,' I said, and threw it high over Aislinn's head. It crashed to the flagstones near Irial's corner. The child was gone in an instant, out into the garden. As Aislinn moved to recover her treasure a figure loomed up behind her, all bunched muscle and furious eyes. The knife clattered to the floor. They fell together, her wildly thrashing form pinned by Gearróg's strong arms. Spectres they might be, but the fight was violent and real, her desperation against his force.

'You killed them!' Aislinn screamed, her voice now ragged and hoarse. 'Your little boy, your baby –'

'Hold your filthy lying tongue!' Gearróg had one hand on her throat, the other holding her arms above her head as he knelt across her struggling body. 'It was an accident! An accident! Don't spit your poison in my ears!'

'Make him stop,' Aislinn gasped, and her eyes rolled towards me. 'Call your brute off or I'll see to it that the Normans come up the hill as easily as that kinsman of yours did, the one you weren't sensible enough to go off with! I've done it before and I can do it again. All it needs is a word, a snap of the fingers – get your filthy hands off me, pig! Don't just stare at me, do it, Caitrin!'

Perhaps I was staring; her veil had come off completely as Gearróg grappled with her, and her hair spread out across the library floor, long, shimmering, the hue of ripe wheat in sunshine. I recalled, uncomfortably, how Nechtan had longed to touch it.

'It was an accident,' Gearróg said again, and such was the difference in his tone that my heart skipped a beat. 'I didn't do it. It was an accident.' What had been furious denial had turned to stunned recognition. He remembered now, and knew this was true. Something had changed here, changed profoundly.

New figures in the doorway: the wise woman of the host, and behind her the two others who had gone with her to the garden to wait. They crossed the library to kneel by Orna. As Aislinn quieted in Gearróg's grip, more and more folk came in to stand around us, watchful, expectant. There was no doubt, now, that what we could hear from down the hill was a song. It sounded out through the brightening air of morning, jubilant, strong, not quite in unison: *'Swing your swords proudly, Hold your heads high, Brothers together, We live and we die!'* Someone shouted: 'Lord Anluan!' and many voices answered: *'Lord Anluan! The Tor!'*

'It's over.' Gearróg might have been witnessing a miracle, such was the wonder in his voice. 'They've done it.'

And at the same moment, the wise woman said, 'I'm sorry; we cannot help her.' She laid Orna's still form down and stood to face me. 'Her neck is broken. A quick passing and a valiant one.'

It was too much to take in. The battle won. Orna killed. Perhaps, when the men came back up the hill, we would learn of more losses, more brave souls who had given their lives so that Anluan could win back his own ground and theirs. Strangest of all, Aislinn quiescent on the library floor, no longer spitting insults, no longer struggling.

'Tonight is All Hallows,' the wise woman said. 'A hundred years since the accursed chieftain of Whistling Tor first called us forth.' She turned her shrewd gaze on me. 'Did you find what you sought?'

'It's in her book,' I said, and as I spoke, suddenly Aislinn moved, writhing like an eel, slipping from Gearróg's grasp, diving across the library to seize her journal. She rose wild-eyed, with the book clutched in her hands. Her golden hair was dishevelled, her clothing disordered. Gearróg lunged towards her. 'No!' I said, obeying some impulse I hardly understood, and he halted in his tracks.

'But –' Gearróg protested as Aislinn opened the little book and started, with feverish strength, to rip each parchment page from its stitching, tear it up and drop it onto the flagstones.

'Leave her be, Gearróg.' I could almost hear her thoughts. Though her face was a frozen mask, they were in her eyes as she wrenched apart what she had held close for a hundred years, the cherished repository of her secret knowledge. *How dare you over-look me? How dare you speak as if I were invisible? I am a sorcerer. I am powerful. I will destroy you. I will destroy you all.* And at the same time, the voice of a girl just come to womanhood, a voice of long-ing, yearning, promise: *Look at me. See me. Love me.* It seemed to me that she had been caught up in her own curse: she had loved, hated, lost each one of them in turn.

Tiny scraps of parchment, here two words, here only one . . . They lay all around her, scattered like the fallen leaves of autumn's first gale. Aislinn took the empty covers of her book and tore them in two. 'He can't do it now,' she said with perfect clarity, her eyes on me. 'There's no banishing the host without the spell. You won't end this so easily.' She turned and walked out into Irial's garden, and the folk of the host moved back to let her pass.

I stood numb, watching her go. Gearróg was opening and clos-ing his hands, as if he needed to do some damage with them. 'Are you all right?' I asked him.

'Yes. No. You going to let her go, just like that?'

'For now.' It seemed Anluan had won his battle. Once he was back on the hill and learned the truth, he could hold her in check. And it was All Hallows' Eve. 'She's wrong,' I said. I looked over at the wise woman, and she gazed calmly back at me. 'It doesn't matter that she tore up the book. I think Anluan can do this with-out it.'

Gearróg's eyes widened. 'You mean . . .'

'If what she wrote in her little book really is the counter spell, he can use it. I believe he can release you all.'

He sank to a crouch, his hands over his face.

I knelt down beside him. 'You'll be with them again, Gearróg,' I said quietly, laying my hand on his shoulder. 'The ones you loved; the ones you lost. I truly believe it. Now come. I have another task for you.'

We did not go back by the inner door, but made a solemn pro-cession through Irial's garden. The women of the host went in front, and then came Gearróg with Orna in his arms. I walked last. Not alone; the ghost child crept in from a corner of the garden, embroidered bundle in hand, to walk close beside me, brushing against the skirt of my borrowed gown. Suddenly I felt the full weight of this. If the counter spell worked, we would be saying goodbye to all of them. Cathaír. Gearróg. The little girl. Eichri. Rioghan. A catalogue of tears.

As we went through the archway something made me turn to gaze back over the empty garden. The cool autumn sunlight lay on a drift of fallen leaves, the empty birdbath, a blanket of moss softening the stone seat. A lone bird sang in the bare branches of the birch. And down by the stillroom there was a shifting and a folding. I saw nothing moving, but I had the sense that someone had stepped back, set down a burden. This garden had always felt like a safe place. It came to me that someone had kept watch over it, someone who had loved all that grew here. He had lingered beyond his time, knowing there was a duty to be done, a guard to keep; after all, he had seen his son become a man. The unseen tenth in the circle: the invisible presence revered by all. Here, not by the compulsion of a fell charm, but by his own selfless choice. He had been a good man, deserving of eternal rest, but love had held him here until he knew his son would be safe. I fixed my eyes on the place where a rake rested against the stillroom wall, with a hat hooked over the top of it that surely had not been there when I first entered the garden, and I whispered, 'Farewell, Irial. Go home to your Emer. I will watch over him now.'

chapter fifteen

I t was a day of triumph and of loss, of jubilation and of mourning, a day that would furnish fuel for a hundred years of fireside tales. Anluan led his ragtag army back up the hill and into the courtyard with his head held high. The men of the settlement marched behind him, shields carried with pride, weapons gripped in hands more accustomed to wield hay fork, scythe or fishing net than bow and spear. The men of the host came after, with a new light in their shadowy eyes. They had held fast; they had stood by their comrades. They had obeyed their orders and kept to the plan. Rioghan looked stunned. Perhaps he had not quite dared to believe that this time his audacious strategy would bring victory and deliver his lord home safe and sound.

The makeshift infirmary filled up. The stunning success had not been achieved without casualties, and the spectral monks went to and fro with their basins and bandages, splints and potions, tending to the wounded from the settlement and from the force Magnus had brought for the surprise attack.

I had barely time to greet Anluan before he was surrounded by a press of excited folk. As I moved across the courtyard, the

tale came to me in fragments. All across the Tor folk were talking, talking, trying to put it together. The chieftains of Whiteshore
and Silverlake, with their remaining troops, were even now dealing with the ragged remnant of the Norman army. Cleaning up, I
heard someone call it. The horses having bolted, the enemy was
fleeing on foot, disordered and terrified. No doubt Stephen de
Courcy had heard the tales of Whistling Tor before he decided to
lay siege to the place. That was not the same as waking from sleep
to find oneself doing battle with an army like Anluan's. Magnus
was of the opinion that Lord Stephen would already have decided
against claiming the hill for his own. Just in case he had not, Brión
of Whiteshore and Fergal of Silverlake were out there reminding
him of the wisdom of such a choice.

Anluan's first party, led by Cathaír and made up entirely of
spectral warriors, had entered the Norman encampment while
the enemy was sleeping, then manifested abruptly, spooking the
horses and causing general pandemonium. Though the Normans
had greatly outnumbered their attackers, they had not had time
to assume their fighting formations or establish sufficient order
to strike back effectively. While the host was still wreaking havoc
among them, the substantial forces led by Brión and Fergal had
mounted their surprise attack, driving the enemy up onto the hill.
There Anluan's second force, under his personal command, had
fallen upon the Normans with much screaming and wailing, van-
ishing and reappearance, trickery and surprise, not to speak of
the traditional use of arms – by all accounts, the warriors of the
host had put their combat skills to fine use. The men of the settlement had played their part bravely. Fighting alongside those
who had been the stuff of their worst nightmares had been a challenge, but their time on the hill had prepared them for it, and they
were proud of their efforts. I did hear several men ask how long
it would be before they could go back down to the settlement and
see what was left of their homes and belongings. They had lost
four of their own, and one of them was Tomas the innkeeper. We
would be burying him and Orna side by side.

Olcan's face warned me of a further loss. His ruddy cheeks
were ashen, his good-natured smile quite gone. Four men of the
host carried Fianchu on an old door. The dog's breath rasped in

his throat. He lay quite still save for the laboured rise and fall of his chest.

'What happened?' I asked, going over to lay a hand on Fianchu's neck. There was life in the small eyes yet, but it seemed to me they were clouding, dimming by the moment.

'He saved Lord Anluan's life,' one of the bearers said. 'Leaped forward as a poxy grey-shirt swung his sword, took a heavy blow to the back. Where should we take him?'

This last was addressed to Olcan, who pointed towards the house. I was stunned. I had thought both Olcan and Fianchu would go on forever. Somehow I had not imagined an ordinary death of this kind could befall either – they had been on the Tor forever, or so I had believed. I watched Olcan follow his dying friend to the front door and inside. The courtyard was full of folk and abuzz with talk; the forest man moved through the crowd as if he were quite alone. Anluan and Rioghan were surrounded by people from the village. Eichri was deep in conversation with another monk, not one of his spectral brethren but a flesh and blood cleric who must have accompanied the wounded up the hill. I hesitated, thinking of Aislinn and the news I must impart to Anluan as soon as I could extricate him from the crowd. Olcan must not keep this last vigil without friends by his side.

Magnus came up beside me. He was clad in full battle gear, his garments showing the stains of a fight well fought, his hair dark with sweat where the leather helm had covered it, his grey eyes calm. 'Poor old Fianchu,' he said.

I nodded, holding back my tears. A chieftain's wife needed to be strong at such times, and if I was not wed to Anluan yet, I would be soon. 'I'm going inside to keep Olcan company,' I said. 'But I need to talk to you, and to Anluan, Rioghan and Eichri, as soon as possible. It's urgent. Even if Fianchu is dying, I'm afraid this can't wait.'

Magnus glanced towards the steps, where the chieftain of Whistling Tor was facing a new kind of siege, from folk who realised at last that here was a leader who could help them, and were now asking all the questions they had been saving for years. Beside him, Rioghan was attempting to maintain control, while Cathaír stood guard behind. 'We might have trouble getting him away,' he said.

'Tell him it's about the counter spell.'

'It is?' His brows rose. 'I will, then. Welcome back, by the way.'

'You, too. You've achieved remarkable things here while I was gone; I can hardly believe it. Magnus, I need to warn you about Muirne. It may be hard for you to believe, but she tried to poison Anluan. Certain things happened while the battle was going on, and that's what I need to explain to you all.'

In fact, word of my discovery was spreading like wildfire through the host, for Gearróg had been unable to hold back the news. I heard them murmuring one to another as I crossed the courtyard with Magnus at my side – *she's found it, maybe tonight, she thinks we can all go, at last, at last* – and in my mind I repeated the words of Nechtan's Latin charm, on which it all depended. I wondered why Aislinn had risked keeping any part of the answer written down. She was clever; she must have realised that even those fragmented scribblings might allow a scholar, someone who knew Latin, to find the answer to the puzzle and lift the curse she had laid on Whistling Tor. It would have been far safer to keep the charm in her memory, where only she could find it.

But no. I recalled that terrifying moment in the vision when she had tried to speak the words that could free her from Nechtan's spell. Dying and unable to remember. Dying and unable to save herself, even though she had discovered the remedy without her mentor's aid. When she found herself, after death, entrapped in her own curse and bound to each chieftain of Whistling Tor in turn, likely she no longer trusted her own memory. So, instead of destroying the book that held the feverish notations of that earlier self, the one who wanted above all to impress the man she idolised, Muirne had hidden it away, locked in the special place where she thought nobody would ever look. Even Irial, who had used the stillroom regularly for his work, must not have known it was there. She was clever, no doubt of that. I hoped she had no more tricks to play on us.

We found Gearróg and charged him to make sure the message was passed on to Anluan as soon as possible. Then Magnus and I made our way to the kitchen where, as I had expected, Fianchu had been laid in his familiar corner by the fire. He had a blanket over him, and Olcan sat cross-legged by his side, murmuring.

In his soft undertone I heard a catalogue of Fianchu's good deeds, his many acts of kindness, strength and loyalty. I settled myself beside the forest man, my eyes streaming. Magnus, ever practical, busied himself putting on the kettle and clearing the table, saying nothing. The women from the village had gone off to start packing up for the return home, which would happen as soon as Fergal and Brión sent word that it was safe to leave the Tor.

We stayed as we were awhile. Olcan's voice made a steady counterpoint to the laboured sound of Fianchu's breathing, each rise and fall a harder mountain to climb. Always a little slower, a little fainter . . .

The others came in one by one. Eichri was first. He knelt to lay a comforting hand on Olcan's shoulder. 'Remember that time he saw off a whole pack of wolves?' the monk said with a little smile. 'They didn't rightly know which side was up and which was down. You've got a big heart, Fianchu.'

The dog lay quite limp under his blanket; it was by no means sure that he could hear any more, though Olcan kept murmuring to him and stroking his neck. 'Brave boy. Dear old friend. Best dog in the world. You have a good rest now, that's it . . .'

Magnus stepped over and passed me a handkerchief. I mopped my face and blew my nose. We waited.

It was not so long. Against all expectations Fianchu lifted his head for a moment, and Olcan bent to whisper in the dog's ear, so softly that I could not hear what he said. Fianchu put his head down again, relaxing on the blanket, and Olcan bent over him. There came a rattling and rasping as the dog's breathing faltered, and then silence.

'He's gone,' Eichri said. 'May he rest well; he deserves no less. A valiant hound, loyal and brave.'

'I'm so sorry, Olcan,' I managed. 'He was a wonderful friend to all of us, so gentle when he needed to be, yet fierce and strong enough to play his part in battle . . . I'm sure there's never been another like him.'

Olcan muttered thanks. He had moved so Fianchu's head was on his knees. The dog lay limp, the tip of his tongue protruding from his mouth. Olcan's hand continued to move gently against the hound's neck, but he was silent now.

Anluan and Rioghan came in soon after that. Anluan looked dead on his feet. His face was a mask of exhaustion, the bones prominent, the eyes too bright. He had not even had the chance to change his clothes. I wanted to throw my arms around him, to weep against his shoulder, to tell him over and over how proud and relieved and happy I was. But this was not the time for that. I simply looked at him with all the love I had in me.

Anluan put a hand against his leather breast-piece, over his heart, and smiled his crooked smile. The weary eyes softened; I had never seen such a blend of pride and tenderness. Then he went over to Olcan and Fianchu, and crouched down beside them.

'I know there are things that need to be talked about,' Olcan said. 'Go ahead, don't mind me. I'll just sit here a bit.'

'You put up a brave fight down there yourself, Olcan,' said Rioghan. 'Expert hand with the axe.'

'Did what I could. Wish I could have saved him.'

'Fianchu showed exemplary courage,' said Anluan. 'He was a dear friend to us all. I owe him my life. I owe the two of you a debt of gratitude that can never be repaid. This is not your struggle.'

'Ah, well.' Olcan accepted the ale cup Magnus offered him. 'Maybe it's not, but I feel like part of your family now, and so did he. He was a good dog, Fianchu.' His simple epitaph spoken, he lifted the cup, drank, set it back down. 'Welcome home, Caitrin. Didn't think to say it before. It's good to see you.'

'Gearróg said you had urgent news for us, Caitrin,' Anluan said. 'He's standing guard beyond the door there, and we've sent Catháir round to the other side, so we'll be warned if anyone comes. Tell us what has happened.'

We seated ourselves at the table, though Olcan stayed on the floor. I told them the tale of Nechtan's experiment, so nearly successful but turned awry by the girl who had not wanted to give up her life so her mentor could have his uncanny army; her discovery of the counter spell, her delight at her own cleverness, her despair when she could not use the words to save herself. The curse pronounced in silence, the curse whose form I knew because the obsidian mirror gave me a window into the mind of whoever had written the text that lay beside it. One hundred years of ill luck; one hundred years of sorrow; one hundred years of failure.

'And she had the power to make it work,' I said, as my audience sat around me hushed and still. 'She had learned far more from Nechtan than he probably ever realised; she was as apt as he was at the casting of spells. *I will shadow your steps and those of all you hold dear*, that was part of it. She has done so for four generations, stirring up the host and whispering words of despair to each chieftain in turn. She has used her skills in sorcery to add to the chaos.'

'But . . .' Anluan's arm was tense against mine. 'How could I not see this? How could I not recognise it? You're saying all of it, the voice they fear so much, the frenzy that causes them to lose their minds and attack at random, has been entirely her doing?'

'I believe so,' I said.

'Great God, Caitrin!' exclaimed Anluan. 'If anyone other than you had told me this I would have dismissed it as sheer fantasy. *Whispering words of despair*. That rings true. I have been all too ready to believe them. To claim them as my own. I must have been blind.'

'I suppose,' I said, 'that part of her skill may be in making others see her as perfectly harmless.' She hadn't tried very hard with me; her enmity had been plain from the start. Still, it had taken me a very long time, almost too long, to realise the extent of her malice and her power. 'It seems your father spent time with her, perhaps even seeking her help with his botanical work and welcoming her companionship after your mother died. But . . . well, there's something I found that I think you should read now. It was stored away with Muirne's personal things.' I fished Irial's last notebook out from the pouch at my belt, opened it at the first page and gave it to him.

In the silence that ensued, Magnus got up and poked the fire, I refilled people's cups, and Olcan sat quietly with his old friend. Rioghan and Eichri looked at each other across the table, the shadow of a looming farewell removing all trace of their customary sardonic humour. When Anluan had finished reading, he sat in silence for a little. Then he said flatly, 'She killed him. He wanted to live, and she killed him.'

'I believe so. Your father died from the same poison she used on you.' I glanced at Magnus, whose eyes had widened. 'In this letter, Irial writes of making the decision to step out from his fog of grief; he tells the shade of Emer that he will never forget her, but that he will watch her live on in Anluan. It is not the message of a man about to kill himself from despair. Aislinn – Muirne – chose to keep this from Anluan, and from you, Magnus. She loved him, and she wanted to keep everything the way she believed it should be here on Whistling Tor. It was bad enough that Irial loved Emer as he could never love Aislinn. When he wanted to bring hope to the Tor and the folk who lived here, when he wanted a life for his son that would be better than his own, Aislinn must have seen it as a betrayal. She couldn't bear it. So she ended it. I believe she was responsible for your mother's death as well, Anluan. That could never be proven, of course.' I said nothing of Conan and Líoch. This was more than enough for now.

'Holy Mother of God,' muttered Magnus. 'The uncanny fire; the way nobody saw a thing until it was too late . . .'

'Fire without smoke; smoke without fire. The method is in one of those grimoires. As I said, she was – is – an able practitioner of sorcery.'

Anluan had bunched his good hand into a fist. His eyes were cold as frost. 'There is no doubt that Nechtan wronged her,' he said. 'But this is indeed a long and bitter vengeance. Where is she now?'

Seeing the fury on his face, no less alarming for the obvious control he was imposing on himself, I was glad I had not mentioned that Aislinn had threatened me with a carving knife. 'I don't know,' I said. 'But she'll be watching. We need to be careful right up until the words of the counter spell have been spoken. She doesn't like things to deviate from the pattern she has established here. She will fight to keep her curse in place, though I think it has caused her only misery. She tried to make me give her the book by tormenting Gearróg, and then by hurting the little girl. In the end I passed it over and she ripped it up.'

A silence; five pairs of eyes were turned on me in question.

'So she believes we can't do it,' I said. 'She saw me using the obsidian mirror with her book open; she must know, or guess, that I've seen the ritual. But from what she said, it's plain that she doesn't credit me with the wit to remember the words of Nechtan's invocation after one hearing and a glance at her book. The counter spell is very simple: the chieftain must speak the Latin invocation backwards. I imagine the other elements of the ritual would need to be the same, the pentagram, the snake circle, the herbs and so on. There is a woman of the host who might be able to assist with that.'

Anluan was still staring at me. 'You memorised it? All of it?'

I nodded. 'And now you must do the same,' I said. 'In private, behind closed and guarded doors. Aislinn won't want us to do this. If she believes it's a vain attempt based on little more than guesswork, we might manage to finish it.'

'Are you certain this will work, Caitrin?' Eichri's voice was unsteady.

'Not certain, no. But I am sure I have the words correct, and I am sure about the form of the ritual. What remains to be tested is Aislinn's conviction that the counter spell is something so obvious. It seems surprising that Nechtan did not think to try it.'

'He probably didn't want to,' Magnus put in. 'He may never have given up the idea that he could some day turn the host into the mighty army he wanted. And if that was his thinking, he probably never told Conan the words of the original invocation – why would he? Most likely, there was no written record of it apart from these notes of Aislinn's. Of course, there was the book Nechtan got it from in the first place, but Conan may not have known about that.'

'Besides,' I said, 'she did pronounce the curse, a hundred years of sorrow and so on, and perhaps the counter spell wouldn't have worked until that time was up.'

'Which it is tonight,' observed Olcan from his corner. 'All Hallows' Eve.'

'If Muirne – Aislinn – is as clever as you say,' Eichri said, 'she must know that. Why is she fighting against it?'

I could not think how to put it into words: my conviction that Aislinn was trapped in her own spell, that her wish to punish and hurt each chieftain of Whistling Tor in turn went parallel with her love for them. I imagined her dropping the poison into the jug as tears welled in her eyes.

'Aislinn is not part of the host,' Eichri pointed out. 'The counter spell might not work on her. She might linger on forever, casting a blight on the Tor and all who dwell here. Don't look at me like that, Caitrin.'

'She will be gone from here before the sun rises again,' Anluan said, his voice like iron. 'As for the threat today, while I am on the Tor Muirne must comply with my will. We must prepare to enact this ritual, and when we need her to come, I will summon her.' He looked at the others, each in turn, his eyes resting last on Eichri and on Rioghan. 'You understand that I must do this,' he said.

'Ah, well,' said Eichri with a forlorn attempt at nonchalance, 'I'd best claim on that last wager, Councillor. Pay up!'

Rioghan thrust a hand into his robe and drew out a shining silver coin. It danced across the tabletop into his old friend's hand.

'What was that one for?' I asked, blinking back tears.

'Whether you'd be back before or after Anluan won his battle.'

I stared at them. 'You all believed I would come back?'

'You belong here.' Anluan's fingers tightened around mine. 'Sending you away was the worst error of my life, as our friends here have been reminding me regularly ever since the day we found you gone. I did not consider that in losing you, we lost our beating heart.'

'It was right for me to go. And right for me to come back.'

'Did you find that sister of yours?' Magnus asked. 'I liked the sound of her.'

'There's a whole story there, part sad, part happy, part in between. When we have time, I'll tell it.' I glanced at Anluan. 'I should teach you the charm. It's in Latin, and you have to say it backwards.'

'Brighid save me. We'd best start straight away.' Anluan rose to his feet. 'Or almost straight away; I must wash and change, at least. Olcan, will you need help . . .?'

'I'll help him,' Magnus said. 'You've more than enough to do. Brave fight. You showed your colours as a leader, in my opinion.'

Anluan inclined his head in acknowledgement, his cheeks flushing red. Magnus's words had been akin to a father's recognition that his son had proved himself a man.

'We'll be needing to receive Brión and Fergal up here some time later,' Rioghan said. 'Word is that they'll report in person once the Normans are driven beyond the borders. Since you'll be busy, Magnus, I'll make some arrangements for that; look out the best mead and so on.'

'Thank you,' Anluan said. 'Caitrin, I'll send Cathaír across for you as soon as I'm fit for company. I want you to keep Gearróg with you at all times. Call him in now; stay in sight of him.'

Then he went away to his quarters, and Eichri headed off to look out the mead and some other supplies suitable for visiting chieftains. After speaking quietly to Olcan, Magnus called in two burly men of the host to help lift Fianchu. I gave the hound a little kiss on the nose, and Rioghan grasped Olcan by the arm, saying, 'A grievous loss, old friend. I wish you strength.' Then they bore the dog away for burial.

Rioghan and I were alone in the kitchen save for Gearróg standing guard just inside the back door. It felt necessary to do something, to keep my hands busy, so I found a cloth and wiped down the table, thinking that if Orna had not volunteered to come with me last night she might still be here stirring a pot or ordering her assistants about. I hoped their losses would not sit too heavily on the folk of the settlement. It would be important to maintain the extraordinary trust it seemed had developed during the time of the Norman threat. Anluan would be very busy indeed, and so, I supposed, would I.

'Caitrin.' Rioghan had seated himself at the table again, long hands clasped before him. He sounded unusually tentative.

'Mm?'

'Do you truly believe this will work? This counter spell?'

'I hope so,' I said. 'As I said, there's no certainty to any of it. But I believe we must try.'

The silence drew out. I turned to look at him, surprising a strange expression on his pallid face. He looked as if he had found a long-sought treasure, and at the same time as if he were about to lose what he loved best in the world.

'You've helped Anluan achieve something truly remarkable today,' I said. 'In the eyes of the outside world, his winning that battle must seem the stuff of an impossible dream.'

For a long time Rioghan did not speak. Then he said, 'I'll miss him. I'll miss you. I'll even miss that disreputable excuse for a monk. I used to think that if the counter spell was ever found I'd fight it with all my strength. But . . . I think perhaps I'm ready to go. Today was a stunning success. My plan worked perfectly. But I don't feel jubilant. I don't feel vindicated. I just feel tired.'

'If it works, you might see him again,' I said softly. 'Your lord, Breacán. For certain, you will not go back to that in-between place. Not after this.'

'You think not?' His smile was doubtful.

I sat down opposite him, reached across and took his hands in mine. 'I've seen what a good person you are, Rioghan. Loyal, brave, kind . . . You've been strong in your support for Anluan. I truly believe your past error will not haunt you beyond this point.' After a moment I added, 'This place won't be the same without you.'

'Ah, well.' He shook his head as if to rid it of doubts. 'All I can say is, thank God you're here, Caitrin, to keep our boy company. As for the rest of us, we're probably best forgotten.'

'Don't ever think that,' I said with a lump in my throat. 'If nobody else sets your stories down in writing, I surely will. You're part of the history of the Tor. Now stop this or I'll be crying too hard to act like a lady when these visitors get here. And I want to make a good impression.'

Anluan and I spent the next hour or two shut up in his quarters together. Doubtless the folk from the settlement had their own ideas about what we were doing. We did not emerge until Anluan had memorised the form and words of the ritual, though he did not practise saying the counter spell aloud. He would do that only tonight, when all was ready. We talked at length about what must be done and came to one conclusion. We could make every aspect of the ritual as close as possible to last time, but there was no knowing whether the result would be as we wished. All the same, we must try.

There was a great deal to be done. The wounded still lay in what had been the chapel, and needed attention. The folk of the settlement were getting ready to go home, bearing their dead with them. And the materials for the ritual must be prepared. Fianchu had been laid to rest down at the farm, and now both Magnus and a red-eyed Olcan turned their attention to helping with the preparations. Magnus collected the herbs we needed. I remembered the names of only two or three of them, but the wise woman offered her grave advice as to which would aid the transition between worlds. Olcan obtained clean sand from a supply at the farm. Under my directions he marked out the pentagram with its enclosing snakelike circle. The wise woman went to harvest the herb called goldenwood. No matter, she said, that it was not the sixth day of the moon – gathered with the correct form of words, the herb would be equally effective. She was away for some time before walking out of the forest with the small branch across her outstretched hands.

These activities halted for a while when Brión of Whiteshore and Fergal of Silverlake came up the Tor to greet Anluan and to tell him Lord Stephen's forces had withdrawn from all three territories. The two chieftains drank some of our mead and spoke of the future. If there was a slight unease in their demeanour, it was well concealed, and their manner toward Anluan was both courteous and respectful. Anluan agreed that a council should be called before winter weather made travelling too difficult. Stephen de Courcy would likely be only the first of many upstart foreigners wanting a bite of good Connacht land. Mention was made of Ruaridh Uí Conchubhair, and of how things might be different if one of his sons took his place as high king. The local leaders must stand strong and united until that time came. I listened intently as I smiled and passed around the mead, but my mind was on tonight, the ritual, Aislinn. Where was she? Did she still possess some means to undo our efforts?

The visiting chieftains did not stay long. Each was keen to head home with his fighting men now the job was done. Anluan thanked them for their support and expressed his deep regret for their losses. Brión left us two healers who had accompanied his army, since he knew our household was small and would be stretched in providing the necessary support for those who lay wounded. When our visitors were gone, we bade farewell to the folk of the settlement, who were ready to leave the Tor. Tomorrow, Anluan said, we would go down and attend a ritual for their dead. After time for mourning, he would be wanting to speak with them about the future. I saw that already new leaders were stepping up to take the places of Tomas and Orna. Duald, who had once been so afraid of a wandering scribe, was one of them, and Orna's friend Sionnach seemed to be speaking up on behalf of the women. There would be a path forward for all of us. If the counter spell worked; if Aislinn had been right about it. If I had remembered correctly. If nothing else got in the way. Seeing the hope in the eyes of Gearróg and Cathaír and the others, I prayed that I had not made a terrible mistake.

As dusk fell, the host began to gather in the courtyard: men, women and children in little groups or alone, waiting. The buzz of excited talk that had broken out earlier in the day was gone, replaced by a hush of anticipation. Anluan had told me he wanted to talk to the host before the ritual began, and he was doing so now. He wasn't making the kind of grand speech people expect a victorious chieftain to deliver on his return home. Instead, he was walking among them, a tall figure clad all in black, giving each in turn what time he could, listening to each, telling each how sorry he was that his ancestor's ill deed had condemned them to a hundred years of misery. I watched their faces from where I stood with Magnus by the circle. I saw no anger there, no sorrow, only respect, acknowledgement and a dawning hope. *Tonight, this very night we will be at rest.*

'This must work,' I muttered. 'It has to.'

'What if Muirne doesn't make an appearance?' Magnus asked quietly. 'It sounds as if it can't succeed without her.'

I had discussed this point with Anluan at some length: what Aislinn's part must be, whether she should stand in the centre again and what would happen to her if she did. She would not be willing. She'd have to be coerced to take her place, and that felt wrong to me.

'She'll do it if I bid her,' Anluan had said. 'Caitrin, the girl is a murderess several times over. She must be banished with the rest of them. If Nechtan's spell of summoning required her to stand in the middle of the pentagram, then we must do that again.'

'I suppose she will come if Anluan calls her,' I said now. 'She has always obeyed him.' But still, in the depths of my mind, I wondered if this was right. Anluan had not seen that last vision in the obsidian mirror. He had not felt Aislinn's utter terror as she realised Nechtan would not save her, that he didn't want to save her, that her life was the price of his success. Yes, she had performed evil acts; she was a killer. Yet I knew that if it were up to me to make her step into the centre tonight, I would not be able to do it.

I made my own farewells as dusk darkened to night. The cool light of the moon shone down into the courtyard, illuminating the wan faces of the host. The wise woman: I thanked her for her calm assistance and she bowed her head in grave acknowledgement. Why this self-possessed, serene creature had found herself amongst Nechtan's host, I could not understand. The monks, who now emerged from the chapel to join the others: I thanked them for their skill with the wounded. 'And for your singing,' I added. 'When I heard that, it seemed to me that God was present even here, in this place folk call accursed. I remembered that when we go astray, he leads us home.'

'Bless you, child,' said one, and the others said, 'Amen.'

Anluan was talking to Eichri now, a hand on the cleric's shoulder. Rioghan stood alone, his red cloak a bright note in the moonlight. I walked over to him, remembering the day the two of them had met me on the road and showed me the way.

'Rioghan.'

He had never been given to smiles, and he did not smile now, but there was a warmth in his dark eyes. 'Caitrin, lovely lady. You've brought our boy great happiness. Be happy yourself, my dear. Live your life well.'

'I will, Rioghan. You've been a wonderful friend. I want to thank you for your loyalty to Anluan.' Curse it, I had thought myself strong enough not to shed tears; there would be time enough for them later, when this was done. 'I wish you could stay with us. I hope you find what you most long for. Surely you have earned that by now.'

'You've a great deal of kindness in you, Caitrin. May the world treat you as kindly. As for what unfolds next, for me, for that wretch of a monk,' the glance he cast Eichri's way was affectionate, 'for the rest of this motley bunch, who knows what we can expect? A different ending for each of us, perhaps. You are right to use the word hope. That is all we can do.' A shiver passed through him, and he pulled the cloak more tightly around him.

Next, Catháir. He had changed since the day I fled the Tor to confront my own demons. His eyes still darted about; his pose remained restless, the weight shifting from foot to foot. But there was a purpose in his face, a strength and repose in the contours of it. He had been at the very forefront of the attack today, leading the warriors into the heart of the enemy camp. He had played a vital part in the victory. I saw confidence in his look, and a new self-respect. Anluan's trust had transformed him.

'You will be glad to go, Catháir,' I said.

'I have waited long for sleep, lady. Yes, I will go joyfully to the land beyond the grey. Yet I would not have been without this day. These last days. Watching the Tor come alive again; singing the song of battle . . .' He fell to one knee before me. 'Lord Anluan is a true leader. It has been an honour for me to serve him. But you . . .' His voice faltered, then grew strong again. 'You came here with love in your heart. From the first we were real to you, as real as when we wore the flesh and blood of our living bodies. You did not look on us with judgement, but with compassion. You gave us hope.'

My tears were really flowing now. I laid my hand on his shoulder. 'You're a fine man, Catháir,' I said. 'You've served him with great courage. I wish you peace.'

This was getting harder and harder. I caught Anluan's eye as he clasped Eichri in an embrace. He smiled, and I saw that if it was a trial for me, it was far more for him. He had lived amongst these folk all his life. They were his family.

As Anluan moved away, I went up to Eichri and, abandoning the conduct of a chieftain's wife, threw my arms around him. A chill embrace, but my heart felt only warmth. 'Dear Eichri, I'll miss you every single day. I'm so sorry you have to go, you and Rioghan.' I stepped back, my hands on his shoulders. Immediately I saw that something was different. The strange necklace with its cargo of bones and unidentifiable shrivelled objects was gone. In its place my friend wore a strip of leather from which hung a plain wooden cross.

Eichri saw me looking and grinned. 'Never thought you'd see the day, did you, Caitrin? No doubt I convinced you I'd forever remain a sinner unrepentant. I almost convinced myself.'

'How did you . . .?' I could not find the right way to ask the delicate question.

'Brión of Whiteshore brought a priest with him to tend to the injured and speak prayers over the dying. We talked. I had been asking myself certain questions for some time, Caitrin; going over my past errors. We are taught that God forgives sinners. I did wonder if a sinner such as myself could ever be deserving of such mercy. I haven't been sure, in the past, that I even wanted it. Something changed in me while you were gone. Perhaps it was the pattern of goodness that you brought with you. Perhaps it was the flowering of hope on the Tor. At any rate, I spoke to Brother Oisín of my past. He listened and gave his opinion that I was wrong about God's mercy. So I'm working on repentance. Just as well, as it turns out. I pray that this ritual does not condemn me to a hundred years more in that grey place halfway between here and there. More than the fires of hell, I fear boredom.' He regarded me soberly, then flashed his big teeth in a new grin. 'And no, I didn't ask Brother Oisín about a certain secret library. He seemed the kind of man who would be deeply shocked by such a notion.'

'Anluan will never seek it out,' I said, glancing over to where the chieftain of Whistling Tor was now bidding a grave farewell to Rioghan. 'He will conduct tonight's ritual because he must; nobody else can make it work. I believe that after this he will shun the least exercise of magical arts. He fears becoming his great-grandfather all over again. I think he will destroy the grimoires.'

'Mm.' A look of speculation entered Eichri's shadowy eyes. 'This place is full of magic, Caitrin. Whistling Tor was a place of eldritch tales long before Nechtan came along to dabble in sorcery. Such a long cloak of uncanny history is not so easily cast aside. Anluan should keep his books, just in case he needs them. That's my opinion. Farewell, my dear. Look after that fine man of ours.'

'I will.' I scrubbed a hand across my cheeks.

'It's time.' Anluan's deep voice sounded across the darkening courtyard and a hush descended. Magnus lit a torch from the little brazier and climbed the steps to set it in a socket near the door of the house. The flickering red light sent Anluan's shadow across the ritual circle to touch the empty space in the centre. The people of the host began to gather between snake and star, five silent groups of men, women and children. I had wondered how the spaces Olcan had marked out could accommodate so many, but there they were within the lines of sand, a sombre, shadowy throng. Rioghan slipped off his red cloak, dropping it onto the flagstones where it lay like a pool of dark blood. Eichri was waiting close by. The two old friends embraced, looking long into each other's eyes.

'I'll wager two silver pieces we end up together again, Councillor,' Eichri said, and Rioghan said, 'Done, Brother!' But all they exchanged was a smile. Eichri's brethren were forming a small procession, their lips moving in silent prayer. He stepped into the line, and they moved into the circle as if entering a chapel. Rioghan placed himself with the warriors, who clasped his hand in greeting and farewell, each in turn.

Gearróg was at the foot of the steps, keeping guard over Anluan until the very last moment. I went to stand beside him.

'Thank you, Gearróg,' I said. 'For keeping Anluan safe for me; for courage beyond the call of duty. For being yourself. I hope you will see your dear ones again soon. I wish you happiness, my loyal friend.'

If he could have spoken at that moment, he would have. I could see that there was too much in his heart to allow words. He gave a nod, then moved away to take his place amongst the host.

On the bottom step close by me a small figure crouched, head down, shoulders hunched, bundle in her hands. Trying to be overlooked; trying to be invisible.

'It's time, Caitrin,' Anluan said, glancing at the child, then at me.

I sat down on the step beside her and put an arm around her shoulders. It was like plunging my arm into ice water. 'Sweetheart,' I murmured, 'you have to go now. You need to step into the circle with the others. Time to say goodbye.'

Frost-white face turned up towards mine; shadowy eyes fixed on me. 'Go where?' she asked.

'Somewhere good,' I told her, feeling like a liar and a traitor. 'You might see your mama again, maybe.'

'I want to stay with you,' the ghost child said, her little voice clear and true. 'You can be my mama.'

A spear straight to the heart. I could not find an answer, for none was right.

'Come, little one.' The wise woman reached out a hand. 'Step over to me. Take care not to set your feet on the sand; lift them up high, as if you were dancing.'

The child did not look at me again. She walked across, stepping neatly, carrying my mother's embroidered kerchief and the last fragments of Róise, token of my sister's love. She stood beside the wise woman, between two points of the star. Her eyes stared into nowhere.

'We're ready to begin,' Anluan said quietly. Magnus stood on his left. I wiped my eyes on my sleeve, then took up my position on his right. Olcan was by the brazier. 'I will call her.'

But there was no need to call. From the archway to Irial's garden Muirne stepped forth. The neat concealing gown and veil were gone. She wore an ancient garment that had once been white, a high-waisted gown with an embroidered hem. Its skirt wafted around her as she approached. Her hair was loose, a shimmering waterfall. A little wreath of greenery crowned her head. Her eyes shone in the moonlight. 'I'm here, my lord,' she said.

My skin prickled. Aislinn come of her own accord to help us? Aislinn already clad in her ritual garments, calm and willing? We had been certain Anluan would need to summon her, and that she would have to be forced to play her part. We had anticipated reluctance, fury, perhaps fear. Not this.

'There is much I could say to you, Muirne,' Anluan said, keeping his tone level; no trace in it of the bitter fury I knew he bore towards her for the deaths of his beloved parents, the attempt on my life, the long years of suffering. 'But I will say only this. For the wrong my great-grandfather did you, I am sorry. For the wrong you have done to me and my people, God will judge you.'

She watched him calmly, not a flicker of emotion on her face.

'Tonight is All Hallows,' Anluan said. 'One hundred years have passed since you cursed the family at Whistling Tor, and it is time for the doom you set upon us to be lifted.'

'You are no Nechtan,' Aislinn said. 'Try, by all means. Try and fail. You're so good at that.'

Anluan took a deep breath, held it a moment, released it slowly. 'Take your place in the centre, Muirne. Regrettably, it seems we need your assistance.'

'It seems so,' she said, and turned to walk across, lifting up her skirt so it would not brush the ritual markings out of place. The folk of the host shrank back as she passed, and someone hissed. In the very centre of the pentagram, Aislinn halted and stood facing us, hands clasped demurely in front of her. 'I'm ready,' she said calmly. 'Attempt your little spell by all means.'

Anluan fixed her with his gaze. 'You will be silent,' he said, and she was. The faint smile that played on her lips troubled me; it was as mocking as her words. If she was prepared to stand there, in the very spot where she had suffered betrayal and death, she must be quite certain we would fail.

Olcan had strewn the ritual herbs on the brazier, and the air was filling with their scent, pungent, compelling, startling the mind to wakefulness. Anluan commenced his slow progress around the circle, pausing at the quarters. I knew from the grimoires that for a spell of banishment the circle must be cast the other way, so he walked contrary to the sun's path, and the form of words we had chosen was different, too.

'Mystical spirit of water, we honour you!' Anluan moved past the ghost child, who stood beside the wise woman in the west of the circle. The little girl had bowed her head and was staring at the ground. 'Purifying spirit of fire, we honour you!' He passed the warriors, who stood tall in pride at today's achievement. 'Life-giving spirit of air, we honour you!' He walked by the monks, who knelt with hands together in prayer. Several ghostly women were supporting one another with joined hands or arms linked; their eyes followed his progress. 'Nurturing spirit of earth, we honour you!'

Anluan had completed the circle and now began to pace out the lines of the pentagram, walking with care so the sand was not disturbed. In keeping with Nechtan's ritual nobody stood within the points of the star, but all huddled in the spaces between, save Aislinn, alone in the very centre, looking like a winter princess from an old tale, all white and gold.

Anluan's slow walk was done. He turned at the final point, standing where the lines joined in the north; he lifted his arms and spread them wide. 'Divine essence of the soul, source of all goodness and wisdom, we honour you!'

He paused, drawing a deep breath. It was time for the counter spell. His voice rang out anew, deep and compelling. '*Erappa sinigilac oigel! Mitats ihim erappa!*'

A shiver went through the people of the host, a shadow of memory. The words held power. They hung in the air, conjuring the unknown.

'*Egruser!*' Anluan called. '*Egruser!*'

He waited a little, and the air grew colder around us. He spoke the words of banishment again. I sensed a darkening, though no cloud had covered the full moon. As Anluan opened his mouth to speak the words a third time, it seemed to me that something was pulling towards the circle, as if it would draw us all into that world beyond death. My jaw was tight; my heart hammered. *Now . . . now . . .*

'*Egruser!*' Anluan cried, and the spell of dismissal was complete.

Silence. Nothing stirred. Nothing changed, though the bone-deep chill remained over us all. Then Aislinn's laugh came like a peal of bells. 'What did I say?' The look she turned on Anluan was almost affectionate, like that of a wife teasing a husband for his endearing clumsiness. 'Caitrin got it wrong. You got it wrong. You are no sorcerer.' She turned in place, surveying the folk of the host, folk who had just seen their dearest hope dashed. 'He's failed you,' she said. 'You were fools to expect anything else.'

'Shut your poisonous mouth!' roared Gearróg, stepping towards her with hands outstretched as if to take her by the neck and throttle her. Others moved too, the old warrior Broc, one or two of the younger men.

'Hold still!' called Anluan, and they did. 'Do not disturb the pattern!'

'This is over, Anluan,' Aislinn said. 'You can't do it. Admit it. Your foolish woman there has made a promise you can't keep. This does not end so easily.'

'Be silent!' Anluan roared. Out in the circle the ghost child began to cry, a little, woeful sound.

'What do we do now?' muttered Magnus.

Think, Caitrin. The Latin words had been right, I was sure of it. The pattern was right; the herbs were as close as we could get them. The elemental greetings had been carefully worded – Anluan's reluctance to tread the path of sorcery had made that essential. This was the right place, the right time . . . I gazed across the circle, desperate for an answer, and met the limpid eyes of Aislinn. I remembered Nechtan's lust for her, the way he'd seen her every move as an invitation. She'd been young, pretty, desirable – for him, perhaps more desirable because she was also clever. That girl in the first vision had begun to lose her conscience, but she was far from the evil being who stood amongst us now. Nechtan had wanted her. He had chosen not to bed her. He had known that to do so would ruin his great work of magic.

And that was the answer. There was only one thing wrong here, and it was not the spell of banishment. 'Anluan,' I said, 'we must do it again.'

He looked at me, face ashen white in the moonlight, the irregularity of his features more marked than usual.

'But not with Aislinn in the centre,' I said. 'That's why she was so willing, because she knew it was wrong. When Nechtan was preparing for the ritual, he needed her as an innocent, a maiden untouched – he resisted temptation to keep her that way. That must have been a requirement of the spell. After the evil she has wrought here over a hundred years, Aislinn can no longer play this part. Someone else must stand there: a young girl who is untainted by sin.'

A restless whispering among the folk of the host. A stir in their ranks, and the ghost girl was pushed gently to the front.

'No!' I cried, finding it suddenly hard to breathe. Not this little one, so frail, so tender. She had trusted me, whispered her sorrow to me, taken refuge in my bed. She had asked me . . . My heart skipped a beat. Dear God, this was what we had to do. This, which felt so wrong, was the way to work the counter spell. It was the opposite of what had happened the first time. This was no living girl, but a spirit. If she stood in the centre, she would be left behind, left in this world when the others departed. And that was just what she wanted. 'Anluan,' I said, 'I think this is right. But first we must make the child a promise.'

His eyes were on Aislinn, and when I followed his gaze, I saw a dawning horror on her face. 'I'm sure it's right,' I added in an undertone.

Aislinn moved, lightning quick, bolting out of the centre heedless of the pattern. Sand scattered. Before she could break through the folk of the host, two pairs of strong arms halted her flight: Cathaír's on one side, Gearróg's on the other.

'A promise,' Anluan said. 'What promise?'

'That if she stays, we will be mother and father to her.' I considered the long years ahead with a child who could never get warm, a child who would remain as she was, five years old, while Anluan and I grew old and weary. She was a spirit; how could it be otherwise?

'Men, hold Muirne there,' Anluan ordered. 'Olcan, please step into the circle and remake the pattern for us.' The authoritative tone gave way to a gentler one. He moved down the steps, stood by the outer edge of the pattern, squatted down. 'Little one,' he said, 'come forward.'

The child approached, careful to keep her feet clear of the lines of sand. Not too close; she was not quite sure of him.

'We need you to help us,' Anluan said. 'You'll have to be very brave; as brave as Olcan's big dog who saved me today. Can you do that?'

A bob of the thistledown head.

'The others are going away,' he said carefully. 'Cathaír and Gearróg, Rioghan and Eichri and all these people, they're going to another place. If you want, you can stay with Caitrin and me. You can stay here. We will be your mother and father. Is that what you want?'

'*No!*' Aislinn's scream cut through the air, brittle as fine glass. '*You can't do this!*' Held fast in the two men's grip, she thrashed and fought, her fair hair flying.

'Be still, Muirne! Hold your tongue!'

She obeyed; Anluan had always been able to command her on the Tor, and his control still held, though her eyes were desperate.

'Don't be scared,' Anluan said to the little girl. 'Just whisper it to me, yes or no. Will you help us? Would you like to stay?'

The child nodded, her solemn gaze locked on his pale face. She whispered something, but it was only for Anluan's ears.

'Very well,' he said, rising to his feet. 'You must go over there, to the middle of the big star, and stand very still until I say you can move. Can you do that?'

Aislinn's lips were moving, though she made no sound. I imagined her words: *Don't send me away, please, please! I love you!* But Anluan was watching the little girl as she picked her way across the lines of sand.

The child stood in the centre, feet together, bundle tight against her chest. The moonlight shone on her gossamer hair. Olcan had swept the sand back into place, then retreated to the brazier; the pattern was remade. Anluan came back up the steps, turned, raised his arms. The host stood ready once more.

'Erappa sinigilac oigel! Mitats ihim erappa!'

A shifting, a swirling all around the circle. The chill was as deep as the harshest frost of winter. Time seemed to falter in its tracks; sudden cloud extinguished the moon. The child gave a wail of terror and dropped the embroidered kerchief. An eldritch gust caught the little bundle, skidding it across the flagstones to an inner corner of the pentagram, close to the spot where the two warriors held Aislinn captive. Quick as a heartbeat, Aislinn's foot came over the line to kick the bundle beyond the child's reach.

'My baby!' shrieked the little girl. 'I need my baby!'

'Come and get her, then,' taunted Aislinn, her voice reedy and ragged, as if it cost her dearly to disobey Anluan's command. 'Come on, you're supposed to be brave, aren't you, little spy? Just run over and grab your precious baby. Didn't look after her very well, did you? She's only a bundle of rags now.'

The little girl stood shaking, trembling, full of the urge to rush across and snatch back her darling, but holding still because she had promised. Beside me, Anluan drew an uneven breath. All hung in the balance. One word wrong, one gesture out of place and we would fail again. We could not ask the child to do this a second time; there had been a note of utter terror in her voice.

Gearróg muttered something and let go of Aislinn. Cathaír held firm. Gearróg stooped to retrieve the bundle, then moved into the centre of the pentagram, kneeling to put the kerchief in the child's hands. She was sobbing with fright. He picked her up; settled her on his hip. 'It's all right, little one,' he said. 'We'll do this together, you and me. A game of pretend. We're pretending to be brave dogs on guard, like Fianchu.' He gazed over at Anluan and nodded as if to say, *You can go on now.*

No going back. No thinking beyond this moment.

'*Egruser!*' Anluan called. '*Egruser!*' and as he spoke the ritual words a scream ripped across the circle, a wrenching wail of anguish: '*Nooooo!*' Even as she fought against the charm, Aislinn faded. Shadows danced. The torch blew out, leaving the circle in near darkness. The wind gusted again. The leaves shivered on the trees; the pattern of sand went whistling away across the flagstones.

From one breath to the next, the host was gone. Between the points of the ritual star the spaces were empty. In the centre, a stalwart figure stood with feet planted and head held high, and in his arms was a smaller person, whose hair was no longer gossamer-white but dark as fine oak wood.

'Magnus,' said Anluan in a voice unlike his own, 'light the torch again.'

'Gearróg?' I stepped down, not quite sure what I was seeing there, but knowing I had just witnessed an act of such selfless courage that it took my breath away.

Light flared as Magnus touched the torch to the brazier and lifted it high.

'By all the saints,' he said in tones of awe.

Gearróg set the child down and she ran to me. Her hair shone glossy brown in the torchlight; her face was rosy. When I lifted her, she felt warm and real. Gearróg was examining his hands, moving his feet, touching his face as if hardly able to believe he was still here.

'I'm . . .' he said, disbelieving. 'I can . . .'

Without a word, Anluan strode across to throw his arms around the guard. Olcan fetched another torch, and it became apparent that something truly astonishing had occurred. Here before us were two living beings: a little girl of five, a sturdily built man of perhaps five-and-thirty. Blood flowed beneath their skin; their bodies were solid flesh. Gearróg put a hand against his chest.

'Beating like a drum,' he said in wonder. 'Sweet Jesus, my lord, you've wrought a miracle.'

'If this is a miracle,' Anluan said, his hand on Gearróg's shoulder, 'it is not my doing. I cannot believe such a wondrous change could be made by speaking a charm whose origins lay in a dark work of sorcery. This . . . this transformation was not wrought by my fumbling attempt to reverse Nechtan's spell, but by your act of selflessness, Gearróg, and by the child's loving trust.' He looked across at me, and at the girl in my arms. I saw that after the long and testing day, he was close to tears. 'We must find you a name, little one,' he said. 'We cannot have a daughter with no name.'

'It's late,' I said, struggling to grasp onto the real world with its practical challenges and its comforting routines. 'She should be in bed.' Emer, I thought as I carried our new daughter indoors. If Anluan agreed, we would give her his mother's name.

Nobody had much to say. The immensity of what had occurred had set a deep shock in all of us. We were too stunned to feel joy at our success, too awestruck to absorb the consequences of this night of deep change. Each of us took refuge in ordinary things, the little things that help us deal with what is too large for our minds to encompass. Gearróg carried the child over to Anluan's quarters while Magnus found a small straw pallet and a blanket or two. She was asleep even before we laid her down in this improvised bed. I tucked the embroidered bundle in beside her. Anluan went to the chapel to check that all was well with the wounded and their attendants, and returned to say that even the most sorely injured was holding his own. Gearróg offered to stand guard overnight while we slept. Anluan thanked him gravely and said he would not dream of it. If Gearróg was concerned for our safety, we would promise to bar the door until sunrise. 'You, too, must sleep,' he said.

'Sleep,' Gearróg muttered in astonished tones. 'I haven't slept in a hundred years.' A vast yawn overtook him.

'Come on, then,' Magnus said from the doorway, where he stood with Olcan. 'We'd better find you a bed. The three of us might share a jug of ale first, eh?'

Anluan closed the door, pushed the bolt across, stood very still a moment without turning.

'Are you all right?' I asked him. Magnus had brought us a candle; its wavering light sent shadows dancing around the chamber. Someone had tidied the place, straightening the bedding and removing the remnants of that desperate effort to save Anluan's life. The memory of it would be with me forever.

'I think so, Caitrin. So much has happened today, I may spend the rest of my life making sense of it all. Such immense change. I feel as I've been turned inside out and upside down. And yet . . .'

I sat down on the edge of the bed and began to unfasten my bodice.

'And yet, all I seem to be able to think of is what an opportunity I will be missing tonight, since I am too weary to do more than climb under those covers, put my arms around you and fall fast asleep.' Anluan sat down beside me and bent to pull off his boots.

'There's always tomorrow,' I said. 'Let me help you with that.'

SUMMER

Irial's garden is full of colour: honeysuckle cloaks the walls, the beds of lavender are alive with bees, the grey-green foliage of the giant comfrey bush shelters our heart's blood plant, which has sent up five stems this season. The birdbath hosts a crowd of chattering sparrows. Streak, the terrier, races madly around the path, pursued by a muddy-looking Emer. Our daughter is growing apace; her hair is long enough for plaits, and she has lost two baby teeth. Nechtan's All Hallows rendered death to Aislinn. Anluan's All Hallows has given our daughter and her protector full and natural life.

I watch them through the library window. More than a year has passed since the day I first came up the hill to Whistling Tor and met a man with hair like fire and skin like snow, a crooked man who shouted at me and almost frightened me away. Now here I am. That crooked man is my beloved husband. We have our daughter and another child on the way. And I have my first commission, copying a book of classical verse for Fergal of Silverlake. Fergal wants decorated capitals, ornate borders and a touch of gold leaf, and he will pay appropriately. The work is going well. It is a joy to take up my craft again after so long, to lose myself in the

402

intricacies of it and to see a thing of beauty flowering on the blank page before me. I've had to ban Emer from the library. With the best intentions in the world, she enters any room like a miniature whirlwind with Streak generally not far behind, and there are precious items here, Irial's notebooks, my writing materials, and the other documents now stored away in boxes. We have put the dark history of Anluan's family behind us, but we will never forget.

Gearróg is in the garden now, a basket over his arm. Emer likes to collect the eggs. Olcan, who will be working down at the farm this morning, loves to see both the child and her little dog, for he still misses Fianchu. Gearróg takes Emer's hand and they go out through the archway with Streak dancing around their feet.

Ah, Gearróg! He's only talked to me once about that night, and how it felt to give up the chance to be reunited with his loved ones in the place Catháir called *the land beyond the grey*. He wanted it so badly. I still remember the way he sank down, hands over his face, when he learned it was possible. But Gearróg is a practical sort of man. He knows there's a place for him here. Anluan has put him in charge of our household defences. The Normans may have lost interest in Whistling Tor itself, but that doesn't mean the threat to our part of Connacht is over.

Besides, Gearróg added when we spoke of this, our household is short of helpers for just about everything, and he can turn his hand to milking cows or carrying messages or digging the vegetable patch. As for his family, he will see them eventually. Perhaps God means it to be that way. Maybe he needs to live out the rest of his life so he can make up for the things he got wrong before.

The fine weather is bringing everyone into Irial's garden today. Here is Maraid in a broad-brimmed hat, with a basket of sewing, and behind her the newly walking Etain, her small hands held firmly in Magnus's big ones. Proud of her accomplishment, the baby beams as she wobbles and staggers along the path, and Magnus's smile is almost as broad as hers. Maraid speaks to him, turning her head, and if she cannot see what is in his eyes as he answers, I surely can. My sister came in the spring, for our wedding, and she has stayed on far longer than she intended. She still grieves for Shea. But time is slowly healing that wound, time and the love that surrounds her and her daughter here at Whistling

Tor. Magnus is a patient man. Already she likes him greatly; his strength and gentleness are exactly what she needs. In time, I believe she will come to love him.

'Finished for the morning?' Anluan is standing in the inner doorway, one hand up on the frame. I wonder how long he's been there, watching me without a sound.

I rise and walk across the library, and he stretches out his arms to receive me. He's looking tired, but it's a good sort of weariness, caused by long days of work rebuilding our ties with the community beyond the Tor. He, of us all, has borne the heaviest burden and continues to do so. The host may be gone, but there are fresh challenges, those every chieftain of Erin faces in these troubled times. Leaning against him, warm in his embrace, I say, 'Emer told me she heard the horse again last night. A neighing sound and a rattling of bones.'

'It misses Eichri, no doubt. As do I, more than I can put into words. And Rioghan; I had not realised quite how much I depended on his friendship and his wise advice. I hope they are content, wherever they have journeyed.'

'They'll be seated opposite each other, trading quips and making wagers in the place beyond death, I expect.' It's hard to summon a smile, but I do so for Anluan's sake. 'Come, let's join the others for a little before you and Magnus go to your meeting. Did you know the heart's blood is already in bud?' Maraid has told me she'll try to make ink when the flowers are ready. That pleases me, since it implies she will stay until autumn at least. 'Anluan,' I say as we pause on the threshold.

'Mm?'

'They would be so proud if they could see you now. Irial and Emer, I mean. Our children will have the future your father wanted for you.'

'I believe they keep watch over us,' Anluan says, surprising me. 'Our good spirits, the souls of our departed ones. I sense my father's presence in the garden. He must be glad to hear the voices of children here, to see folk busy about the place, to know the curse that shadowed the Tor for so long has been lifted.'

A wailing from the garden as Etain takes a tumble. Magnus scoops her up and cradles her against his shoulder as if being a father were as simple as making a good pie. For him, perhaps it is. The baby is already quieting in his arms.

'Come out here, Caitrin!' my sister calls. 'Magnus and I are in disagreement about a method for preserving eggs and we need you to arbitrate.'

Anluan takes my hand and we go out together into Irial's garden.